QUEUES LIKELY

Lee Kerr

Copyright © Lee Kerr 2014

www.leekerr.net

The right of Lee Kerr to be identified as the author of this work has been asserted by him in accordance with the Copyright, Designs and Patents Act 1988.

ISBN 978-1-291-78383-4

This novel is entirely a work of fiction. All characters in this publication are fictitious and any resemblance to real persons, living or dead, is purely coincidental.

All rights reserved. No part of this publication may be reproduced, stored in a retrieval system, or transmitted, in any form or by any means, electronic, mechanical, photocopying, recording or otherwise, without prior written consent from the author.

'Queues Likely' sign and slogan are crown copyright and contain public sector information licensed under the Open Government Licence v2.0.

'Life is a journey,

not a destination.'

Ralph Waldo Emerson

American essayist, lecturer, and poet.

For all you career climbers –

Don't forget why you're doing it.

1

'Get back to Joanna's place!' I shout, as our small group is forced to split in two. We had only a second to consider so very few options. It wasn't enough time to make any real decisions, let alone the right one. We had to divide up the evidence, that's what we agreed in the lift on the way down. It was the only thing we really agreed upon.

As soon as I see him crawl out of that door, his injuries nowhere near as bad as I had hoped, I take her hand into mine and we run. She's reluctant at first, perhaps unwilling to leave our friends behind, or perhaps she's as stunned as I am by our touching. It's the first time I have properly held any part of her, our bodies finally connecting through something that isn't fuelled by my hormones and as the panic surges through my body, I become distinctly aware that it could be our last small embrace.

I push us forward but the pain deepens with every pounding step and I know that my wound will not help our escape. She stops for a moment, so she can rip the shoes off her feet and I instantly wish that my injury could be fixed just as quickly. It still gives me a second to catch my breath and look back, just long enough to see that he's in pursuit, charging at us like a raging bull.

The others are behind us now; our friends who are already defeated, with their arms in the air as they are quickly surrounded by more enemies than we ever knew we had. I look at that poor boy, as he fights against two men both twice his size, and I vow that I will somehow make things right.

We keep running until we turn a corner, but it doesn't help our escape. There's nowhere to run and no place to hide. We bang on doors in desperation, hoping that someone will find the courage to offer us sanctuary in such early hours of the morning.

Our cries go unanswered and as he comes closer I realise just how helpless we are. I grab her hand again and pull her close to me, hoping that I will somehow find a way to protect what now matters most. I look up at all the tall buildings, my tired mind hoping just one person will be leaning out of their window; that someone will at least be a witness, if not our protector. I see no one as I finally appreciate that all those wrong choices in my life have led to these last twenty-four hours. I know that the moment of judgement is here for all of us, regardless of what we did or perhaps didn't do.

As he gets closer he slows down and I know that he wants to turn those last few paces into my agonising wait for his revenge. I look him straight in the eyes and we both know that this will be our last fight. On some level I might even miss it, knowing that once I make my stand then nothing will ever be the same.

He moves quickly, his mind probably aware that there isn't much time. I punch him with all I've got but the force of the swing does nothing. I feel like I've just hit a brick wall, with all that stored up hatred seeming to tear its way back down my arm.

'Is that the best you can do?' he says, as his body stays on course.

He hits me hard and I step back, already knowing that my body will tire before he gets bored of pounding me into the concrete. I spit out some blood as I look over at her. It takes only moments for me to realise that my most single regret in this short life is that she has to be here now, suffering from my countless mistakes.

We look at each other but her face doesn't show defeat or anger. She doesn't look ready to give in as easily as me, but then she hasn't suffered at the hand of this man for as long as I have. She simply smiles, somehow telling me that she really believes that we will be okay, that we can somehow get out of this. She soon turns her attention onto our attacker as she projects a long and fearless scream. Her shoes are held in each hand with the heels angled out, the designer tones and intricate styling lost as they are now fashioned into a pair of street weapons. She runs at him and makes her attack but against his huge frame she doesn't stand a chance, as his hands meet with her body, quickly forcing her to the floor.

I shout out her name as I stand up but it just gets me another slap, forcing me backwards.

A car pulls up and his eternal accomplice gets out. His usually slick hair is messed up, which feels strangely satisfying. He limps towards us, one of his shoes stained with blood from a high heel that passed through leather and skin, leaving a scar that will last forever as a constant reminder of all the things he has done and what he is about to do. It's not enough but at least she caused some damage before we ran.

She is soon lifted from where she landed and thrown into the arms of the new arrival, leaving me alone to fight my eternal enemy. He simply laughs at me as all these threatening words pour out of his mouth. And when several punches to my head follow, I know that I've been beaten. My selfish drive and blind obsession have become my undoing and the damage he so obviously plans on causing will remind me of this moment forever.

However hard my next punch is it proves to be useless, as I feel his thick hands grab each side of my head, pushing us both deeper into an alleyway as my feet barely touch the floor. As his next blow knocks me to the floor I think back through my short career, to the sinister world that unfolded around me as I saw only that shiny ladder. The climb to the top was all that mattered for the entirety of those precious few working years and only now that I've hit rock bottom do I realise what a pointless waste it all was.

I don't bother to try to get up and as I taste the dirt that's laced with my own blood I wonder if he's still hitting me. I feel nothing now and as my vision fades I don't just realise what I've lost, but I finally learn what I could have had. As the darkness finally takes hold and my mind falls quiet, I can only wonder why I didn't figure it all out sooner.

Three payslips, sixty-two long commutes, two hundred hours in traffic, four tube delays and one apparently minor operation earlier...

2

I'm standing at one end of a long table. The people I'm here to impress are sitting at the other end, with all the products I'm required and desperate to shift spread out in front of me. Most of this gear remains untouched, the packaging still unopened, which is never a good sign when your client can't even be bothered to take a look.

Our promising poster-stands are built up and strategically placed behind me, acting more as shadows than guides. They're covered with bold slogans and photos of happy families, healthy children and germ-free pets.

When I say it's a long table you might get the impression of an antique oak affair, stretching to the other end of the room, with people sinking into oversized seats. But it's not. It's just several different tables joined together with a muddled assortment of chairs; simply functional – the best a NHS meeting room could ever justify.

I'm halfway through the pitch and the only indicator I have as to how I'm doing is from my boss, Mitchell, who's sitting to my left. He offers the whole room an odd grunt or growl, giving us a full and frank insight into his thoughts. His heavy frame has enveloped the small plastic chair that's required to hold him; the long creaking noises from his regular shuffling becoming the backdrop to my well-rehearsed speech.

But it's the people opposite who worry me the most. They seem barely alive and scarcely interested in anything I have to say. They just want to know the price, the shipping requirements, the package sizes and whether they can be easily integrated into their current set up. There's no excitement and no passion for all that I bring to them. And so I refuse to give these most basic of details until the end, until they've listened to what I have practiced all night, somehow feeling determined that I'm better than that. Better than all of them.

The only person truly interested in me and perhaps what I'm saying, is Joanna Richardson. She's sitting directly opposite me and in the middle of her harem of prematurely balding men – the sort of middle managers who are relied upon for their ability to find enjoyment in the most soul destroying moment. These are the kind of obscenely long-nosed and small-minded guys who almost squeal out in horror when they spot what they deem to be a significant hole in your cost-ratio analysis.

Joanna sits there, leaning back in her chair, smiling curiously at me as I try to pin an age on her. That face has to be mid-fifties at the earliest, but she's still well maintained. Her salon-proud hair flows downwards, the creation of a designer with talent. Some of the curls settle calmly on her neck line, almost pointing the way to her plump tits that are pushing their way out of her dress. And this is what puzzles me – her face doesn't match her body.

I soon realise that Joanna has asked a question, which I've failed to answer. 'Packing formats, please?' she asks again, as she looks at me with raised eyebrows and her chair tilted to the side, offering me a very pleasant view of those bubble breasts.

'The formats come in our own bespoke sizes, larger than the standard but with all our own fixings,' I say, slipping into my standard corporate speech.

'Larger than standard?' she asks and winks, much to my astonishment.

Mitchell mutters under his breath as I choose to ignore what I've just witnessed, putting it down to my tired ears hearing utterly the wrong thing. I continue to explain the benefits of our products above the competition, making sure I get out all those important facts now that the opportunity has presented itself. Not many people want to hear it, so when the chance comes I start reciting everything from our glossy brochures that claim to sell the ultimate protection in this bacterial-riddled world.

My company, The Global United Eradication Corporation, or G.U.E for short, has only one aim: to coat every surface of the globe with our sticky, translucent product that promises to kill anything remotely bad. Cover your children with it, spray it on every surface and even bathe your dogs in it. We sell everything from hand sanitisers to worker protection kits, from nasal sprays to personal sickness tests. Our aim is to make your small world a sanitary one and to educate you along the way, so that you keep it real and sustainable. Today is our chance to get into three South London hospitals, helping us to fuel the ongoing quest of my company to disinfect the entire planet – to rid us of every known germ and deadly bug. And only then will we be safe to lead our apparently happy and risk-free lives. We'll also have immunity to virtually nothing and the next deadly virus that comes to say hello to mankind will probably end up wiping us off the planet.

But who am I to question our mission? I look at the products spread across the table and I think of my new BMW parked outside and I realise that I'm doing alright out of this. I sometimes wonder if I will look back on these days and think that I've played some small part in the end of humanity; that it won't be the kick-ass super bug that kills us, but rather the fatal inability of the next generation to go play in the dirt.

I look over at Joanna as I watch her team pass notes down the line. I'm seeing the hierarchy in play but I'm not seeing someone who's casting a keen eye over the deal as much as she should be. She's the consultant – the middle woman – tasked with pulling in the numbers and doing the deal, but today she hasn't asked anything remotely challenging, instead having spent most of the presentation staring at my crotch.

I continue to throw in as many facts as I can before someone tries to stop me. This standard drivel is flowing out of me now, as she starts to drive a pen in and out of her mouth. She plays with it so obviously, showing me what looks like proper technique as this object travels the entire length of her tongue. Everyone sees this, as this entire room filled with her loyal accountants now become shocked onlookers as I wonder which one of us has truly lost it.

A welcome question comes in, this time from baldy sitting next to her, but it catches me off guard as I stare into her eyes, which are still focused on my tackle and the only notes on her pad in big writing say 'larger than standard.'

The room falls silent as the seconds tick by without an answer. Only the sound of the struggling air-con offers me any comfort as my mind remains empty and Joanna simply smiles.

I shake her out of my head and prepare my apologies, but before I can ask for a repeat, one of my team sitting behind me stands up to speak. It's Jerry, the only one in the team who's not allowed to speak. He slowly walks forward, his arms spread outwards as everyone in the room suddenly turns to someone double my age. The number crunchers look eager, as if the old face taps into the wealth of experience that I clearly lack. But I look over at Mitchell, as he looks like the world is about to end, his eyes wild and his arms tense as he starts smacking his mobile phone on the table.

Jerry's confident entrance into the deal quickly turns into mumbling. He's desperately trying to seize his moment of glory, planning to stretch it out more than is needed, longer than he'll ever get. I try to give him this precious moment, knowing how much it will mean to him, as I consider the point at which I can cut him off without appearing rude; where it looks like he's had his opportunity to add some value and now I continue the story. But he's started with information no one needs, smiling to everyone around the room as he weaves his yarn. This moment can't last for much longer and everyone, except Jerry, probably knows this.

Mitchell stands up, towering above both Jerry and me. 'Look, Joanna,' he says, as he holds out a thick hand to silence Jerry. 'You know these products are fucking good and I know the price is better than any of those other bastards will have given you, so let's not fuck about. We've said enough, so you've got twenty-four hours to decide, otherwise we all move on with our miserable lives.'

Without another word he storms out and as the door slams behind him I watch the various document wallets close and people stand up to leave. Joanna winks at me and leads the charge out of the room, as I wonder if she has gone mental, or if I was never informed that this shrewd businesswoman is also a slightly unhinged sex pest.

I look down at my trousers, almost wondering if I have wet myself, or if there is some stain in the most unfortunate of places. I see nothing and decide that the reputation of this woman that had preceded her for many years, and that had built up such anxiety in my mind, was now in tatters. I came here to sell some shit and this will most likely be the first pitch I have ever lost.

I head outside to find Mitchell, just in time to see him throwing one fag to the floor and then lighting another. I walk over to him but as soon as he spots me he closes in, his eyes forcing their way into mine. He soon dominates me, by height and bulk, with long slicked-back hair, staring down at me. 'That was a complete fuck up,' he says, his breath stale and his eyes full of anger.

I try to speak, to justify my inaction and to assure him that I really was all over this, but it's clear that he's not interested as he places a hand on my shoulder and tenses his grip. I look away and it somehow feels good, like the firm hold my dad used on me all those special times somewhere between my last school football game and my first proper interview. I know that I'm not in school anymore and I need to fight my own way through the world, without the endless reassurance of a parent who will always side with you. But now I'm entirely on my own, with only Mitchell's dark eyes for comfort, making it clear that I'm not doing well.

'You know that we need access to more hospitals and they have the big research facilities we want to get close to. I told you how important these are, didn't I?'

'Yes, Mitchell, I know that. It just didn't go how I expected it to.'

'It didn't go how you expected it?' he says and pokes my chest, pushing me backwards. 'What did you expect from a sales pitch? A red carpet and a welcome blow job?'

I shake my head, seeing no point in arguing. 'It's just not what I expected from Joanna.'

His eyes narrow as a grin spreads across his face. 'Let me tell you something about Joanna – she's not as special as she thinks she is.' He takes a long and painful puff from his cigarette before throwing it on the floor. 'She's slowly losing the plot and her reputation along with it.'

'What?' I ask, not seeing this. All I've heard about her tells me she is an industry professional at the top of her game and today shows that she can rule a room and walk away untouched.

He moves closer, one foot resting on mine. 'She's vulnerable and weak, which means you need to strike hard. Do you understand me?'

I nod, not really knowing what he's talking about, only wanting this conversion to end.

'You seal that deal, Ryan,' he says, his belly touching my chest, his husky voice ringing in my ears. 'Are you hearing me? Whatever it takes, you seal that fucking deal.'

*****

She's staring at me from across the room as she pours the wine. They're not small glasses and she's not stopping at a respectable point, which sends me a clear message about how the next couple of hours are going to go.

I look around Joanna's apartment – the living area is an open plan affair with soft lighting and easy tones on the walls. There's obvious money here but it's all a bit bland and outside of my assumed tastes of her generation. There's nothing floral, bold or dark – just simple whites accessorised with the odd canvas print, sculpture or lost relic from her world travels. It's what I'd expect from a top floor apartment of a nondescript building in Hampstead but it's not what I'd expect from her. I had always assumed that when I finally met this woman her personality would live up to the exuberant reputation that's talked about by all. But now that I'm in the lair I feel a little disappointed.

I didn't expect there to be so much silence, either. But what her words fail to convey she gives away in her regular glances in my direction. She walks over to me, her heels tapping on the wooden floor. She's still in the same skirt and blouse combination from earlier but with another button undone and her jewellery removed.

'So, Ryan, how do you think you did today?' she asks, slowly handing me a glass, pulling it back slightly, making me work just a little harder.

I laugh and then attempt to describe how I thought things went, trying to capture the essence of what I thought was a pitiful presentation filled with her unexpected sexual innuendos. I try to assure her that it really wasn't my best as she leads me to the corner sofas that line up below a pair of large bay windows. The blinds are all closed, making it the darkest side of the room, lit only by candles. There are no open windows, no mercy of fresh air to cool me down.

She listens as we walk and talk, nodding at just the right time, her eyes seeming to know everything, surrounded by these dark shades of experience that tell me she's been here before and she quite liked it. She smiles as she sits me exactly where she wants, just on the edge of the fold in the sofa, putting herself within arms-reach.

I make myself comfortable, not really out of my depth being with a woman in a strange apartment. In any other moment this would actually be fun, as I take charge of personally guaranteeing her satisfaction. I've never had a bad evening with wine and a woman, but if I ever got bored I would normally make my excuses and find something better to do before the evening drew to a close.

But I know that I can't leave and I cannot assume any control, my being here still unclear and the context of this still a mystery. I start sweating, which I'm sure is from both the obsessive amount of candles and Joanna's probing glare, accompanied by this permanent all-knowing grin.

I open my mouth to continue my pitch, or my plea – I'm simply not sure, but a hand goes up before I can say anything.

'Let me give you some feedback, Ryan,' she says, her hand covering my mouth, silencing me in the most patronising way possible.

I nod and put one leg over the other, making sure I sit back on the sofa; calm and relaxed – my best not-really-bothered look.

'First of all, you have the confidence and the presence to pull things off. You turn up in my world with those chiselled looks and that tight-fitting tailored suit,' – she leans forward, eyeing me up and down – 'You're clearly good looking.' Her eyes are beaming yet her voice doesn't falter for a moment, like she is stating an unemotional fact with zero flirtation.

'Thank you,' I say, ready to politely accept her flattery. But that hand quickly reappears, as a finger runs down my face and almost breaches my lips. She throws back more wine, the effects already starting to change the tone around us.

'You're cool and calm, backed up with sound knowledge. You know your stuff, but' – she pauses to look at me, that grin arching from ear to ear – 'You're incredibly arrogant.'

I sit back as she continues to look me up and down.

'I mean, come on, you know you have the looks,' she says, squeezing my leg, a little closer to the goods than I would have wanted. 'You've clearly been trained to recite all that corporate crap they fill your head with, but it means you've got nothing left for a real personality, darling.'

'Really?' I say, wondering how much this is actually worth my time, or my career.

'I think it's fair to say that you lack substance.'

We sit in mutual silence. I think about getting up and leaving, planning all the things I could be doing right now. I start to wonder how I have allowed this woman to quickly assume such power over me, something a woman has never done before, not even my own mother. She is right though – my looks get me whatever I want but I'm not going to sit here and justify it.

She soon laughs. 'Sometimes you have to hear the realities of life, Ryan,' she says, leaning close to me again and pinning her face near to mine. Up close I can see the detail that no amount of makeup could ever hide. The blusher is overdone; the obvious reapplication before I arrived does nothing but put another fake layer on top of her aging spirit.

We keep the silence going for a few more minutes as I drink my wine. I'm paralysed by my raging thoughts. I need this deal and I can't even begin to tell myself how much my world relies on making this happen. It doesn't matter how hard I have worked to prepare for today, or how much I tried during that thirty minutes of hell. All that matters now is that Joanna can put a pretty big nail in my coffin.

My world has become so complicated and so intertwined into the mess I am now in that making a clean break will mean losing everything. My rented flat, my leased car; my few real possessions are scattered amongst the things owned by organisations. My whole life is on loan and Joanna silently threatens to close them all down as reality finally knocks at my door, reminding me just how much I enjoy the life I have created, with this lingering air of uncertainty threatening to take it all away.

But something surges inside me, telling me that I can find a way out of this. My charm can work its magic, even in Joanna's world of brutal feedback. I get up and collect the bottle of wine from the fridge, pouring the remaining liquid into her glass before she can stop me. I smile, leaning closer to her as I force the glass into her hand and then gently towards her mouth. 'Joanna, I think you know our offer is a good one. We can get the infrastructure set up quicker than anyone else –'

She puts another silencing hand up, this time using it to push me away. 'We've done all of this and I know that your product works. Christ, there's more alcohol in it than a bottle of vodka.'

'Then why am I here?' I ask.

She quickly frowns. 'He said you knew? That you understood?'

I shake my head, having a fairly good idea where this is going but refusing to admit to myself that it will really come to it.

She runs a finger down my chest, the act of pure intimacy breaking down all barriers between business and client. 'Sealing this deal means doing something more,' she says, her eyes wide from the wine. 'Mitchell promised me a good fuck.'

I take a deep breath, as the reality of what is required of me finally finds its way into the open. I find myself staring into space, my mind lost to the simplicity of the transaction agreed between our potential client and my boss. It's not the act of sleeping with a woman double my age that bothers me. I have my standards but I'm honest enough to admit I'll sleep with any woman, and the thought of the pleasure I'll give the powerful Joanna feels like a game worth playing.

But this doesn't seem like a deal I can win through a subtle dominance of her emotions – teasing her aging desperation to the point where she doesn't know if I will bid her goodnight after the next drink or take her to the bedroom and fuck her brains out. It's the brutal movement of the boundaries that worries me the most. I'm the team leader responsible for sales of our corporate products throughout London; the guy in charge of cracking the capital, and I know this comes from a mix of hard work and some arrogance, rather than just pure skill. I admit that I slept around a lot on my way to the top but I didn't sleep my way to get there and now it seems that is all I'm good for. The competition has clearly got better so Mitchell had nothing else to throw at Joanna, except for my cock, so that's exactly what he did.

'You were aware of this, Ryan, weren't you? It's part of the non-verbal agreement.'

I say nothing and all I want to do is to slap her, to push her onto the floor and tell her that I'd be the best shag she would ever get but it would only ever be on my terms, at a moment of my choosing. She looks at me as my face mirrors this journey of emotions I'm going through. It isn't even the morality of what is being held over me, not even the fear of what Mitchell will do to me if I fail to deliver. It is the very simple fact that this woman who has always seemed so powerful now looks so pathetic.

I finally nod, never having agreed to this but somehow knowing my affiliation with Mitchell would eventually bring me to this moment.

She lets out a small scream. 'Good! I'm glad you're on board with this,' she says, patting my knee. 'It's not the norm, as you can imagine. But I'm really not getting any younger.'

I nod again, wondering how my promising career could have sunk so low in just seven years. I decide it's time to focus on her breasts, thankful that they look so much younger than her face. And as I look into Joanna's eyes I can tell the moment is coming. I'm so bitterly disappointed that it hasn't come about from an evening of flirting, as I slowly tease her emotions until she begs for more. Nothing moves in my trousers as I flash forward a couple of hours to see myself scrubbing every inch of my body in the shower. I think about how the anger at what I'm being forced to do will soon be replaced by that dirty feeling, as I prepare to break a personal code I didn't ever see the need to create.

She lurches towards to me, straddling herself over my knees as I lean backwards. She quickly pushes my back into the sofa, as my hands instinctively hold her in position. She leans closer to me. 'Global Germ Scrubbers, or whatever you guys call yourselves these days, are already the cheapest,' she whispers as she freely kisses my ear and cheeks. 'Getting my signature is based entirely on your performance tonight,' she says and smiles before she suddenly leans back and rips open my shirt. Her eyes look wild as she grabs at my pecs and then my stomach like I'm hers to own.

I try to force her away from me as subtly as I can, to somehow hold back the desire that seems to be swelling within her. Her shoulders are tense, her mouth gaped open, as she continues to poke at me like I'm some sort of toy, her hands pulling my shirt further away and then trying to squeeze around my biceps. I tense my arm, giving her everything to feel good about whilst desperately throwing myself into the moment.

'I haven't been screwed by a thirty year old for twenty years and I can't remember the last time I saw a six pack,' she says, as her hands claw at my stomach. 'Whether you will enjoy this or not you need to put on a performance. Life is all about an act,' she says, as a hand reaches into my trousers. 'So a quick fuck simply won't do.'

*****

As I lie on Joanna's breasts I feel relaxed. My head is gently resting on them, my noble neck taking the strain. It's a classic picture of two lovers, soon time for me to return the favour and have her snuggle up on my chest as she teases the few hairs on my stomach. I feel much less violated than I expected and more content that I've felt in a long time. It's a sense of almost liberation and I'm entirely clear as to the reason why.

I'm not sure if it's the expensive bed, the mood lighting or the sound of her heart beating, but something made this very different to my usual sexual experiences. I run a finger up and down her body, tracing the curves and marks of a world of experience, thinking about how the sex was better than I could ever have expected. She didn't play dead like many of the other girls, their heads always propped up with a cushion, expecting me to do all the work. She dominated and demanded, forcing me to raise my game, pushing me to do more, constantly stretching my boundaries.

I smile as I look up to catch her eyes and kiss her on the forehead before trying to pull some of the covers over me, ready to cuddle and sleep for a while. But the duvet doesn't move as she holds it firmly around her, offering me only the shake of her head.

'You need to get rid of that,' she says, looking down to the condom still wrapped around my cock.

I laugh at her creased face, accepting that she probably hasn't seen one of these in a long time and my usual trick of subtly removing it under the duvet would be lost on her.

'Properly, in the toilet' she says, pushing me away from the bed.

I do as I'm told and head for the bathroom, getting rid of the goods and doing the standard check of my hair and teeth. I rinse my mouth with water, thinking about how much I need to impress her, and when I think about how much I have to lose I make the effort to find some mouthwash.

When I walk back into the bedroom I see that she has wrapped the duvet firmly around her, cocooned within several layers of what looks like disgust. 'You need to go. My husband will be home soon.'

'Your husband?' I ask, my random lust replaced with anger at her betrayal to what I thought was our special moment. I had always wondered if Joanna was married but the moment she had me entirely naked and pinned to the coffee table, its contents thrown over the floor, my naive assumption was that she was another perpetually-single career woman.

'You've got to be kidding,' I say and stare at her for a few seconds, standing naked in the middle of her bedroom. She says nothing in return as I finally start to retrace my steps to find my clothes. She soon gets up to help, wrapping her body tightly in the top sheet. As she finds my socks she throws them on the bed and then runs into the hallway to bring back my shoes.

'What about the deal?' I ask, as I try to button up my shirt that no longer has buttons, seeing absolutely no remorse in her eyes for that lustful moment. 'Do we have a deal?' I ask, as I play with my suit in an attempt to cover up my chest, already thinking about the last tube being long gone.

But she says nothing. I consider asking her to call me a cab to get from Hampstead to Canary Wharf but I see no interest in her eyes. I don't see regret either, but more of a contempt that seems to be aimed entirely at me, like I'm something dirty that needs to be removed from her life as quickly as possible.

'You've used me,' I say, as if it's some sort of revelation, as if she isn't already fully aware that this is something she had planned from the moment today began.

'You can let yourself out,' she says, before walking into the bathroom and slamming the door shut.

3

The door opens and he pulls me into the office. His face gives nothing away as he drags me into the centre of the room, his thick hand easily reaching around my arm. He allows us both to settle into this place, into this moment, where he towers over me. His stare tells me he could hit or hug me and you never know which one is coming with Mitchell – such are the mind games he plays. If you read any decent HR manual this would be defined as *bullying by your manager* but not in his mind and not in our manual.

'So?' I ask, as he continues to stare down at me.

'Well, what do *you* think?' he says, walking over to his desk.

I follow and sit down opposite him, not wanting to be his puppy but not wanting to stand like some desperate loser in the middle of the room.

He suddenly laughs as he starts some celebratory banging on his desk. 'You nailed it. Well, more accurately, you nailed her!'

'Can we keep that bit quiet?' I ask.

'Sure, sure, that goes without saying,' he says, holding out his hands and offering what seems to be slight empathy to my situation. He suddenly falls into a coughing fit from too many cigarettes this morning; his lungs all set to give up way before lunch. He gets up and walks around the room, thumping his chest like he's beating any lingering decay out of him.

He sits back down and transfers the contents of his throat into a tissue. 'I ain't dead yet,' he says, grinning over at me.

I nod back, knowing that I couldn't be that lucky and I'm also entirely aware that last night will never be just our secret. The only thing that will possibly hold this together will be if Joanna demands that Mitchell tells no one and since she is married that is likely to happen. She will have more luck than I ever will, I think, as I calculate all of Mitchell's daily senior cigarettes breaks and all those regular chances for him to ruin my career in one short puff.

He leans back in his chair, knowing I'm deep in thought. 'It's between you and me, Ryan,' he says before propelling himself forward. 'You did good.' He taps his nose and I know it's not just between us and it never will be. I know this will come back to get me and it will be at a moment of his choosing.

Mitchell suddenly becomes absorbed in the papers on his desk, a pen tracing its way along the writing, his oversized and clumsy hand forcing the red ink onto the page. He soon looks up and throws the bundle of papers at me, which I realise is the contract for the deal, with different parts of the pages underlined and circled. 'Get your team on the stock shipment plans and get this contract down to legal before that bitch changes her mind.'

I nod, knowing my place and knowing how the next few weeks will go. Mitchell and his no-eye-for-detail strategy will mean he harasses me every few hours with no idea as to what I'm doing. He'll overpromise everything to his boss and then have me summoned up to Raj's office to explain my apparent failures. Mitchell will hold me to this moment – the time when he highlighted the major concerns in big red ink. Except that he won't have highlighted anything of significance and if anything does go wrong then he will feel no remorse in making it clear that the disaster could have been avoided, had I took heed of his original markings. The document now in my hand would, of course, never be found.

'There is one more thing,' Mitchell says, as I'm already near the door, the contract clutched in my hands. 'Two things, actually.'

He stares at me as I make my way back towards him, his face void of any life as he waits for my body to connect with the chair before he starts.

'Jerry,' he says.

I sigh. It's the name I didn't want to hear and the bollocking I thought I'd escaped.

'He was a complete and utter fucking nightmare yesterday.'

'He was trying to help,' I say, knowing my defence won't do anything but anger Mitchell just that little bit further.

The dreaded pointed finger soon appears in front of my face, his long arm stretching across the desk as if it can extend as far as it needs to, his hairy wrist coming away from his suit to bring him just a little closer to my head. 'If you hadn't lost your mind in the middle of the presentation he wouldn't have had to speak. And besides, you assured me that fuck-wit wouldn't speak,' he says, his voice getting louder and deeper in equal measure. 'I'd have rather listened to the cogs turning in your tiny little brain than him mumbling his life story that had no fucking relevance to anything.'

I open my mouth to answer but he tilts his head, silently growling. 'That bloke has had his day and all the best things in his sad little life are long behind him. If he thinks he's going to hang around and wait five more years for us to retire him off then he can fucking think again.'

'Pride,' I say.

'You what?' he says as his pen snaps in half, spreading ink all over his desk.

'He still has pride in his job.'

'What the fuck?' he starts yelling. 'Fucking pride?' His heavy head starts to shake violently, his mind unable to direct all that built up anger at me and sort out the mess he has just made. I know this reaction, and I know what comes next as the stress becomes too much, with him trying to maintain an evil stare at me whilst thumping the keypad on his desk phone.

I laugh, which results in the bleeding pen suddenly hitting my shirt, ink splattering over the crisp white cotton.

He stands up. 'Pride doesn't replace his complete and utter idle incompetence. You fucking deal with this situation.'

And after a few moments of glaring at each other, his secretary is soon fussing over the table, breaking up another round of fighting.

'You have a problem with that, Ryan?' he says, his body hunched over the desk as I remain seated comfortably.

'You said two things so what is the other thing?'

He strokes his un-kept beard, grey patches all over it, keeping his gaze on me. 'By that I assume you are clear?'

I nod. 'The other thing?'

His eyes narrow, his mind probably deciding if my slight insubordination should be further challenged or if he will let it go this time. 'You have a new team member joining today. She's part of the solution, if you get me? Which I really hope you fucking do.'

I nod again and then throw myself out of his office before he does, surveying my multiple wounds as I make my way down the corridor and into the sanctuary of the lift.'

*****

I get to our work area to find the three of them laughing. Jerry is on the edge of the conversation, desperately trying to join in, but the other two are not allowing him any chance to break his way in and hijack their morning with irrelevant tales from before they were born.

He sees my arrival as the perfect opportunity to get air time, as he draws attention to my ink-stained shirt and the fact I'm approaching with a folder in my hand. He immediately hushes the other two up as I throw the paperwork onto my desk. He's only ever this bold when there is something of interest, which in this case is me.

The other two laugh as Jerry starts to interrogate me. An outsider to our group would find this a confusing situation, as Jerry stands up and surveys the mess standing in front of him, finding the confidence to take a rare centre stage. This is one of those unique moments when he uses his age as a senior status, just slightly overstepping the boundary of who really is the boss. He asks if we got the deal, telling me that he could have done more, would have done more, had he been allowed.

I waste no time in announcing that we got the deal, which results in a cheer from all of them. I'm about to give details when Jerry interferes again, still using what he perceives as my vulnerable position to personally acknowledge the work he did, those ten seconds of stumbled fame apparently changing the course of history.

'It's time to shut up now, Jerry,' Tina says, stepping in just before the point where I declare that I've had enough. 'No one was supposed to speak except for Ryan.'

I nod over at her, quietly thanking her for saving me from pointing out the obvious.

But she doesn't nod back, refusing to offer any acknowledgement, instead focusing her energy on Jerry. 'It was a specific instruction from Mitchell, so he had someone he could firmly blame when things went wrong. And since you intervened you probably stopped Ryan from getting another kicking, which I personally think is a real shame.'

Jerry doesn't answer or laugh, instead choosing to finally back down and retreat to his desk.

I watch as Tina follows him and continues her morning assault, muttering how much of a shame it is that I have survived to fight another day, as she recites the moment Jerry stuttered his way into a serious presentation. I rarely pay attention to their complex friendship, but today I choose to observe, seeing that Jerry agrees with just about anything that comes out of that woman's mouth, which makes him either very stupid or utterly spineless.

When I first joined the business I thought Jerry was the CEO, or the Chairman, or at least a Head of a Department. During those first few days he had tried to take me under his wing and had even given me a book that explained how you should always act as if you already have the job you desperately want. He dressed like the boss and acted like the boss, but had no power and virtually no respect, mainly because he spent more time acting like a key player and less like the little cog he needed to be.

The day I became his boss was the day I think he realised that he really was just a number and that he was no further forward in the queue for a big bucks position than he was ten years earlier. Passed over for yet another promotion, the reality had finally hit him that he was a fifty-eight year old relic of the eighties, being managed by a thirty-two year old career-climber.

'Tina, enough,' I say, feeling a sudden wave of guilt for not letting him speak, as well as a slight and increasing concern for his heart, which has already failed him once. Jerry was born of an era where the idea of grievances didn't exist, so when Tina launches into one of her tirades about his incompetence, I can only let it go on for so long.

'So, we got the contract, despite the randomness of yesterday,' she says, abruptly moving the discussion forward.

'We did,' I say, realising that they have no idea just how random it was. I go about explaining the next stage of the plan, how we survey the hospitals and see just how much slime we can pump into each building and just how many different dispensers one hospital can possibly need.

'You won't get what you promised them on this final figure,' she says, having taken the contract on my desk into her possession. Tina's head is now constantly shaking, her eyes finding mine at the turn of every page, reinforcing what cannot be done and my apparent ongoing failure as their leader.

She starts pacing up and down as I watch Jerry join in, taking the only chance to participate in a real conversation that he'll get today. 'Five thousand dispensers! Do you know how much gunge it will take to fill that many?' she says, in between mouthfuls of an almond croissant.

Gunge is what we refer to as the main product – the mother-ship of all world-known sanitising products. This gooey, alcohol-laced substance is the foot soldier of the G.U.E Corporation's global conquest, coming in a variety of scents that can be dispensed in any format you require.

Tina is pacing around our cubicle area now, her choice of a thick woolly jumper in October not necessary when you consider the padding she is already carrying. I know that by the afternoon her hair will be matted with sweat, causing it to curl and stick to her forehead, accompanied with a sickly smell of what she calls eau-de-hard-graft.

But there is a very clear reason why I tolerate the panic, the smells and the grief on Jerry's old heart. The fact that she's already returned to her desk, hunched over her oversized calculator as she taps in numbers and ratios to make the deal work, more than makes up for the immense baggage that follows her. She mutters figures that don't exist in my world as Jerry leans over, nodding and pretending to have a clue what she is talking about.

I watch them for a minute, wondering if this isn't the moment where I should be giving some motivational speech to the team, setting a clear tone to the task ahead. How can they go off and deliver anything when their boss hasn't given any jobs out? Ken suddenly pokes my arm, pushing me towards the coffee machines. I nod and happily walk away, leaving Tina to solve a problem that may or may not exist, as Jerry acts as some sort of motivator, and at no point does it look like my half-arsed leadership will be required.

'Jesus, that woman just can't help herself,' Ken says, as he starts to pull weird faces towards her. 'Why does she have to turn everything into a major worldwide disaster?'

'The costs are tight so she might be right this time.'

Ken immediately shakes his head as he lets out this laugh. 'Who gives a shit, anyway? I wanna know how you got the deal.' He starts methodically surveying my body language, looking for any sign of a clue. 'That pitch was titanic and we cut it too fine on the product – even I know that. And yet we walk away with a signature from Joanna. So, the question, dude, is how the fuck?'

'We came in on cost. Tina will make it work and by the time we hand over to the production guys we'll be installed and well clear. They can sort the rest out.'

He pushes me, using both hands to put some distance between us so he can get a proper look at me. 'You fucked her!'

He's still talking as I grab his mouth and pull him away from everyone, to the quietest corner of our floor that's crawling with prying ears. 'Ssshhhh,' I mutter, slowly removing my hand.

'You did, didn't you?'

I grab his mouth again as he holds up his hands in surrender until I slowly step away.

'You did,' his eyes are wide, his smile stretching across his tanned face. 'Oh shit, Ryan, you fucked Joanna!' He starts asking me a hundred questions, mostly about her breasts and whether they are wrinkly or still firm, as he has always hoped.

I allow him a brief question time and then I grab his shoulder, pressing my fingers firmly into his flesh until it stops him talking. 'Not a word.'

'It's cool, man,' he says, still smiling.

I look at him, knowing that he will be true to his word, at least whilst he's sober. But the problem with Ken is that he's rarely sober and rarely not under the influence of something, whether it be drugs, money or just hot girls. I also know that I'll need to explain everything in graphic detail at a later date and whenever we're alone this will be a constant source of amusement for him.

The fact that Ken is my best mate comes with its advantages, but distinct problems when it comes to telling him what to do. He just doesn't listen. We joined the company on the same day, after I'd graduated and he'd just moved over from the States. He looked so innocent in those first few hours; his face from the subtle and subdued Japan, but his accent and attitude from liberal and confident New York. When I asked the reason why he chose England as his new home he said it was because he liked only two things in life – blond girls and beanie hats. I knew then that we'd be mates but I never thought I'd have to try to manage him.

I see Ken looking over my shoulder, 'Oh shit, Mitchell is coming and he's got some brunette bird with him.'

'It must be the new girl,' I say, not seeing the need to look around.

We start to walk back but Ken pulls me towards him. 'Hey, I got the stuff,' he says, his eyes wide open as he looks at me for some sort of approval.

'Are you sure about this?' I say, taking a deep breath, not wanting to ever have this conversation in work. 'It's getting too obvious. One of these days someone is going to figure out what we're up to.'

Ken's head is shaking, like the possibility of getting caught simply doesn't exist in his world. 'No, man, it's cool! I've heard that there's some new shit hitting production soon and I'm all over it. Seriously, people are gonna go crazy for this gear.'

I shake my head but he's having none of it. 'Are you in? Of course you're in. You can't back out now, dude.'

'Do I have a choice?'

The only reassurance he offers me is this devious smile, the one he always has just before he does something stupid. 'This party will be our craziest yet!'

*****

'So, this is Sophie,' Mitchell announces to the four of us, rotating his glare between the team, one by one, ending on me. 'And I'm sorry to announce that this man is your new boss.' He watches me for a moment, shaking his head in some sort of disbelief at the complete screw-up that he has employed. It's moments like these that remind me of Mitchell's view of the world – that he is some noble eagle, left hanging around with all the turkeys.

But today's visit to the department feels different; it is different, caused entirely by the new arrival. It's not just how she looks, but how she carries herself, that tells me I've met a woman of substance. The moment they arrived she took a step away from Mitchell, her eyes on us and not on the monster next to her.

'He normally turns up to work in a clean shirt, so accept my apologies on his behalf,' Mitchell says.

'It was just a little accident earlier,' I say, staring straight back at him.

He takes a step towards me, breaching the small little circle that had formed between us. 'You just make sure you report it, Ryan.'

'I'm sure a man like you keeps a spare somewhere,' Sophie says. 'And if not, then it's lucky we're in central London.'

'A girl who has solutions,' Mitchell says, his shadow over me disappearing and his face brightening up. 'I like that and now I'm thinking that perhaps you can sort out the seriously lacking fashion standards in the rest of the team.'

The new girl turns towards him. 'No, Mitchell, I won't be doing that. I'm here to work and be a part of this team, so isolating me from them on day one isn't going to help, is it?'

Mitchell glares back at her as I find myself almost mesmerised by the presence of her massive balls. She doesn't falter, standing there with her dark hair, dark eyes and a black suit with a low-cut top. She's full of so much authority that she completely contrasts Mitchell's fading grey tones. His pinstripe suit and unruly thinning hair seem only to prove that he is a thing of the past, now meeting his match against a solid rock of the future and it feels so good to watch.

He stares down at her for a moment, sizing up his new opponent. I start to wonder if Sophie is perhaps a recruit of Raj's or some internal transfer; any of these options make much more sense than Mitchell hiring someone he couldn't immediately bend to his rule. I only have to look at myself to know how things work around here – our first major conflict carved out a clear tone as to how our relationship will forever work.

Mitchell suddenly laughs. 'Now we finally have someone who can shake things up around here,' he says, looking at me. 'She'll be snapping at your heels soon.' He slowly places a hand on Jerry's shoulder, looking down at him. 'It's always good to bring in new blood, don't you think? It lets us have a clear out from time to time.'

I watch them both, the dynamics of these two men still unknown to me. They never talk and rarely even manage to say hello, yet they've shared a common employer for several decades. Mitchell still has his eyes on Jerry, but the old man won't look back at him. His eyes rest on me instead, almost begging to be rescued.

'I'll leave you to get acquainted with this sorry bunch,' Mitchell finally says, as he walks away, a cigarette already in his hand and primed for burning.

Sophie watches him leave as if she's waiting to check that the trash is gone. She turns around, staring at me. 'I assure you I won't be snapping at anyone's heels.'

Tina laughs first. 'Oh I think you'll be eating his heels for breakfast,' she says and then walks back to her desk, Jerry quickly in tow.

We look at each other, the new girl and me, and we must both know that it's true. If everything happens for a reason, then the arrival of this woman can only be another nail in my sorry coffin. She shakes her head, perhaps trying to tell me that I'm wrong, that everyone is wrong and the only reason she is here is to work hard. I offer her a half-smile and nod my head, silently telling her that I know things are changing.

4

'Are you sure this is the right size?' Toyah asks as she's fussing around me. She's patting the new white shirt like it's some sort of animal, as it flaps on a hanger, perfectly ironed by someone in the shop she just bought it from.

She seems content with her purchase, although her confused face still says she doesn't think it will fit. She looks up to see that I'm topless, with one arm outstretched to hand her the ink-stained shirt. Her mouth drops open as she stares at my exposed chest. In any other moment we'd be screwing by now and we both know it.

'Did I do good?' she asks in this whiny voice, with her head tilted to the side.

I don't answer as I try to take the new white shirt and quickly regain my dignity. She pulls it away, just managing to grab the dirty shirt off me too. She steps back, holding both shirts in one hand so she can tease a finger into her mouth in this weird attempt to be sexy. She's made that pose before in my presence, many hundreds of times and every other time I have found it to be nothing but a complete turn on. She only needs to angle her body in the right way and give me the slightest hint as to what she would do if it was my cock in her mouth and I'd be freely begging. But now her graphic illustrations seem nothing but disturbing, happening in an entirely inappropriate place, her selfish actions freely putting my career in the firing line.

'Oh, tell me I did good!' she says.

I move a step closer, trying to outwit her with an attempt to grab the shirt and to get out of this nightmare.

She pulls further away, that playful face from the depths of my bedroom now haunting me in my place of work. 'You're not shy are you, my little sex monkey?'

I cringe at her, trying to somehow put some sanity into her limited brain. 'I'm topless in the stationery room with the receptionist from floor five, so what do you really think is going through my mind right now?'

'I know that, silly! But you just look good enough to eat,' she says and then throws both shirts on the floor as if she's about to start some dramatic dance routine. She's soon giggling away, jabbing her fingers at my chest, playfully fighting off my hands as they try to grip onto her. I now realise my most fundamental mistake of the day – allowing my regular dial-a-fuck to be helpful. It's me who has crossed the line, asking her to do something different, to be someone she isn't. Toyah thinks everything is a game that results in her either getting a new handbag or a good shag and seeing me exposed in a small room will only ever heighten these primal instincts. Her laughing gets louder and I'm convinced the door is about to burst open, which is just what I don't need.

She suddenly lets out a high pitched moan before running her hands into her hair and pushing her breasts out. 'Show me I did good and drop your pants!'

I'm speechless, knowing that this is a line that even I couldn't cross, not even after all my recent exploits with Joanna. I figure I've got maybe five minutes before someone realises I've been gone too long and I'm still no closer to getting out of this mess. No one but Ken knows I'm shagging Toyah and in my mind it's impossible for anyone else to find out, especially not this way.

'Oh, come on Ryan, please! I'm so desperate for you right now!' She says, pushing her hands down her skirt.

'Toyah, I'm not dropping my pants,' I say, half-hard at the thought.

'Just a little suck,' she says, as she lunges forward and manages to unbuckle my belt. She's soon on her knees, tugging at my trousers.

'Please stop,' I say, begging both my mind and body to find a way to make this stop. And just as I think I've regained some control, her insane giggling still echoing through the room as I fight off these wild hands, I see the handle move and the door swing open.

*****

'It's not what it looked like,' I say, as I follow her along the corridor, a constant and desperate step behind.

Sophie laughs whilst shaking her head. 'So, this is the impression you want to give to the new girl?'

'Let me explain, please.'

To my surprise she actually stops in the corridor and pushes me against a wall – as private as things can get around here. 'I'm really not sure there is any need to explain. I have a fairly good grasp of what was happening.'

'She was bringing me a new shirt,' I say, determined to get something out into the open. 'You saw my other one had ink all over it.'

'And you couldn't have got changed in the men's toilets?' She says and then shakes her head, almost correcting herself. 'And of course you needed Barbie to help you with this incredibly difficult activity.'

I stare back at Sophie, trying to think of a suitable answer, not able to tell her the truth that I was actually making a copy of the contract and in that most unfortunate moment Toyah returned with my new shirt. Things happened too quickly and the shirt was there, fresh and crisp, so it made sense to get changed. It was just a quick trip inside the stationery room and ten seconds of being slightly exposed and then I could carry on with my day. My biggest error was bringing Toyah and her raging hormones into such a confined space.

My innocent actions seem like such a perfect answer to give to Sophie, or to anyone, except that no elaborate story can ever undo the memory of Toyah's squealing voice inviting her in and setting the scene of the two of us in such a wrong place.

'Look, it got out of hand,' I say. 'We were just swapping the shirts over –'

'– and your pants fell down?' Sophie says, holding out a silencing hand. 'And then she dropped to her knees to help fix *that* problem during which time, for some very strange reason, she felt that laughing hysterically would expedite the situation to the point where your cock makes an appearance?'

I start laughing. The more she speaks, the more I like our new girl. 'Look, I've never done anything like that before.'

Sophie doesn't laugh back, she just leans against the wall, this dark stare poking out from under an even darker fringe. 'Great, I'm twenty-eight and I've been working for six years. And in that short time you are the second pervert boss I've had.'

'I'm really not,' I plead.

'No?'

'Please.'

She mimics a stuttering motion back at me, almost tracing the movements of my face. 'Am am am... Am I going to tell Mitchell? Is that the question you're so pathetically struggling to articulate?'

I nod. 'It had crossed my mind.'

She stares at me, probably making sure I know that all the power now rests with her. Forget the thought of her chomping at my heels; she's got my balls in a vice and my career in her palms and all in the space of just thirty minutes.

'I'm not going to tell him, but God only knows why. And for some entirely stupid reason I won't even try to use this against you, not ever. If you want to fuck someone with a bigger bust size than IQ then go ahead, but don't do it on my time, boss.'

I let out a deep breath that says more than words ever could. I hold out my hands in some sort of truce, the fact that I was innocent not even worth fighting for any more. 'I'm sure that you joined this organisation to build up a decent career and I think I need to say now that I'd like to help you with that.'

Sophie only offers me this stunned expression, like she can't believe I'm still talking, like the only option left to me is to shut up and run away. 'You're going to help me with that, are you? And don't even try to flatter me with all the reasons why I pitched up here. Oh, and don't you ever try anything like that with me. Your looks or the snake in your trousers will do very little to entice me.'

'A snake?'

She takes a deep breath and lets out a long over-emphasised huff, the sort where I'm not sure if she is flirting in some sarcastic way that will take some time to understand, or if she is genuinely displeased with me. I think it's going to be a look she gives me often, especially when she's trampled over me and I'm left licking her boots.

'I didn't mean that,' I say, as I hold out my hands. 'I won't try anything with you, I promise.'

'Oh, so I'm not good enough to be fucked over the photocopier?' She says and crosses her arms. 'Well this just gets better. Blondes only, is it? Or is it the fact I actually have an ounce of intelligence and the ability to realise that the stationery cupboard isn't where I should give out blow jobs to all the boys.

'I didn't mean that,' I say, desperately trying to keep up with her growing list of concerns about me.

'I think its best we leave things here, Ryan,' she says and walks away, her long, leather boots squeaking as she makes her way up the corridor, all to the delightful rhythm of her tight, clenching arse-cheeks.

She looks back to see me freely staring at her departure. 'I'll let you go clean up. You've got lipstick on your crisp new shirt.'

*****

I'm sitting in the middle of Raj's office in a chair entirely on its own. It's a good few steps to the nearest desk and even more to the door behind me. They're both staring at me, Raj from behind his oversized glass desk and Mitchell from the corner of the room.

I can't help but over-analyse my all-too-frequent trips to Raj's office. It's always got this minimalist feel to it, offering only a few pictures around the walls, most of them with those apparently inspirational leadership quotes that should motivate you to leave the room ready to run a marathon, obliterate the competition and achieve all your goals before lunchtime. If I'm honest, I'm entirely sick of staring helplessly at these pictures whilst Raj gives me another speech and all the time I promise to be this model employee they think I am. The only picture that ever intrigues me is one of Raj and his family, with all of them standing in front of some big house. It's his home in India, as he frequently tells me, with his smiling wife and three happy children, their white teeth beaming against a red brick backdrop. It's a huge mansion, built from hard work and years of dedication, but he assures me it is only a modest cottage. Blood, sweat and tears are apparently what it takes to get a place like that. Personally, I've always hoped that the acquisitions of my life will come a little easier than that.

I look over at Mitchell who is standing where he always stands, exactly where he intends to be. He's in the corner of the room, deliberately facing side on to me – just outside what you would define as being within the conversation, but still close enough for me to hear his heavy breathing. He's also as far away from his boss as he can get, just about present in the room but not standing united with Raj.

From this obvious position, Mitchell's subtle yet regular undermining of Raj takes place. The constant word play between them is like the ultimate story of how good meets evil and how this particular evil doesn't make any effort to hide his feelings. My time in this room always makes me wonder if Raj even sees Mitchell for what he truly is and if he does, why there seems to be no effort to keep him in check. I remember the day Raj arrived from India and the pride on his face when he announced to everyone that he was the new Country Manager. It didn't last long when the only hand that rose was Mitchell's and the only question asked was how Raj planned to re-motivate the entire workforce after yet another appointment of a fuckwit foreigner.

By the time I recall that faithful day and tell myself that I still quite like the overeager Raj, I realise that I'm now in the midst of a lecture from him about delivering premium performance. It's his all-time favourite topic. I sit here, nodding away, whilst shuffling around in my white plastic chair, looking like a child who's trying to get comfortable. I cross my legs in an effort to defend me from the moat of air that surrounds me, but that looks defensive, so I uncross them and spread my feet out, now looking too relaxed for my own good.

In-between his talking I jump in every now and then, whenever he makes a seldom stop for air. I'm not sure if he wants me to say anything or if he sees it as being rude, but I figure that I'm far more interested than my immediate Line Manager, who is still staring at me with his hands in his pockets, offering only an occasional grunt or cough.

'So, Ryan, why do you think you're here today?' Raj asks, with this big enquiring smile. 'And what do you think about your current position on the performance ladder?'

I pause, partly for effect and partly to ensure that I defend my position as best as I can. I'm also more than thrilled that this isn't turning into an investigation into my alleged misconduct in the stationery cupboard, somehow happy that it's only about my variable job performance. 'I've brought in some good deals lately and I've formed the team that I want, which means that we're really starting to deliver on the foundations.'

'Granted,' Raj says, with a big supportive nod. 'And Joanna talks highly of you and we know she's not an easy woman to please.'

'I'll say,' Mitchell says, offering his first words of the day, reminding me that our private little story is still more than alive.

'You've had some good successes lately, Ryan. Most London hospitals now subscribe to our catalogue of key chemicals and our London big business dominance sits at twenty percent.'

This is one of Raj's key performance indicators, as he calls them, meaning they are what turn him on. His personal target is unsurprisingly one hundred percent, giving no room for failure, which is a bit like aiming to sleep with every supermodel on this side of the equator, except a lot less fun.

'We should also remember our domestic growth strategy,' he says, tapping his head at his almost forgetfulness of how much gunge we can flog to the individual masses. 'Our friends in production are above their quotas on shipment of the new family hygiene kits and pet sanitisers. They're now just waiting for us to deliver our part of the Global United Eradication puzzle.'

'And that's the reason for our concern, Ryan,' Mitchell says, taking a step towards me.

'No, not a concern,' Raj says. 'More of a flag for future performance, simply telling you where you should be aiming for. Both the corporate and domestic expansion plans have very small question marks over all of our performance,' he says, making a big circular motion with his hands.

'And that, in quite a big way, is down to you, Ryan,' Mitchell says.

'Well, I wouldn't get carried away with whom at this stage but more about what,' Raj adds, giving me this little knowing smile. 'When I took this job on this little island I saw so much potential. And this glorious Capital is where our performance picture hangs the highest and since you're a key manager for London then I'm looking for you to grow our dominance.'

Mitchell puts a hand on my shoulder, giving it a gentle yet reminding squeeze. 'What he means is you can't just get into bed with the big NHS trusts,' he says and grins, showing me the back of his mouth that reveals a long row of silver teeth. 'You need to get into the big wide world and get big businesses signing some substantial contracts.'

Raj immediately lets out this large huff and a nod, as if he's reluctantly agreeing with Mitchell that my performance is entirely shit. 'I live for the day that we see our branded sanitisers on every working desk in London and on every hand basin in every toilet. Let me tell you I'd like to see the Queen rubbing her little corgi's down with our new doggie deo. Wouldn't that be the day?'

Mitchell calmly kneels down in front of me, his eyes now at the same height as mine. 'You were supposed to conquer Canary Wharf.'

I open my mouth to speak, to give an update on my progress and to defend my precious position, but he simply holds a hand to my face. 'That's why you're living in that posh pad. You think it's just for the view? Every major business and residential block should have our products being delivered by the boat load every fucking week.'

'Now, let's not use bad language,' Raj says, clearly not having an issue with Mitchell's assessment of my limited accomplishments.

'Of course,' Mitchell says, standing himself back up. 'I'm just hoping Ryan will soak up some of my bottled up ambition.'

Raj walks around to the front of his desk and looks down at me, his head already nodding. 'I think he's probably right and let me tell you we have some very exciting product launches to come. For now you are living in the heart of the financial district, with row upon row of desks and buildings to sell our mighty products to. I mean, the list is endless, don't you think?'

'Yes, I get you,' I say, about to launch into my top five stats about what I've already done to deliver their quest for dominance.

But Raj holds up a hand, now sitting on the corner of his desk. 'Let me tell you a good place to start,' he says and then pauses for effect. 'Your neighbours... If they will convert even to a pocket protector then that's a small but effective start. It won't build the empire but it will be a block on those solid foundations. And then this neighbour tries our toilet pre-treatment, then our patented *Flu Fighter* around their house, realising their cold goes just that bit quicker thanks to the G.U.E Corporation killing all those lingering germs. Then they go to work and tell their colleagues and before you know it everyone is wiping their hands with our products the moment they get into the office.'

He starts nodding again and I nod with him, looking up to see Mitchell is doing the same.

'We need to set sail for premium performance,' Raj says, making a boat motion with his hands.

'Yeah, Ryan, set sail,' Mitchell says, motioning me towards the door, with a firm grip on my shoulder and two fingers digging their way in, reminding me just who has the power.

When we reach the door I look around to see that Raj is already behind his desk, his eyes on his laptop that's likely to be full of graphs that paint a bleak picture of my current sales figures and market penetration.

Mitchell catches me looking over and pulls my tie, dragging me closer to him. 'Bollocks to all this crap about boats and sailing. If you don't want to find yourself quickly sinking you had better pull in some big deals soon, otherwise I'll have you walking the plank off that fucking Shard. Do you get me?'

I simply nod as I get my final insult of the day, which ends up being a double-slap on each cheek and the door shut in my face.

Now, that's what I call motivation.

5

There are days I wonder what the point of anything is. Every day I get onto the same treadmill and run the same race, but what is the actual reason for doing this? It's because I want to make bags of cash and retire by the time I'm forty-five, with my body vaguely intact and a girl on each arm.

Well, that's what I tell myself. I imagine this future world where my time is a constant battle between my New York apartment and my Spanish villa, with my yacht anchored somewhere else in the Mediterranean desperately competing for a slot in my busy lifestyle. And I'm still regarded as hot, which means I'm still kept occupied by fucking young models every day, even more than I do now, and they all love it. Fine dining and fine women; every day until I die. When I was twenty I would tell myself this would all be achieved by the time I was forty, leaving many years to enjoy the fruits of my hard graft. Twenty years seemed achievable back then, but it seems that as you get older your aspirations get a little blurred. Or maybe it's just reality that comes knocking, telling you all the harsh truths that your dreams are often just that and deep down you knew must have known this all along.

My few friends can be split into two distinct groups – those who work hard to keep a family going and those who travel through their totally carefree life in the pursuit of fun and happiness in all their many forms. The likes of Ken and me, who see the world as a chance to make money and shag our way to a future filled with divorce settlements, turn out to be a dying breed by the time our generation have hit their thirties. Whilst we're busy holding onto our wild dreams, most people settle on a realistic compromise by their forties.

Most of my friends measure their success through the age of their children and what they are doing in school that week, counting up all the little victories of their young ones. I watch as their Facebook profile photos become those of their kids; their life slowly morphing into something new and not entirely them. It seems so utterly draining to me, planning your life around a term-time table, trapped by your children for a minimum of two decades.

So, how do I measure success? It's mainly by the distance to the next junction. My journey home is like the final torture of the day; the agonising wait for the traffic lights to change, if only to move forward a few precious metres. It is the perfect epitome of my tedious working life, like one long and arduous queue through the days and weeks of the year, all those hopes and dreams I had are miles in front of me, in a place where I never seem to get any closer to.

From the city office to Tower Bridge there's fifteen junctions to battle through. This doesn't sound a lot to many people, until I force them to appreciate that this is one of the most cramped parts of London. The dark buildings do a great job of blocking out all the efforts of the sun as their endless shadows taunt me all the way home. This is the part of the journey where I reflect and lick my wounds from my time at work. It's when my flashbacks of the day are most vivid, especially where Mitchell is concerned, with the physical bruises often competing with the mental scares as to which is the most real.

Today was no different after it was made quite clear that I'm not paying for my upkeep in the way that Raj and Mitchell had foreseen it. These thoughts stayed with me the whole day and quickly returned when I got into my car, making it clear that all my hard work so far just hasn't been enough. It's not that I necessarily disagree with them, it's just that I hadn't realised that Raj had figured me out so quickly.

By the time I reach Tower Bridge and start to snake my way around to the A13, to what is fundamentally a straight road home to Canary Wharf, I start to accept who I am again. I join the queue behind everyone else who are going the same way and declare that there has to be more to life than this. When I think about the five hundred cars in front of me and the five hundred behind me, all of us queuing for an hour of lost time, I make that one thousand hours of practically dead time. It's like a limbo world of simply existing, where nothing actually happens. You don't hear of famous novels or amazing songs being written whilst queuing on the A13, so let me put it another way – that's 365,000 hours of grinding existence over just one year in one very small part of the world.

When I start to measure my life in minutes and miles I realise just how pathetic it really is. I have put my life on hold to go to work and now I don't know how to get out.

45

I get home to what everyone else tells me is a gorgeous flat and I sometimes think it is what keeps me going. Two bedrooms with floor to ceiling windows, both overlooking the bright lights of Canary Wharf and so close to the towers that I feel I could reach out and touch them. Add to this a living room and kitchen you could fit a small restaurant into and it's all good.

But all this space is for just one person and with the 14th floor status comes the apartment to die for but also the loneliness of an isolated life and the reality that none of this is really mine. It's all on borrowed time and if I don't perform then I'm out. I know it and they definitely know it. I'm trapped by the chains I helped them put around my neck. The thought of the challenge to sell something to the masses would have had me salivating at the thought a few years ago but now, when I have things to lose, it's not so appealing.

As soon as I get in I turn on the TV, just so I can feel there is something else alive in here. I sit down and look around at the life that's been handed to me. I like it, but sometimes I don't feel like I've earned it. I'm measuring my life by a few possessions and the odd dinner party and gathering that are the envy of my neighbours. When I remember that some of my friends are struggling with kids in some tiny starter home next door to some zone 6 ghetto I know I have a pretty cool life.

I think I probably have, except that it only exists whilst I serve my master.

I pour some wine and stare out at the towers laid out in front of me. It's now that I realise how impossible my task is – to try to sell a product that no one sees the immediate need for, in the middle of a recession. I get the whole businesses idea and the fact that our gunge does make them cleaner and safer in this era of corporate social everything, but do normal people's homes need every product we proudly display in our portfolio?

I look down into the windows of the residential blocks around me – into the lives of my potential customers. It's dark now but many of the curtains haven't been closed yet. I look into their living rooms, with their wall mounted TVs flashing away, their own special story in their little slice of life. Sometimes I see kids run into the living room, refusing to go to bed as I watch a diligent parent take them by the hand and lead them out of the room.

I try to avoid looking into what I think are the bedrooms, but I've seen the odd couple fucking, perhaps happy to have an audience. I know I do. The kitchens are of course the least interesting, especially when all you see is people loading the dishwasher. But that's my target market – the people I need to get in with. Whenever skin touches skin or hands touch a surface then that's when we need to get them. You can play on the ever-growing germ fear; what's growing in your dishwasher no one told you about and what's lurking in your fridge, busy licking all your food when you're not watching. However, in this war we have an army of chemicals to help you win, all of which I'm supposed to be selling to the masses.

I take one more look into the open rooms and then close my blinds, not knowing where to start to conquer Canary Wharf.

*****

I hear the giggle before the knock on the door.

I look through the peep hole to see that it's Toyah, one of the only real releases I have – quite literally. She checks her make-up and then pushes up her boobs before ringing the buzzer, holding her finger on it for just a little too long, all signs of her slight desperation.

I stand and watch her for a moment, knowing that she's really not the one for me, not long term. With barely enough intelligence to find her way here, I sometimes wonder how she functions day-to-day. I know she would irritate me beyond belief if we ever became more than we are now. I would bring the cash, organisation and pace to the party, whilst Toyah could only ever bring that endless horny lust she shows for me, coupled with that incessant giggle. It would never be enough to allow her to exist in my future.

But when I look through the hole I find a way to put all of my frustrations to one side, if only for a few hours, as I find each physical part of her worthy of a small obsession of their own. That long blond hair and that slim, supple tanned skin, all setting a backdrop to her huge brown eyes. She's just too good to resist.

I open the door and she lets out an involuntary giggle. I don't even bother to speak as I pull her in and hand her a glass of wine.

'Hey, sexy, are you ready to finish what we started earlier?' she says, throwing her bag onto the sofa and then downing her wine.

I nod, knowing she's my only real escape from my trapped life, even if it is for a few sweaty sessions a month. She knows I'm going to fuck her into next week and she'll leave completely satisfied and that's the deal we made – nothing less and definitely nothing more. I only allowed her to stay over once and I'll never make that mistake again. I remember how she grabbed hold of me in my bed, finding a way for as much of her flesh to touch with mine, before she started a conversation that had no pause or end. It felt like she was literally sucking the life out of me as she talked for the whole night, telling me her life story – patching together all the things I wouldn't have known, but had no interest in ever finding out.

The next morning, after barely two hours sleep, she stroked my chest and told me how amazing our connection was and that we now knew so much more about each other. From that moment onwards I told her that it wasn't a good idea to get too close, all on account of how much trouble I could get into. Although, I always politely assured her that I would pay for her cab home and ensured she got a good seeing to in the process.

This has become our regular, discreet arrangement. The couple of times that she has suggested this could ever be more, I have pinned her to the sofa or put her on the glass table and spread her legs as wide as the reach of my arms, fucking her harder and harder until she replaces those silly little ideas with this constant begging moan. There's no more talking after that, until I dial the usual number for the usual cab to be outside as soon as humanly possible.

By the time I've found my own wine Toyah has already got her clothes off and positioned herself on the edge of the sofa. She starts playing with herself, happily teasing her body and my eyes.

I laugh and pull my trousers down, causing her to groan like I'm already inside her. And as I slowly approach I know that this really is the best routine I have in my life; the only one that I can always rely on for maximum pleasure in return for little effort. I take in a large gulp of wine and dribble the cold liquid down her body. She screams and tries to grab any part of me she can, begging me to come closer. I stay just out of arms reach, knowing that I won't be able to resist for much longer.

    I look down at her and she looks up at me. I'm sure we both want to make these moments work for as long as we can, and when we both finally settle down with a partner we will always look back and remember the lust and inventiveness that we shared for many happy months. I edge my cock closer to her face and realise that right now, in this bleak part of my life, this will do nicely.

6

By the time the weekend arrives I just want to veg out, putting my effort into the acquisition of clothes and gadgets – anything to distract me from the burdens of my apparently promising career. But Saturday morning is always reserved for a trip home. I'm not what you'd call a mummies boy, but I am an only child and have a sense of duty to be a caring son, however tough I find it.

'You work too hard, baby,' Mum says, as we're standing in the kitchen. 'All those hours they make you work, I hope it's worth it. You're just like your father. It's all work and no play.'

She potters about the perfectly tidy kitchen that is the only un-neglected room in the house. I know it's where she spends most of her time, after she asked me to install a TV on the wall and she had it all redecorated, leaving everywhere else in the house stuck firmly in the past.

The whole house used to sparkle just like this room, with new wallpaper going up as often as the seasons changed. Each room used to compete with the other to be the latest look, just like the trends sold in all the home and style magazines my mum regularly collected. First it was wallpaper and then it was paint, which was followed by a combination of paint and feature walls with bold patterns – disposable stuff that lasts a year. My mum used to follow all of these religiously; a total convert to keeping the home fresh and properly accessorised.

Now this one shiny room glows against the darkness of the house, with the view of the dying garden always looming just outside the window – a constant reminder that everything has changed.

'You could get a dog,' she suggests, as she does every weekend.

'Who would walk it?' I ask her, knowing she will never make the trek from Surrey to Canary Wharf to walk an animal. 'How about *you* get a dog?' I ask, getting braver with my weekly challenges back to her, knowing that at some point she needs to find some sort of purpose.

My mum shakes her head, as she does every week when I suggest getting a pet, moving house, joining a women's club, or whatever else I can think of to help. 'Your Dad's in the living room, go say hi whilst I finish your breakfast.'

'I know that, mum,' I say, looking across the hallway to the bleakest of all rooms in this large, oversized family home. The door is slightly ajar with light from the flickering of the TV coming through the gap, but that's not enough of a reason for me to go in there and say hello, goodbye or any number of possible things that I should say.

Instead, I make my usual journey around the house, checking all the lights work and the numerous toilets flush properly; trying to be the man about the house, convincing myself that a woman of fifty-five cannot do such things for herself. I open all the curtains as I make my way around each room, letting light flood into this gloomy place, as if these small and insignificant actions actually serve a purpose other than making me feel slightly useful.

This place is nothing like I remember from my youth here, growing up in suburban Surrey. My school friends have long since moved away and any of those first few girlfriends have either found men or turned out to not be as pretty as I would have hoped. It all means that my life is now totally in London, apart from this one small family anchor reluctantly bringing me back every weekend.

'Why don't you come and move in with me?' I say, when I get back into the kitchen. 'It's got everything you need and there's plenty of space for both of us.'

Mum ignores me as she places three plates of breakfast on the table.

'Mum, why three plates?' I ask and sigh. This is a question I ask every weekend and I vow to never stop asking it until she gives me an answer that I can understand. 'And how is he going to eat that?' I say, when I don't get an answer.

'Oh, your dad's not hungry? I should have known.' She picks the third plate up, the redundant one that has no purpose in this kitchen or this life.

I grab her arm. 'Mum –'

She shrugs it off, pulling away from me and turning her back as quickly as she can. 'I can't believe he doesn't want this now. But you eat up, it'll get cold otherwise.'

I turn to my food and do as I'm told, eating quickly and quietly as she storms into the living room with the plate of food, demanding to know why he's not hungry. I try to focus only on my breakfast and as she starts yelling my eating gets faster, making me only chew what I need to.

She's still shouting but her demands get no answer back as I eat like I'm fourteen again, shovelling the food into my mouth so that I can get outside and play with my mates, my youthful-self never able to stay in the house on such a sunny day.

I picture her in the room just across the hallway and it makes me throw the food into my mouth so fast that the fork smashes against my gum. I don't stop to check the damage and for every word that echoes around the house I pile in more food. I don't coat my bacon with beans, or mix sausage with egg – it all goes in quickly; whatever my fork can pierce first.

A drop of blood drips onto the beans which finally forces me to crack, as tears form in my eyes. I refuse to cry, to allow this weakness to show. I run out of the back door instead, escaping this life made by my parents, soon finding a way back into that lost teenage world.

I go looking for Oliver, my best friend, so that we can hang out. I'll try to buy us some fags from the off-licence and we can practice looking cool, or go get his mum's Grattan catalogue and stare at the women in the lingerie section, picking what kind of boobs we like best. There are so many things we need to explore, so many experiences yet to have.

By the time I figure out that Oliver is long gone and that our tree house was taken down a decade ago by our fathers, marking the end of our pre-puberty years, I'm heading back into the house, into the very different world that exists now.

The house is silent and everything has calmed down. The district nurse is in the kitchen with my mum, steaming cups of tea set out in front of them. She puts an arm around Mum and gives me this knowing nod that I think says I'm doing okay and that I'm definitely doing all that I can. Her gaze tells me not to worry and that this is just life's way of doing things and that at this stage there is nothing more I can do.

I tell myself that this really is what the nurse is thinking, as I kiss my mum on the forehead and then make my way out the back door, not daring to turn around and check if I'm right.

*****

Ken is on fire. I mean, he's just buzzing, like it's the start of his own personal concert performance or something. His face is red from booze and I'm pretty sure he's sniffed some shit in the bathroom. He said he wouldn't do that on a work night anymore, but based on the thing standing in front of me now, running around and screaming, I don't fully believe him.

He's kitted out my two bed pad with the usual party gear. The ten or so boxes of props stored in my flat make a regular monthly outing that normally results in my savings getting a little top up and the cleaners on a full time shift the next morning. This is by far the most exciting part of my business life and I figure it's a win-win for everyone involved.

'It's gonna be sick, man!' Ken says, as he massages his temples, obviously trying to bring both his vision and brain back to something that resembles normal. His jet black hair is spiked upwards and his stubble perfectly timed at five days' worth, which is just about as good as it gets before the unconnected hairs start to look like random patches spread across his face. Apart from sorting out his head and putting a pair of trousers on, this is as ready as he's managed to get.

I look at him standing there topless and remind myself just how lucky he is. Despite my admiration that his face seems to be frozen in time, it is actually the thing that plagues him the most. 'My chest still looks like a little boy's,' he says, poking at his stomach and then falling to the floor to do some push ups.

I ignore his worries, knowing that genetics will always side with him as we compete over the next ten years to keep our definition. I look over at the hundred or more boxes of merchandise piled in the corner of the living room. 'You've never taken so much before.'

'I've never invited so many people before!' he screams, as he jumps up and runs to the balcony doors for some air.

'Well done, those thirty push ups have made all the difference,' I say, as I watch him rub the sweat off his chest with a tea towel.

'This is it, Ryan, you're looking at the mother load! Oh, man, are you feeling it?' he says, grabbing at my crotch.

'You're wasted, man, look at you – your eyes are fucked.'

He starts to do a dance, swaying his hips from side to side and putting his arms up. 'I'm just getting in the mood, baby, just warming up before the beggars arrive.'

Ken calls our monthly visitors *The Beggars* because he believes they are all begging to get fucked by us, or more accurately, by him. The specially selected, by invitation only group usually consists of middle-aged housewives and tired mums, all of them clearly neglected by their over-worked or just plain disinterested husbands.

Ken looks for these poor women, who are trapped in their boring lives, at places outside M&S, or in the car park at Sainsbury's, as he helps them get their trolley of shopping into the car, all the time assuring them that he is here to help. He tells them about our products and the intimate Canary Wharf pad that is the home for our little show case evening. It's like an Ann Summers party, but for the world of disinfecting and sanitising. He calmly leaves them, giving no sign of any threat as they drive off, having already been handed a card that details our website and the assurances that he will be there to personally work with them on their needs. They go home and they think about it, about him; they desperately find a reason to throw that card away and think nothing more about it. But most of them simply cannot resist the offer of youth, of excitement, of something different.

And when the day of the party arrives they all turn up as quiet as mice, like it's some *Alcoholics Anonymous* meeting, most of them sporting a mid-life ladies tyre and drastically sagging boobs. They walk in with red rings around their eyes from those endless household duties, but are always dressed in what they think is their best glamour outfit. It's nearly always some two-tone number from a time when sequins actually looked cool.

But the main thing is that they turn up, have cash to burn and of course they love all things cleaning related. They're basically domestic goddesses in their own right; it's just that they're stuck in a war between time and freedom to be the person they always wanted to be. Well, that's what we tell them, promising that we can help sort out the family needs and protect their little world and still have time to be an independent woman.

Ken is standing by the boxes as I put on a tight white fitting shirt. He's staring at me with this look like the devil just took hold of him and plans on having one mental night with a hundred-or-so ladies. He looks like he's cooled down enough so he's also getting himself into a snug white shirt, accessorised with a skinny black tie, as dark as his hair and eyes. There's no beanie hat tonight and he keeps checking himself in the mirror, twisting those different spikes as he slowly sways around.

'Shit, Ken, I think we should get some coffee inside you.'

'Fuck the coffee!' he says, as he starts opening the boxes and shuffles through the contents. 'This is completely mental.'

I watch him as he organises a pile of boxes that contain the basic gunge, all packaged up under different purposes, but essentially it's that same blend of alcohol and random herb extracts that none of us have ever really heard of. 'We've done this a hundred times and I've never seen you get excited before.'

He opens a box and throws me a pack of the apparently new stuff. 'This is the new shit, baby. And I promise that it is good shit!'

I start smiling once I figure out what it is. 'This hasn't even been released yet.'

'No! Not for another few weeks, so we'll be the first to show it off and these ladies will be gagging at the thought. I told you, man, it's the mother load!' He rips open several of the boxes in a fit of hysterics, throwing cardboard all around him. 'I got all three products in the new *Sex Sanister* range. Can you believe it?'

He throws them into the air and we're soon hugging and celebrating his latest achievement. 'Quick, man,' he says. 'You gotta help me stick the labels on them.' He quickly gets out this bundle of pre-printed labels that say *new product range*. All the goods come unbranded so we can shift them directly to our little band of consumers, claiming that we get them direct from the manufacturer as extra supplies they cannot shift, so we keep the labelling simple and only mention our company when we think it will help.

The fact that they are extra batches of product without a home is technically true, as they come direct as samples from the production plant in China. Ken's previous role was working in the Asia manufacturing division so he uses his contacts to get us several thousand packs secretly skimmed off the production line direct to us, using my flat as the London storage office. The bit that's not technically fair is that we don't pay a penny for them and the G.U.E Corporation doesn't see any of the profits.

So, yes, this could be defined as the acquisition and selling of company products for personal gain. I've read all of this in the company policy manual, somehow hoping I never have to hear it in real life. But Ken's first hand stories about how much gunge gets pumped into the sewers and how many samples there are lining every employee's shelves at home kind of makes our little initiative a drop in the big shiny G.U.E ocean.

Besides, those boxes in the corner are one small piece of my retirement yacht and the party last month conveniently brought that retirement age just a little closer to forty. And Mitchell did tell me to raise product awareness, so that's exactly what we're doing.

Ken is busy kissing every box before he puts the sticker on it as I make myself busy unpacking our standard products, positioning them around the flat. The *Dog Sanitiser* is always popular – a special deodorising and bug killing formula that's supposed to kill all the germs that can transfer to humans. I place a picture of a young boy hugging a Labrador next to the product and of course we've got a few real life horror stories of kids contracting viruses from their precious pets. Some say that this product is like bathing your pooch in a bath of gin, but is that really a bad thing?

I use the tables for smaller products like the *Sanitising Nasal Spray*, which sits next to a poster explaining just how many germs live in your nose. You'd probably be better off and have more fun snorting strawberry vodka, but that's just my opinion.

The Global United Eradication patented *Shower System*, or 'good luck guessing what's in the bottle,' as we like to call it, is by far the backbone of the domestic sales and warrants a pyramid of boxes stacked up in the corner. You could just get your children to wash themselves in peach schnapps but, on some level, that would probably feel wrong.

By the time I'm done, Ken has hidden all the new *Sex Sanitiser* products back in their boxes for the big launch and I've lined up all the free booze on the breakfast bar. We don't scrimp on the basics; the champagne flutes are top-dollar glass and the alcohol is a decent mid-tier variety. We want them to feel valued so we give them a lot of attention, soft music, much laughter and two good looking boys who are willing to flirt, listen and give them all the attention they so obviously lack on a daily basis from their husbands.

And in return all they need to bring is their secrecy and their money. We don't take card or cheques and we don't give receipts. The website address changes regularly and remains deliberately vague, meaning that we rely mainly on word of mouth. Despite this, it's obvious that Ken is good with his marketing, as the room starts to fill up with arrivals, people soon spilling into the hallway. I have to herd them around like lustful little sheep, getting them to squeeze together, making it a little more intimate.

There are a lot of familiar faces tonight, with many previous attendees making a second or third appearance. They flock to Ken and me like we're all best friends, letting the others see them say hello, bragging about their familiarity with us in front of the nervous newcomers. I play it cool, talking nice, totally flirting, each of them getting a look like they will be the one on top of me tonight, panting and screaming as I wrap my arms around them and stroke tits like they're the best I've ever seen.

Ken is busy at the door, telling them that we've got the usual stuff to get their homes both sparkling and completely void of even the nice, friendly germs that probably do us good to sometimes hang out with. He's also telling them that we've got something new, something that will bring back the sparkle in the bedroom.

The hired help comes in the shape of two of our most loyal disciples. We could have gone for two young fit guys, but you have to remember not to alienate or scare away your core customer, so we have Samantha and Kim. They're two yummy mummies who have been with us from day one, happily dishing out the drinks and reassuring the newbies that this will be a fun experience that they will be nothing short of desperate to take part in again.

We start fifteen minutes later than planned, due to the logistics of fitting everyone into one room. Ken gets straight up onto my coffee table which has become his regular little stage. He's whipping them up into a frenzy, picking out names of some of the regulars and doing an obsessive amount of flirting. His tie quickly comes off and his shirt ends up half open, as the sweat pours down his red body. He has knocked back two glasses of fizz by the time he's sold our standard shit, this time keeping it short and simple with the offer of a box of mixed gunge supplies for a hundred quid. If every one of today's visitors took us up on this offer it would make us a cool ten grand in less than an hour's work.

He moves on to the good stuff pretty quickly, leaving out many of our favourite horror stories about how many germs there really are in the average sized family home. Our professional advice, for what shit it is worth, is to send the husband and kids off for a weekend so you can scrub and sanitise the whole house, removing the germs in a systematic way. Hell, there's even a ten-page guide on the G.U.E Corporation website for how to do it. Then, when they return, you implement a consistent routine of self-sanitising. We talk about how to educate the family, so as to keep the germ count in the safe zone. If they make a big enough order then we'll even throw in the standard germ monitor for free.

We need to be sure that they get what this is all about, because if you're going to make this work you need to follow the proven quadruple plan: surroundings, surfaces, skin and saliva. This means a regular need for a variety of products ranging from our driveway germ killer to our total room *De-bugging spray* and our surface cleaners, plus the various shower gels. And don't forget our legendary *Eradication Paste* – it's like cleaning your teeth with a lethal cocktail of bleach and white spirit, but it actually tastes pretty good.

'But what about the bedroom?' Ken asks, with a bottle of champagne somehow making its way into his hand. He's now completely fucked and totally running off script, but it's beyond my ability to stop him now. If I jump up there he'll probably try to fight me off the stage, losing us the credibility that so easily equals cash.

'So, how many of you still get a regular seeing to?' he asks the room. 'Don't be shy ladies... we all need some sweet lovin!' He picks out a couple of the more adventurous women to answer and he's soon whipped the group into this general peer pressure that they are all human beings with needs who rarely get them fulfilled. And the group consensus seems to be that one of the core reasons for lack of sex in your mid-life is that you can't stand the mess. The sweat that oozes out of every pour and the smells – you can always get them with the smells, which leads to unanimous nods. And we've learnt that if we hook them in with the dirty smells meaning dirty, evil, killer-germs, then you've got them on everything else, especially what goes inside you.

'And you have no idea where else he's put that stick of his!' Ken shouts, leading to a tumbling silence as I wonder if this is the moment he has finally just gone that little bit too far, blowing my retirement yacht clean out of the water.

'Does he honestly clean it properly before he inserts it?' Samantha shouts. It seems to work, on some level, as most of the beggars start to slowly nod.

'So, ladies, we are proudly introducing something new to the market,' Ken says. 'And you'll have the chance to take this great trio of products away weeks before the official launch.' He holds the product up high, his arms stretching upwards, like he's presenting it to God himself. 'I give you the *Sex Sanitiser kit*.'

Celebratory music is playing as Ken dances around the table, throwing samples around the room as I turn the lights on and off. The regulars are screaming as the newbies look a little out of place and I start to think we should have kept to shifting the normal shit and held a little more intimate soirée for our loyal converts.

'Firstly, the sanitising *Sex-Spray*. Put this around your room and bed and it reduces germ count by eighty percent!' he shouts, as he's spraying it all over, telling his choking audience just how lovely the fragrance is.

'And then there is the *SaniLube*. Let's imagine for a minute that you're lying in bed and he comes home all sweaty from work, or more likely the pub, and how many of you feel a little randy? It's totally normal, ladies, but how many of you can get him into that bloody shower? And even if he does, is he that thorough? After all, he'd be wearing the same pants day after day if you didn't put new ones out for him.'

The group of cackling women are laughing and nodding, which is always a good sign that he's got them hooked. 'Well, with *SaniLube* you can massage his hard and hot cock before he goes in! And ladies, let's be honest, I'm a man of the world and sometimes it's a bit dry down there, so *SaniLube* not only has the patented germ killer, especially targeted to the nasties that get down below, but it's also enriched with aloe-vera, helping to glide this in nicely with a little extra moisture, plus killing any germs hanging around those difficult to clean areas.'

'Difficult for him, anyway!' one lady shouts, as Ken tries to pick her out in the audience, only managing to shout back in the general direction of his supporter. He starts rubbing the lube over his exposed chest, his momentary absence from the room seeming to be ignored as the crowd watch him find his exposed nipple.

'And what about blow jobs, ladies? God knows I love getting them!' He's rubbing his crotch now, separating his busy hands between a nipple and his pants. 'You'll also be glad to know that *SaniLube* has no bitter aftertaste and is proven to kill all that shitty little bacteria that leads to all sorts of horrors in your mouth. So, once you've rubbed some over his cock it's clean and scent free sucking for you all night!'

Inhibitions are thankfully dropping as Ken starts to talk through the best way to massage it onto the penis, telling them just how he likes it and making wild threats to show them. By now, the dirty and thirsty flock have drunk all the champagne as we reach the final product.

'And now we need to talk about protection,' Ken says, hushing the group for silence, trying to be as serious as possible in his state. 'I know many of you use the pill, but think back to life before it – weren't condoms easier? You don't know what the pill does to your bodies and what about cancer? You just don't know!' Ken is shouting now, talking total shit as I get ready to step in and bring a sense of order. But as I move to the stage he pushes me back into the crowd, horny women soon grabbing at my arse.

'And what about your sons and daughters? Wouldn't you rather they had safe sex?'

He's got an unwrapped condom in his hand now, flapping it around everywhere. 'And you won't believe it but this little baby can actually kill half of all STDs when it comes in to contact with them. How many of your kids are walking about right now with an active STD and don't even know it? We don't like to admit it but the statistics hurt, so just Google it.'

The room falls silent, as the group enter into some kind of reflection about Ken's observations, or maybe the thought of their kids having sex just killed the mood for many of them. I move forward again, openly thanking Ken for his time, ushering him off the stage before we lose everything. I know he doesn't want to go as he winks at me and then lets out this scream as he rips off the rest of his shirt, throwing it into the hungry crowd.

He looks down at me, his eyes wild and the plan for tonight so far away from where we are now. I'm shaking my head but he's just nodding at me, somehow telling me he's right.

He looks around the room, his eyes unlikely to be able to focus on anything as he starts to unbutton his trousers. 'So, ladies, how many of you need a reminder lesson on how to put a condom on properly?' he shouts, his trousers and boxers around his ankles before I can say another word.

7

Monday morning comes around pretty quickly and it arrives with its usual hangover, served with an extra dose of reality at going back to work so soon.

I'm still young enough to remember when I used to love my job, because it was so much more than a job. My working life was always referred to as a quick, popular and envied climb of the career ladder. My ascension to the dizzy heights of Executive was a much talked about event that everyone knew was coming. I picked the right company, small enough but rapidly growing and cleverly in a market that was set to boom. The need to clean everything has slowly evolved over the years, to the point where cleaning just isn't enough. People want every surface disinfected, safe – beyond harm. But even that isn't enough anymore, as half the planet now seems to harbour this paranoid collective worry about what the invisible germs really do to us. The fear of that killer virus that will wipe out humanity has led this demand to sanitise everything we humans come into contact with. In the process we might kill a few harmless bugs, but that's not going to change the world we see.

So eight years and five different positions saw me climb the ranks to be someone important by my thirtieth birthday, all helped by the countless number of virus outbreaks and killer hospital bugs that always make the news.

Against this backdrop it always seemed like nothing could stop me. All I had to do was come up with some ideas and people would always be nodding at me in meetings, enjoying my youthful enthusiasm and go do attitude. Every boss I had simply loved me, some in a more literal sense, but they all respected what I did. And once I'd proved I could sell shit to anyone, I got bigger targets and people to boss around myself.

Maybe it was all too perfect, or maybe that's just how I remember it.

I stare out the window and look over Canary Wharf, wondering if it's all gone wrong. I drink my coffee and look into the different flats, watching people as they charge around, getting ready for work, or getting the kids off to school. I wonder if they are happy, appearing in different rooms as they rush around to prepare for their day ahead. I'm not sure if we can be truly happy in every moment of our lives, but surely the idea is that the exciting and meaningful events outweigh the routine existence. I'm pretty sure that the morning routine isn't something any of us will cherish on our deathbeds, but if this ritual first thing in the day leads to an enriching time later on then it all makes sense. But if the mundane existence stretches across our whole waking day then why do we bother?

This is something I like to ponder every workday morning and so I have made time, at the sacrifice of sleeping, to think about this for ten minutes each time. I do it naked, just out of the shower, when my body and mind are freshest. I let my body dry naturally as I sip my coffee. It's nothing perverted, I'm rarely hard. I see it as my chance to lay myself bare and in front of the world, my body and mind exposed through two oversized windows. I'm not sure if anyone ever looks in and as long as I have looked out I don't believe I've found an admirer yet.

I used to get a real buzz from work; hitting the targets, then hitting the pub, followed by a long and sweaty shag with a hot girl. I put complete and total effort into all of these activities, before pressing the reset button to do it all over again. I used to think I could do it forever, until somehow the chains of my working life started to weigh me down.

I blame one person for this – Mitchell. He quickly changed my world, as on the one hand he gave me this flat and the cool car to go with it, in return for what I thought was hard work. But on the other hand he presented me with this threatening alternative reality that he always promised I'd end up in if I didn't succeed. It was a life of brutal demotion and a failed CV, backed up with assurances that he would pursue me to my next two jobs to tell them how crap I really am. And once Mitchell's claws of reality sank into my flesh I found it all so scary, like the prospect of failure was actually possible and that not delivering the targets had real consequences.

As ridiculous as it sounds, they call him the 'Destroyer of Worlds', because he has this ability to graphically describe how he will ruin everything you have if you don't perform for him. He can help you see just how easy performance management really is and good luck with the tribunal when you can't afford your mortgage repayments. If you really think you have the energy to take Mitchell to court, then you have to think about how much he enjoys conflict and how damn good he is at it.

I want to blame Mitchell for this feeling of being trapped in a world I have worked so hard to create. But it isn't really his fault that the only friend who knows what I am going through doesn't really give a shit and the only person I spend enough time with is Toyah, and she doesn't have the mental capacity to see half of the pressure I'm under.

As I walk into the living room I can see the toll the party has taken on my place, with empty bottles everywhere and brown boxes piled up in every corner. They're all empty too, all signs as to the success of the night.

It was only an hour ago that I kicked two women out of the flat after finding them asleep on the kitchen floor. They had been Ken's chosen ingredients for his threesome and as long as they were blond and filthy he reckoned he could fuck them, despite their saggy boobs and caked-on makeup.

I look over to see he's still on the sofa, lying face down with his head covered by a cushion and his butt wedged up in the air. 'I'm calling in sick,' Ken's muffled voice comes from under the cushion.

'Not today,' I say, focusing my attention on the kitchen drawer stuffed with cash that will be banked in the retirement fund by the end of the day. Half of twenty-grand was an easy night's work and even when we minus the booze and clean up job we were still making three months' salary in a few hours.

Ken pokes his head out from under the cushion as I'm organising the cash into piles. 'I am going sick 'cos that's the beauty of you being my boss. And can't you see how entirely fucked I am?'

'You're coming to work,' I say, thoroughly determined to at least have this debate, although I already know it will do little good.

I carry on lecturing Ken as he stares up at me, his eyes wincing, his mind obviously trying to focus. 'Jesus, Ryan, will you please put some fucking clothes on.'

'I'll put some clothes on when you get into the shower. Is that a deal?'

'No,' he says. 'It's clear that I'm too visually tormented to move now.'

'You've had a lot of days off and I'm struggling to argue that they're all pre-booked holiday. You need to think about the shit you're causing me every time you don't feel like doing any work.'

He looks up from his pit, his eyes on my tackle. 'I'm sick, mentally scared and just a little disappointed with what I'm seeing to be able to come to work or even look at you right now.'

'This is weird. You're weird. Just promise you won't spend any of this cash on blow or prostitutes.'

He doesn't answer as I leave him lying on the sofa. He won't wake up until the cleaners arrive and then he'll probably try to shag them. I start my routine of getting ready, knowing that it isn't a happy part of my day, but I also realise that it's not the worst part and having Ken's absence to answer for again isn't going to make it any better.

*****

'So, you decided to come back?' I ask, as natural as I can. I make a conscious effort not to mention the episode in the cupboard last week. It would have been a very valid reason for her to not return to work and I wouldn't have blamed her if she decided to report her new boss and demand a move to a different department. It's what most people would probably do.

Sophie is sat next to me and I know she is staring at me with this kind of punishing probe that's picking apart all of my failings, even the ones she hasn't found out about yet. 'I thought about it for a while, I must be honest. You didn't impress me at all, Ryan, it must be said.'

I nod, realising that our relationship between manager and worker is permanently screwed. She could sit here and preach to me all day about my conduct and I am powerless to stop her.

She chooses this moment when our eyes lock, that small second where I take my focus off the road, to let her dark eyes connect with mine. 'But the way I figure it, you have a limited shelf life, so I think I'll stick around and see what happens,' she says this with a sarcastic smile, like she could easily be joking. It's the kind of gaze that, if challenged, she could easily apologise and pull away from, making some lame excuse.

I'm not sure if it's my imagination competing with my conscience but I think she's bordering on flirting.

I turn my attention back onto the road. 'Thanks for the vote of confidence,' I say, knowing it would be the same decision I would make if I was in her position. It was like the vultures were circling and all bets were off if I could hold it all together for another few months.

But my biggest issue by far is that she does all of this with Jerry sitting in the back seat. He says nothing, like a young child you leave to his own imagination as you have some adult talk in the front. He's either oblivious to my issue, or he's like my god daughter who said nothing the day Ken and me looked after her, but stored it all up to go home and ask her dearest mummy what spit roasting means.

Regardless, Sophie has returned to work and is sitting next to me, and with Jerry in the back seat we queue our way to yet another business meeting. The job of my team is to find new clients – to hook them with the corporate speech about just how many germs are out there and how the next killer bug could wipe out half their workforce. But sometimes we have to shift to client management, normally when one of our loyal regulars decides that perhaps they don't need as much gunge as they thought, or perhaps when the realisation hits them that a bar of soap could do the same job in many situations.

When that type of call comes in it's when Mitchell normally loses it, shouting around the office and demanding that I get in the car and travel to the client so I can personally beg on his behalf.

So this month's less than impressed regular is a cruise ship company and it's unthinkable just how much product we pipe into them every month. Just imagine three thousand germ-ridden, walking virus incubators, locked into a steel container in the middle of the ocean. The potential to spread just one tiny strain of any number of deadly diseases is just so unbelievably possible that we have a catalogue of horror stories.

So, when I left the flat this morning, the first voicemail I listened to was Mitchell leaving me with a very clear message that I need to solve this problem. By any stretch this shouldn't be my issue to solve; I didn't recruit this business and I haven't been the one looking after them. For some reason this still landed on my phone, meaning every other job on the list was on hold until this crisis was resolved.

'Are we stopping for coffee?' Sophie asks, even though she must know we're already running late.

'This traffic is crazy, we don't have time.'

'It's rush hour, what do you expect?' she asks, almost like she's baiting me, pointing out the obvious.

'I expect these cars to move out of my way,' I say. 'Why does rush hour exist anyway? And why does everyone get on the road at the same time? It's stupid.'

'You've given this a lot of thought, haven't you?'

'I spend a lot of time in traffic,' I say, as we come to a stop again, bumper to bumper as far as I can see. 'When you travel the roads enough you know how many junctions you've got to go before the open road and you know just how long you'll have to queue for between each one And, most of all, you have plenty of time to contemplate if it will all be worthwhile when you get there.'

'Oh, that's very deep, Ryan. That's at least a shallow grave of deepness. I didn't think you had it in you.' She kicks her shoes off and settles her feet on the dashboard. 'You don't mind, do you?'

I take a deep breath and crawl the car forward, not knowing if this is the sort of subtle battle I should fight, or just give in and let her slowly grind me down.

'So, why are we going to this place anyway?' Sophie asks.

Jerry immediately leans forward, proving to me that he hears everything but only ever responds when he thinks he'll get an audience. 'Because Mitchell has strained this relationship with a valued client of many years. He has tried to push costs up every time and given them nothing in return and that's not how you manage a loyal client partnership.'

Sophie turns around to get a proper angle on Jerry. 'It sounds like you know a bit about business.'

I see from the rear view mirror that he's nodding, but he's also got this smile on his face as he stares at Sophie and then out the window. It's one of those moments when an old guy's face creases up, showing the lines of his age and the smile that accompanies it tells a hundred tales of experience. It's moments like these that Jerry is normally left to fend for himself, the story told only to strangers, anyone who knows him choosing that moment to walk away.

But not Sophie. She tugs at the seatbelt so she can turn around a little more, willing him to continue his tales of business the Jerry way. He tells Sophie all about this client and how they were one of the first he signed up – his greatest deal back in the day. He talks proudly about how he got a big bonus for the extra business they brought in and how they opened up our world to more than just hospitals and the other obvious institutions.

'And now Mitchell has managed to piss them off,' Sophie says, talking like she knows our business and our team. Ten hours on the job and she clearly thinks that she has got us all figured out, especially me.

Jerry gives a solemn nod. 'He's forgotten the number one rule in business, which is to keep your good customers close.'

'I'm sure there are many other rules that you can tell me about some time,' Sophie says.

It makes me want to throw up but Jerry doesn't take it that way. He's laughing now, showing more energy than I've ever seen from him.

'So why has Ken gone sick?' she suddenly asks, turning back to me. 'In this moment of crisis a team should stick together, don't you think?'

'I don't think that's any of your business.'

'Does he go sick often?'

'Again, that's none of your business.'

'At least once a month,' Jerry shouts from the back to his new ally.

I brake deliberately hard as we join another queue. 'I think you should let me worry about the other people in the team.'

'I'm sure you're doing a great job of that,' Sophie says.

There's a silence in the car as we crawl over a roundabout to see that the reason for today's tailback is a queue on the M1, which is of course the exact route we need to take. I see on the sat nav that we're going to be late. It's flashing red everywhere to inform me of all the delays we're yet to encounter – advance warning of all my future despair. As I see time tick by on the clock I start to realise that this really isn't how I thought my life would turn out.

*****

He's pacing up and down his office as I sit calmly and watch him. Actually, his pace is pretty slow and he's getting annoying. He's an old bloke who looks full of frustration and regret. Sophie is next to me, our heads slowly turning as we watch him move. The only difference between us is that she's got this big grin on her face, like she's either really enjoying this or quite willing to push the boundaries on her first client visit, despite this being only her second day on the job.

'We've been with you for years and don't forget that we were one of your first clients,' he says, staring straight into my eyes, as if it's all my fault that his sales are plummeting and his profits are sinking. But he's right, of course, and so I nod in total agreement. A few decades doesn't sound like a long time, but when you consider how long soap and washing powder have been around then you realise how new our market is.

Modern germ defence for a modern world – that's what we sell, and as a cruise ship company it was one of the most logical clients to go after back in Jerry's day. I talk about Jerry's day like it was fifty years ago, but the reality is that he was a slightly bigger player just a couple of decades ago. He'd been brought over from another company at an apparently senior level and was supposed to spearhead this grand expansion they had planned. His job was to recruit a winning sales team and get out there into all the big companies, spreading the fear as much as the product he carried in little tubs in his briefcase.

That was until Mitchell arrived, with one of his first management decisions being to shelve Jerry in the *far too fucking old* bracket. In Mitchell's world how could you have a dynamic new sales team headed up by a guy who had just turned fifty. So, as it turns out, Jerry won the bid with this cruise company and lost his battle with Mitchell.

Sophie taps my arm as I realise the old guy is talking to me. 'You've forgotten about the small guy,' the old man says, now sitting behind his desk, staring reflectively into a boat in a bottle. He is right, again. These guys have a few boats but nothing compared to the big players. And although you can pump a lot of gunge into a ship on every deck, morning noon and night – there's not much more you can do for them.

I stand up, ready to attempt an apology on behalf of his lack of ability to lead his company to better shores, but he cuts me off. 'You were probably picking your nose in school when we signed the original deal and ever since then you've just screwed us down. And as for her,' he says, looking at Sophie. 'I've not even seen her before. You people keep getting younger but there's no substance in what you say or do, it's just words on an email. No handshakes and no backbone.'

I'm about to answer his second barrage of abuse when Jerry steps forward. 'Derek, I signed the original deal and I take responsibility for it not being right.'

The old man looks at him and Jerry looks back and it's like they're communicating in some silent language, both their faces tanned from decades of summer holidays. Maybe it's the language of the old and lost but it seems to be achieving the desired effect.

He nods at his dear friend, like this big wave of relief has swept over them. 'Jerry, we've had three outbreaks of Norovirus this year and your chemical mixture is supposed to make the odds of this happening near to impossible. You guys are supposed to be the industry leaders!'

'I know, Derek, I heard,' he says, rushing towards him, his body hunched like he's about to grab his old mate and comfort him in his last breath. 'I know that's not good for business.'

Derek's head is now in a constant shaking motion. 'It spreads around a ship like wild fire and it's like you guys are watering your stuff down or something.'

Jerry's hand is held out, all denying, as I start to wonder if this is actually true. Jerry's busy quoting manufacturing standards as I decide to butt in and assure the guy that just because it comes from this new world called Asia, it's still the same standards.

He's clearly not having any of it as he politely pushes Jerry out the way to get a look at me. 'I don't want to hear from Mitchell's pet dog,' he informs me, before reminding me that he built this company from scratch and all they have is their reputation. To me, this means he's pretty much fucked, since his latest little cleanliness issue was all over the papers the whole weekend.

I sit back down with the ever-silent Sophie as I watch Jerry go to work, doing something I never thought he was capable of. He pulls up a chair to the side of Derek's desk, as he excitedly pulls documents out of his old leather briefcase. They chat in their little code about things agreed years ago and before long they've settled on new contract terms based on our new enhanced product, and even some free samples of our *Sex Sanitiser* range for select customers to find in their cabins. As they shake hands I look at the old guy and he seems genuinely happy, perhaps even pleased.

And as for Jerry... well, he looks like a new man. It's like he's found his niche – looking after the older clients. It's complete discrimination but it works, because they come from the same time and they get the same things. In a single moment I see that Jerry has a future, that he has actual potential to add value – that he's hauled himself off the scrapheap and somehow got back in the game.

It's such a shame I have to fire him this week.

8

When we get back to work Jerry practically runs into the office, with his big briefcase swinging around him. As soon as we get to our floor he barges past Mitchell, who is waiting outside the lift. I let Jerry run wild into the office, like he's just rediscovered his lost youth, leaving me to face off an ever-angry Mitchell. Sophie decides to stay close to me with this permanent grin on her face that soon results in Mitchell looking her up and down. I can tell he's ready to give me my dose of daily grief but I'm pretty sure Sophie isn't invited.

I subtly push my hand onto Sophie's back as I mumble about me seeing her at our desks in a few minutes. I'm expecting her to give me this signature smile I've already grown to like and then make an excuse to leave, but instead she violently shakes her body, pushing my hand off her. I move away as she stares at me.

'Doesn't take a hint, this one, does she?' Mitchell says, towering above both of us with this big grin planted on his face. 'Sophie, why don't I make it a little more direct,' he says, angling his body towards her. 'Take your pert, little arse somewhere else so I can talk to Ryan without your flapping donkey ears prying in on his latest bollocking.'

To my surprise she doesn't move at first. She just looks Mitchell up and down, almost sizing him up without the slightest bit of probationary period fear. I quietly watch as these two stare at each other, eagerly waiting to see which one of them will overstep their respective position. I'm hopeful that something is going to happen; desperate to see someone else in the ring with him. But after a few seconds she's all smiles again, soon making her polite excuses and tapping her way along the floor. I can't help but sigh as I see her walk away.

Mitchell quickly grabs my arm and I see no use in me trying Sophie's dramatic tactic as he squeezes tight. 'So why's he so fucking happy?'

'He saved the deal,' I say, as I try to pull away, soon feeling his grip tighten even more.

'He saved what?' Mitchell spits back at me. 'Jerry couldn't save a fish from drowning and you're telling me he saved a deal that didn't need saving.'

'He did the original deal with the same guy, so it made sense for him to renegotiate terms, especially since we failed to stick to the last lot.'

With this extra information Mitchell's eyes are now rolling around as his grip gets unbearable. He's soon pushing his fingers into my arm that he's somehow managed to twist upwards, tensing my muscles to increase the pain. I pull away, considering whether this is the furthest he has ever gone and at what point I'll need to punch him to get free. Maybe that's what he wants – I hit him and get sacked for it and he gets a new beating bag to break in.

The pain is too much and I'm about to make my move when Mitchell decides to push us both into the disabled toilet. I fall backwards, propelled by his force until my face is soon attached to a cold mirror. 'He's the one who fucked up the deal in the first place, you moron. Anyone can get a deal if they promise the world and it's taken us the last ten years to renegotiate decent terms where we actually make some fucking profit.'

'But I thought Jerry was coming along to act as the original link. He's the one with all the knowledge and we had to do something, otherwise we'd have lost the client.'

'And you think that's a bad idea?' he says, as he's bumping my head against the mirror, quite gently, for effect as opposed to causing me any lasting damage. He's playing with me, I know that much. 'And don't tell me you let that Muppet sign on the dotted line?'

He releases his hold to allow me a solitary nod before fully letting go. 'Well it's no wonder he's happy. You're supposed to be giving him notice and instead you're letting him make this decade's monumental fuck up.'

'Why didn't you tell me all of this before I went to see the client? He blames you for what has happened and you sent me to fix it, so I did.'

Mitchell's head is shaking as if its movements could simply block out my observations. 'We'd be better off losing that client than sign another dud deal. Fuck knows what Raj is going to say about this and as usual I'm left picking up the pieces.'

I hit the wall, entering into a world I didn't know I had in me. 'The deal is fair – they're a loyal client and you're being ridiculous, as usual. I'll go and justify what I did to Raj right now and I think he'll get what I'm saying.'

I start to walk towards the door before a predictable arm blocks my path. 'You don't want to test me on this, Ryan. You might think Raj is the boss but let me make it clear that it's just a figurehead position. Doing our bit on the brown front for diversity, if you get me? You've screwed up again and you're running out of options, my friend. Your best choice now, as I see it, is to fall into line and do as I fucking tell you.'

There's this awkward moment that follows this revelation. It's a silent moment that follows every revelation he ever makes. It's this time again where we both wait to see if I've found a backbone, or if I'm still willing to roll over and let him kick the verbal shit out of me. I think about my life of possessions and the routine I'm forced to live by and I realise that I have no other choice. I can't break free without the two things I need the most – money to help keep my lifestyle or the free company stock to feed this desperate need for money. So I give him my best nod – our silent pact for me to keep my cowardly ways in exchange for him to happily accept my apparent flaws, even if most of them are created by Mitchell himself.

'Just make sure you fire that fucker,' he says as he stands in front of the mirror so he can straighten his tie. It's a bold, stripy thing that has somehow managed to survive in Mitchell's wardrobe for many countless years. It stretches far below his belt with this big flappy bit that probably stretches lower than his cock. It's partnered with his trademark thick, pin-striped, dark suit that's a size-or-two too big, even on his heavy frame. As we stand in this small room we're like the two most opposite men, decades apart, who have suddenly been thrust together. But my well-researched style and tailored suits are no match for a man who manages from the seventies and that's why I lose every time.

He pushes me towards the door. 'I need a shit and you need to go and sort out the crisis Tina is in the middle of. She's having another one of her fits.'

I stare at him for a second, my mind wondering what has gone wrong in her world now.

He gives me this gentle slap on the face. 'Why haven't you fucked off yet? Do you want to watch me fill this toilet bowl?'

I quickly make my escape, all the time wondering if we have any boundaries left that he hasn't already invaded and destroyed.

*****

I can hear her shouting as I reach our desk area and as soon as I get close she makes a run for the ladies toilets. She always does this, with no concern about making a drama in the office until someone more senior comes along to stop her.

Ever since I've had a team to manage I've read every type of leadership book there is. People don't often believe it but I try to be a good boss; I try to do all those things that a good manager is supposed to do. But how do you lead your way through the dramas of a short, slightly-psychotic woman running across the office, screaming at someone down her phone?

I decide that the rule book for this hasn't been written yet, but that today will be one of decisive action. I've allowed this to happen too many times, partly because I have no idea what to do and mainly because when Tina isn't in a crisis she's bloody good at what she does. I gaze over to the seating area to see Jerry is still telling his story to a small crowd who have gathered around him, all of them clueless as to the fuck up we've jointly made this morning.

I soon find myself knocking on the toilet door, deciding I'd rather deal with Tina than burst Jerry's bubble, although I know his time will soon come.

There's no answer as I hear Tina shouting, 'You can't have him so go and fucking die!' I assume this is still into her phone and so I wait another couple of minutes until I'm certain that any other female in the toilets would have retreated by now. Besides, Jerry's crowd have abandoned him in favour of watching my performance, so I decide to knock once more and go in.

As I enter I realise she's made her way into a cubicle, making me think she's going for an innocent pee and some chill time. I decide that this needn't be another possible disciplinary investigation and I start to retreat outside, but before I get to the door I hear crying coming from her direction and since I've come this far I decide I'm here for the long haul this time.

I slowly walk up to the door, the sound of me calling her name echoing off the tiles in this small room. As soon as I start knocking she makes this gross sniffling noise as I imagine her sitting on the toilet seat, her small frame filling most of the cubicle.

'Ryan, is that you?'

'Yes, Tina. I'm here, in the ladies toilet, trying yet again to fix whatever the issue is today.'

'You're a little out of your depth, boy, so I suggest you toddle off back to your desk.'

I think that she's probably right, but I decide that something needs to get done today. 'I'm not going anywhere until you come out of there and tell me what's going on.'

To my surprise she unlocks the door but doesn't open it. I wait a second before realising I need to push it. It's like some symbolic moment between us – if I want to know her issues then I need to find the guts to open the door and unleash hell, in the form of whatever issues she is harbouring. I realise I could still walk away with our eyes never meeting in this place. She'd have a little cry and then come back to her desk, no one ever knowing what happened and us never needing to speak about it again. That is until the next time she loses it, slowly edging to the point where one of us gets called to Raj's office.

I push against the door, letting it slowly slide open to see her sitting on the toilet seat, her fat arse hanging over the sides as she stares up at me. She soon starts sobbing as I stare down at her, not knowing where to start. She's dripping with sweat, her curly hair all matted and even damper than usual, her trademark thick black polo neck almost strangling her big neck.

The sobbing turns to full blown tears as I stand and watch this grown woman, this mature person, have a good blubbering cry. I don't know where to look so I just stare down at her, thankful that she's fully clothed, although I can imagine her doing this at home whilst taking a long dump. She throws a used bit of toilet roll on the floor and starts grabbing for more, until we both see that the holder has run out, wet and mangled pieces all around her, like she's created her own little nest of pity and self-loathing to fester in. She's now frantically pulling at the empty holder, almost begging it to supply her with more tissue.

I walk to the next cubicle and grab a whole bunch of them, before standing near the sinks, trying to beckon her out of the mess around her. She shakes her head at first, wiping the tears off her face, as the limited makeup smudges its way across her red cheeks.

I usher her out one more time, deciding that I'm not going near her again. It's like a doorway to my own personal hell, with this woman babbling away about random shit that means nothing to me or to the business we work for. The only people really qualified to deal with this would be another woman or a gay man – both of them immune to how this most ugly scene could put a man off the opposite sex forever.

She finally stands, grabbing at the doorframe with both hands to pull herself up. This short and stocky excuse for a person is soon standing in front of me, her beady eyes looking me up and down whilst she holds out a demanding hand for the tissue. I oblige immediately, feeling hopeful that some bog roll will somehow sort out the monster face in front of me. She's soon taking long blows of her nose, slowly clearing each nostril with this grand summoning of every bit of snot and phlegm she can find.

I start my lecture as Tina makes her way to the sink. I'm reciting a speech I've had prepared for a while. It's one about how she does a great job, a truly exemplary job, but that doesn't make up for her complete freaky fits that are getting more and more frequent. As I start to hit her with the reality that this moment isn't normal she doesn't really seem to hear anything, or be remotely interested. She washes her face, which I think is a good thing, but then she starts rinsing her hair and giving it a proper soaking, which is just plain weird. And before I can say anything her head is under the hand-dryer. Her hands are busy ruffling through her short locks, trying to bring some order as I continue with my lecture, choosing to compete with the noise as opposed to stand here and look lost in the wrong toilets with a woman that frankly scares the shit out of me.

When she's done Tina walks straight passed me, clearly heading to the door. I call her back, demanding that she doesn't leave me alone, almost turning this whole episode into my problem. 'Are you staying in here?' she asks.

'You can't go out there until you've told me what the problem is,' I say, anchoring myself to the sink, refusing to let this pass.

'There's no problem. Don't you worry yourself, sweet man.'

'No problem? Look where I found you?' I say, looking over to the cubicle and then looking back to the sink, willing her to remember and admit to what I saw.

'You went looking for a problem, Ryan. If you pry into everyone's lives then you'll find a lot more of them. Or perhaps you want to go digging into everyone else's life and find their issues? Maybe it stops you finding your own.'

'We're not leaving here until you tell me what is going on. We've reached that point.'

She stares back at me, one hand on the door handle and one foot angled towards me; two options that both now seem to be appealing to her. For a second I think her tensed arm has won the battle and forced her out of the room, but then she starts crying again and makes a run for me. This small bundle of blubbering bulk is soon wrapping her arms around me, with her bobbing head level with my pecs. I'm completely lost for what to do; the hug feels almost intimate, like a girls embrace after a quick fumble in a place where we shouldn't be. She starts to squeeze tighter, almost trying to push a response out of me. I pat her head, somehow thinking that will help, but it feels such an obviously patronising thing to do. She soon gives up looking to me for any form of comfort and starts to release me.

I wait for what seems a long time before she fully lets me go and steps back. 'I needed that', she says, letting out this long sigh and staring at the floor before sizing up my body, her gaze ending on my chest.

'You need to tell me what's going on because I'm getting really freaked out by your random mood swings. You do realise that none of this is normal?'

She starts to shake again, like she's about to start a big crying fit that could rival all others – like I've pushed a button that should never be discovered, let alone pressed. But my patience is gone. It left many months ago, when these trips to the toilet became all too regular and were always followed by apologies and quiet, sobbing requests to leave early.

'Just fucking tell me!' I shout and stand in front of the cubicle, my arms stretched out, banning her exile back in there.

'They can't take him away,' she says, suddenly calm and void of any new tears. 'They can't take my boy from me.'

9

We're sitting outside a bar for what everyone else thinks are celebratory drinks. We have even got champagne on ice, which Jerry bought for everyone. I'd hoped we could avoid this and the announcement that we got a deal that apparently no one senior to me ever wanted. 'We shouldn't have touched it with a barge pole,' was the parting message from Mitchell, which could have come a little earlier. Apparently, providing sanitary protection for a few thousand humans confined in a big metal tub is something even we should charge more for.

I offered to buy the first round of booze, hoping that it would cancel out all thoughts of triumphant bubbles, but Jerry insisted on something more fitting than a pint of lager for this glorious moment. He finally thinks he did something right in the last ten years and he has to buy his own fizz. It really says everything.

Jerry is busy telling Ken his story of turning around today's client meeting against what he is selling as being up against all odds. What I now know is that I was supposed to be correcting his fuck up in the first place, so by me waiting idly by I've made the same fuck up, except its worse when you make it twice.

Mitchell has already told me I'm for the chop. He believes he made things completely clear that I was to go fix Jerry's mistake and not offer the same ridiculous terms. I was supposed to be bringing Jerry along so he could sit in the background and see how it's supposed to be done.

The thing that strikes me the most in this moment, whilst Jerry is telling the world how fucking awesome he is and I'm contemplating the final bullet to my head, is that Sophie is sitting opposite me with this evil stare. She's not interested in Jerry's story or the catalogue of past achievements that he's now flaunting. She seems only interested in making sure I'm still aware of how much she hates me and everything that I stand for.

Even though I don't know her that well, I already know what she's got a sulk on for. As her glare moves between me and Ken, I know she's pissed that he has turned up for the post-work drinks but didn't show up to do any actual work today. I look at her and

I know I'm on pretty dodgy ground here. Jerry and Tina have always turned a blind eye to Ken's regular disappearances and my complete mismanagement of what the policy manual describes as *short-term persistent absenteeism*. I mean, if I read the manual correctly, then Ken should have been sacked three times over by now. But he's my mate and he's helping me sort out my future exit plan, so he's not going anywhere whilst he's on my watch.

So, if I can't sack him then all I can do is listen to his endless promises that he will get better, for both of our sakes. Of course I know that this will ultimately mean I have to make up more elaborate business trips that he has been on, just so I can cover up his increasingly frequent drug-fuelled, post-orgy, come-down days. Now that Sophie is on board I know we're both totally fucked. She's here to spy on me, I'm sure of it, and it won't take long before she's got an arsenal of entirely shocking information against me. She's already caught me in the cupboard with the resident blond bimbo and now she's sussed out Ken, so it won't be long before she figures out the extortionate amount of stock we're shifting on the side and then its game over.

The strange thing is I don't feel as worried as I should be. I look at her, as she's still giving me this disapproving bitch-stare that tells me how shit I really am, but all I really feel is majorly turned on. Her dark killer eyes against a backdrop of pale white skin and black hair tell me I'm a screw up. But, despite the death stare, I just want to climb into bed and beg for her mercy. She's like that spider who eats the male once she's done with him but even knowing this I can't bring myself to leave her web. I don't want her forgiveness; I'm talking about full blown beg her to bring me to ecstasy and then rip my heart out. I'm so entirely turned on by this creature opposite me that for the first time since I was fourteen I actually worry about whether I can perform enough for a woman.

And there's something more than just letting her walk up and down my back in her black leather boots. I want her approval, too. Not just in the workplace or in the bedroom, but in my whole life. She's the first woman I can't just have and it's driving me insane.

My penis has told me the reason for this is that she is obviously a lesbian – there can be no other explanation as to why we've not already jumped into bed. I have to admit, my manhood is totally arrogant but it's nearly always right.

It's my heart that tells me that it could be worth more and that she could be the one, if she just got to know me outside of work. My head has already warned me that Sophie is simply a brutal business woman on the fast track to an Executive position and she has full authorisation to trample on a few mere mortals whilst on the way up. I think I used to be in that club, until Mitchell became my boss. And now it's like having Satan as your direct line manager; I'll never please him, never do enough.

I know my head is right and that I should make a swift exit whilst I can, but it's my dick and heart that are wrestling for who should win. I want Sophie to be my cruel mistress, to dominate and own me. I've never had these thoughts before but I'd work for it, for all of it. I would try for an eternity to gain her approval and her love.

I can't stare at her any longer without wanting to run away to nurse my hard on. I don't want to look away, either, but I can't think of anything to say. She continues her probing stare until I angle my head into Jerry's storytelling, finding out that he's still busy bending Ken's ear. I try to pull a face to get a laugh from her but there's no movement – not even a twinge at the side of her lips. I move closer into Jerry's conversation, pitying myself for needing to hook onto the old man's tales, just for something to hide me from her.

He's talking like a director now; it's all business speak with long pauses to allow his powerful observations to sink in. In return, all Ken is doing is drinking. He's finished the bubbly and is onto a pint he got himself before we arrived and I know the moment he finds the bottom of his glass he'll make a quick exit. Jerry continues to relate everything he did back to the perfect sales techniques of the last three decades, like he's written his own book on it and is now plucking out the key strategies to give Ken a dose of what he should be doing.

It doesn't take long before Ken disappears without even announcing his exit, but to my horror Sophie follows him. I know she's going to ask what he was doing today and I curse myself for not coming up with some clever story that gives Ken the clear direction he will need. I watch him disappear into the bar, followed by Sophie, until it's just Jerry and me.

It's never just Jerry and me.

I try to avoid these situations as much as I can, as it's entirely obvious that I have nothing in common with the man. His career pretty much failed twenty years ago and he's been on that slippery slope to retirement ever since. I don't even know if he's married. He never mentions a wife or kids and I never ask. I know that's bad and I should make more of an effort but that's just the rules in the jungle. You don't see the alpha-male lion – head of the pride – worrying about what the old smelly granddad cat is doing, so what's different for us? He gets paid to do a below average job and I never go after him, so by other peoples standards he has survived longer than he should.

Well, that is until now. The pressure will be too much not to fire him. I'm out of options and he can't remain a passenger any longer. I look at him, as he's busy speaking at me but I have no idea what he's saying. He'll be chatting away about his business triumph as I'm busy assuring myself that his redundancy payment plus his pension will be more than enough to keep him comfortable in the latter years of his life. I know he'll be okay, with his years of service and his extensive pension – he'll be laughing all the way to the bank.

I think about telling him now, just getting it off my chest and putting him out of his misery. We'd both feel better, eventually. If I just tell him now then I'll sleep so well and he can start planning his retirement. I'd be doing him a favour, really. After all, Jerry has a permanent tan from regular holidays so he'll be able to spend all his time away, seeing more of the world and maybe he can even write that book on business he's been talking about.

Even though Mitchell would be pleased I did the deed tonight, I decide not to. I've not had the HR assessment through yet and, to be honest, the bloke looks pretty happy. He's got more confidence than I've ever seen since I've known him. His face still looks worn and haggard, with those endless bags under his eyes that speak more of restless nights on babe chat rooms than they do of late night preparations for boardroom meetings. But killing someone at their happiest doesn't seem the right thing to do.

'Can I give you some advice, Ryan,' he says, as I finally start to pay attention to him.

'Sure, why not,' I say, ready to smile and dismiss whatever drivel comes out of his mouth this time.

Jerry sits back and starts to cast a watchful eye over me, like this one day's success has suddenly given him the sixty years wisdom he's been searching for so long to find. 'I know you look at me like I'm some old coot who doesn't know what he's doing.'

I quickly shake my head, trying to convince both of us I'm wrong, but he quickly holds out a pointed finger. 'You should pay me more respect, young man. I was doing deals in London before you were born and believe it or not I was just like you.'

I stare back at Jerry, genuinely impressed that he's found a backbone and slightly sad it's come ten years too late. 'I do respect you, Jerry.'

His hand quickly smacks the table, sending the empty champagne flutes into the air, with only me making the effort to balance them. 'You don't respect anyone and that will be your downfall. Do you think you are the only power hungry man in history? Just because you think my past is back in the eighties it doesn't mean I should be valued any less. You need to learn about the people in your team and how to get the best out of us, not just playing little whispering games with Ken. It's pathetic to ever have to bear witness to.'

I nod, thinking that this quietly fading man is actually serving me some honesty and it feels damn good. 'I think you're right, Jerry. I haven't respected you enough.'

'You agree with me?' he says, with this look of shock mixed with a cautious glare, like I'm drawing him into a trap.

'Yes, you have a past, but it's left you now. I've heard the stories and I've seen the old spreadsheets. You used to pull in the deals and do the business but that was a long time ago, you have to realise that.'

He's shaking his head now, openly and desperately denying my thoughts, like I'm telling him a truth he knows but won't ever accept. 'I'm an integral part to the business and that's why I'm still here. It's not just about the young men like you, with all your energy and stamina, but it's also about knowledge and experience back at the base.'

'Oh, you think?' I say, not sure how much further I want to push him or why I'm even doing this. I could just sit quietly and nod, meaning this would all soon be over.

'Yes, I know it. Any good business knows it and Raj has told me so.'

'He's told you that you're an integral part of the business?' I ask, so blatantly showing my hand that I clearly don't agree. Raj has never once told me this, so I'm not sure if it's disbelief or jealousy that has now taken over me.

Jerry is busy nodding at his bold statement as I prepare to ask the killer question, the one that blows his wild theory out of the water completely. 'So why aren't you in my job, or higher up?'

He smiles, the long wrinkles in his face stretching up his cheeks and surrounding his eyes. 'Because Mitchell Hunter showed up, that's why.'

It's my turn to nod, knowing how completely capable Mitchell is of ruining any career he so choses. 'I kind of figured that but I never found out what happened between you two.'

Jerry pours us the remaining champagne, almost relishing the chance to tell someone the story – his side of the story, something that's probably rarely heard. 'I was doing quite well, you know. I got some good deals and slowly climbed the ladder in a few companies, until I saw that this tiny chemical company was looking for some high flying sales executives to sell some very different and cutting edge products. Did you know that the first sanitising gel was made in the sixties but it was the nineties when the idea of mixing antibacterial solutions with all manner of gadgets really started to take off?'

I look at Jerry and maybe, just maybe, I get a glimpse of myself. 'And you were the man to sell a lot of it?' I ask, now throwing myself into Jerry's little adventure.

'Yes, but it wasn't like that back then. It was about networking and building up long term contacts that led to those big deals. I've never really been motivated by making lots of money. My skills lie in tying down those real intricate relationships that take a long time to create, but ultimately you get that special signature.' He takes a moment to smile, to really grin and look at the whites of my eyes. 'I'd already been there and done that, as you are now, Ryan. When I was your age I was doing all those deals, getting that short and momentary buzz, like you're selling a house. You eventually get bored selling houses down the same road, in the same place, and so you want to do a little more with your life. I was in my early forties when I joined this promising little company that had such big aims for the future.'

'And they were looking for maturity and experience?'

He quietly nods, one of those reserved indications that I'm so bloody right. 'There was only a few of us at the start. The research department was based in an industrial estate in the North, making it nice and cheap, whilst the rest of us were in poky offices in east London. The business grew quickly and every week there was a new person joining. We got some good deals. I got some good deals! We expanded and moved up to new and better offices in central London and opened production plants all over the world.' He pauses for thought, lost in his past that so few in the company will ever know about. 'Before I knew it we were a PLC, with shareholders and corporate targets. It changed us a lot but it also opened new doors, especially when they advertised for a Sales Director. I thought straight away that it was my job, the one they had been grooming me for, but I was very wrong. The day Mitchell Hunter walked in and took this job from me I knew my future was over.'

'You've had him as a boss too?'

He quickly shakes his head. 'I headed up a smaller district sales team, focused on our loyal London clients. I tried to fight against Mitchell, tried to fight against the loss of our culture that people like him were causing. It was when they told me I was fighting against progress that I knew it was over. Mitchell had come in with the idea that instead of just selling to big businesses we could sell the idea of personal sanitising to everyone. It turned out that he was right. It caught on and before you knew it everyone was walking around with little bottles of lemon scented fluid in their pockets and handbags.'

'He came up with that idea?' I ask, with obvious shock at the big brute Mitchell actually having a good idea.

'Well, he took the credit, that's all I know, and before I knew it he had absorbed my team into his and appointed a manager above me, so that he could be sure he didn't need to ever talk to me. And since then there have been a lot of people like you, Ryan.

Young people who he can scare and manipulate so that he can keep me at arms-length.'

'He's not manipulating me and what makes you think he's even bothered about you being around?'

The pointed finger comes back again, telling me to pay attention. 'I know a lot more than you will ever know and that's why he keeps me away from him. He doesn't want to remember all of his past and I'm the person who can bring it all flooding back. You aren't the first young and naïve guy he has beaten around the office and you won't be the last. He'll use and abuse you and then throw you out when he's done with you, or when he needs someone new to blame.'

'Well, thanks for the vote of confidence, Jerry. I'm a little more important than you give me credit for.'

'Oh, really?' he shouts, now openly laughing at me, like I'm just this young fool. The thought of him being right about anything just scares me and nevermore than the truth of where I sit on the ladder. 'You're just a little cog, Ryan, a little bigger than I am now but entirely replaceable. I must inform you that I think Mitchell is getting ready to burn you.'

'Burn me? I think these opinions are a little above your pay grade, Jerry.'

He just laughs again, like he's had these conversations with many of my predecessors; like he waits for his moment to pounce before coming out of the shadows with his vile observations. 'I've seen it all before and why do you think little miss perfect is here?'

'Sophie?'

'You will end up leaving soon and Sophie will already be in situ to take over. She'll shake things up a lot, I think. Ken will follow hours after you depart and Tina will be gone within a few weeks. She'll be transferred, as no one can deny she has skills, but it can't go on being mixed in with her wild tantrums, however hard I try to help her.'

'And you, Jerry?' I say, genuinely wanting to hear the end of this tale. 'What will happen to you when we're all gone?'

He finishes his drink, savouring the moment. 'I'll survive as I always do. I've clearly shown Sophie the value of what I have achieved today. All I need to do is keep my head down for another five years and then I'll retire to the Philippines just before my sixty-fifth birthday.'

'Oh how exciting, Jerry. Please do tell me why the Philippines?'

'I have my reasons but I can't go until I've got a little more cash in the bank. It's my plan and I will survive it until the end.'

'What makes you so sure of that?' I say, trying to sound a little angry but inquisitive, without giving away the very different future I know is coming his way.

'It's simple. I'm such a small cog. With head office now in China and Raj being sent here to head up the UK operation, and with him slowly tightening the screws down on Mitchell, it's clear that he will be too busy preserving his job to worry about little old me. It's you that will get the chop, especially if they find out about the excessive amount of sample stock you are getting through.'

'I don't know what you're talking about,' I say, far too quickly, trying to keep a straight face and not showing my shock that Jerry of all people is aware of what we're up to. It's simple in my mind – if Jerry knows then everyone else already found out months ago.

'You're just a pawn in a big boy's game, Ryan. You need to learn the lesson that anyone is dispensable, especially when you play with fire.'

I nod, slowly taking in his observations, giving nothing away as I finish my champagne. 'At least I'm still in the game, Jerry. All you've done for the last decade is sit on the side lines and criticise everyone else for trying. You've wasted your life and now the little that's left is behind you.' I lean over the table, the most sinister part of me in charge now. 'Good luck with your retirement, you'd better hope it doesn't come too early.'

I get up and walk away, leaving him open mouthed and in contemplation that his exit plan, which is so obviously crucial at his age, might be under any kind of threat.

*****

By 9pm Jerry was gone. We'd thrown that hammered old man in a black cab and written down his address. Despite my incident with him I had only stormed off to the bar. I didn't hold anything against the guy, even to the point when I gave the cabbie a handful of twenties to get him home. A lot of what he said made sense and only reinforced my need to get my own exit plan moving. Why play the game of shadows with an employer when you can get out there and make your own life? Perhaps a lot of people have that thought but so few manage to escape. I know I will be different and with Sophie on board I know I have no choice but to find a way out.

By 10pm Sophie was gone, too. Ken and me had both tried to ply her with alcohol, Ken openly stating his reason was that we could all go have a threesome, with my motives being a little more sinister in that I wanted to know all her deepest secrets, especially in relation to me. But she said nothing of any substance, as if the wine was water. My head got fuzzier as her stare became more determined and she left without giving me anything to cling on to.

Now it's just Ken and me and within minutes I've given him the low down on Tina's latest crisis, followed by Jerry's observations on my career survival likelihood and then finished off with my deepest fears that Sophie is out to get us both. He just smiles through all of it, which makes me glad I omitted my other feelings for Sophie.

The only bit that gets him excited is my announcement that Tina apparently has a son and that she's hidden this fact from everyone for years. He starts screaming wildly at the gossip, announcing loudly that it's simply impossible for such a whale to actually carry another body inside her for nine months. It takes only seconds for me to regret telling him the things she told me under duress, surrounded by her snotty tissues and pent-up desperation. I promised I'd keep it quiet and that I would take my duty of care for her seriously, which has clearly managed to last less than a day.

Ken soon changes the subject to his 'big party to sell more shit than we've ever sold before'. He's planned it all, getting the new secret products and more hungry and gagging women than we've ever entertained in my flat. He's talking about renting a hotel conference room because people apparently spend more money when it looks official.

I try to calm him down but he's not listening to me. I think he's already done a line in the toilet and all my rational thoughts about keeping the party low key and exclusive are simply not sinking in. As I try to sound reasonable he's just talking over me, around me and instead of me. He's not interested in keeping it safe and simple. He's thinking big, because big risks equal a big load, as he always tells me.

But I'm too busy trapped firmly in reality, thinking only of my job and what happens if I lose it. I'm trapped by the security that my career has given me; the posh pad and the regular wage – they keep me in line, in check and in desperate need to do my masters bidding. I start to wonder how far away I am from my big plan and how scary it is that things can easily get in the way. I'm simply a prisoner in a cell I moved into of my own free will and now I can't leave it, can't give up all that I've achieved.

After all, if I don't have my job title, my car and my flat, then I've got nothing.

And having nothing means starting the climb all over again.

10

I finally chose to give in and go to the doctors for something I should probably have had checked out a long time ago. Even when I'm in work, during those long days, I still manage to forget about it. When I am naked and alone I see it – the lump. It doesn't hurt; it just silently grows, probably more in my mind than real life.

I assume that it's cancer and with good reason. What else can it be? The first thing that came to my mind when I saw it was that it will probably kill me and way before work drives me to a heart attack. But sometimes the lump disappears and since when does cancer do that?

'It's a hernia,' the doctor says, no sooner than my pants are around my ankles. I stand and stare at him, wanting to tell him he's wrong. I was too prepared for the other word that I don't know what to say. I don't even know what a hernia is.

I think he can tell that I'm waiting for more so he fills the awkward silence by checking my balls, kind of out of courtesy. He has a good feel, pulling them around a bit until he's completely satisfied that I don't have anything else of any interest.

As I pull up my trousers and desperately think of what I can ask, he sits himself down and starts tapping on his keyboard. He's young, no older than me, with a decent figure-hugging shirt that matches his trimmed stubble. It's the first moment that I've even noticed him or the pictures of his travels pinned around the room. To come to think of it, it's only now I've realised that I'm dealing with another human being; someone with as many hopes and dreams as me and maybe just a little trapped in this small den of regular bad news.

A wave of relief guides me to a seat next to his desk as I silently wait for him to be done with whatever he needs to tell the computer about me.

'Won't be a moment,' he says, with this smile. It relaxes me as I start to realise this might be one less problem to worry about. He soon swivels around, facing me with all the beaming energy that smile can offer. 'So it's an inguinal hernia, quite common in fact.'

'Aren't hernias for old people?'

He laughs and nods, just enough to tell me I'm more right than wrong. 'It's normally caused in men your age through external factors, as opposed to any internal issues. Have you been straining anything lately?'

Only my mind, I think, before quickly shaking my head.

He stares at me for a second and I think he's sizing me up. His attention and all that energy seem to be directed at my head and not to the physical issue I came in with. I stare back, determined that I'll stay strong for at least another minute. Despite my desperation to keep my life as normal as I can, I still think about the other options. I think that if he asks me the right questions, with just a little probing beneath the surface of my tired brain then I might just crack. Getting signed off sick doesn't seem like a bad option. The work-related stress sick-note could easily be followed by a harassment case against Mitchell, whilst all the time I try to find another job.

I wonder if there will be a similar position that puts me in a top Canary Wharf pad, another job that gives me status and the ability to pursue my bold end game? I think about going to war with Mitchell, about the damage he has already promised he will do to my next two jobs after him and I think that it's just not worth it.

'So, do you go to the gym a lot?' he asks, his fingers poised back on that keyboard. 'Or perhaps you are straining on the toilet? Either of these can cause the hernia.'

'Maybe,' I say.

'Maybe,' he says back, before doing this silent thing on me again. 'Maybe, which one?'

'Maybe both,' I say. 'Look, I really don't know. So what do I need to do? Is it a course of drugs or something?'

He gives me this smile again, which is becoming more patronising than understanding. 'Do you know what a hernia is?'

I shake my head, acknowledging out loud for the first time that I actually don't.

He nods back and starts explaining what it is, telling me things I hadn't even thought of. I half-listen and only really pick up what he's saying when he tells me it will need an operation, which in turn means time off work.

'An operation?' I say, almost pleading with him. I want to argue with him, to argue against logic and the facts presented before me. 'I can't take time off work, not now.'

He stares back at me again, silently waiting to see if I plan to elaborate on that, and when I don't he starts printing some stuff out for me. They look like factsheets, telling me all about this most unglamorous of ailments and one that Mitchell will entirely fail to understand.

'The waiting time will be a few weeks to months, anyway. That is unless you go private, in which case they can see you a lot quicker.'

I think about the private medical option, using the insurance the G.U.E Corporation kindly contributes into and then I think about being away from work for any more than a long weekend. Every day I'm away means Sophie can snoop freely into my activities whilst Mitchell plans my demise. They will work together to ruin whatever is left of my career. 'I'm going NHS,' I say.

He nods back and starts tapping into his keyboard. 'The recovery time is usually two to three weeks but I'm afraid after that you'll need to avoid the gym for a while.'

I don't answer as I stare at the printouts he has given to me but I'm not really reading them. I'm just silently contemplating which of my six-pack or my career I'll lose first.

'Is there anything else?' he says, giving me that one final chance to come clean on all the other issues.

I shake my head. 'I think I've done enough for today.'

*****

I'm standing in Mum's kitchen. I'm ready to break the news that her little boy needs an operation – that he's going to be knocked out and cut open. Even if it is only to push my intestines back inside and do some quick repair job on the muscle wall, it's still the stuff of nightmares for every parent, no matter how old the child.

For me, it's more the inconvenience, with no gym or partying. As for Mitchell it was a complete and utter travesty. No driving anywhere and a minimum of two weeks recovery time, which he soon told me, through gritted teeth, would have to be taken as holiday.

But for my mum there is nothing. No shock, no standing up and giving me a long hug. I expected a thousand questions, until she was satisfied of how minor it really is, but there was only a short gaze in my direction before turning back to her whatever task she has found the energy to do.

Carol is in the kitchen, taking mum through some financial stuff. Carol is mum's best friend and someone I've known for most of my life, making her and mum the equivalent of what Ken and I will become, if he doesn't eventually abandon me for someone better.

'We need to sort out the pension and accounts,' Carol says. 'We've put all of this off for long enough,' she looks at me as she makes this statement, as if I should have been all over this.

'We haven't got a money situation,' mum says, looking at me with this smile of satisfaction.

'Do you have enough?' I blurt out, as if I have found some purpose in all of this.

'Yes, there's enough here,' Carol says, as she shuffles through the paperwork and then takes hold of mum's hand on the table, comforting her as I never could. It's a well-known fact that women are better at the emotional sort of thing and they'd probably never dispute that. But that means the men should be good at the practical and important things. Those are things like having the no-bullshit chat with my dad when I had the chance. Facing up to the uncertain future we all have and getting signatures on the right documents.

Both me and my old man failed to do this. We never talked about the practicalities of what happens in any number of scenarios where mum, the person who doesn't work, needs to know that the roof over her head is comfortably covered.

'I suggested that mum comes to live with me,' I say, looking directly at Carol. I watch and wait, wanting to know her thoughts on this most ridiculous idea.

'Your dad won't like that one bit,' mum says, her head shaking as she stares up at me. The rings around her eyes are nearly black, clear signs that the exhaustion is winning the battle for her mind.

Carol rubs a hand along mum's shoulder, pulling her closer for a hug. 'I think it's something you could consider, even if it's just for a few weeks.' She gives me a cautious look before turning back to mum, making sure she catches her eyes. 'It might be good for you to both spend some time together.'

Mum stands up and pushes her oldest friend out of the way as she storms over to the sink. 'Well, I can't just leave him. Who will do the cooking and the cleaning? You two just don't think about these things.'

Carol walks over to the sink, her resolve not faltering for a moment. The conversation that seems to be on repeat and that has defeated me many times over is still a battle Carol wants to fight. 'You know we've talked about this before,' she says.

Mum throws everything she is holding into the sink, her mind clearly as equally ready to battle this out. They stare at each other, locked into the ultimate battle of right and wrong; what is wanted against what is needed.

I know that I should join in, perhaps even take charge. I am her son and it is my duty to sort this. But I choose not to and instead I make my excuses to leave. Mum doesn't hear anything as I head for the door, retreating far too many times than I can recall in the last few months.

Carol simply nods as she accepts my leaving again. I'm not sure that she agrees with my unwillingness to see this through but she seems to understand why, which is good enough for me right now.

Thank God for Carol, is all I can think, before I go into the garden and start on the weeding that I'll never get to finish. Once they've cut me open I'll be no good to anyone. I'll just be another burden for someone to look after and the list of those able to help is getting less as the weeks roll by.

11

As soon as I arrive in work I'm summoned to see Mitchell. The blinds to his office are already closed, setting a clear divide between what is happening in there and the far nicer outside world.

I shut the door and turn to see Mitchell is standing next to me, forcing his face towards mine. We're now sealed in his world and those on the outside can only guess what is happening. Anyone on this floor will know I'm here and they'll assume I'm getting a bollocking of some sort. It's a well-known fact that I have never journeyed up to this floor and left with a smile on my face.

'What's this hernia crap all about then?' Mitchell demands. 'Sounds like some modern bollocks illness, if you ask me. It's all in your bloody head.' He's towering over me and prodding my forehead, breaking all boundaries and breaching all rules about how you're supposed to treat an employee.

He doesn't wait for an answer, instead walking over to his desk. There isn't anything I can say that will placate him and I doubt that the need for an answer is why I'm here.

I slowly follow him to his desk, taking up the seat opposite him. His office is big but it's empty, just his oversized desk and a few filing cabinets. There's a round meeting table in one corner but I've never seen it used for anything except piling paperwork on. It makes me laugh that it's round, somehow symbolising a moment in time where there might be a constructive meeting where everyone listens to each other, ultimately finding agreement and compromise.

It's the blinds that frustrate and scare me the most; a product of the past that should now be illegal. They're nothing more than a symbol of shit management from an era where bullying got you some sort of respect. If you have to hide what you're doing then you know it's wrong, but I'm not sure beating obedience into your employees was ever legal, in any era. But here I am again, in Mitchell's office and doing nothing about it.

'So, come on then, explain this operation you apparently need,' he says and stares back at me, demanding an answer.

'It's a doctor's diagnosis, not mine,' I say, cursing myself for not coming up with a better answer. I knew this moment was coming and all I can do is blame the nice doctor who would happily have signed me off had I told him a quarter of the shit I get.

Mitchell doesn't say anything in return. He just stares at me and in return I stare back, calmly looking at his probing eyes that are so unbelievably grey. Any hint of brightness or a healthy blue glow has been driven out over years of him hating everyone and now they're just dull, with no life left in them.

We both know that the fight still goes on. Despite how long the silence lasts he is still opposite me, in my face, his recent cigar and coffee breath poisoning me from across the table. His beard is a total mess too, nearly all grey. Those last few strands of the man he once was still try to hold on and make an appearance but they're losing the war. I swear that in some of our longest stand offs I've been able to watch the transformation of black to grey hair, counting those few solitary dark hairs fighting to keep a little bit of who he used to be.

'Two weeks off is bollocks,' he says. 'I had less for my chop and I did half as much whinging about it.'

'I've not done any whinging,' I say, realising there is no point in arguing.

He pushes a long accusing finger into my face. 'You're just putting off what you need to do.'

'I'm not putting off anything.'

'So you're telling me that you've sacked that worthless piece of shit?'

'He's not a worthless piece of shit,' I offer back with a long and restless sigh.

'So what you mean to say is that you haven't sacked him and that you have no intention of doing so any time this fucking century?' He walks away from his desk, muttering under his breath before turning his hulk of a frame around like he's trying some new effect on me. 'You really don't want to push me on this, Ryan. Jerry needs to go and you need to remove him as quickly and quietly as possible.'

'What exactly am I sacking him for? For being too old? I'm pretty sure a tribunal will be interested in us sacking him before his retirement is due? Or maybe you're pissed because he just pulled in a good deal and kept a loyal client and you can't stand that? Let's get rid of him whilst he's on a high!' I'm on a roll now and I just can't stop. It's all coming out and I wonder at what point this won't be about Jerry and it will be about me.

Mitchell is coming towards me now like a lion charging after its prey, but I still don't want to stop. 'Or maybe you'd like me to remove him because he reminds you of your shady past. I've heard all the stories –'

I can say no more as Mitchell rips me out of my seat and stands me up, like some kind of action-hero doll he's playing around with. I try to back myself away, to get a better look at what is happening but I quickly find myself on the floor. A sharp pain pulses through my stomach as the realisation hits me that there isn't anything this man won't do.

I try to stand up, to gather myself back together and prove to him that I won't cower on his office floor. I can see his unpolished shoes, the scruffy leather coming apart from the heel, as I push myself up. I force my eyes to follow the trail of his pin stripe suit, vowing to find his eyes. As I look past his bulk of a stomach I think about hitting him, perhaps a hard jab in the bollocks. I've never been a fighter but I'm not a wimp and I know I've got enough beneath my skin to wound him and yet I never use it.

It's too late for me to make a decision as I realise I'm rising up quicker than my legs can ever move me, as Mitchell pulls me up then gets my head wrapped between his bulky arms. I can smell the sweat through his shirt as he lifts my body off the ground like some sort of wrestling match. I'm just waiting for the tombstone move that will finish me off as it dawns on me that I'm not fighting back. His grip tightens and it feels like he's forcing the very last breath out of me; like he's pushing every remaining bit of willpower out of an overinflated cushion.

'If you don't deal with him then I'll deal with you and then I'll deal with him myself,' he says, no more than a whisper in my ear. 'That cruise ship deal was a fuck up. He overstepped the mark and has cost us money. This means what he did was misconduct because he failed to follow your exact instructions to liquidate the contract, so along with all of his other documented fuck ups, that gives us justification to terminate his employment.' He tightens the grip a little more, now freely choking me.

'I hope you really get what I'm telling you,' he says, before finally throwing me across the room.

By the time I get myself up he's sitting back behind his desk, looking down at some paperwork and making no effort to look over at me. It's one of those moments that doesn't need anything else to be said. I'm supposed to have lost and now I should brush myself down and leave the room, silently acknowledging all that must be done.

His message to me is clear and I'm really not supposed to argue anymore because I've been beaten. Literally. I should now retire to lick my wounds and do the deed but in my head and heart I know it's wrong. I also know what will happen if I don't do it and I wonder if I really want to defend an old guy who's reached the end of his usefulness? Jerry must surely have enough savings to retire to his dream shack in the Philippines and live out his days with as many happy-ending massages as his heart can take. He's got his exit plan all lined up and now he's just hanging on for a greedy couple more years.

And what about my exit plan? It isn't even in its infancy stage yet. I'm too young and I've got everything to lose – I'm still in my survival plan.

'I have one question,' I say, the battle between right and wrong still raging in my mind.

Mitchell stops writing, his body not moving. 'I haven't given you the option to ask any questions,' he says, not even looking up at me.

'If you want me to do your dirty work then you need to allow me this question.'

He finally looks up at me, not actually giving me the decency of acknowledging that I can ask my one thing. For him to say yes would be to admit that little bit of defeat to me, and to say no would stop that curiosity of the game that I know deep down he loves.

'Has Raj signed this off?'

'Raj!' he shouts, standing up and leaning over his desk. 'What the fuck has Raj got to do with things?' His face is all creased up, the anger written all over it. 'Who do you think runs this department? I fucking call the shots around here, Ryan, not that Indian baboon.' He's banging his chest now, like he's having some monkey moment of his own.

'Any dismissal has to go up to Raj's level.'

Mitchell slowly makes his way around his desk, moving towards me. I'm not sure if he's about to strike again or just get closer so he can do that murmuring thing that's supposed to have such a dramatic effect; the big words said in a small tone – the most sinister of moments dumbed down to an almost silent movie.

To my surprise he sits on the corner of his desk, the other side just rising slightly off the floor. 'Are you quoting the rule book at me now, Ryan?'

I go to answer but he pushes a hand towards me. 'Raj is quite clear that there are serious issues with mismanagement in your team and that it stems from the leader which, in case you haven't quite grasped, is you. You're living in that posh pad, taking all the money but you ain't delivering the goods. Raj believes at this time this is because you are dealing with the shortcomings of Jerry and that once he's dealt with you will focus back on penetrating Canary Wharf and its rather lucrative surroundings. Sophie, who I really would like to penetrate, is Jerry's replacement and it's all part of a strategic manpower plan that we have agreed. But should you fail to deal with Jerry it will make things all too clear that you are also part of the problem and the failures are riddled throughout your team. Don't deal with Jerry and that's fine. I'll deal with you and then I'll dissect each of your team until I find out what they've really been up to. You'll all end up in the job centre together and ironically the only one who will survive is Jerry, who'll be off on his early retirement, laughing at the rest of you. So, it really is Jerry or you and everyone else. So what's it going to be?'

I take my time to pause, to think about how quickly Mitchell will uncover what Ken and I have been up to. Ken will get sacked for what he's been doing and I can't do that to my best mate. And I can't say I like Tina but she works hard and makes a lot of shit happen. I find that all too quickly I am making my decision to throw Jerry to the sharks, my weak mind soon won over by the ugly reality that Mitchell threatens me with.

I still haven't answered Mitchell before he throws a brown folder at my chest. 'This is a full copy of your numerous performance discussions you have had with Jerry. I think we understand each other.'

I take hold of the fictitious folder that will be Jerry's demise and make my way out of the lair. I'm already telling myself it's the right thing to do, for everyone except Jerry.

*****

So who else could I call?

The answer is anyone but her, but it's too late for those thoughts now. She's already on the balcony, admiring my rented view. She looks good out there, staring across the London skyline through her oversized shades, leaning just a little too far over the rails to catch that corner view of the Shard, whilst pushing her tight skirt further up her thighs.

I watch all of this happening from the kitchen, freely perving at her whilst I prepare some champagne. Sophie expressly said she didn't want to drink but in my opinion that was just what women say when they pretend they don't want to get laid.

I'm struggling with the fact that I let my confidence take a dip and that for one short moment I actually doubted that I could lure Sophie into my home and my bed. Of course she fancies me and of course she wants me. And now, looking back since her arrival, I can see that what I lost in faith has more than been made up in the thrill of the chase.

I told her that I need some help with Tina's latest crisis and that a woman's perspective would be most helpful. It turned out to be just enough to get her here, into my flat, outside of working hours. 'It's a great view,' I say as I step through the doors and onto the balcony. 'Every morning and evening I come out here and feel so fortunate I can look at this.'

'What the fuck do you think this is?' she says in return, refusing to take the champagne flute from me.

I hold it out further. 'Look, I know you said water but it's nearly the weekend.'

'Do you drink to forget your troubles, Ryan?' She says whilst fixing this look of total frustration on me, her suit jacket still done up and her arms folded over her breasts like they're protecting some forbidden zone.

'Look, it's just a drink.'

She steps towards me, her high heels tapping on the wood, and finally takes the glass from me. I let out a slight sigh, not enough for her to notice – more of an inward sort of celebration. I think of this moment as a small victory, considering I've never had to work so hard for a woman before – not even a group of women. She's like an impossible barrier to break down but I'm taking the little gestures as a good sign.

I hold up my glass to prepare a little toast, just something about new horizons and new people working together, but before I can start to speak she throws her champagne over the side and then calmly puts the glass on the table.

'I said water.'

'Oh, Jesus! You really are a barrel of fun, aren't you?'

Her head's now in this constant shaking movement, like some perpetual denial of anything to do with me, or us, that she regularly launches into. 'I know what you want. It's what every man wants. You think we'll sit out here and casually talk about work, about the office politics and about what I really think of Mitchell. And as we make all of this small talk the first glass will slip down easily.'

I decide to sit down to enjoy this story as I put myself in the path of the remaining sun. Its final dull heat of the day rests on my back as I knock back my champagne in one, trying to look just a little less interested or desperate than I really am.

'You'll then go and get the bottle from the fridge, putting it into the handy bucket you've got on the side in the kitchen. The ice has already conveniently found its way in there and I wouldn't put it beyond the realm of possibility that you manage to rustle up just a few little snacks from the fridge. Not enough to keep me sober but enough to ensure that you don't get me entirely wasted before you try your next move on me.'

I laugh but don't speak, as I refuse to give her any more ammunition to support her already killer observations.

She looks down at me through those brown glasses and all I see is the reflection of myself; the image is a small man staring back at me, reduced to nothing more than a cast off in the eyes of someone else. I think about what I will say back, about whether it will be a justifying speech or another attempt at poor flirting. I look at her and wonder if she knows half of what I'm going through.

Before I can say anything she suddenly moves towards me and pins herself over my legs, her head level with mine as my thighs are forced to take all of her weight. I gasp as I feel my dick double in size. It's involuntary; uncontrolled and so completely unlike me. I am always the one in control; the master of ceremonies as the charming host and the perfect lover.

She's so close now I can feel her breathing, the calm and constant motions of her breasts just above my chest. I look at her skin, as I smell her sweet perfume like it's dripping from her neck. 'And then, Ryan, what will you do then?'

'When?' I gulp.

She's lingering all around me now, moving around my head, slowly going from side to side, her breath teasing my ears. 'When you've got me drunk and at your will, what will you do with me then?'

'It's not like that,' I say, trying to push her off me. She refuses to move, using all her fragile balance to keep me weighed down.

'Oh, please, have I got all of this wrong?' She says as she grabs my cock. I try to sit back as her small hands seem to take hold of everything, my thin suit trousers doing nothing to protect me from her sharp nails. 'Then your brain will move to your dick, where it seems to live most of the time. You'll inevitably try to fuck me and I'm sure it would be a great shag. Don't get me wrong, every inch of you bulges through those tight white shirts and slim trousers you wear. I'm sure you'd take me to heaven and back.'

She lets out this half-hearted laugh before putting her other hand around my throat as she pushes my head to one side, so easily bending me to her will that I feel like begging her to fuck me now. She leans close to my ear. 'But this side of you embodies everything I stand against. I'm not a cheap fuck and you'd sincerely have to impress me if I was to ever even consider you as something more than a caveman dressed in Gucci.'

We spend a moment staring at each other. I know it must be her chance to look into my eyes to find some shock and maybe some validation, now that I have seen what she is capable of doing. But when she starts to release me, to step away, all I can do is think about how I want more. I need this dominance, this control and this powerful person to make me see me for what I really am.

'So, how do I impress you, if not through sex?' I ask, thinking only about how I can serve this woman in ways I have never considered before. It's like a whole new species has been created before my eyes and it's one that deserves my ultimate respect; the sort of woman worth fighting for – my primal instinct taking over.

'Well, not with that,' she says and points her gaze at my crotch. 'You wanted some help, some advice and to hopefully form a closer work-related relationship with me.' She starts to straighten up her skirt and walk away. 'I'm going to visit the bathroom and you are going to order a Chinese and make me a white-wine spritzer. Make sure I get some spring rolls, the spritzer is easy on the wine and find some proper issues to discuss.'

As she walks into the flat I remain seated and still, my mind racing as I wait for the slow retreat that should be happening in my trousers. Time ticks painfully by as I let the realism settle that I will never do enough to impress this woman, this new breed of man-eater who has been sent to test and to defeat me. I settle my mind on the reality of why she is here and the serious decisions I need to make over which Chinese menu stands the best chance of somehow saving this evening.

*****

The knock at the door comes at the most inappropriate time.

We're both lying on the carpet, our glasses of undiluted wine on the coffee table, within reach but no longer dominating the night. We've finished the takeaway, we've chatted about work and we've laughed far more than I expected us to.

Above all we have relaxed. I'd like to say it's just Sophie who has relaxed, with her suit jacket off and her blouse falling open a little more than she knows, or cares to cover up. But it's me who has truly calmed down as I enjoy the company of a beautiful woman without nursing a constant throb in my pants. Of course those feelings are there, the stirring that comes when you least expect it, but I'm enjoying the chat and the mild flirting, balanced with the sharing of our two young minds.

This is a new experience in itself, for me. I'm a thirty-something man and only now am I seeing a woman in this new light. The only other woman to have ever pushed these buttons was Joanna, but we both knew that would need to end in the bedroom for everyone's sake. And besides, the moment it was over she tossed me to one side. I wonder if this is what the start of love is like. Maybe the first opening comes with your mind and not your heart and maybe that makes you just as vulnerable.

The second knock at the door echoes through the flat again and I know it is Toyah. That well-used knock at the most undesired moment.

'Aren't you going to get that?' Sophie asks, her probing stare coming out again as she slowly manoeuvres herself from the relaxed embrace of the rug to a sturdier business-like pose, ready for any shock visitor.

I think about saying no, my mind desperately trying to think of any excuse not to walk the few feet to the door. I curse myself for ever meeting Toyah, for all those lonely times when all I could think about was getting a long, hard fuck, and for inviting her over so many times that the doorman would let her in without ever buzzing up to me.

'It's probably the wrong flat,' I say, to the backdrop of that knock again, followed by Toyah's whiny voice shouting my name.

I give in and head for the door, with Sophie already standing up and straightening her skirt, then fixing that blouse button that turns out was a step too far. I close the living room door, as if that will help, as I try my best to think of how I can get this distraction out of here as quickly and quietly as possible. I look through the peep hole to see that sure enough it is Toyah. But this time she's wearing just a laced bra and an almost non-existent thong, shivering and whining as she hugs herself, her arms not knowing which part of herself to cover up first.

I open the door just before she knocks again, her face instantly lighting up as she thrusts herself onto me. I try to push her off but she just wraps her arms and legs around me. 'You make me wait like this!' she screams, as I try to keep a hold of her. I gently wrestle with her, trying my best to prise this fragile thing off my body with as much dignity as I can afford. But she just keeps giggling and trying to kiss me, as if the locking of our lips will cement her being here and validate the risk she took in practically stripping in the hallway.

'I thought I'd return the favour,' she says, pulling the small string of her thong further down her leg.

'Look, Toyah, this really isn't a good time,' I say, as I manage to finally lift her off me and put her feet back onto the floor.

'I can see,' she says, her body frozen, as I soon realise she's not looking at me but instead towards the living room.

I turn around to see Sophie dominating the doorway. She looks at me and I look at her and it's as if we both know that I've just ruined what was becoming a great night. I don't think she even looks angry, but more disappointed at a possible *something* that could one day find a way to turn into a promising relationship, but that's just been strangled at birth.

I knew we wouldn't be sleeping together tonight, or maybe any night soon. But I felt fine with that. A peck on the cheek and a knowing smile the next day that would have been enough to fuel my interest, my suspense and my willingness to not look at another woman until Sophie made up her mind.

But now her own mind is clearly made up, her head shaking and her eyes looking a little more moist than I ever wanted to see. We're both speechless, both a bit lost.

And so it's Toyah who breaks the ice of the moment. The small, yet loud and cheeky, and so utterly insignificant, Toyah. I hadn't considered her in all of this, as she stands there barely clothed in a moment she didn't expect to find, in a place where she's been fucked in every corner and position imaginable. My eyes, my thoughts and my heart hadn't once reminded me of her, despite the fact she is still clinging to my arm.

We both look at her as she lets out that signature giggle. 'Is this a threesome night?'

12

Today is the day.

That's what the message told me this morning. My usual wake up routine was shattered by Mitchell's name appearing on my phone just gone 7am. His voicemail was angry, as I would have expected the conversation to go – another message of pure hatred that I must remember to record.

So I trudged across London with the other thousands of corporate drones, heading to their desks with coffee cups in hand. Not many people ever look happy to be heading to work, or do they just hide it better than me? I always wonder how many people deep down hope that something will save them. I imagine that all of us long for some higher power to tell us that we don't need to go to the office today, that what we slave over for sixty hours a week really is quite insignificant and that we should get the hell out of here.

If we suddenly got blown up, or invaded by aliens, or just a random outbreak of a contagious virus, you wouldn't find many people declaring that they simply must get to the office to clear that email pile-up that's been haunting them all week. We work simply to get paid and we must have something to fill our lives with, but lately I wonder if there isn't perhaps something else we should be doing with our precious time.

When those days do come it feels like the universe is all eyes on me, watching what I will decide to do. And I think today could be one of those moments.

Sacking Jerry isn't particularly the nicest thing I will ever do but it will certainly be remembered for a long time to come. This wasn't the way he wanted to go. This wasn't how he wanted to see out his days in the place he has committed so much of his life to. There will be no glorious speeches of his achievements; just one sad and lonely old man being brutally pushed out the door he wanted to walk freely out of in just a few years time.

And why has this happened? All because one man doesn't like him and because of a past between them that no one remembers. I know Raj is aware of what is happening but at his level it's just numbers; he doesn't care how hard Jerry does or doesn't work. Mitchell says this was always inevitable and that if it wasn't me then he'd have someone else doing what he claims must be done.

I read the folder Mitchell gave me a hundred times last night. I read every page and every testimonial to the fuck-ups made by just one person. This dossier of the fictitious failures of one quiet old man proved to me beyond doubt what the corporate machine can do when it turns all eyes on you. It's like everyone touched it in some way, with Raj approving the need for change, Mitchell leading the witch-hunt and the cogs of human resources ticking away with the blatant breaches of policy.

Then there is me – the Line Manager. I'm the one guy who has his prints all over this work, despite the fact I first caught sight of it a matter of hours ago. But if I don't make this happen then all the team will suffer. We'll all go, except for Sophie, the girl who I now know was always planned to replace Jerry at my side. But maybe that's where I want her to be, by my side for everything that is yet to come. I walk towards our building and keep repeating Mitchell's last words to me, 'this is about doing the right thing, which sometimes means you need to do things wrong.'

And so for Jerry, today is a choice – a half-hearted goodbye package or a fight for his pride.

*****

The moment I walk into the office I see him at his desk. He looks tired, but it's Friday and it's been a long week for us all. I start to wonder how tired I'll feel by Friday when I'm double the age I am now.

I look at him, the man who hasn't been appreciated for a small eternity. No one asks him what he's going to do for his weekend yet he's still finding the energy to smile. It's one of those lingering smiles that make me feel genuinely sorry for him. It's the kind of smile that carries on when the other person has gone back to their work, the smile that begs to be noticed just a little longer. He always comes back from a long weekend a deeper shade of orange but no one teases him about the excessive sun beds or probes where he has been. He doesn't really exist to most people around here.

There have always been rumours that he was a married man once and that his wife left him for another man; just another shade in his web of rejection. However, there's no one in the team that knows the face before the one here now. That younger and more agile Jerry would have been at the top of his game, but now it's just rubbery skin and deep frown lines left behind, and those eyes – buried in two large craters as dark as his suit.

Before I know what I'm going to say Jerry is sitting in front of me. Time moves agonisingly slow as I position us on either corner of a large table, in the biggest available meeting room at the furthest end of our open-plan office. I know that deep down I've not finished wrestling in my mind with the reality of what I have to do. I've not found those other options, that win-win outcome that works for us all. I'd imagined falling into bed with Sophie last night, in a half-drunken embrace where I take her into my confidence. I try to visualise how shocked she'd be at first, but how quickly she would come around and how her even quicker mind would think of the perfect result.

Instead of Sophie firmly at my side, I have Jerry and this folder – that brutal masterpiece that was only created to destroy him.

'What is this about, Ryan?' he asks, more casually than I would expect. He leans towards me whilst keeping his back straight, making the chair do all the work. He swizzles and adjusts it until he's got the perfect angle on me, almost like it's now his meeting with me. No matter what the nature of the meeting Jerry has always come across as this senior director type, the sort of person you'd like your granddad to be. There's no mumbling of words or unsteady movements. I watch him, his eyes following mine but with a steady smile on his face and I know that this is all an act.

The longer the silence lasts the less his persona can hold. His shirt fits his slim frame well but the dullness of the colour shows his lack of care; his tie tries to shout trend but it's held back by this bronze tie-pin. Everything about Jerry smacks of the past fighting to somehow be recognised in the modern world.

He's frowning, in some sort of open opposition to the moment. Maybe he knows. Maybe he has seen it coming for a long time. I take a deep breath and say the line I've been practicing for days. 'We need to talk about your performance.'

Once it's out there I don't feel any better. I'd convinced myself that once I said the first few words the rest would just flow naturally, all leading to the point where I crush him then quietly escort him to the door. Jerry is staring at me open mouthed and I'm totally clueless as to what he thinks. 'You've probably been expecting this, Jerry,' I say, hoping that I can make him do the hard work of explaining the situation we're now both in. It's a dirty trick I learned from Mitchell and now I find myself doing it.

To my horror, Jerry suddenly smiles. 'The cruise ship deal,' he says, grinning and smacking his hands together. 'I knew it!' he shouts, as he starts walking up and down. 'I knew it was the big one. It always has been and now it's finally been noticed.'

I nod, not sure of what to do.

'Well, it's about time I got some recognition, Ryan. It's been years in the making.' He suddenly opens a folder of his own as he licks his fingers to help him fumble to the right page. 'I have a lot I need to talk to you about and now seems like the time to do it.' His glasses are no longer hanging off his neck but now posed on his nose, his face angled to let him look through them and to see me at the same time. 'Do you know how many people go on a cruise every year, Ryan?'

'No, Jerry, I don't. And I don't think it matters.'

'Doesn't matter,' he almost shouts. 'That one deal was the tip of the iceberg, if you excuse the pun. What about sanitary precautions before the trip? What about a simple shot of concentrated *Double-Eradication Fluid* added to a normal shower gel to help kill the nasty bugs before you travel?'

'Jerry, no,' I say, not wanting to go there, not wanting to hear any of this plan.

He grabs my arm, frantically trying to join his gaze with mine, clearly desperate to find a common ground and an ally to spread his idea. 'Cruise ship companies will pay to issue it. Imagine a special welcome pack going out to every passenger due to set sail and all the extra product samples we can send them.'

'We need to talk,' I say, as our moment of frustration reaches a climax when I'm staring at his finger on the page of some complex report and he's staring at me. It's this look of triumph mixed with complete and all-consuming anxiety that really scares me about Jerry. This is the moment he's been waiting for. The moment he should have had when his suit was last fashionable; when he last meant something to someone.

He's soon thrusting the report in my face, his obvious anger at my lack of interest. We enter into this sort of civilised paper-wrestling match, where he's trying to force feed me the information and I'm desperately trying to make him close the folder and forget any idea he has of career revival. 'Jerry, we need to talk,' I keep repeating through gritted teeth.

The folder suddenly hits the floor, an array of graphs and figures strewn all around our shiny shoes. He's soon crouching down, trying to pick them all up, telling me he simply doesn't understand what's got into me.

And that's where I tell him. This guy whose laid his whole life bare in front of me, on his knees and desperately trying to scoop up the one lifeline to anything successful. 'Jerry, you're fired.'

He instantly stops shuffling. In fact, he just stops moving. I get up and walk to the window but soon find myself storming back towards him. 'You knew this was coming, you had to know. You have a past that you cannot get away from and we need to move forward. You had to know this was coming, Jerry.'

He doesn't answer as I find myself lecturing this old man, still on his knees, his mouth wide open. He listens, trying desperately to take it all in.

'No, Ryan, once you see these plans you'll see that I'm onto something. We can't ignore it.' He tries to force these bits of paper into my hands as I close them up, refusing to take anything from him, the paper getting crumpled and torn. 'Please, just look! You have to look.'

I grab him by both arms and pull him up so we're eye to eye. 'It doesn't matter what you do, Jerry. They don't want you here anymore.'

'You mean Mitchell doesn't want me here and you're the poodle doing his dirty work.'

'It doesn't matter about Mitchell,' I tell him, knowing that he'll never believe it. The one common thing we both share is that everything is about Mitchell and the power that he can wield over those unfortunate enough to meet him.

'Oh, yes it does, and I haven't lost to him yet. He might think he's won but I'm taking this to the top.' He starts walking towards the door, his precious surviving paperwork stuffed into his folder.

'You don't think that he's won? He won years ago! Can't you see that?'

'No, no, no, no!' he shouts, banging his fists on the table, his head in this constant shaking moment, refusing to admit the reality he's been stuck in for so long.

'You are no longer needed!' I shout, just above his hysterical banging. 'Your capabilities have let you down and you just cannot see it.'

He still continues to ignore me as his eyes dart all around the room, his banging coming to a slow stop as he clearly starts to runs out of energy.

'You are useless.'

He stops all movement completely. Everything falls silent as he stares at me.

I pick up my folder. 'In here it details all the things you have done wrong and all the times the business has tried to improve your performance. But it doesn't have to be like this and if you leave quietly then you still keep your pension and you get a decent pay off. It's a good deal, Jerry.'

He takes a couple of slow steps towards me. 'What about my pride? How do I leave without that? How do I live knowing I was booted out?'

I sigh, summoning an answer somewhere from the depths of my empty stomach. 'Things change and you can't always fight back the tide. Just go and enjoy your retirement and do all that travelling you have always talked about.'

He quickly grabs the folder from my hands and throws it across the room, paper landing all over the long table and the floor. 'No. I'm not going anywhere. We have never formally discussed my performance, meaning all of this is utter nonsense.'

'It *is* happening. You will be leaving.'

'How does it feel, Ryan? How does it feel to be so utterly incompetent at managing people that someone else has had to make up a folder of all the conversations that were supposed to have happened between us? You are that spineless that they only exist in someone else's mind.'

'I tried to help you, Jerry. I tried to make you part of the team and to feel valued, despite the zero value you add to us. You survived here a lot longer than you would have done without me. So don't go blaming me for being a relic that no one else wants.'

He circles around the desk. 'Well, how noble of you, being a pawn for someone else. Don't ever think any of this was of your doing. You're just a boy who does what his master wants.'

'And you retired twenty years ago!'

He doesn't reply. He just falls into one of the big black chairs and starts sobbing. A handkerchief soon comes out of his pocket but he just holds onto it whilst letting the tears flow freely down his cheeks and onto his shirt collar. He looks at me a couple of times with this expression like my parent's dog used to give me when it went for a shit in public – kind of silently wishing I'd leave him to it, but don't go too far as this really won't take long.

'I just wanted people to like me and to respect me for what I can do,' he says and takes a deep breath. 'I've become everything I feared and now I can't even leave here with my pride intact. Why, Ryan, why can't I just play out my last couple of years? Why can't I do one thing on my terms?'

I sit down next to him, pulling the chair closer, wondering if this is one of those touching moments. 'If you don't go then the team will suffer. If you go then you have your pay off and full pension and the team don't suffer. It's the only choice I have.'

He suddenly stops crying, his mind taking back control as he looks at me. 'No, Ryan, it wasn't your choice. You could have made it my choice.'

*****

'You total and utter fucker!' Sophie shouts at me with a pointed finger that keeps brushing against my nose. She's wearing this look of complete horror, like her face has become twisted and warped at the thought of what I did. 'You really are the lowest form of life and it's entirely clear to me that you don't care about anyone except for yourself.'

I'm shaking my head, almost like I'm in complete and utter denial at what she's saying. I mean, the evidence is all there – Jerry is at his desk right now calmly placing his personal things into a brown box with everyone crowded around him. They have come to listen to his story whilst hugging him or at least giving him a firm pat on the back. At some point most of them take their time to stare into the office I'm hiding in, to give me this look that says what a wanker I am. When most of them do this it makes me want to laugh, because they never said a word to Jerry in all the years he's hung around and now he's finally been dealt with they somehow want to show how much they apparently care. The only thing they really care about is that it wasn't them – all those pats on the back are really saying, 'I'm glad it's you and not me, mate.'

I stare back at Sophie, the only person whose judgement means anything to me. She is the one person I thought would understand, because if she was truly here to replace me then getting rid of Jerry is something she'd end up doing herself. As I stare at her soft face I start to wonder if I've got it all wrong and that perhaps things could have been different. She's not speaking anymore; she's just staring at me. It's not even an angry look but one that I think resembles pity. I know she's really pissed, the feeling I know won't ever be forgotten easily.

I just want to be with someone who will acknowledge what I have done, to tell me that although it was difficult it was also right. I need her to hold me and tell me all the reasons why Jerry never adapted, never moved forward and ultimately sealed his own fate. I don't want someone to just listen to me; I want someone to say to me all the things that I need to hear, that true validation that comes from an intelligent mind. But instead, Sophie has stormed into this meeting room and opened all the blinds, bringing light and openness to the room where I just hid in as I ruined Jerry's world.

'Well, what do you have to say?' she asks, as I stare across the office to see what Jerry is doing. It suddenly dawns on me that I'm going to miss this guy; that he has been a part of my life for long enough that there will be a hole, however small and insignificant he is to the corporate cogs of the G.U.E Corporation. Maybe it's not just the work you do but the other things you bring to those around you.

'By your silence I'm assuming you have nothing to say?'

I look at Sophie, at the beauty that comes from her simple face. It's her dark eyes that draw me in every time I see her, and when they're joined by that ever-so-slightly stunned expression I know I can't resist her. 'Can we talk about last night, please?'

It takes just seconds for her body to start convulsing. It's like these shock movements take over because she doesn't know what to say. Her head is shaking, her arms are flapping and her mouth keeps jamming with these words that can't quite make it out. 'Jerry is so insignificant to you, so completely unimportant, that all you can think about is asking why I didn't stay to join your fuck-fest last night?' She quickly heads for the door, her limits obviously reached. It looks like I'm now officially a lost cause, someone she can't even bare to be in the same room with.

I hold out a hand, gently grabbing her arm. 'Please don't go, not yet.'

To my surprise she stops and silently stands in front of me, her face looking at mine. She grabs my hand, taking it into her grasp as she starts to play with my fingers, her own weaving through mine. I feel a rush of excitement surge through my body as I watch her every move, my entire mind in a state of disbelief. She's positioned herself perfectly to block our embrace from the outside world but I can't help but look through the window to count how many people are watching.

Her fingers start to tease their way up my arm as she strokes the underside of my wrist. This smile has appeared on her face and although this is the most inappropriate place for this to happen, it feels so right. She grips my forearm, trying to fit her grasp around the muscle, testing my strength whilst I can only imagine this happening again tonight, in my bed as we kiss and explore each other's bodies. I soon realise that I've released all control to her, the weight of my arm held up by her grip, my entire body and mind wanting this.

'Close your eyes,' she says.

I think about this for a minute, about the people watching from outside, the casual glances they're making to see what we're doing. But still, I obey. I'll always obey Sophie from this day onwards – our own private moment that can usher in a new way of living for me.

'You can open them now,' she says.

I quickly do as I'm told, half expecting her to be standing here, totally naked, without a care in the world as to anyone outside this room. It's only as my eyes open that the pain hits my cheek. It's like I feel the slap without seeing it, before she lets my arm fall back to my side and leans in closer to me. 'You'll never have my respect. You'll never have my body. And you'll never have anything special with me.' She takes a moment to stare before turning around and walking out, whilst all I can do is watch her leave me with the life I so desperately convinced myself I deserve.

*****

I sit at the table and look around the room that's full of these raw emotions. Jerry's paperwork is still scattered over the table and the floor, all those promising plans and strategies meaning absolutely nothing now. They'll never come true, not under Jerry's careful eye. The thoughts and ambitions of one old man were dashed in seconds. The whole thing took a lot less time than I had expected, with the feelings of regret and disgust at myself lasting a whole lot longer.

Now this place feels like my tomb. I don't want to be in here, remembering the last few hours, but I can't face going outside, either. Jerry is still at his desk, still looking for pity and attention from anyone who will give it. He's looked over at me a few times but I don't think it was a look of begging; it's definitely not the sort of look that will see him pleading for his job back. It's not the sort of expression that says he wants revenge either; it's a look of disappointment – in me. I don't think there will be any crossing of words when he leaves, either. I think he'll just go and I plan to stay in this office until he does just that.

I look out across the vast office in desperate search for allies. I quickly see Ken, who has predictably managed to avoid all conflict. He's my best mate and my partner in crime. All our future business ventures will be together and yet he can't even bear to walk in and show me some support. The fact is that I still need someone to validate what I've done, to tell me that it needed to happen. I keep telling myself that there was no other decision, that there was only the possibility that Jerry leaves and we all survive. It means that what has happened today will be a win-win situation until the day I die.

But now I'm abandoned with these thoughts. I fully expected Ken to back me and I always hoped that Sophie would get this; that she would offer me her unconditional support born out of her brutal mind having calculated all the options, knowing that Jerry was ripe for sacrificing in the name of the greater good of our team.

As for Mitchell – I expected to be abandoned. He left me with no choice but to sack Jerry and now he will distance himself as much as he can. I think about the conversations that we had with all those assurances that this was the only option and the fairest situation for everyone concerned. But then I look at the paperwork lying hopelessly around the floor, with all those made up conversations between Jerry and me. This complete work of fiction is what will ultimately ruin my career and keep me in chains to Mitchell forever. I sit in silence and contemplate the illegality of what I have done, let alone the morality of fucking someone over who was just trying to skip the radar until he retired in peace, with his dignity somehow intact.

I'm now finding layers I never knew I had and I don't want to meet them. And as I sit here wondering who will save the day, it's Tina who walks into the room. I had hoped it would be Mitchell who would burst in here, bellowing at everyone to get back to their menial work. He'd soon be towering over me with his husky, deep voice booming through the room as he tells me to grow a pair and get over it.

Instead of him it's Tina standing here and even with me sitting down there isn't much chance she'll ever tower over me. I look at her and she looks at me and I can't even begin to imagine what bombshell she is going to drop now.

'I need to leave early,' she says, her usual rough tone not giving much away, always sounding a little too harsh, whatever the situation. I try to gauge some reactions from her face but she doesn't seem to look bothered either way.

'That's fine,' I say, entirely relieved that it is as simple as that. 'If that's it, I've got some paperwork to do, so I'll be out soon.'

'You mean you'll be out when Jerry has been escorted from the premises?' She laughs, looking over at Jerry and then back to me. 'You'll be out when he's finished packing his miserable little life into the three brown boxes he has been allocated and then he's sulked his wrinkly butt across the office to the lift. And as those doors slowly close on this sad chapter of his life, that's when you'll be out?'

I give her this look but she just laughs. 'Did you know, Ryan, that at Jerry's grade you are allocated just three brown boxes. You *can* buy more if you want to.'

'I really have nothing to say to that.'

'So you're not going to help the old man carry his boxes to the cab? Shame on you.'

I look at the door, signalling for her to leave. 'I'm not in the mood for this.' I've never thrown someone out of an office and I figure that today isn't the time to start, especially if I want my limited popularity to ever improve.

But she doesn't move, choosing to comfortably anchor herself next to me. 'You've got some messages,' she says, her enjoyment of this moment so completely obvious. 'The first one is from Mitchell, asking if you've sorted out the problem yet. I assumed the problem was Jerry and the fact he has been dribbling tears all over his desk for the past hour dictates that you have sorted it out. So I told Mitchell yes.'

'What did he say?'

'He told me to tell you that you need to find some testicles of your own and call him yourself.'

I nod, knowing that he won't come down here to rescue me. Maybe that's a good thing as I can escape to his office, to the protection of a different floor with different coloured carpets and different people – those who might not yet know what I've become.

'The other call was from human resources asking to give them the paperwork they need. I assumed this paperwork also related to the problem, so I told them you're dealing with said issue and you will send the paperwork when you've stopped cowering in this office.' She looks around the room, surveying the damage, the whole thing seeming quite intriguing to her. She finally lets out a big sigh.

'If that's everything then you can leave me to it.'

She nods, but doesn't move, still staring at me as she analyses my movements. 'What do you want me to say?' she asks after a minute or so of silence. 'Would you like me to tell you that you're a total bastard? Should I inform you that you've most definitely ruined Jerry's life? I mean, you have definitely ruined that poor bloke's life, but let's face it he's completely shit at his job and the chop came from above.'

'I'm glad you understand,' I say, starting to find this unlikely of allies somewhat relieving.

'Oh, I didn't say I understand or that I agree with it. We'll all be wondering who's next, and since you spend so much time eating out Ken's ass and Sophie is the perfect new girl, I can only assume it's probably going to be me.'

I quickly realise that this is going to become her latest crisis, her next issue to get obsessed with. 'You do a good job,' I say, thinking that I could say more, something a little on the motivational side.

'I do know that,' she says. 'I am literally the sticky glue that holds this team together. I'm completely clear on that and if you even try to pull a stunt like that on me I will bury you.'

I stand up, trying to gain some height so I can defend my position. I can't face any more conflict and her threats seem strangely sinister and entirely truthful, coming from a woman with some serious anger management issues.

'You know I've got a lot of shit to deal with, Ryan. So don't let my issues become your issues. My advice is let me get on with my job and you focus on Sophie. After all, she's your replacement, so I'll be making sure her and I are getting on just peachy.' With this revelation she finally moves towards the door but turns at the last minute. 'And if at any point you'd like me to send in Ken to give you a big man-bro type hug, then you just shout.'

As she slams the door I realise that I'm nodding, my mind telling me that's exactly what I want her to do.

13
DEAD END AHEAD

The old man couldn't stop staring at me. I swear to you it was like he was licking his lips as he looked me up and down. I always know the ones who've been drinking before I get there and yeah, that was definitely him. He spoke normal, Queens English for proper, but some of the last words slurred out of his mouth and like fell off his tongue.

He was in a suit – a nice one too, probably Marks and Spencers. It fit him well, like. But here's the thing, I'm not detective material or nothing, but it's gone six in the evening and the suit must have been on him all day, so why was the shirt so crisp and clean? I remember smiling at that, thinking to myself that he's one of those hygienic guys who have a shower and put on some fresh undies and a new shirt before putting the posh suit back on. I like them ones, especially when they're that old. I have enough problems with the wrinklies, let alone when they stink.

Now, I like my career types and I like them a little older than me. They've got all these stresses and strains from their jobs, with a posh city pad and a secretary, plus a proper degree and all that. The straight ones are the best, when they've got some bulging muscles and a day's stubble. They give it large all day but you know all they're thinking about is getting home early so they can sit me on their rock hard cock. They're often home late so I'm left waiting outside, having a chillin spliff. I remember once this one guy had me naked in the lift and threw me into the shower. It was all primal instinct, but it fucking hurt though!

But this guy? Well, he was a lot older than I normally allow and he looked like the city had literally sucked the life of him. Man, it looked like he was in need of some major chillax time. I mean, it was obvious he'd been chewed up and spat out a fair few times. That didn't bother me cos I was convinced I'd hit the mother load. He had to be a boss of some big international company. I'd tried to Google him before I got here but I found nothing, but that's no real surprise as they never give their real names.

So, I was watching this guy and he was watching me. He had some hair left, which was cool considering he was like bordering on pension territory. And he had this tanned face that was nearly orange and so wrinkly too. He either loved the sunbeds or travelled the world for his job. I chose the second option, thinking that maybe I could have him as a regular and get to know him and really fuck his brains out. Then maybe one day, when I still kindly visit him in the old folks home, he'll give me all his money. He could totally give me his passport too and I'd happily travel to all the places he's been, like I'm reliving his life for him.

'What do you do then?' I asked, suddenly taking an interest when I mainly glaze over at this point. I don't really remember what he said, just that it had the words 'senior' and 'director' in it. Of course that sounded good enough to me but I knew something weren't right when he said it. And trust me, I've faked enough moans in my time.

I was about to ask some more questions and figure this guy out but then he hands me my money, in an envelope, like it's all official. Everyone does this bit differently. Some pay up front and I've even had some say they'll only pay when I deliver the satisfaction I promised them. And man, when they say stuff like that it drives me wild. But this old man didn't have the balls for that, so he just looked down at his dirty beige carpet as he handed me the dosh.

'You like skinny boys then?' I asked as I'm standing there in just my undies. This is the bit I love, when their eyes are all lit up. I made sure I brushed my hair over my face as I said it and of course I'd angled my hard cock to push along the side of my tight pants. Skinny and hung, that's what he ordered.

He gave me this nod back, but he didn't look that convinced and as the rock in my pants already started to shrink I think he realised he'd just dumped on our moment. 'I like you, of course I do, but I rather have a thing for men of Asian origin.'

'Why the fuck would you like them?' I asked, trying to remind myself that loads of guys like the Asians. 'Is it the little willys?' I asked, quickly pulling my snake out of my pants and shaking it around.

But he did nothing. Now was his chance to get my monster stuffed down his throat, but he just stood there with this stupid old crystal glass full of brandy or whiskey, or some other old man's drink. He looked at me, like into my eyes, as far away from my cock as you could get. 'When you get to my age you need to think about finding someone to take care of you. I never really expected my life to end up like this, I truly didn't. So now, I have to be practical and start to think about the reality that I'm not going to find a life partner, but rather a mutual arrangement.'

I started laughing at him and I promise I totally didn't mean to. I think I was laughing more at myself, at the fact that I couldn't do what one of those Orientals could. Like the thought of only sleeping with him and having to sponge bath him as he gets like really old, and what if he lived until over a hundred? He'd have to be mega loaded to make it worth my while, except I don't need a visa and they'd be begging to get over here. But as I looked around his flat I thought that he ain't got much that would appeal to them. His place was like beyond minimalist.

'So when are you importing one then?' I asked him, not really giving a shit now.

He paused and made this big huff, like whether he was considering if it was worth telling me. I think he must have known I wasn't really interested and my limp cock was even less bothered, but he decided to tell me anyway. 'My plan is actually to move out to Asia. Why bring what you want here when you can go over there. You see, my latest business venture is to start a gay retirement home abroad and to attract other similar thinking men to join me. I've been talking online to a lot of male nurses out there and they are very interested.'

'And you don't think they'd be more interested in getting out of their shithole country and over here to some young white cock?'

'Young man, I'll assume you've never been to anywhere in Asia?'

I shake my head. 'Rice and spice don't interest me, mate.'

In return he shakes his head and any minute I was thinking he'd be demanding his dosh back. 'I see why you old guys dig them though, they deffo like taking care of people.'

'Well this country cannot support continuous migration, so taking business out to these countries is most definitely a viable option for the future.'

'When are you moving over there?' I kind of interrupted him, just wanting to get to the end of his little story and start the sex.

But that's when he just stares at the floor, at his manky old cream carpet that needs some serious kick-ass from a bit of laminate flooring. 'I've had some complications come my way today.'

'So that's why you called me?' I asked, as I was suddenly all around him, kissing his forehead and massaging his neck. He downed that brown juice and kept looking away as I brushed myself against him. I was hard like super quick, but there was nothing happening in his trousers. I kissed his forehead again, but it was all sweaty and tasted like salt.

He quickly ran away, mumbling something about needing another drink. He disappeared to the kitchen so I looked around the living room, but there weren't much to peak my interest and even less to swipe. He had this super old telly. It was big but the back stuck out for miles. His living space was basically a sofa, a small table and chairs and a few old-timer ornaments, plus this hanging picture of what I reckoned was his ultimate paradise – hanging above the fireplace.

'Are you, like, busy packing?' I asked when he finally came back, all crazy looking and dripping with sweat. I looked around the room again, so bare, with these boxes stacked up next to the sofa.'

He looked over at those same boxes and then back to me. 'That's all they gave me.'

I moved closer again, deliberately breathing over him, kissing the back of his ears. I was raging hard and I figured now was the time. I really didn't think things would last long and that maybe I could get away with finishing him and saving my load for another job. His face was pretty red now and he was still pulling away from me. He had to have done this before but he seemed to struggle with how it all worked. I wanted to tell him that all he needed to do was plant his lips around my boner and I'd do the rest.

'Remind me, how old are you again?' he asked, as my pants landed around my ankles and I started pulling his shirt off. It was a clumsy mistake cos he was too fragile and dazed, as the ice from his drink went all over his shit carpet.

I used my classic line, the one I'll use until the very end of my teens. 'I'm as old as my cock is long in centimetres, if you get me?' With this bold revelation I started my kissing frenzy all over his chest, which was firmer than I expected, but just as orange.

He gave me this dazed look, which I thought at the time was down to his confusion. Of course the old guy was a feet-and-inches type dude, so I forgave him. But the sweat that was pouring over his forehead was just sick – I couldn't kiss him there without thinking this is what age and decay must taste like. I decided to take his spare hand and force it to wrap around my cock, 'Nineteen centimetres, just so you know!'

His hand didn't stay around my shaft for long though, as it kind of lost its grip and fell to his side and then the glass in his other hand hit the floor. I was busy working on his nipples and only stopped when he let out his grunt, which I thought meant he didn't like it, which shocked me as most old geezer's love a bit of nip pulling.

I looked up to see what was going on and that's when I realised he weren't with it. His legs like gave up and I really tried to catch him but, come on, I ain't built for heavy lifting. I managed to kind of help him land a bit softer than he would have done on his own, but I wasn't sure if that helped much. He was like clinging to his heart as I was shouting at him. 'I'll get you some water,' I said, like that would ever have helped where he was going.

And that's when I saw it, what I reckon was death knocking on his door. He made these couple of croaking noises and then his eyes just disappeared. And all I did was watch, not really that scared at all. I didn't touch him after that, thinking my prints would be all over him.

For the next few minutes I moved quickly, first pouring more of that brown stuff down his gob, figuring the alcohol would get rid of any trace of me. I then wiped down his body with a manky cloth from the kitchen, just hoping it would brush off any of my hairs and stuff.

Once I'd put my clothes back on I didn't rush out the door, instead I just stared at him, his mouth wide open and his head angled towards those boxes. I decided to look in the top box, which was full of stationery and shit. But on the top of it was this photo, not in a frame or nothing, just the print lying there. It was a photo of a guy but he wouldn't have known this photo was being taken cos he was dancing with his shirt off and a huge bottle of champers in his hand. And man, was that guy fit! You could see each of his abs tracing their way up his hot smooth chest. It made me wanna get my dick out right there, until I remembered the dead guy was just behind me. I then thought maybe this photo was the old man, like, thirty years ago, but then I realised everything behind the guy was too new, like recent times. See, I told you I could do detective stuff.

Don't ask me why I decided to do this, but I cradled the photo in between his hand and chest, like next to his heart. How sweet, eh? Maybe it was his boyfriend or a lover or something. Anyways, it just felt right. I still took the money cos, after all, he put me through a load of shit. I didn't go hunting for more cash as I don't steal from the dead and besides I didn't need my prints anywhere else. And so I wiped over a few surfaces I probably never touched and then I took one last look at the old geezer. He looked sad, but I figured I wasn't the only one who ever thought that about him.

I closed the door and left him, and for all I know he's still rotting there now.

14

It's the Monday of a brand new week in a brand new month and today is a big raging deal for the business. It's one of those symbolic moments that we're supposed to have engrained on our souls forever.

I'm at the annual Global United Eradication Corporate Conference, so I'm struggling to see what the eternal and ever-lasting gossip will be that hasn't already been leaked in the form of the entire range of products that Ken can attach to his penis. There are always loads of new products at these events – shown to us just before they go live so we don't tell everyone too soon. But I'm really not sure how many of us really have the time or inclination to be spies for the ever-growing competition. It's just new shit to sell to the same people; protection money against a danger you can't even see or begin to understand.

The scientists and technologists are all here, showing us how they've made previously unsafe chemicals now fit for human contact. It's also a proven fact that where the techies go the marketing department follows, giving us all that bullshit as to why they think this is the best product we've ever pushed out there.

The *Sex-Sanitiser* is of course the most talked about product that everyone has heard of, despite a complete embargo on even mentioning its existence. It's said to be capable of revolutionising the billion pound sex industry as we bring obsessive hygiene control to one of the most intimate things in the world. And that is exactly what this woman is telling Ken and me as we're standing at the *Sex-Sanitiser* stall. He's busy laughing at all the products, picking them up and playfully attaching them through his clothes to various parts of his anatomy whilst an mass of gathered geeks just stare at him in disbelief.

They probably think he's laughing wildly because he's grossly immature, which is completely right, but he's actually laughing because he's already had a go, way before anyone was allowed. 'How the fuck do you think they tested it?' he shouts at me. 'Slap one on and away you go'. He grabs my arm, his eyes full of devious intent. 'If this is the kind of shit that goes down in product development then I'm getting a transfer. Shit, man, they can put as many chemically coated condoms onto my dick as they like, as long as I get to pick the babe who jumps on for the drive.'

I push him forward, onto the next stall, every word that leaves his mouth oozing with childishness. Take Ken on holiday or down the pub and he's a blast, but take him to somewhere that requires any element of professionalism and he goes into total self-destruct. If I've not said it before, Ken only has a job because he is with me and he is my only ticket out of this hell.

Over the course of today we'll pick up as much free shit as we can. Any possible stuff that we can sell or hand over to our loyal fans will be gathered up. Giving away free samples to the ladies always goes down well as it helps to build up trust, as Ken puts it. They feel safe because they're getting corporate goodies, all properly branded, but it's given away by two local young businessmen, so everyone wins.

Everything we take must have a value making it worth our time and the obvious risk. Take too much stuff and you'll get noticed, so we plan it between us and load up Ken's car at every opportunity we get. Even the goody bags get pillaged at the end of the day, with nothing for us and all for the cause.

I think it's the reason why I came by train today. I just didn't want the pressure of Ken finding some spare boxes full of gunge-coated goodies that he decides to swipe and load into my boot. He is getting too greedy and we both know it.

We soon get seated in the big auditorium, specially kitted out for the day. We sit as a team, our first time together without Jerry, which doesn't seem as weird as I thought it would be. He never really made much of an impact on the world around him when he was here and looking at Ken or Tina they don't seem bothered that he's gone.

It's Sophie who, on some weird level, seems to care the most. Her interest seems hypocritical to me, since she knew him for only a matter of days. She has made sure she has sat the furthest away from me, still barely speaking and only really using full sentences when her death stare won't quite cut it. Most things work related are now communicated through Tina or an email that starts with 'Dear Ryan, my ever-spineless boss.'

I look at our relationship, or rather what our relationship could have been, and I feel pathetic to my core. I should have made it more than this and I lost someone who I actually had feelings for. Not just lust or passion, but something more – something that isn't easy to put into words, which makes it special in my world. What's really worrying is that I still can't move on from her. I'm entirely obsessed with this woman and even when she looks at me like I've just crawled out of the swamp, I still want to do something to make her like me.

My looks have always got me women and my personality always attracted people to me, but now my actions proved just how far I could make them hate me. I don't blame Toyah for turning up the other night; it was my own fault for entertaining the silly bitch for so long. I should have cut ties months ago, as soon as she started asking to go on dates or for me to meet her precious Daddy. To her, I *was* her boyfriend. I just never quite committed to be the one who she could show off to people just to get them jealous.

According to a woman's brain if you fuck them out of their mind three times a week then you're madly in love, or else why would you put in so much time, passion and energy into making them scream? But to a man it's just raw sex – a chance to offload and expel some energy, which made Toyah the regular fuck that got out of hand. I remember during the last few shags she just lay there, staring dead into my eyes as I pounded away – she must have known that's all it was.

My thoughts are interrupted as everyone around me stands up and starts applauding. I follow a few seconds later as Ken yanks me to my feet to see the arrival of our CEO on stage. I clap but I can't say I have any energy or connection to this anymore and when I look around at the hundreds of people in this huge building, I realise that I'm still just a small cog in the big corporate war machine that's oiling up for more battles.

I really thought I was more than that. I was the guy sent to sort out Canary Wharf; the guy they gave that huge apartment to because I apparently climbed the ladder enough to deserve it. When people above talked to me I thought I really was the one – the guy they chose to do great things. When Mitchell used to ask me to do stuff I thought it was because I was special, skilled and appreciated, but when you're on the payroll everything you do is for someone else and never really yourself.

I watch as the big boss paces around the stage, his busy mouth barely stopping for breath as he tells us how great the next year ahead will be. It's all about the new stuff, never the past and rarely the present. When you think of a CEO of a pharmaceutical company that has poured literally all of its experience into a bottle of clear liquid, you'd expect a short and unassuming guy to grace the stage – a geek, a secret scientist. Not in this case – our Top Gun is a tall thin guy with the biggest clump of black spiked hair I have ever seen. It's like all his power is kept in this perfectly formed tuft, gaining him the most original name of *The Quiff*.

The *Sex-Sanitiser* is up first but it's apparently not the main event. Something has upstaged it, something even Ken and I weren't aware of, and there's this serious side to the whole thing, like it really is the next possible cure for everything on the sinister side of sex. There are no fit models parading around the stage; no topless men or women in skin-tight bikinis who playfully weave around our leader. Right from the first word, the top boss makes it clear that this is a significant advance in chemical research and development that has made it possible to make sex considerably cleaner and a whole lot safer.

Instead of taking a taboo subject and making it a turn on, he reduces it into a process that carefully details the stages you should follow to ensure the safety of all involved. Any stirring in my pants disappears as he talks with no emotion about these key processes, starting with a consistent home attack and eradication routine – the backbone to any possible hope of safety and a long life. You need to be regularly using our *Eradication Gel*, our *Dental Rinse*, our *Bacteria-preventing Deodorant* and of course all of our six-step home chemical treatments.

And then, when you are both ready for sex, because apparently we all know when this will happen, you should give the lubricated gel ten minutes to work and ensure that the condom is applied only by hands that have been washed in our patented *Hand Sanitiser*.

So, what do you get for religiously following this routine and for giving up any possible sign of romance or spontaneity? It kills all surface and airborne viruses, which means you can't catch about half of all known STI's and it closes the big gaping hole in your otherwise thorough cleanliness routine. By this he means if you're already hooked on sanitising your home, car, pet, office, mouth, partner and body with our gunge then the only problem left is those few moments of dirty love.

I listen patiently and soon realise that this isn't going to be something sexy. This is something clinical and scary, born out of the fear generated that we're all going to die from something we will never know is coming. It will be something that makes us bed-ridden without even seeing it – something that kills us ever-so-slowly.

He paces around the stage, slowly and methodically catching the eyes of as many of the front row as possible. 'However, there is another way and that is the Global United way. Follow our thorough and precise way of ensuring that you get fewer colds, that you are less likely to catch that violent stomach bug all your friends have and you might just survive the epidemic that kills all of the great unprepared.'

Pictures flash up on the screen of our regular customers, the millions worldwide who have sold a large chunk of their freedom to a routine and an over-priced product that will enslave them forever. For if they were ever to stop using it then all those years of protection will be wasted.

Video clips start to play of concerned mums packing their children off to university with a *Sex-Sanitiser* kit in their case, and of clearly responsible adult couples who diligently discuss that this is the best way to ensure a relaxing experience, knowing that they are protected by what cannot be seen.

In this case it isn't the sex that sells, but rather the fear of what it brings. This is the ugly side of something beautiful, targeted at the millions who no longer lead those carefree lifestyles. This product isn't aimed at those who climb a fence at midnight for a quick shag in the park, or the ones who leave their keys in the bowl, just hoping it's a good lay. The people who will buy this don't fuck; they make love, on an irregular basis and have shared their lives for decades. It is those around them they will buy this for. It's the thought of what it does, not what you do with it that matters.

The videos stop and the Quiff announces that the modern world isn't where we're aiming this product at. 'There will be no active selling of this product in the United Kingdom,' he says and then waits for these words to be soaked up by his audience. 'In fact we won't try to make this product big anywhere in Europe, where our customers will become easily complacent and think it stops the spread of everything. Of course we'll target our existing customers by mail and web sales and many of them will make a purchase, but to make this a wholesale product launch will leave us open to too much scrutiny.'

After a few more minutes of listening we find out that the main market for this stuff is the developing world. If we can start to bring this range into Africa, India and China then we can grow the widest market penetration.

I look at Ken and his face is a picture of complete horror. I know what he's thinking, that sex sells and this isn't a sex product – it's now an evolution of exposing our bodies to the least amount of fun as possible. He was convinced that he'd be spending his time travelling around gyms and universities, chatting to loads of hot young women and personally showing as many of them as possible how to use it.

'And this is just the start,' the Quiff says. 'Within the next five years our scientists will have evolved a better way to kill all sexually transmitted infections and diseases, as well as stopping most viruses from ever harming us in the first place.'

There's loads of what sounds like confused clapping, with no one quite sure if we've stumbled on the cure for AIDS or if we're just going to cover every known surface in pure alcohol and hope it does a decent job of not killing us. It turns out, as the Quiff explains, that there is already a next day shock-injection to take if you've had unprotected sex, so our job was to find a way to transport this safely in a gel whilst not making half the planet infertile.

'So, if we start in the developing world then within the next two decades we will live on a planet where sexually transmitted infections are a thing of the past. And then I want to take this further, so that the next generation will be born immune to all disease.'

He says 'born' way too many times, like the clone war is ready to go. 'Although we are not pushing the sex sanitising range, the product I bring to you will be something very relevant to this country,' he says, giving the audience no time to keep up. 'We live in a pressure cooker of disease and travelling viruses, all of them evolving and adapting to new ways to attack innocent and unwilling hosts. It doesn't matter how many people keep their homes safe and even if you apply all of our regular routine, you are exposed to thousands of deadly bacterial microbes throughout your working day. Now something will change that, as safety takes on a whole new meaning from this day forward. Ladies and gentlemen, I bring you our new and patented *Building Guardian*!'

A video takes over from where the Quiff leaves off, showing people at work, some of them healthy, some of them sneezing. One of the actors runs into the toilet with some obvious bowel issues, whilst another coughs up something you wouldn't give to your worst enemy. As each of these things happen it shows the germs flowing freely through the air – all computer-simulated but nonetheless still representing real fear. The germs grow and some die as they hit surfaces, but others multiply and we watch them get inhaled up some guy's nose. The camera even zooms in on the germs gently landing on fresh food, as people tuck into what they think is a safe and tasty chicken salad. He doesn't know that it's just become the lunch from hell.

'We can stop this and we can stop it now. Our patented *Building Guardian* will become the new sign of a safe and stable workplace. Think of all the employers who operate from within big buildings, full of their most important assets. Their people are exposed to millions of daily germs, and imagine the absence cost to a typical head office of five hundred people and then think about how many people go off sick every week with a deadly stomach bug. Now this number will be vastly reduced for anyone who is protected by us.'

I stare at the big screen in this daze, seeing that whenever anyone enters the building they pass through a scanner that seems to detect any sign of illness through infrared monitors. The Quiff talks through what we're seeing, as each person has their clothes sprayed with powerful jets of air that claim to kill any air born or surface bug. He claims that all of this takes just seconds and won't harm anyone. On every floor, in every lift and within every toilet, simple *Bug and Bacteria Eradication* delivery devices will be fitted, which let out a regular flow of harmless chemicals.

'The future is here, ladies and gentlemen. And in any new building these can be fitted directly to the central air-conditioning supply, and anywhere else they can be discreetly installed, all controlled by radio frequency, making no sound or scent.' He looks around the room, his long black spikes pointing up at the screen. 'Safety now comes silently and systematically, thanks to our *Building Guardians*.'

The stage goes quiet and one single lights shines down on the boss. 'Once we're in, then we have literally thousands of potential personal customers. Let me assure you that we will protect this planet, one building at a time.'

I listen as the Quiff tells us that all companies who purchase a *Building Guardian* will also be able to pay discounted subscriptions on our *Six-Step Home Eradication kits*, vastly reducing the germs their employees come into contact with, ultimately reducing their absence costs. My head is shaking. My disbelief is so apparent for all to see, but I'm not sure if it's due to mine and Ken's future projected loss of income, or the fact at how hard we've now got to work.

*****

I'm waiting not-so-patiently for the train.

Coach B, seat 21A. I keep repeating this to myself as the train pulls into the station. I do this because all I really want to do is sit down and be left alone. I simply want to get as far away from the conference and as close to home as I can be within the next few minutes. I think about all I've heard today and I don't know what to do first. There's much to think about and the small confines of my little train seat are far from perfect. I decide that once I've settled into a wine or two then I'll focus on the future and I'll start with my date tonight.

Ken has been constantly ringing me since we left the conference but I haven't answered. He'll want to discuss what stock we've swiped between us and what theme we'll set for the next party. He was desperate for me to drive back with him, to complete an inventory of the stash en route to London, taking into careful consideration our future supply issues with the *Sex Sanitiser*. When we parted ways he was already plotting a trip to the factory in China so we can go direct to his contacts in production and then store the goods at a friend's place in Japan. It is such a bold plan for such a pointless exercise.

I couldn't face him or the car journey, and so I lied to my best mate and told him I was heading off to another meeting and then getting a later train. He chose to believe me with no further questions, his short attention span not offering a care in the world as to the detail required of my position within the business.

In the distraction of another call from Ken I can't find coach B, so I find myself fighting to get onto the train, jumping onto the next coach. The train is packed with people and I already know that by the time I manage to find my seat, I will need to turf some muppet out of it who hasn't bothered to reserve.

The train gets moving quickly but I've not managed to get out of the coach C hallway with ten other people squashed into the place where you only bother to occupy on the local trains. This one's travelling for the next couple of hours and the panic has already set in, as the woman next to me mutters something about no one buying allocated seats anymore.

'Anyone for coach B?' this guy asks, as everyone around me yells that they are.

Within seconds this young spotty guy arrives from nowhere, as if he has drifted gracefully through the crowd to appear before us. He's got this name badge that says *Terry* and I notice that the job title on his badge says *Train Manager*. This clearly places sole responsibility on him to explain this situation and to find a solution. After all, that's what management is all about and I'm convinced that I shouldn't be the only one who suffers at the hands of unrealistic demands and expectations somewhere from a book you've never read.

'Coach B has been removed today, folks,' Terry calmly announces. He doesn't manage to finish what he is saying as an announcement goes out, with something of a similar message. Both Terry and the tannoy soon get drowned out by the mob around me asking a hundred questions that all want the same outcome.

'Like I said, coach B has been removed.'

'What, from existence?' this woman next to me asks, which gets a laugh only from me.

'You'll have to stand up or fight for a seat, I'm afraid,' Terry says in this completely calm tone, as if a battle for the last remaining seats is a normal afternoon task for a hundred-or-so tired and weary passengers. Before anyone can challenge this thought he's already making his way through the smallest of gaps to confront the next batch of dazed passengers, all holding out their tickets in some faint hope of a resolution.

Several of the people around me start to move into the carriage, the search for the great unreserved starting in haste. I can already see over their heads that there aren't any free seats. The family next to me start moaning, as three kids weave around the adults.

'Go find your seats,' their dad shouts.

'Our seats don't exist no more,' one of the kids shouts back. They still try and the moment they disappear the small remaining group shuffle around, happily growing their own precious personal space.

The dad quickly starts heading back my way as the train reaches the next stop, so I jump off and head towards the rear carriages, the thought of the next two hour journey propelling me further and further away from the family from hell.

I jump into the back carriage, into that space between first class and cattle. I'm immediately surprised to see that no one has had the same idea, as I find just one other guy in here. I settle into this sort of jump-seat and give the black youth who just became my journey companion a cursory nod. He's not paying me much attention, just calmly eating, with a carrier bag resting on his lap. It's full of stuff, like he's already set up for the return journey.

I settle into my small, padded seat, with only the wall to rest on. He looks at me a few times through these oversized glasses and eventually takes off his headphones to ask why I'm here, as he looks down at my pointy shoes.

I explain my issue but he just nods. 'Major bummer, man.'

A phone call comes through so I decide to politely ignore him and get some work done. For some reason I notice that my desire to reflect on life has been quickly replaced by the adrenaline of the hunt for carriage B, and by the burden of my rather pointless job of disinfecting all of Canary Wharf.

It's tonight's date on the phone. The restaurant is closed, all boarded up. I repeat back everything she's saying, as if I'm hearing it wrong; as if stating what I'm being told will somehow change reality. It's totally covered in wood and that there is a note on the floor that probably explains the issue, but it has fallen down. I even find myself speaking out loud the bit where she tells me the closed down restaurant likely sets the tone to what she believes will be a bleak date and that she should probably stick to her gut instincts in that tonight is just a poor show that will lead to a poor fuck.

She doesn't want me, I tell the youth, as he sits attentively listening to my drama. Within seconds of me hanging up he's telling me that it's all good. He sits back in his seat and just looks out the window. He's talking to me yet still taking in the view of the world around him. Everything he says is calm and relaxed, like he has zero pressure to give me his answer or to appease any part of the world that he resides in. He simply grins and chills in his bit of space as he gives me his urban view on my lack of a Friday night shag.

The truth is I really did fancy a shag – a really good one, lasting well into the night. But a part of me genuinely hoped for more this time. My way in with women is always through my body and I know that. I have already admitted that my arrogance and lack of effort on anything other than polishing my abs and perfecting my fucking would mean the most dedicated of women will eventually lose interest.

When a woman first undresses me they love what they see. They spend countless hours looking and touching, like they're trying to burn the vision of my body into their mind forever, somehow knowing things will come to an end. And after a few months, sometimes only weeks, it happens, and we don't see the same thing when we both look in the mirror. I come back from the gym and check the fruits of my hard labour – and as I run a finger down my stomach I'm proud of what I've created, knowing that it is my hard work and dedication that built each rock where fat could easily thrive. They're my best ever creation; individual gems in my otherwise uneventful existence. But they look at me and they think I'm vain; they don't see that I'm celebrating one of the only things I've ever battled for and managed to keep. They just stare at me from the bed and silently demand more of a reason to stick around; something more than simple parts of my anatomy with some chilled champers on the side.

'You're all buff, my man,' he says, as I realise I've not said anything in my head since I landed in this seat.

The Train Manager offers me the pleasure of a wine before I need to answer the guy. It's not complimentary but it is cold and so I take two mini bottles, also offering the kid a drink. He declines, showing me his 2 litre Evian bottle, the label all torn off from him refilling three times from the tap. I don't dare ask if he means from the toilet opposite.

As the journey continues I drink my wine as fast as he gulps down his water. We're soon chatting and laughing and before I know it I'm half-cut and learning how to hijack the first-class wifi. Winston, as his name turns out to be, is teaching me how to be street. He thinks I'm cool, but I'm not in the club and if I want to climb the ranks I need to be a little less uptight. He recommends that I should lose the belt and let my slacks hang lower, as well as getting myself some cool shades. He thinks I clearly work too much and that my lack of long-term success with the ladies is because I'm using my animal instincts to impress women who want a range of emotions that I'm clearly not stretching to.

By my third bottle of wine I think he's completely fucking right.

When he asks what I've achieved this week I quickly convince myself that he really is my personal messiah, sent from heaven to help me. He shares half of his chunky KitKat with me as I explain everything, from sacking Jerry through to losing Toyah and Sophie in one night.

'Sex and stability,' he says. 'Now I get you.'

'But I've never had Sophie,' I quickly explain. 'Not in my bedroom or in my life.'

'So do you want her pussy or her friendship?' he asks.

But I don't manage to answer. I've drifted away into thought and I soon realise that I'm happier out here in the corridor. I'm not in a numbered seat; I'm just in the place where everyone passes me on the way to the toilet. As the train picks up speed I look out the window and realise that I'm simply passing life by. There's so much more to see and so much time left in my dreary existence to make something different happen. It's like the wine has removed the haze of tiredness that constantly surrounds my tired mind and now I just need to figure out where I should go.

Winston puts his headphones back on but he's still muttering feel good facts at me. I don't fully hear what he's saying and he can't hear my replies, but I don't think that matters to either of us. I know there's more if I want it.

It's a slight liberation, however short-lived.

15

'Let me put an angle on this for you, Ryan,' Raj says, sitting on that favourite corner of his desk. 'If you would permit me to sum up my view of your recent performance the only word I can really use is 'confusing', wouldn't you agree?'

'We've built up some solid touch-points and now –'

He holds up a hand, clearly not finished. 'But Canary Wharf is so big and we're still so small. You have a proven track record but your current numbers don't really stack up.' He takes this moment to stare at me, making sure our eyes connect before he lets out this little huff. It's not like the huffs Mitchell uses, which normally precede a torrent of abuse, but more from a place of ever-so-slight pity. He continues to look at me, his big brown eyes looking me up and down like he's some sort of snake busy deciding if I'm worth swallowing whole. 'I think it's important that you tell us the view from your window.'

I sit in silence for a moment, not really knowing what to say, but seriously wondering if I should ask to step down, or perhaps just resign now and save us all some hassle. For the first time ever I think about telling him that I cannot cope; that I'm not as good as I thought and that perhaps the reality is I have been over-promoted. I feel so small now, like I'm just some weak body wrapped up in special *Hugo Boss* armour that's just a little too big for me.

It doesn't take long for my arrogant side to take back dominance, as it reminds me of all that I have achieved and to look back at how well my career proceeded until the day I met Mitchell. 'We've already made contact with the top twenty businesses but with such a small team I can't –'

Raj is quickly standing over me, this ticking finger telling me to shut up again. 'Can't simply breeds consistency, Ryan. Consistent failure! You have to create the vision of what you want to achieve and lead your way to that legacy, whether you are a lone salesman or if you have a team of a thousand, in the end it makes no difference.' He paces for a moment then perches himself back on the corner of his desk, pulling his trousers up to show these socks with pound signs stitched into them. 'I'm not sure whether you are carrying people in your team or if you just need a big dose of passion pills, but whatever it is I do need some quick results from you. All eyes are on us with the new *Building Guardians* and it's important that we're both on the same page with this.'

A grunt of laughter comes from the corner of the room. 'I'm not sure if this one's in the right fucking book.' Mitchell walks towards the middle of the room but instead of coming to me he chooses to stand next to Raj. It feels like unfamiliar territory, the two of them side-by-side, both staring down at me with their individual looks of anger and confusion.

I decide to look behind them and I see the sun pouring in. It makes the outside world such an inviting place to be. The trail of light is making its way across the office, casually crawling towards me. Since I've been in this room I have watched it get closer and cover more of the floor space and within a few minutes I know it will be over my face, causing me to squint and eventually block out the two of them. I will then be able to deliberately close my eyes and only have to listen to the long list of my failings.

Mitchell throws a folder onto the floor which lands in front of my feet, the first few pages falling out and showing what looks like bills. Raj shoots him this disapproving look that tells him he has gone too far, but it doesn't have enough punch in it to show that there will be any consequence. It doesn't matter either way as Mitchell is still staring down at me as if Raj isn't even in the room. 'Aren't you going to take a look?'

I lean down to pick it up and then start scanning through the pages to see that it's full of rental bills for my apartment. I always knew roughly how much it cost but I'd never had to sign anything or ever see the reality of this detail. The only thing that had ever mattered to me was having the keys to my dream flat and dream car; the fact that my entire life was on loan never really occurred to me.

'Do you see how much your luxury lifestyle is costing us? I bet you didn't know it was a small fucking fortune.' Mitchell walks closer to me, his chest moving up and down as his heartbeat speeds up, like it's trying to break free of his chest, his whole demeanour showing no care or thought for the fact Raj is in the room. It feels like it's just the usual two of us, as he circles around me, deciding when he is going to strike that killer blow to the back of my head, or when he's going to lock his thick arms around my neck. 'You swan around in your happy bachelor pad, taking all the hand outs we give you, but not delivering any of the goods. I mean, did you think you could ride on the glory of your past endeavours forever, just taking the money and screwing your way to the top? And you do seem to be happy to fuck your way up the ladder.'

Thoughts of my time with Joanna come flooding back into my head and I stand up, desperate to bring order to the conversation and to stop Mitchell from having all this control. He's still shouting but I can't hear what he's saying anymore, as I prepare my deepest thoughts that will shortly become my loudest confessions. I know he's about to go over the edge as my own mind frantically searches for the right thing to say – that one thing which can break Mitchell and force him to hit me or make any permanent damage that Raj will not be able to ignore.

My rage is pushing me forward and I know I'm willing to tell Raj everything, from me shagging Joanna all around her flat to sacking Jerry simply because I was told to. But through sharing my darkest secrets they will inevitably become overshadowed by my revelation that Mitchell really is a complete and total nutter. I square up to him, my chest pushing against his and in the corner of my eyes I can see Raj grabbing at his arm, trying to pull him away.

His hulky body pushes against mine and he sends me a step backwards. 'You really need to learn a lesson in respect.' The threat comes through gritted teeth and I know that this is it – the moment in time that will change everything, giving me back my freedom and taking off the burden that this man has put on my shoulders for far too long.

'Enough!' Raj shouts, far louder than I would ever thought him capable of doing. He steps in between us, his arms outstretched and a smile spread across his face. 'Look at the passion that you two bring to the job! There is so much care and energy flowing between you that I can see now why you work so well together.' He places a hand on each of us and starts to pull us together and even Mitchell moves a little. 'It's like the perfect father and son relationship, you both tell each other how it is and I'm sure a firm handshake is all it takes to move on to the next chapter of your adventures.'

'He's not my father!' I shout, feeling more anger at this one single slip of Raj's naïve tongue than any hundreds of unfair and unwarranted discussions around my capability.

Mitchell doesn't look happy either, as he stares at Raj like he's from some other planet. We shake hands, as Mitchell predictably makes his grip far firmer than it needs to be. He doesn't take his eyes off me as Raj perches himself back on his post. The sheer fact of what I have just seen proves that he plans to remain both neutral and deliberately clueless as to what is really happening.

'Now, Ryan, let's hope you can put this slight performance cloud behind you, because we really can't carry passengers. It's your chance to get out there and prove us wrong, to which you should thank Mitchell for your one month extension.'

'A month?' I say, the reality hitting me that it's now make or break for my life as I know it.

Raj calmly nods. 'After which time I'm afraid there can be no guarantee of you remaining in position without a solid set of figures.'

Mitchell grins, 'Go on then, Ryan, thank me.'

'I have my operation in two weeks and it's a minimum of two weeks recovery,' I say, putting it out there and not knowing what level of empathy it will get back.

'What are you today?' Raj says. 'Some sort of failure monkey?'

'Looks like you've got two weeks to get your house in order then,' Mitchell says, with this obvious smile on his face, like he's already planning my demotion whilst I'm off sick, my return finding Sophie at the helm of a ship where I'm clearly not welcome.

Raj simply claps his hands once in some single act of agreement and final judgement. 'Remember, Ryan, there isn't a monopoly on the exceptional, so get out there and show us all what you can deliver. Time, in this instance, really waits for no man.'

I can only nod, unable to find anything remotely suitable to say to that. Mitchell is already making his way towards the door, his body hunched forward as if it will get him there quicker.

When I get outside he's waiting for me. I try to leave the door open a little but he just reaches around me and slams it shut, before moving his head to be next to mine, almost like he's moving in for a kiss, which terrifies me more than his threatening death breath. 'So now you really see what a spineless twat that man is. The sooner I get him shipped off back to Pakiland the better.'

'You do know he is Indian?'

'What the fuck are you talking about?'

'You said 'Pakiland' which I assume you think is something that's actually acceptable to say and you think he's from Pakistan. But Raj is from India, although I'm sure you knew that.'

He grabs my throat as his thick hands work like claws, digging deep into my flesh. 'I'm going to burn you, boy. I'm going to stand and watch your miserable life fall apart. You have no idea what's coming and by the time that fucker is back on the banana boat and I'm doing the job I deserve, you will be nothing more than an unpleasant memory to every miserable wanker in this place.' He pushes me away, watching me regain my balance and walk straight back towards him, ready for a fight.

'You know your problem, Ryan? You give no thought to the rich tapestry of the past. You think it's all about you, as if everyone else's story started the day you walked in here. A lot of shit happened long before your balls dropped and the sad thing is that if you were less absorbed in your own fucking life you could have unravelled it all.' He doesn't stay to hear my feeble comeback, pushing some poor office interns out the way as he bludgeons his way to the lift. He half turns around to catch me in the corner of his eye. 'My advice is focus on packing up, because you ain't ever getting enough business to put yourself on the new G.U.E map.'

*****

What is the definition of despair? I think it looks a little like trying to get somewhere without a map and whatever you do it never quite works. I think it is doing the same thing day after day and expecting something different to happen.

I've seen two completely packed Tubes go past and my despair at being stuck underground has turned into total determination to get onto the next one, no matter what the cost. I chose to travel to work by Tube today and I'm left realising that it's no better than the car.

Queue down here or queue up there, but whatever I do, queues are likely somewhere. It's like my entire life has become one long tailback, from the moment I left university until the moment I fought my way down the escalator and onto this platform with a few hundred other angry, tired and worn out people.

As I push my way onto the train I feel the build up behind me, people forcing me to go forward, giving me no choice but to fight my way onto the carriage. The people around me want the same thing and any choices I had disappeared the moment I stood down here. My life is now on the path that I chose and there is no way of getting off without seriously damaging everything I have worked for. The door slams shut as everyone squeezes into what little personal space they can find – most people are shoulder-to-shoulder, forced to embrace their situation, whatever the smells and sights they are made to endure.

As I position myself between two fellow city guys I feel the true weight of my burdens. The conversations of the last few days and the thoughts of my future seem to pin me to this very spot, as I wonder how many other people on this one carriage feel as I do. Of the hundred or so people, how many of them don't want to leave this quiet, metal cylinder to return to their busy life in the city above?

The Tube joins a queue, the driver telling us that we're waiting for the train ahead to move out of the platform. It's one set of people queuing behind another set; thousands of people not moving, simply waiting in these underground caverns. I suddenly feel trapped, like this is the journey that will never have the end to it that I planned. My early retirement and everything that goes with it are falling away, lost to my arrogance, my greed and my complete lack of any conviction. Of all my failings the biggest has to be that I've spent all my time in the wrong places. All my ambition and optimism were projected into the future, to the life I wanted, with nothing in the moment where I could have found meaningful love. Instead, I kept the present filled only with meaningless sex and the pursuit of a life I never really owned. And what about the past? Well that's where I've left all the people that should have mattered most to me, whist I was off creating my future without a care in the world as to theirs.

The Tube finally empties and I get a seat. I see my reflection in the window opposite but I don't see the person I used to be. I see the person I have become and it truly scares me. The bags under my eyes, the pale and greasy skin and the stubble that has gone from designer to desperate; this new me doesn't hold the attractiveness I used to feel.

This girl comes into view. 'You seeing anything you like over here?' She gives me this wink as she uncrosses her legs and leans forward. 'It's my stop next.'

I close my eyes, shutting her out and letting the desperation creep in. Perhaps all I am actually good at is picking up girls and giving them a night of pleasure. It wouldn't be a bad life and I could probably earn decent money from it. I'd be my own boss and could choose my own hours.

'Arrogant fucker,' are all the words I hear as the doors open. I expected her to declare to the other passengers that I was gay, after all that is the normal response from any cute blonde that I reject, which I have to admit rarely happens. Instead she chose to capture the very essence of who I am. Those two words from a stranger perfectly summed up what everyone who knows me must think and it couldn't have been better timed.

*****

As I finally reach home and step out of the lift I decide that I should downgrade my despair to something like desperation. It's like one shade lighter than complete and utter hopelessness, where it really is all over. I feel close to the dark, to giving in and crawling away from the iron fist of Mitchell, but I know there is little left. I still have some stock, I still have my tenuous position and I'm still an arrogant fucker.

The moment I turn into my corridor I see her, wedged in between the door and her big weekend bag, like it's a barricade that's keeping her safe. Her long legs are folded into her chest and she's just staring into space with a fag in her hand, not really aware I've arrived.

'Toyah, you can't smoke in here.'

She doesn't look at me and there's none of her normal smiling or screaming, no effort to leap into my arms. Instead she takes this long drag, all the time looking at the floor. She's got this makeshift ash-tray made out of tinfoil perched on the bag and looking at it this isn't her first smoke of the evening. I take my chance in the silence to look around, soon seeing a half empty bottle of Malibu next to her; even in her own dark moments Toyah still takes the mild approach.

When her eyes finally meet with mine she flicks the cigarette towards me. I stumble back and instinctively protect my suit, shouting a little. In return, she cries. It starts as a whimper, her body moving up and down to the rhythm of her little moans, but soon turns into this total wailing as she slaps her face and tries to pull her long curly hair over her eyes.

I move closer, tapping her gently on the arm, but this has no effect. I make the mistake of leaning down and her arms are soon around me, forcing me into some kind of James Bond move as I cradle her in my arms and carry her into the flat. Once we're inside I realise my next fatal error, as she shows no interest in letting go, with her legs and arms wrapped around me like some sort of hungry love leech. As I try to pull her off the grip just gets tighter, her head buried into my neck so she doesn't have to see the look of complete frustration on my face. Or maybe she's considering biting me, I'm really not sure anymore.

I stumble towards the sofas, having no patience or interest in her games tonight. I try to sit her on the back of the sofa but it doesn't work. As I feel her tears streaming down my chest I use all the strength I have left to launch her body towards the padded cushions. Not only is this the most unsexy thing I have ever done to a woman, it was also completely stupid as now I have a blonde, hysterical, tormenting ex-lover shouting at me, with the addition of blood streaming down her face.

'You threw me at the coffee table!' she shouts and then starts screaming, the kind of howl that will bring every neighbour in this block running to her rescue. This is the girlfriend beater scenario being played out in court, the evidence against me utterly overwhelming. I run over to her but she frantically crawls away, her face full of fear as her mind is clearly telling her that this is an attack. The woman I have made love to on every bit of furniture and floor in this place is now in some sort of horror movie of her own making and no matter what I say or do she just tries to pull herself further away from me.

I finally manage to touch her face, to stop the bleeding with my hand. I start to feel some sense of calm as she pulls her small handbag closer to her body, hopefully finding some tissues. I smile at her as the screaming turns to heavy panting, but it's not the tissues that make an appearance.

The moment we look at each other my eyelids are suddenly closing, the pain searing through my eye sockets and into my mouth. I start choking as I fall back, my fingers desperately rubbing at my eyes, but this only makes the stinging worse. I can taste the attack in my mouth and I'm not sure if it's blood or just the cocktail of chemicals.

I try to hold back my own screaming as I get up and stumble towards the bathroom, or perhaps the kitchen, I'm not sure where I'm going but I know I need a sink. 'Toyah... water!' I run forward, trying to mentally picture where I am, trying to figure out the best way to help myself. All the time she says nothing and after I hit a wall and fall down she still doesn't come to my aid.

I lie on the floor, rubbing my eyes, desperately waiting for the sting to leave me. I can sense her shadow over my body but she still doesn't speak, not even her normal whimper in a time of crisis. Instead of doing whatever she came here to do, her final parting gift is a sharp pain in my stomach. Her foot strikes me again for good measure, the force far greater than I would have thought she was capable of, probably helped by her thick pointy boots, the kick months in the making.

I lie still, perhaps playing dead, perhaps not able to figure out what to do. I wait to hear the slamming of the door but even then I can't find the courage or purpose to move.

16

It's the call I've always dreaded but I knew that one day it would happen. I had convinced myself that it would come from a friend or a neighbour, having forced their way into the house and faced a frantic and unfair need to juggle between summoning me and calling for proper help. In this case I was right, with the call having come from Carol, the dutiful and caring friend. What I didn't expect was the place where I was being called to and not at eleven in the evening.

I have barely got the sting from the pepper spray out of my eyes and the dent knocked out of my pride, before finding myself racing across South London to get to Sainsbury's. I've had no call back from Toyah, giving me no chance to explain that I wasn't trying to hurt her and no understanding as to why she turned up in the first place. Whatever the reason, it feels like we've finally had our closure – through blood and pain. After months of wild sex I'm not sure it was the ending I wanted, but it's probably what I deserved.

As I get closer to the store I realise that this is something else that I could have stopped from ever happening, especially if I had just spent some time in the present – being the caring son that I should have been.

I park up, finding a space right near the front of the store. I can hear her before I have even got inside; the voice is undeniably recognisable, but the hysterical screaming is something I am not used to. And all of this is coming from the mouth of my timid mother. She has barely spoken anything coherent for months and now she is yelling at some poor bloke who's dressed in an oversized and dirty suit.

As I approach I try to assess the situation, assuming he is the Duty Manager, probably more used to throwing out alcoholics and druggies than my poor mum. She is busy holding onto a shopping trolley full of stock, literally piled high with groceries and on the other side there is this security guard three times her size, trying to pull the trolley away from her. Carol has a hold on my mum's arm but it's doing no good and as the struggle gets worse I tell myself that this is it. This is the breakdown that's been looming in the nearby shadows for too long.

'This is my food!' my mum shouts, trying to pull the trolley closer to the exit. She looks quite willing to take this guy on as she struggles to prise his iron grip off the metal. 'I have to get this home before Harry wakes up.'

'This isn't yours!' the guy in charge shouts for what looks like the last time. 'You haven't paid for it.'

'Mum!' I say as soon as I'm close enough, which immediately gets a mixture of confused looks from the staff and a sigh of relief from Carol, as I see her hands release much of their grip on my mum's arm, symbolically ready to hand over this immense burden. But my mum doesn't hear me, instead taking the opportunity of the distraction to pull harder at the trolley. She somehow manages to get it away from both Carol and the guard, as she starts running with it towards the door.

'Take her down!' the manager shouts to the guard, who in turn nods and starts to move towards her. With this look of determination he quickly catches up with her and rips her hands from the trolley, before he pushes it out of the way. It travels further than I would have expected, as it slowly rolls its way along the entrance area.

The instinct to protect my mum takes over my whole body, no doubt fuelled by my mind's reminders of all the times I have failed her of late. As his heavy, outstretched arms get ready to swallow her into his giant mass I run towards him, throwing myself into this six-foot hulk of muscle. Much to my surprise and probably his, I manage to force him off his feet, as we both fall into the flower display. Buckets of plants crash everywhere, quickly covering us in water as it pours all over the floor. We struggle for a few moments as we both try to fight each other off and stand up, no one helping us as they watch in amusement at how this evening is progressing.

By the time I regain my balance it's all too late, as I find him towering above me, his suit covered in mashed up flowers. He takes one look at me before planting his fist into my face. I feel the blood streaming from my nose as my head hits the floor. My vision becomes blurry as I see black shoes pacing in front of me and I feel Carol's frantic hands shaking my arm. She's calling out my name, a mixture of shock and exhaustion so obvious in her voice.

As I drift out of consciousness the last thing I see is my mum, pushing that trolley, making it out of the door and into the car park, the wheels rattling as she battles along the solid concrete floor. She doesn't look back as she tastes the cold night air and finds her freedom.

*****

Mum is busy unpacking her groceries, inspecting each and every item as if they are a collection of prizes that she has won. She has literally fought for them; these small treasures in her big hazy ocean of confusion. In this moment, as I watch her, she actually seems happy. She's focused on something, which could actually be a good sign, if it wasn't for the fact that she had attempted to steal everything that she is now meticulously organising into the cupboards.

She is ignoring both Carol and me, as she goes about her business. I paid for the groceries, the flowers and the privilege of nursing my nose with a bag of peas as Carol tells me how it all happened. She had only popped in for a couple of bits and found my mum with the trolley full of stuff. When she asked my mum why she had so much food, the reply she got back told her there was serious trouble ahead and so she called me. There have been many times of late that I'm thankful she has my number. I always thought it would be her that called me and so I keep her name in bold letters accompanied with the loudest ringtone my phone has, like some crisis hotline right through to my innermost fears.

'I really don't know why your mum needed so much food,' Carol whispers, as she looks at my mum and then back to me. She has this constant worry frown whenever I find her in this kitchen. It's like she doesn't want to be here, but like any good friend she does what she can for a family she has known for years. She does the washing up and she makes the tea and all the time she fills in the gaps I have failed to notice. I know she's as lost for words as I am and she tries to avoid the same conversation. The one that finds my mum in the past, remembering a world that no longer exists.

I look at Carol and I know that this experience has aged her more than my mum. She's beaten and she doesn't want to hear this any more than I do and she certainly doesn't want to confront what is lurking in the living room. And so she visits daily, coming in through the back door and never going anywhere except this one room – the only one that isn't closed off to the outside world.

'She just kept saying it was for a big dinner with you and your dad,' Carol says and then takes hold of my arm. 'I'm so sorry.'

We both look through the hallway, to the living room door that is half open and we both know that one solitary light is all that illuminates what was once such a bright place.

'I can hear you both,' my mum says without turning around. She's busy putting stuff in the freezer but then she stops, looking puzzled for a few seconds. I look back at the hollow shell that used to be my mum, as even the most basic of domestic chore is taking its toll. 'Oh, there you are, Ryan,' she says, turning around to me. 'Wait until I tell your old man what's happened,' she says and grabs the peas off me and then packs them away into the freezer.

Once the food is gone she asks Carol if she's staying for a cup of tea. Carol looks at me and I look outside. 'Mum, do you know what time it is?'

She looks outside but she doesn't seem to register how late it is. She puts the kettle on and sets out four mugs, all the time humming to herself.

Carol gives me this look, the face that says she's seen all this before and she can't see it again. These are the moments I have successfully managed to avoid for some time now. The fear of what I'll hear and the impossibility of what needs to be said work together to drive me away from the person I should be helping the most. Carol's tormented gaze moves between the assembly of mugs and the back door and as the kettle starts to boil the intensity on her face grows.

When the teapot slams on the countertop it proves too much and Carol stands up. She finds both Mum and me staring back at her, both with different thoughts but surely neither of us really wanting her to leave. I look back to the living room and I'm not sure if I can do this alone, but I know it is my fight to have. I know that this should be family only and with one simple nod I release Carol from her responsibility. She disturbs my mum's tea pouring as she forces a hug upon her and then flees into the night air, my mum shouting after her to come back for lunch later, after all, we have enough to eat.

As soon as Carol is gone I can feel the tension between mum and me. It hasn't been just the two of us for a while and I don't know what to do. I never knew what to say when it happened and I never quite got a handle on what should have been said since. And now, even months on, I still don't know what to say to someone who denies everything.

She's staring at me now, through two dark pockets that somewhere hold those hazel eyes I'm happy I got from her. She used to be a stunner, my mum, with bronzed skin that glowed and a smile that made every journey home so worthwhile. Now all that's left is this pale looking shell that used to be the most important person to me.

'Fetch your dad this cuppa,' she says, holding out the mug. She stares at me, silently demanding that I do the impossible, like some sort of demon has taken control.

I shake my head, the subtle move telling her I won't be a part of this lie any longer. 'You know I can't do that, Mum.'

'Of course you can, he'll be dying of thirst in there.' She tries to force the hot mug into my sealed fist, trying to get me to take the handle. Tea spills over my hand as I resist but she doesn't notice, doesn't seem to care, as she forces me to play along. 'Take it,' she cries, as her mind is only focused on making my fingers relent, forcing her twisted reality upon me.

I take the mug off her and throw it into the sink, pieces shattering all around the kitchen. She gives me this look of horror, like I'm the one who's wrong in the head. It's all gone too far now and the bold destruction of his favourite mug must have a follow through. She goes towards the sink to tidy up but I pull her back to me, my hands gripping her shoulders as I look into her eyes. 'If he's thirsty then why doesn't he come out here and get a drink?'

Her head shakes as I keep a firm hold. Determination runs through my veins as my heart feels like it will beat out of my chest. This is the change that has been a long time coming – it's the future we must both experience, must both share. 'Why don't you call him and we can have tea together out here?'

'You know he's busy, Ryan. You know how hard your father works.'

'Worked,' I say, as my eyes bore into hers. 'How hard he worked.'

Her eyes examine my face, as she looks for a sign of a lie. I start to think I'm getting through, as I hope that her world will finally fall apart in front of me. I hope the tears will come and go a hundred times, so that we can finally start to rebuild on what is left.

'Why are you being like this?' she says and then screams, just like the night it happened. She looks at me just like she looked at that policeman, a thick blanket draped over her as the rain battered down. She refused to get into the Police car and she refused to leave the crash site. It was an evening that should have changed her world but she refused to accept any of it.

'We both know how hard he worked,' I say, still holding onto her. 'He did everything he could to provide for us. He drove up and down the country for hours and you know that coming home to you kept him going.' I pinch her shoulders, hoping to get through to whatever is left. 'He always looked forward to a decent meal and a glass of brandy in his favourite chair. You'd do the washing up as he settled in to the evening, his favourite programmes planned out before him.'

She suddenly smiles, already pulling away from me. 'I'll cook him something now. I'll cook you both a fry up. That'll get you set for the day.'

I pull her back towards me. 'He doesn't need food where he is now. He needs us both to accept what has happened.' I start to drag her away from the kitchen, my determined mind settled on the door ahead. I feel nothing but fear as I look forward, my eyes set on that small crack where the light from his small reading lamp still shines through.

She fights back as I pull her through the hallway, as only my desperation to hear her say something different, something that resembles any level of acceptance, pushes me forward. It would be easier to do nothing – to embrace her denial; to keep our little secret, fuelled by our ever-silent pact. She starts to kick and scream; no doubt begging me to end this horror, clearly not wanting to know what awaits her. I'm relentless now as I put my arms around her and carry her into this twisted version of reality, my back pushing the door open. We're in the middle of the room before the smell hits me; the layers of dust and lack of daylight for months have left behind the lingering scent of that past life we all shared.

We both stand and look around, as a strange sense of calm takes over my mum. It takes me a second to find the courage to turn around and I find weird that I'm okay looking at the fireplace but not what is behind me. I eventually turn to see that same black leather chair in the corner, the one small lamp on the table next to it the only thing still here that has any purpose. In the dimness of the room it takes my eyes a moment to confirm that he isn't sitting on that chair, waiting for his supper whilst he chats away about his travels that day, about the horrors of the M25. About his most hated sign: 'Queues likely.'

But everything is as it has been for some time, nothing touched since his last supper. I take my mum's hand just before she manages to escape and run out of the room. I gently pull her back as I refuse for her to accept anything but the truth. 'When did you last cook him dinner?'

She stutters out some random words, as her mind staggers to find any answer that won't be the truth. 'He'll be home soon,' she says, still pulling away from me.

I drag her to the fireplace, taking careful hold. 'He is home,' I say, forcing us both to look at the urn on the top of the marble surround. I stare at it, seeing the past, present and future of one man now entwined together; what is left behind now in the care of others.

I refuse to take my eyes off it, not willing to let this moment pass until I know that we understand what has happened. We must both accept what life has thrown at us and we must both work together to keep his memory alive. More than anything he would want our lives to continue; to start a new chapter, to make our own time in this world matter.

I look at my mum and see tears rolling down her cheeks and I hope that she finally understands what has happened. This one silent gesture tells me that she is starting to accept that her world has changed. As I feel my eyes fill with tears of what feel more like joy, I realise I have been denying all of this as much as she has.

17

I always feel better when Ken is my wing-man. The queues don't seem to matter as much. The clients don't matter that much, either. In fact, all of life's struggles seem to matter far less when he is around.

We're speeding up the motorway, having found the freedom of the open road at the beginning of the M1. Those first few miles as we leave London are always a pleasure without many other cars to contend with. We chat and laugh all the way to Milton Keynes and even with its array of roundabouts and identical roads I still find my way through the chaos.

There's no crazy traffic today, which I'm convinced is due to Ken being here and not the fact that it's half-term. It's my lucky charm sitting next to me, telling me everything is going to be great. He's never been a great listener; a few choice questions will tell you that, but if you want energy and excitement, then he's your man.

He takes a long sniff of the blow that he's lined up along the dashboard.

'Really, Ken, on a work day?'

He just laughs, his eyes already starting to glaze over. 'This is a BMW. It's expected in one of these.' He bangs the dash, the left over powder filling the air. 'It should be complimentary!'

I catch the scent of the blow and I cough, trying to clear it out the way. My head doesn't need any more of a haze over it today, however tempting Ken's corrupting ways can be. It's at times like this that I realise my personal motivator is also my personal liability. The policy manual clearly details that the possession and consumption of any illegal substance is gross misconduct and that I should suspend him on the spot. I used to laugh about these sorts of things but now I just frown as Ken tells me to lighten up. It is slowly dawning on me that when we go into business together I won't have the threat of that manual anymore. We'll be truly alone – just me, Ken and his many crippling vices.

When we finally arrive at the possible new client's offices Ken falls out of the car and starts laughing. Most people think he's full of life but I know he's just full of powdered happiness. He stumbles a little and then manages to stand up. 'Chill out, man,' he says, as he puts on his suit jacket and then lights up a cigarette. He carries on lecturing me about how uptight I've become. It's one of those conversations he has with a fag hanging out of his mouth, as he takes a long look at me, his already narrow eyes getting a little more judgemental.

I ignore him and look at the concrete encampment around us, each building as nondescript as the other. I start to realise that this place is my own personal hell – a congregation of several young and hopeful corporate entities, all with their clever logos and promising slogans, trapping many hundreds of people inside them.

Ken looks at me and inhales deeply. He doesn't see what I see, doesn't care about the things that should matter to both of us. Ken flicks his cigarette and we walk into the reception area that offers little hope that this will be a lucrative deal. But I need this to be a deal and a good one at that. I need the business now more than ever, as the ticking clock continues its brutal countdown and any signature will do. It won't be a contract; it will be the signing of a petition against my brutal and planned departure.

The only good news is that they have asked for me, which shocked me in the first place and now as I stand in front of the entrance desk I start to wonder if I'm a little too late. In the corner, there is one simple coffee table and two chairs that must be cast offs from a dental reception. This place smells of defeat and the brown boxes piled up everywhere tell only of what it used to be, with one shitty canvas on the wall trying to sell this place as anything remotely successful.

'Sorry, we've just been acquired,' this guy says as he makes his way out of the lift. He's short and thin, with a full rug of hair, all spiked and styled. His suit looks a little too big, a supposed tell-tale sign to a lack of style, but at his size I'm sure that's always an issue. He strides towards me, his confidence setting a presence where his stature never could. 'You must be Ryan,' he says, as he gives a firm handshake full of effort. 'I'm Todd and I'm sorry about the mess.' He looks around, surveying the apparent damage. 'The acquisition happened quickly and we're, errrr, still recovering from it.'

'This is Ken and it's not a problem. We're here to talk about how we can help you guys.'

Todd nods as he ushers us upstairs, his energy spilling words out quicker than they make sense, as he explains that no one saw it coming and that the new interim boss had barely got settled in before calling for us.

'Most probably a *Building Guardian*,' I say to Ken, as he mutters under his breath that it clearly won't be anything to do with sex.

'A building what?' Todd asks, as he pushes us into a small meeting room.

Ken places a hand on my chest, his face full of smiles as he tells me that he's apparently got this. 'A *Building Guardian* is our patented protection system for ensuring that every part of your office space is discretely sanitised and protected against all known airborne and surface germs.'

'Really?' Todd says, with this frown poking out from under his big fringe.

'That's not why we were called?'

He holds out his hands, his face shaking. 'I have no idea why you guys were called. All I know is the new boss took over and one of the first orders she barked was for me to get you up here.'

'And here we are,' I say, just as the new boss bursts into the room.

'Ryan, Ken, please meet –'

'We've met before,' I say, everything clicking into place as I already regret the most pointless journey and a wasted morning in the car.

*****

She's staring at me from across the table and I can't believe that I'm here, with her. I should be enjoying this moment but I don't know how to. I'm not sure this is even allowed and I have no idea if I'll be able to claim the cost back.

When I think about expensing this, I think about the look I'll get upon putting the receipt on Mitchell's desk, assuming Michelin star restaurants are now significantly above my pay grade. When I was on the upward climb these were the questions I never asked myself. I never had to, but on the fast track back down I feel compelled to do all I can to save myself. I look across the table one more time, to see that she's got the oysters, whilst I've got the economy-flavoured soup.

'You're not hungry?' Joanna asks.

I smile and stare down at my food. 'I'm starving,' I say.

'Well, darling, get yourself something bigger. After all, a strapping young man like you needs more and believe me when I tell you that the main course will be even less substantial.' She gives me this long stare, her eyes taking in every part of me on show to her. 'Bread is the key,' she says, as she fills up my wine glass.

'You're pouring this yourself,' I say, as at least three waiters catch her doing their job.

She laughs and throws the bottle back into the bucket. 'Never forget that I'm in charge.'

'Don't I know it,' I say, before this long silence falls upon us. I finish my soup as Joanna slurps down her oysters. She digs around the big bowl with her fork, searching for that last one, her attention entirely on the hunt.

When she's finally finished she carefully surveys the damage around her lips, making sure she wipes away any of the juices before clutching her wine glass as she plants this long gaze upon me. It seems like a long time passes between us speaking, as this silent exchange does nothing for my confidence. 'I had a lot of fun that night,' she finally says.

I slam my spoon into the bowl, this single action silencing the tables around us. The soup does what you would expect it to do, covering the white table cloth and my shirt with orange stains.

Joanna playfully tuts. 'You'll have to get that shirt off, darling.'

I can feel the rage growing within me; anger at her for being one of a few women to ever get inside my head and make me feel something other than simple lust for the opposite sex, and pity at myself for not letting it happen with someone far younger and within my league. She's still smiling back at me with this ear-to-ear grin, the sort that shows the game for what it is. This feels like one of those moments where you calmly finish your wine and leave, throwing down some notes for the food and the waiter's trouble. Except that I'm not that kind of guy anymore; I no longer have the status or cash to pull it off.

'So, you didn't have fun?'

'I had fun as much as you had control.'

She sighs and then pauses, taking it all in. 'Would you like an oyster? I saved this one just for you,' she says, holding it in her fingers like it's some prized gift of life. I shake my head but she ignores me and stands up, moving around the table with the shell still in her hand. 'Would you like this?' she says again, now towering over me. Half of the waiters stare at us as she grabs the back of my head and tries to force it into my mouth. I fight back as she pulls at my hair, her nails scrapping my head. It lands on the soup-stained cloth, looking like some poor slug that's been left to shrivel and die.

'Now, that's control,' she says as she sits back down, taking her wine glass back into her hand. 'And besides, how do you conclude that it was me who had control that night?'

I take a deep breath and rub my eyes, trying once again to see if I'm really asleep. I've dreamt of Joanna many nights since we met, but this is the stuff of nightmares and right now I can't figure how I'm going to get out. 'I wasn't doing that to you, was I?'

'Darling, it was you who had your dick in me!' she shouts and then laughs, looking around for agreement as other diners whisper amongst themselves.

I get up to leave but she's way ahead of me, with a fork sticking into my knee under the table, her head tilted as she watches me. 'I'd stay seated if you want this deal to happen.'

I must give her this look of horror because all she does is laugh. I grab the fork from her hand, as we start to wrestle under the table. 'I'm sick of you and Mitchell playing mind games with me. You've done it once and I swear it's not going to happen again, so whatever game he's got you playing it's now over.' I stand up again, this time without the threat of a stabbing. 'I don't care about the deal and I don't care what you two try to do to me.'

I push my chair under the table, trying my best to act with decorum, hoping one day to return here in a very different situation.

Instead of fighting with me she starts to plead, as she stands up and gently grabs my hand. 'Please, I don't want to fight for your attention. You should stay if you want to hear about Mitchell.'

A waiter approaches as I sit back down, the temptation too much to avoid. He asks if we're okay, but only I answer, as Joanna instead chooses to start a silent vigil, constantly looking into my eyes. The main course passes us by but there is still no answer or confession of all that I need to know about the man who's been slowly fucking with my mind for months.

'Do you know how much control you really have?' she finally asks.

I say nothing as she shakes her head. 'Darling, you have all the power. You're what, twenty-eight?'

'Thirty,' I correct her, as if it makes any difference.

'At your age I think you have a fairly good idea of how many women want to bed you and that is what I would call true power. What I had over you was never really control, it was just a short-lived fantasy. I tried my best to capture it, so that I can remember every moment of our time together, but the truth is that it's already just a fading memory.' She suddenly bangs the table. 'And I want it every day. I want you, in every possible way, as you really are the boy I never had but totally deserved. I should have spent less time working and more time living and now that I'm in my fifties I want more than anything the one night that is slowly slipping away.'

'So you used me?' I say, my voice barely a whisper compared to her loud dialogue and desperate tones, shared freely for all our neighbours to hear. 'You used your position to sleep with me just to say you'd done it.'

'Yes, Ryan, we fucked. Please feel free to use the big boy vocabulary any time you like.'

Her outburst finally attracts an array of tutting from the table next to us, but it doesn't stop Joanna as she leans over. 'Darling, if you'd had his meat in you I promise you'd be talking about it until the day you die.' She leans back over to me. 'I'm at the point in my life where I really don't care. No one can hurt me, do you see that?'

'What do you want?' I ask, knowing that there can be only one outcome. I already imagine that she's got a room booked upstairs. The waiters will happily have our wine moved to the room, chaperoning us to the door to give everyone else a rest. And she'll either insist that we finish what we started in private, or fake a need to lie down. Either way, I give it ten minutes before I'm trapped between her thighs, our strange game continuing. All I know is I want it. I want her now and I want her screaming with pleasure. She's simply the most powerful woman I've met and whatever she's trying to do to me, being forced to bring back her youth through using mine is something I'm willing to play my part in.

I look at Joanna and I think about Sophie, as I realise that in my mind they are the same person, just separated by twenty years. They both make me feel so different to any other woman I have ever met and I would happily take the younger or the older, or both.

She smiles and leans back, taking me all in. 'I'll always remember our time together, it was simply my best and you were, as I'm sure you know, quite amazing.' She suddenly laughs. 'Did I just catch you nodding? Modesty is still a virtue, darling.'

I laugh back, now in the game, feeling just a little power coming my way. 'You should know that I had to put in a lot of effort that night. You definitely made me raise my game.'

'Well I'm glad, but it will never happen again.'

I pour the wine, already planning on another bottle. 'Oh, really? I'm sure there's some way you can persuade me.'

She grabs the glass from me, throwing its contents onto the carpet, confirming to me and all those around us that she's finally gone mad. 'I just told you it will never happen and I meant it. We could easily go and fuck right now, but don't you see that it will be your way of having control again?'

I shake my head, wanting this crazed woman now more than ever.

'Our possible future is as sad as it is obvious,' she says. 'We'd meet a few more times, in discreet locations, the sex getting longer and more intense as our bond together grows. You see, I know I would force you to do more and more, finding and stretching whatever limits you have. It's what I'm good at. And trust me... I'm very well equipped to do just that.'

I stare back at her in agony as she starts to massage my hard cock with her soft foot. I don't know what to say and I can only think about having her right now, in every possible position. I don't care who's watching as I start to count down the seconds to when we will be naked and rolling on a bed.

Her face is giving me no such reassurance as she pulls her foot away. 'And then at about the same time that I fall in love with you, you'll stop answering my calls. There will be some valid reason, most likely that you've found a girl your age, or you've decided to travel the world for a year or two, which turns into a half decade of you sleeping and drinking your way around the globe. As you're busy finding yourself, I'll simply age further away from you, until the day you return back home to find what you will immediately think of as your grandmother waiting to greet you. It's not the life I want.'

'That's a nice story,' I say, flicking my fingers for a waiter. 'Shall I get the bill?'

She laughs once more. 'Ryan, we're not going to fuck.'

'Perhaps you'd like to discuss this somewhere more private, Madam,' the waiter says.

I nod back at him, wondering why it's taken them so long. 'Just the bill,' I say and turn back to Joanna to find she's already out of her seat and heading towards the door.

No one gives chase as I leave my card and catch up with her in the lobby. I take a hold of her shoulders and pull her close to me, her head soon buried into my neck. 'I'm sorry. I don't mean to have any control over you.'

She pulls away and wipes her eyes and then guides me to some seats, putting a small table firmly between us. 'You must promise me something, Ryan, and you must mean it.'

'Anything.'

'Oh, for fucks sake, this isn't the bloody movies. Say it like you mean it, like you realise even half of the mess you're in.'

I frown and then slowly nod, not really wanting to know the mess she's thinking about.

'Promise me we will never have sex again. Promise me that whatever happens, you will not try to sleep with me and any advances I make will be completely ignored.'

'You really want me to promise that?'

In return she simply looks back at me with these pleading eyes, through a gaze that finally shows her true self. 'Promise me, because the only way we can stay in touch is if I know that nothing sexual can ever happen. And believe me, we need to stay in touch.'

I finally nod, agreeing to something I disagree with. I am easily able to separate the fact that it would just be sex, but I've learnt so many times that to a woman it's not that simple. 'I promise that we won't be doing it.'

She takes my hands into hers. 'Good, it's the right thing. For as much as I lust for you, what I want more than anything is to put things right. It's the future that matters now and there are things you must know about Mitchell.'

I find myself leaning forward, listening to every word that she says and somehow knowing that this next hour could be worth more than a hundred shags.

18

Ken has gone.

He said he had to leave straight away. It was one simple phone call that told me nothing more. He didn't even seem high. In fact, he seemed calm, possibly in control. This is a big deal for several reasons. Firstly, Ken never goes away and if he ever does it's with me, or with a girl or two in tow. Secondly and by far the biggest issue from all of this is that it's party time and as the women start to arrive in my flat I realise that I'm quite alone.

I send him one more message, but I expect no reply. I realise now that I'm going to be flying this one completely solo and it's scaring the hell out of me. Several of the regulars have already asked where he is, which isn't uncommon, as many times he would have still been in the bathroom, doing another line of coke before making a bold entrance.

It's some of the newer faces that concern me the most. They start asking if it will be another live demonstration, their expectations set at a level I'm unwilling to go to, as they stare at my crotch like its public property. These events have become all about lust and the perversions of these filthy-forties women and nothing at all about the product benefits.

Ken's left me all the merchandise we have and I vow to sell every last bit of it. I think about keeping his half of the income too, after all I've done all the work today and I don't even know how far my boundaries are yet to be pushed. I look around the room to see them all laughing, most of them looking at me and then giggling in their little groups. This is when women are at their most dangerous – when in heavy numbers and where champagne flows like water. These sales nights are like their release and last time Ken pushed the boundaries beyond what any of us expected and for my ego to leave this unbruised I know I need to do the same.

I push my way through the crowd to get into my bedroom, the one place that no visitor is allowed. I find myself at the en-suite sink, washing my face and staring at myself in the mirror. I'm not sure I recognise who's staring back. There's nothing behind the looks anymore; just a pretty face and a lost soul. My life is going nowhere and I know it. All those grand plans and big dreams – they all went silently on hold, until my ambition turned into this lonely and lingering anxiety.

I tell myself that my career has well and truly turned to chaos, as I find the one small bag of blow I had hidden away, just enough for one emergency line. It's purely for the most desperate of times, something that would make me break my five years of freedom. I always knew I would screw it up for something big and tonight is the night. I sniff it all up, telling myself I'm going to sell, strip and then shag my way through this weekend. I will be alone but it will be epic.

By the time I come outside the music is playing and the women are chanting my name. It's all about me and it feels good. They all stare at me, their lustful little minds telling them what they hope they will see. As I reach the small stage I've got my sleeves rolled up and a bottle of champagne in my hand.

If they will buy some shit, I'll show everything they really want – it's our special deal. These events have probably always been about that. It's just Ken and me who thought these people actually wanted clean and clinical houses, but in actual fact they wanted some fun, some desire and clearly some flesh.

I gulp back some fizz until it spills out of my mouth and down my shirt, which only fuels the chants of 'Off, off, off!' I try to flirt but end up quickly obliging with my shirt coming off, keeping the t-shirt on underneath as I desperately try to control this moment. I even try to talk about the benefits of the *Sex-Sanitiser* and how the supplies are limited, which is no lie.

As I take my t-shirt off I can feel my heart beating in my chest and I'm not sure if it's the mix of fizz and blow, or if I'm genuinely the most aroused I've ever been. There are so many eyes on me, the closest of them pulling at my trousers and chanting for more flesh. 'It's time for a demonstration, ladies!' I shout, as I unbutton my trousers and throw the belt down. I notice Samantha and Kim leave, all of this probably too much and never what they signed up for. I have to admit that it's nothing like any of us planned, but it's too late now. My body is all I have to offer and I'm going to sell it to the highest and most desperate bidder. Someone in the crowd hands me a kit and someone else pulls my trousers down. I look down to see I'm harder than I thought, as I try to keep my balance and tease my way into my pants.

I'm ready for the big reveal – the moment I bare all. I've already promised myself that this is a good idea, that I've already broadcast sex online and been to numerous orgies, so by comparison this is just an extension of that liberation. In many ways it's far less eventful.

I'm no longer looking at the crowd as I put a hand down my pants. The room falls silent and the music stops, almost as if destiny has brought us all to this moment. I embrace my small shot at fame like it has been coming all my life; my soul purpose in this wasted journey now obvious as appeasing the unfulfilled desires of many women all at once. They all look at me, desperate for more as they beg me to take this to the next level. I keep my focus ahead, looking only at the door and in just two short seconds the whole meaning of tonight changes.

My boxers don't drop, but my mouth does, as I see Sophie standing in the doorway. She doesn't move, this permanent grin fixed across her face. She looks quite comfortable, leaning against the wooden frame. My confidence leaves me as quick as my hard on, as I'm busted again by the one woman who keeps finding me at my lowest.

*****

We end up sitting on the balcony. I guess that neither of us wants to stay inside the living room and get a constant reminder of tonight's events.

Sophie can't stop laughing. She looks over at me and bursts into a fit of giggles. I don't really understand her motive, but I'm thankful for getting this reaction, if not slightly shocked she has bothered to stick around.

'You really are quite pathetic,' she says, suddenly all serious. 'I can't believe you've ended up selling company stock and stripping in the same evening. I think it's taking multi-tasking a little to the extreme.' She pats my head and lightly slaps my face. 'Is this the lowest point in your life? I can only assume so. And as for the theft of company stock... well I'm quite sure Mitchell will fire you out of a cannon when he finds out.'

I gulp my wine back and think about how that conversation will go. She's right, it will be exactly the ammunition Mitchell needs to finally ruin me. I think about my bank balance and all the illegitimate earnings that they will come after, pushing me to pay it all back. I don't even think about this evening; I'm not even slightly embarrassed. If anything I'm annoyed that I still have stock left to shift and that Sophie could at least have had the decency to discover my escapades once my fans had left me with a big pile of cash. As it is, I have plenty of illegal stock and no cash or fun to show for it.

'Such a predicament,' she says, shaking her head and staring at me through this long fringe. I offer no answer back as I watch her for a moment, noticing the littlest of details, such as her perfectly styled hair and her figure-hugging dress that's just a little too formal for her to just randomly pop around my flat on a Saturday night.

'So, are you going to confess, or am I going to have to tell them? I really hope you don't put me in that position.'

'I can't do this anymore,' I say and then walk away, too dazed to fight back and too exhausted to plead with her.

'What's wrong?' she asks, following after me.

'What do you care, Sophie? And why are you even here? Why don't you go and sharpen your knives at home. I'm quite sure you'll get enough entertainment on Monday and by the end of the week you'll have my job.'

'I think I'll stay for now. It's far more entertaining here,' she says, as she piles some of the merchandise boxes together and sits on them. 'And besides, whoever said I want your job?'

I find myself kneeling on the floor in front of her, my shirt hanging out of my trousers and my forehead drenched with sweat. I'm a mess, but I'm too exhausted to fix it, even in front of the one woman I want the total and unwavering approval of. She has seen me at my lowest – in fact we've both witnessed it together and now I have nowhere to go. The tears start, as I wonder if this is my full breakdown coming a few decades too early. As I cradle my head in my hands it doesn't feel like this has suddenly crept up on me, in fact completely the opposite; this complete failure has been banging the door down for some time.

Sophie doesn't say or do anything as I comfort myself. She just stares down at me with these dark, robotic eyes that seem only interested in evaluating what I will do next. She tilts her head to get a better view of my sobbing, but does nothing to show any compassion to a fellow human being, however much of a prick she thinks I am.

'Everything is fucked,' I say, not particularly to her, since I've already figured she isn't in the least bit interested. It's more of a statement to the world, telling anyone who cares that I know it's all over. I make a pathetic glance up at Sophie and in return she offers me what I can only assume is this satisfied stare – I've got what I deserve. I look back down, knowing she's right.

'You know, all I want in life is to be successful.' I look around the flat and despite the mess, the place is a palace that many people would beg to live in. 'I want a place like this that I can call my own. I want to earn it, not fear for when they are going to take it away. I want to be my own boss, to be good. And I want a decent woman to share it with.'

'Like Toyah, you mean?' she says, all too quick, all too clear.

I sigh, I frown and I cringe.

'So, is it over?'

'It was never on!'

'In your mind, perhaps, but not in hers,' she says, as she starts pacing in front of me. 'She loved you and you failed to do anything about it. You failed in the most horrific way in the most important duty any man has – to make sure you do something when they fall in love.'

'She didn't love me, she fancied me. And there's a big difference.'

She raises her hands. 'Oh, well, why wouldn't she! I mean – just look at you.'

I move closer to her, as close to her face as I dare get. 'You think looks are my fault? Don't you think I want to be known for more? I am more than skin deep.'

She just laughs and runs a finger down my chest. 'Oh, poor Ryan. Everyone holds his looks against him, when all he wants is someone to love, but for some reason he keeps getting caught with his pants down. Quite literally.'

I push her hand away, harder than I meant to but not enough to make me regret it. 'Why are you here? Haven't you seen enough? Go and put some champagne on ice. I'm sure you'll need it next week once I've made my confessions.'

She sits herself down at the breakfast bar, rummaging around the party remains, laughing at the scene spread throughout the room. 'You're right, I have seen enough, but none of this really interests me. What I'm far more concerned about is the allegations that there is a spy in the camp.'

I stand myself opposite her, putting the countertop between us. I take this moment to pause, to reflect on what I'm hearing and then the panic sets in. 'Well it's not me, if that's what you're thinking.'

She just laughs. 'Shouldn't you ask what the spy is supposedly looking for?'

'All you do is play games and this is your latest one.'

'Actually, this is no game. Someone is selling our secrets and both Mitchell and Raj are worried about what exactly is getting out there.'

I look around at the immense amount of evidence spread throughout the apartment. 'So now you think it's me.'

She laughs. 'Actually, no, I don't. I think you're selling our stuff, but judging by tonight's techniques, I don't see you capable of selling G.U.E secrets. But where is Ken? Shouldn't he be here tonight? After all, you can't possibly make a fool of just yourself every time.'

'He's not selling secrets,' I say, fairly certain that I'm right.

Sophie's eyes suddenly squint, as she watches my every move. 'Tell me what you know.'

'Tell you what? Last time I checked I was still your boss and you decide to come here and ask me questions.' I take her by the arm, ready to throw her out, but she doesn't move willingly as she keeps herself firmly on the seat.

'You know things about Mitchell, don't you? How much do you know?'

I look at her, as I desperately try to fight through the haze so I can put it all together. There are so many new parts to a puzzle I didn't know existed, like where is Ken and what do all the things Joanna said actually mean. All I know right now is that I don't have the energy or the patience for this. My sole purpose this weekend was to hide away as much of the game-plan money as possible and then pack up my things. I don't care less whether Sophie is here or not now, so instead I grab an unopened bottle of bubbly and head to my bedroom. If, for some strange reason, Sophie decides to follow me then it would be a bonus. Otherwise, I consoled myself that a night alone could be just what I need.

Much to my enjoyment, she follows me, the tide finally turning in my favour. 'You're not interested because you think I'm going to tell Mitchell what I've seen.'

'The thought had occurred to me that a heartless bitch such as you will do exactly that. And all I can say is good luck, as I'm off to bed.'

'What if I promise to tell no one? What if I promise to walk away and pretend like this never happened? And in return all you have to do is to know one more thing.'

I turn around, which I'd like to say is due to intrigue, but the truth is that I am too desperate not to. 'You're willing to make that deal?'

'I have no interest in your little side business. There are much bigger things at stake.'

I start gulping down the champagne, finding it all a bit too *Spooks* for my liking.

'Tina is the key to all of this.'

I spit across the room, unable to control the laughter rising from my stomach. 'Crisis Tina! You have got to be kidding me. This is a wind up?'

'She'll need your help soon. It won't be out of choice, but she really has nowhere else to turn. And all I can say is don't fuck it up.'

'And what exactly will she need from me?'

She takes the bottle from me, sipping it like a lady, taking her time to sell this ridiculous story. 'You have one fundamental thing in common – you both hate Mitchell and he genuinely fears what you can both do to him if you work together.'

'Mitchell fears nothing.'

'That's where you are so wrong. He feared Jerry more than you knew, but you didn't listen to anything that poor old guy said. And now he has left and he was the one man who could tell us so much from the past.'

I take the champagne back, the thought of Jerry making me start gulping it down. I've wondered for a while how his retirement is going and I'm pretty sure he's already took his flight to the Philippines and has his face buried in some Asian boy's ass. Like we didn't all know. 'Jerry's gone. We should all move on.'

'Why did it have to be you?' she says and shakes her head. 'Just remember to look out for Tina. She will reveal everything if you look after her properly.'

I start to walk to the bedroom. 'Yeah, right, Tina.'

'And Ryan, thank you.'

'For what?'

'Thank you for showing me the real you tonight. You might just have been the most pathetic excuse for a man I have ever seen, but at least I know you have some layers.'

I simply nod, my hands going down my pants no sooner has she closed the door.

19
DIVERSION AHEAD

His big arms are all around me, those hairy hands groping all over my body like I'm this little plaything that he owns. He rubs and presses his chin against my neck and his filthy stubble scrapes at my flesh like he might just tear it off.

I shudder inside but I don't think he notices. More than anything I hope his cock doesn't get hard again. It's such an ugly thing, which barely went in, even when it was standing to attention. Now it's completely hidden by his belly, all this fat draped over it. I guess I should probably be thankful for that.

I try to move away but he pulls me back, literally sucking me into his body. He tries to spoon me but all those layers of flubber around his stomach push into my back, his wet floppy cock touching my skin as he somehow manages to arch his way around me. My heart starts beating faster, but I don't think it's in a good way, and as his arms close around me, sealing me in, I practice the very helpful technique my therapist taught me. She told me that whenever I feel trapped I should close my eyes and take my mind to that very special place.

I soon find myself far away from Mitchell and his heavy breathing. I'm on a beach and the only noise I can hear are the waves lapping along the shore. The sun is beating down on my skin and the heat feels good and I feel it slowly bronzing me all over. I suddenly feel someone running a finger down my stomach. It tickles and I immediately imagine that it's Ryan, with his smooth, lean body touching mine. Those gentle strokes, caressing and teasing me in all the right places, as his sword slowly rises to the challenge.

God, it was big. And God, how I miss it. I swear there were times he slipped it in without me even realising; my body distracted as he caressed my neck and his tongue found parts of my body I didn't know existed. The second time was always the best – it went on all night once, to the point where I couldn't take a second more, however amazing it felt.

'Did you leave it where I told you to?' this husky voice breaks into my thoughts, quickly crushing down all the walls I built around my happy place.

I open my eyes to see that I'm still entombed in this godforsaken hell hole with Mitchell. His chubby hands are pulling at my breasts, which he clearly thinks I should be enjoying. I flip over, which I immediately realise is a great move, since his wandering hands are now on my back. I also figure that I need to be able to see him, to see what his eyes are telling me.

'Well, did you?' he demands.

'It was horrible,' I say, as I suddenly start shivering, my mind casting back to that awful moment. The instant I saw it last night I knew it would haunt me forever. And no matter how many times I tried to go to my happy place, it just wasn't possible after that.

Mitchell just laughs. 'What did you expect? The bastard was dead!'

I start crying. I just can't help it. I never thought I would ever see a dead person, let alone someone I recognised. I mean, it's not like I knew the old codger much, but I still don't want to remember his pale and mangled face staring up at me. I start to feel faint, as this haze comes over me. I try to wrestle my way out of his grip so I can get to the bathroom. I need to get my head between my legs so I can calm down. It doesn't help with my new diet of no food after midday, but I know it's the shock that has caused all of this.

Mitchell doesn't let go – he just keeps telling me to calm down. I try to listen, I really do, but I know that I need some space and a cigarette and then I'll be okay. He suddenly grabs my throat. 'Calm the fuck down. You're acting like a maniac and it won't help the situation.'

I push and pull at his huge body but he doesn't release me, so I really start whaling, my best tantrum screams coming out. Fuck him, I think. If he wants to bully me then I'll show him what a brat I can be. 'You're just like Ryan,' I shout. 'He tries to beat me and now you're doing it too. You men are all the same!'

He suddenly lets go, but he doesn't have a look of shock on his face, instead he has this big smile on his face. 'Oh, Ryan tried to beat you, did he? Well I never thought he had it in him.'

I bite my lip, knowing I've said too much. 'Well, I'm not really sure what happened. It was just a big misunderstanding, so please forget I ever said anything.'

His eyes narrow and he grabs my hand closest to him. 'You know that's not going to happen, don't you? Not without a very good reason.'

'Can I go to the bathroom, please?' I ask, desperately needing to get out of this before I say something else that I shouldn't. Besides, I really need a wee and a wash and the chance to get his sweaty scent off me.'

He's on top of me before I can do anything about it, his heavy frame weighing down on me as he starts to kiss and bite my neck. 'You can go to the toilet when I'm finished with you. I bet you didn't slope off halfway through when you were with lover boy, did you?'

I shake my head. I never left Ryan's side, if I could help it. I always worried that he wouldn't be there when I came back. And now it was all over, all because I couldn't be the woman he needed me to be. I laugh at that thought of not being the woman he needed me to be. I still can't understand it all... how the sex could be so good and yet he loved someone else. It had to be a mistake, it just had to be. I look at Mitchell and then back at the bed, all the time wondering if I should tell him.

'There's something else,' I finally say, knowing deep down that this isn't a good idea. 'There was a photo of Ryan, perched on Jerry's chest, just cradled in his arms.'

Mitchell leaps up, moving quicker than I ever thought was possible. 'What? This just gets better. He died clutching a picture of his dearest Ryan.' He lets out a celebratory cough, bringing up all the snotty stuff that Mummy always taught me to sort out in private. It makes me feel sick to my stomach but he doesn't even notice, as he starts picking his nose. 'This is just perfect, and you left the hairs just where I told you to?'

I look back at Mitchell as he stares down at me. 'Did they really love each other? It's just, well, I still can't quite believe it. I mean, I would just never have seen it coming –'

'You're being a pathetic, silly bitch, again, aren't you?' he says and grabs me, pulling my face close to his. 'We've been over this a hundred times. If they didn't love each other why wouldn't Ryan be with you now?'

I think about this as Mitchell holds me tight. It's difficult to focus my thoughts with his fire-breath on my face but it does make sense. It was all the sex but none of the commitment. 'We had such an orgasmic time together,' I say, now realising that it will never happen again, no matter how much I want it.

'That little prick fucked you but loved him. I warned you about this and remember all the other evidence I told you about. And now you tell me that there was a photo of Ryan on Jerry's dead, wrinkly body and' – he runs a hand down my cheek in the most tender way he has ever treated me – 'he badly beat you.'

I shake my head, denying the possibility that Ryan could ever hurt me. 'It was just the one time and he didn't beat me, things just went a little weird.'

Mitchell holds a finger to my mouth. 'That's what you're telling yourself now, but in a week's time you'll remember other things and before you know it you'll see Ryan for the total bastard he is. You just remember that when he finally gets what's coming to him.'

I violently shake my head, not wanting to be any part of this anymore. I just want to get my things and go, to leave this mess and remember only the good times.

Mitchell imprisons me back within his solid frame and I can feel something stirring beneath his belly. 'He finished Jerry off and he was probably going for you next. I bet he fucked the old git to death then left him lying on the living room floor.

I'm still shaking my head as he pulls me on top of him and I think he's trying to sit me on his cock but it's not working. 'Jerry's last thought was probably how much his arse hurt,' he says and slaps my bum. 'He's out of control, that boy, and after all I've done for his career.'

I don't say anything as I lay motionless, my slender body arched around his huge tyre. I close my eyes again, hoping that this time I can stay a little longer in my special place. It was the place where I was happiest; in Ryan's arms and in a time where none of this was real. A time where he didn't love Jerry and I didn't have to screw Mitchell once a month just so I'm not on the next redundancy list. If Daddy didn't need the help with the mortgage payments I'd be out of here and as far away as possible from all this mess and all that's to come.

I suddenly wonder about when they actually did it and how Ryan found the energy. I picture them together and I imagine Ryan's face as he climaxes. I can think about nothing else but Jerry's twisted face and I wonder if they did have sex just before the end. Just as I think about their last time together, I think about something else, something even more confusing. 'How did you know that he was on the living room floor?'

'What the fuck are you talking about?'

I don't turn around to ask this, I don't dare look into his eyes. 'You said earlier, that he was lying on the living room floor. But how did you know this?'

'How should I know? You must have told me and forgot about it.' He leans in closer and I know what's coming. 'You've been stressed and you don't know where your head is, so who knows and who cares. All that matters is you've got me now.'

He slowly licks the side of my face as I feel this slight jab in my back again. I close my eyes and wince. The second time is always worse and as he grunts and pushes, I'm thankful as I hear those calming waves lapping against the golden shores. I soon see Ryan coming towards me in his red beach shorts, with his arms casually rising up as he jogs my way, his muscles flexing in all the best places. I take a deep breath and keep my eyes on him and I know the sun will need to beat down on me for some time to come.

20

I'm shocked that I'm actually enjoying my usual morning coffee. The views over London are crystal clear as the sun makes its way through the morning sky. My neighbours are up too, going from room to room as they get ready to enjoy their day. I stand at my window, naked as always, taking it all in, just hoping I'll delight at least one of my viewers.

Everything feels different on a Sunday. I always feel different. If I choose to do some work, it's exactly that – it's a choice. I used to love clearing my emails and checking all my figures, every bit of me ready to take on that ever-looming Monday. It was the satisfaction of all that I had achieved that made me do it; the growing career, the Saturday night out and the relaxing Sunday afternoon with a beautiful woman. All of these comfortably delivered me back to work feeling ready to fight and win another week, but now it is pure fear that has made me get up early, as I still cling on to the faint hope that I can save it all.

I stare out across the sea of towering blocks and think about how I can conquer this place, as Raj so aptly puts it. I don't really want to do it. I just want to carry on leading this lifestyle; I don't want to lose the status the fourteenth floor of this building gives you but I'm no longer willing to sell my soul to keep it. I want it all for nothing in return.

I think about the different ways I can sell a product that I don't really see the point in. I get how it works and I get how the big corporations will want to sterilise everything so that they put this shelter around their employees, minimising sickness and thus maximising the blood, sweat and tears from each of us. I've seen enough people carrying around our little sanitising bottles and I know that human nature will ultimately lead us to the point where we put this bubble around us, killing anything that could ever think of harming us.

Now that the hospitals and clinics are hooked, I agree that the next best place is the corporate world of Canary Wharf, with its perfect mix of big business and the little guy. What I don't get is how I've ended up flogging it. When I started with G.U.E I saw it as a fun thing to do for a couple of years. I never really got the nobility of it; protecting mankind from all the bad bacteria on the planet seemed like mission impossible to me. But they paid very well and let me travel around, rewarding my creative thinking with bags of cash and shit stock-keeping that allowed Ken and me to do our little bit on the side.

I climbed the ladder quickly and got Ken a job in my team. I earned my first bonus simply for selling little bottles of our most basic product to people on the street and that led to the next logical step of selling the same people a bigger bottle that sat on their desk. Within my first two years the *Pet-Protector* had earned me twenty grand in bonus payments and once the *Eradicating Nasal Spray* and *Personal Sickness Test Kits* were being loaded into my boot I was already upgrading to a better car.

I'd like to say it all changed when Mitchell came along, but I think it happened before he ever crapped on my life. The moment I graduated and got my first job was one of the happiest days of my parent's lives and everything that followed just made so much sense. My dad was a travelling salesman until the end of his days and his only kid was out there in the big wide world too, doing the same job as him. He used to say it was like I was made to follow in his image. He'd laugh at the fact I was selling alcoholic hand wash and I would eternally admire him for selling hot tubs around the country, no matter what the weather threw at him.

We'd chat for hours on the days when we were both in the long queue. He'd be fighting around the M25 as I'd plough my way through central London; neither way any better. Sometimes we'd be racing back home, to Mum, to see who got to the dinner table first. She'd always be at the door, laughing wildly at the best of those days – the ones when we got home at the same time, fighting our way up the drive.

When I got this Canary Wharf pad things changed a little, as I'd be racing home to a girl, maybe Toyah, or maybe two. Dad would always laugh and remind me that I needed a reason to be doing all the hours in punishing traffic, especially on those days when the big sale had just managed to evade you. Those were the days when he told me I needed a good woman to come home to and my youthful lust would change to a longing for something stronger as the years went on.

In my ignorant pursuit of this happiness I hadn't realised just how many sales had evaded my dad in those last few months. We were both on our journeys home, chatting away as I proudly told him I had shifted ten thousand units of the brand new *Home Sickness Test Kit*. There was none of his normal cheering and beeping of his horn, telling the hundreds of cars in front and behind him that he was the proudest man ever. Instead, there was just silence, as I assumed the Friday night traffic had taken one too many tolls on him.

When I heard a crashing sound I knew it was an accident; the car behind had probably gone into the back of him. It was only when the line went dead I thought it strange that he didn't tell me everything was okay and that he would call me back. Everything was always okay with my dad. I knew no different.

The train had tried its best to stop and a couple of brave people had fought their way into the car for as long as they could, but time was never on their side. He couldn't see that he was on the track, trapped between the two hazard gates. They had tried the doors, begging him to open them, but they said he couldn't see anything as he clutched at his chest, his body shaking. By the time they had smashed the window there was only enough time to have one try at getting the seatbelt off him and it turns out that once wasn't enough.

The stress of the job took his heart and everything else that followed will never be more than an unfortunate set of coincidences. And ever since I lost my dad, I have also lost my love of the game. I can no longer see the purpose in my life being on hold whilst I sit in sales meetings, in client pitches and most significantly, in the car, stuck in another queue.

After I lost him, it all became about the future, about the end game of retiring early. I realise now that the present only involves sex, drinking and helping my mum live in her world of denial, as she spends her time firmly rooted in the past.

The phone suddenly rings, breaking me out of all my thoughts. When I see that it's Tina calling I can hardly believe it.

'I need your help,' she says. 'And I don't want any of your shit.'

'It's a Sunday,' I say, hoping that it will somehow put her off.

'No shit, Sherlock. I'm on my way up to your flat now. And Ryan, for God's sake, put some clothes on.'

*****

'We could see you from outside,' this kid says, standing next to Tina in my hallway.

'He does it for kicks. He thinks people watch him.' She pushes past me, dragging this boy along with her as she makes herself at home in my living room, setting several bags down onto the sofa. 'It's probably a matter for the police but we won't let that bother us now.'

'Tina, what are you doing here? And who is this?'

She pushes the boy in front of her. 'This is Elliot, my son.'

'We need your help,' he says, smiling up at me with these big goofy teeth.

Tina starts to unpack, barking orders at Elliot and half-telling me her issues. None of it makes sense when all I want to do is get back to my reflection and my self-pity. She hands me the odd bit of food that needs to go into the fridge, as she tells Elliot that he can't watch too much television and that he must get his homework done.

'Wait, where are you going?'

She ignores me, instead making the poor boy recite all the homework he needs to do. He misses his English spelling assignment and makes a big huffing sound when she reminds him.

'I've got some serious stuff to deal with, Ryan, and since you sacked my last babysitter, then you'll have to do for now.' She kisses Elliot and without another word she runs past me and out the door. I try to follow but she's already got into the lift, this big grin spread across her face as the doors close.

*****

He sits opposite me. I'm conscious that I'm staring at a young kid but I'm frankly fascinated. He's in a strangers place, with all the best views of London outside and the only thing he's interested in is his games console.

He looks up at me and I look down at my breakfast.

'Problem?' he asks.

'You,' I say.

He sets his console down and takes a deep breath, brushing his blond fringe back as he sits forward. 'Mum said you wouldn't be happy with me being here. She said you'd be kicking out some girls when we came knocking.'

I laugh at how much my life is changing. 'Well, normally I am.'

'So,' he says as he looks around, finally paying some attention to this place. 'Are there any girls in here?'

'What are you, like nine?'

'I'm twelve!' he says, with this youthful attitude that suddenly makes me feel old. He also reminds me of myself, which I kind of warm to, but I have no idea what a twelve year old boy should be like. I have no frame of reference other than knowing I was fondling girls at thirteen and shagging some of the better looking ones at fourteen.

'Well, there are no girls in here and besides, I don't want to break any of your mum's rules,' I say, looking down at a sheet of paper next to me with an extensive list of these rules.

'Rules, rules, rules,' Elliot says.

I can only laugh at him. 'The attitude doesn't suit you, what with your dimples and floppy blond hair.'

He starts ruffling his hair, messing it up. 'Mum said you were cool so I'm just trying to fit in, is all.'

'I've got an Xbox if you want to play that?'

He looks up at the giant, wall-mounted television, his face lighting up for a moment, before he looks away. 'I'm not allowed.'

'Man, you have too many rules.'

'My mum says you don't have enough.'

I nod, totally believing that. 'And what else does she say about me?'

'She says I'm not allowed to tell you.'

'I knew you were gonna say that, so there's some ice cream in it if you tell me everything.'

His face creases up, his arms folded. 'Are you actually going to bribe me with ice cream?'

I rub my eyes, realising how I pitched that completely wrong. 'What about some girls?'

He's suddenly pacing up and down, his face all wrinkled. 'Porn, man? That's disgusting! You wanna watch porn with a kid of my age!'

'I meant real girls, and besides, how do you know about porn?'

He tilts his head, smiling. 'The internet.'

'Fair point,' I say, as I think about the extreme parental controls that Tina must have placed on his computer. 'So are you coming, or what?'

'I can't leave this flat, remember?'

'If you ask me, your mum needs to lighten up. And this place is only down the road so we'll be back before her. She'll never know, okay?'

He smiles, running towards the front door, carrying his trainers with him. 'I'll put them on in the lift,' he shouts, as he disappears around the corner.

*****

As it happens, Elliot does like ice cream. We're sitting on a wall, staring through some faintly-tinted glass. He's eating his cone and I'm sipping a latte, both of us squinting to look inside. If you stare for long enough you can make out the forms of the different women, finishing their stretches. It's a perfect after-show to all that I've just shown him; we cool down in the outside breeze, as they cool down in the studio.

'Man, this is awesome,' he shouts, his legs kicking against the wall. 'I can't believe they wear so little when they're dancing around.'

I laugh, as I can't quite believe he has enjoyed some amateur dance group practice as much as he did. But then I think back to when I was his age and how I used to love looking through my mum's lingerie catalogues, picking out my favourite ladies and fighting the constant debate in my mind as to what part of their bodies I liked the most. In an age before the internet it was a constant risk carefully cutting out the page of the one I loved the most, hiding it in my room for a lot of future use.

I watch Elliot as he stares into the studio and I realise that it's a definite step up from paper and virtual ladies.

'How do you know so many women?' he asks, as I think I've just found my first fan.

'We sponsored this dance group through work and when it ended Ken and me decided to keep in touch. Purely from a support point of view, you understand.'

He laughs. 'Yeah right, whatever. So have you slept with any of them?'

'One or two,' I say. 'I can't really recall.'

'I'd sleep with all of them at once,' he says, as he keeps his prowling eyes on the room.

I can only laugh, knowing I was probably just as randy at his age, if not more.

He suddenly turns to me, this grin on his face. 'Quite a few of them asked where Ken was today.'

'Yeah, I did notice. So what does your mum say about Ken?'

'She says she wouldn't leave me with him, not if hell had frozen over and he was the last human being left on earth.

'She's probably talking some sense. Being responsible isn't one of his strengths.'

We both stare back into the room, as I remember how much I used to love these moments when Ken and I would stand at this wall. They always knew we were watching and when they had showered and finished, this flock of ladies would then come running down the steps to see us. We'd all head to the park; two men and their tribe of young women. Those with boyfriends would eventually peel off after an hour or two and those who stayed got a lot of attention, right up until the early hours of the morning. Those were the carefree Sunday's, the time when we partied hard and made the most of every spare second of freedom.

Elliot is suddenly standing up. 'We need to leave now,' he says, pulling at my shirt.

'Leave now?' I ask, as he starts dragging me away. 'But the girls will be out soon.' I look around for Tina, thinking she must be stalking us.

I start to think of my excuses but it's all happening too quickly. He's taken hold of my arm now and we're walking quickly as his eyes scan everything around us. I look down at his face and he looks scared, which triggers something inside me, making me feel protective as I desperately look around to find the threat.

We're in the crowds now but I don't see what is worrying him. He stops us, with people all around. It gives me time to look but I don't see the danger. 'Elliot, what's wrong?'

He pulls me in one direction, making us move again, but then he turns and his body collides with mine. I hold him still, to let us both get our bearings, and that's when he appears. Out of nowhere the Quiff from the conference is in front of us.

The Top Dog of the G.U.E Corporation walks towards us, this big grin on his face. 'Well, hello, it's Ryan, isn't it?' He holds out a hand, as I try to take in what's happening and find out who he's with. He looks to be alone as I shake his hand and I'm shocked that he actually knows who I am.

'I heard you live around here and that you're the man who will be penetrating Canary Wharf with our new *Building Guardians*.'

'Yes, that's right,' I say, as I try to figure out how I stop Elliot from pulling me away without ruining whatever's left of my career.

He looks down at the boy. 'Hello, Elliot,' he says. 'I haven't seen you in a while.'

'You know each other?' I ask, confused that the CEO knows Tina has a son and I didn't. It probably says very little about me but a lot about him.

'No!' Elliot shouts. 'I'm not allowed to talk to him!' He starts to walk away, no longer anchored to me for safety. He breaks into a run before I can stop him and pays no attention to me calling out his name.

I look back at the Quiff to see his eyes following where Elliot is running to. He looks for another second before turning back to me, his grey eyes examining me all over. 'You know, Ryan, you should really try to pick your sides more carefully. Mitchell has tried to be a good and fair boss to you and this is how you repay him.'

I start to move away, knowing only that I need to get to Elliot before anyone else does. 'Well, you know, Bob, I report to Mitchell who reports to Raj, so I don't see how any of this should be your concern. So, if you'll excuse me, I need to get going.'

'Be careful, Ryan.'

'You too, Bob,' I shout back, hoping I've got the balance between preserving my career and sounding remotely like I know what the hell is going on.

I break into a run, Elliot far in front of me, and as I turn the corner I look back at the dance studio and realise just how much I miss those lazy Sundays.

*****

'You did what?' Tina shouts at me, as she paces up and down the living room, never quite leaving my field of vision.

The Xbox is in full swing now and Elliot is absorbed in the big screen. The moment we came back I decided that his homework could go to hell and that I'd broken so many other rules that a few hours of bloke time on Fifa was just what we needed.

'I only took him for ice cream,' I say, figuring that the absence of the performing women was a half-truth I could live with.

'I asked one thing from you,' she says, with this pointed finger at my face. 'Just one thing.'

'You didn't really ask, Tina. You just turned up.'

She gives me this stare and then lets out a scream, putting her head in her hands. 'You know, Jerry always helped and did as he was told.'

'But Ryan's way more fun,' Elliot shouts from the sofas as he wrestles with the controller.

'You be quiet!' she bellows at him like it's something of a habit. 'You're not allowed an opinion on this.' She walks over to him and grabs his ear, pulling him up straight. 'And you should have known better than to agree to his stupid ideas.'

He doesn't turn around as his release from her grasp allows him to return to the ball. England is winning two-nil so I can't blame him for not stopping. It's Tina that worries me as I see her silence has given her time to start crying.

She quickly wipes her eyes and walks over to me. 'You should have known better! You shouldn't have taken him outside!' She starts slapping my arm but it barely hurts and I have no intention in stopping her, thinking it's probably no less than I deserve.

When she eventually runs out of energy she takes a seat in the kitchen area, beckoning me to follow. 'I can't be away from him for a second, Ryan. You have to understand that if they catch me doing anything wrong then I lose custody of my little boy. If that happens then I've had it and so has he.'

I sit next to her and lean across the breakfast bar, quickly looking back to see that Elliot is completely absorbed in the game. 'People keep telling me things, like stuff I didn't know, but none of it makes any sense. So, I'm asking you now, what the hell is going on?'

She grabs the roll of kitchen towel and starts wiping the excess tears and sweat from all over her face, placing less faith in an answer to me than her own lack of social graces. 'If only you hadn't sacked Jerry.'

'What?'

'If you hadn't sacked Jerry then we wouldn't have had to involve you.'

'Involve me in what? You have to tell me what's going on.'

She shakes her head, an almost involuntary reflex that says she doesn't think I'm fit to know these secrets, as if I'm not good enough for this responsibility. 'It took a long time to figure out where your involvement in all this lies, Ryan,' she says and jumps off the stool. 'And now I've realised that you and Ken really are just here for the fucking money.'

'Don't forget I'm your boss, Tina.'

Much to my surprise, she just nods. 'That's all you are.'

'Then why are you and Elliot here?'

'You fired Jerry, remember? And since he's gone quiet I had little other choice. We'd concluded you weren't in on it so I figured you would be the last place they would be looking. I was obviously wrong.'

'Who is looking?' I say, my frustration far overtaking my curiosity.

'It's best you don't know. Just don't trust Mitchell or that wanker who turned up today.'

'The Quiff? Why is he involved in anything?'

Her face gets all scrunched up again. 'I could think of far worse descriptions. Just try to avoid both of them and this will all be over soon. I can't promise what will happen to you, now that Mitchell probably thinks you're involved. Looking on the

186

bright side, you'll be off for your operation soon which will distance you from what's to come.'

I laugh, all of this starting to sound a little too crazy. 'Does anyone actually remember that I'm the guy in charge?'

'One of many team leaders, Ryan. You're just one of many cogs that have turned over the years, some of them doing big things and some of them just filling a gap. You're sadly just one of the ones who filled in for a while, which I think you should be thankful for.'

'I've achieved a lot in my time here,' I say, demanding my respect, from the wider world and not just the person in front of me now.

She pokes my chest, her anger rising. 'When are you going to realise that this isn't about you. My biggest advice to you is to take your bonus money and all the stock you've stashed, and get out while you can. The past is coming back and it will haunt many of us that were around a long time before you and your cock turned up.'

I decide to stay silent, immediately cautious of yet another person who claims to know about my dodgy dealings. I start to wonder if just one of them found out, or if Ken and I were so crap at hiding our tracks that half the company knows. I start to realise that it's probably the reason why Ken has ran away, leaving me to handle the sinking ship.

'How's Jerry?' I ask, deciding that a change of subject would probably be best for all.

Tina lets out this big sigh that carries all her frustrations with it. 'I've heard nothing from him, so I assume he's left the country. I can't say I blame him, as we both knew they would never really let him just disappear. I used to have a key, but we both agreed that changing the locks was the best thing. I've knocked a couple of times, but there's never any answer.'

I start to consider that they were closer than I thought. Not just Tina and Jerry, but all of them – Mitchell, Raj and clearly Bob, too. Whilst I've been deep in planning my own future it seems like they have all been busy with their pasts, with things that have escaped my attention since the day I joined. I start to wish that there was more time to figure out the puzzle, but then perhaps some things are best left where they are.

Tina chooses this as the time for her and Elliot to leave and as I give him my best bloke's high-five and close the door on them, I decide that the present is firmly where I'm staying. And I mean my present, with my issues. It's my life I need to fight for and no one else's.

21

Of all the days I've been expecting, this isn't the one I've been looking forward to.

It's a simple operation. That's all I've heard since the day they told me. Despite all the reassurances that a hernia repair is one of the most commonly performed procedures and that I will be up and about in no time, it still does nothing to calm me down.

The fact that I will be away from work at clearly the lowest point in my career has most likely caused the majority of the burden on my mind. Whilst I will be recovering on my sick bed, Mitchell and several others will not only be plotting, but probably causing, my downfall.

As I look around the outpatient's clinic, I console myself that it's exactly what this place is – a clinic for procedures that don't keep you here all day. In at 6am and out by midday, without any need to see a hospital ward.

I look around to see that I'm not the youngest person here and therefore probably not the only one with those consoling thoughts at the forefront of my overstretched mind. What these younger boys and girls do have that I don't are their mums. For every scared and fearful teenager there is an equally worried mother, all pretending to be calmly reading their magazines as they watch the activities of every nurse who walks through the long, sterile corridor. They make casual chit-chat with their offspring, talking all about the future, as their Dad's start to turn up, having finally found a parking space. These aren't just accompanying adults; they're solid family units who are supporting one of their own.

My accompanying adult finally looks up from her magazine, but says nothing. Joanna simply smiles at me, taking very little of this in and giving me even less back. In the run up to this I would have been happy to do it alone, to get a taxi home and suffer with being bedridden for a few days. Now that the reality of the moment is here, I am glad to have her with me, although I had no choice but to have a responsible person to bring me home and stay until I can move about.

As soon as the nurses announce that they are ready to check people in for their operations, a queue forms out of nowhere, stretching from the reception desk to the far end of the waiting area. I laugh at the fact I'm joining the back of it. 'Story of my life,' I mutter as I slowly shuffle along with everyone else.

The nurses pick people off one by one; different doors for different procedures. By the time I get to the front I'm told that I'm the last for a hernia operation today, giving me the longest wait. I start to think that this really is what my life is all about – being the last at everything that matters. I have simply found my way to the biggest queue and waste my life when others are onto the next big thing in their world.

'I'll be right here waiting, darling!' Joanna shouts and then eagerly looks around for observers. 'I feel like your mother!'

I nod back, finding no energy to do anything else. Despite the awkwardness in the necessity of asking a woman I barely know to be with me, I know that it's a better alternative to dragging along the scattered and damaged shell of my actual Mum. I take one final look at the woman I could call Mother and lover in equal measure, and then disappear into the depths of the endless and identical corridors.

When I'm finally given my own little cubicle, I sit down on the one small chair and realise that this is life stripped bare. I'm in a green plastic gown, my clothes in a bag next to me, with nothing to do and no one to talk to me. This is existence in its simplest form, just without the distraction that daily life coats it with.

Once someone comes in to mark my leg, politely reminding me that this is really happening, I become certain that there is no going back. My life has to change; it has to be full of things that matter and above all else have a purpose that makes it all worthwhile.

I walk in a daze towards the anaesthetics room – the next stage in the process and the last one I will see before the calm. A solitary nurse guides me past all the endless doors as I think about nothing but my pointless existence up until this point. I know that I've hurt more people than I've helped and that if it wasn't for me then Jerry would still be happily employed.

As I lie myself on a bed I ignore all the casual chit-chat, knowing that if something terrible goes wrong – if the surgeon makes the wrong cut, or the drugs prove to be all too much – then I will have absolutely nothing exciting to tell my Maker. Away from my suits, papers and all that corporate weaponry, the excuses for my actions make very little sense.

And so, if my judgement does come at the harsh end of a scalpel then I can do no less than confess my sins. I realise now that I'm a self-obsessed, arrogant and spineless shadow of my former father and I deserve no mercy. For too long I have tried to walk along the same path as my dad; a great man who tried to lead me to even greater success – to follow in his footsteps and continue the family path. Instead of listening and learning, I have robbed and wasted my way through the greatest gift, leaving me with nothing to show for it.

As the drugs finally start to pump through my veins I'm eternally thankful. I welcome the haze that comes over me and as my eyes start to close I thank fate for finally giving me a break.

*****

I wake up to find that I'm alone.

In the past twenty-four hours I've woken up many times, dripping in sweat, falling back to sleep just as quick. Each time I have checked my wound, just in case it's not really there or if I've bled to near death all over the bed. As it happens the dressing is the same as it was, with just a little more blood soaking through.

The last couple of times I woke up I remember Joanna being here, giving me water and painkillers, her usual smile spread across her face as she asked if this was a codeine moment, or if regular paracetamol would suffice. I can't recall much else of the last twenty-four hours but I do remember her wiping my forehead and neck with a cloth, her caring actions leaning more towards a motherly concern, as opposed to anything a loving partner might do.

I half-expected her to be here now, celebrating the fact that I am finally awake, the cocktail of drugs and the extra torment now understood by my body and mind. I listen but is only silence around me, as I look around the unfamiliar room, my senses giving it proper attention for the first time since I arrived here.

I immediately feel lonely and convince myself that this is a bad idea. I want my friends around me and I want to be in my flat, around my things. Most of all I want my mum; the need for something constant taking priority over the practicality of my selection of Joanna.

I look around the large room, with its floral feature wall and chesterfield sofa in the corner. It's battered and bruised but somehow matches the tone of Joanna's world – the modern meets the past. All in all, it's pretty trendy and I start to realise that I need a regular woman to put these touches into my life, or what's left of it.

I move myself towards the edge of the bed, the pain searing through the middle of my body. I think about lying back down; I could sleep for another few hours, hoping that everything will sort itself out in my absence. I know that I need to face the world and that I cannot stay in hiding forever, and so I force myself to stand, making my arms do all the work.

I soon find myself hobbling down the corridor, the left side of my body taking all the strain. Everything is quiet as I make my way towards the living room, with each door I pass closed and off limits. I wonder if I'm alone and I start to feel like I really shouldn't be here.

'Darling!' Joanna shouts, the moment I walk into the room. 'You're finally awake. How do you feel, dare I ask?'

'I'm actually okay,' I say, feeling proud that I've managed to walk a whole fifty paces.

'Well, you look like shit,' she says and then pauses, as if seeing my anxiety sitting just below the calm answer. She suddenly rushes up from her seat and pulls me into the room, finally making me welcome in a place that feels so far from home.

She sits me on the sofa, in the exact spot where we first kissed, and pulls cushions all around me in some attempt to make me more comfortable. As she fusses around me I catch her sweet scent, her face brushing past mine. 'You need a shave,' she says, as she puts the remote control in my hand and moves away.

I sit and flick through the channels but all I can really think about is the last time I was here. My first visit to this place found me being seduced by this woman – forced to have sex in the name of getting a deal. Yet again I cannot move from this spot; the pain holds me here when last time it was Joanna sitting on my knees, pinning me down, keeping me occupied.

Joanna walks back in and catches me looking down at my crotch. 'Nothing much will be happening down there for a while, big boy. I have made you some soup, but if you want something more, then your wish is my command.' She places the tray on my lap and I see that it's got a padded bottom with a floral covering, with handles on either side – the true icon of the sofa dinner.

'This is yours?' I ask.

Joanna starts to laugh. 'Hell, no, I bought it especially for looking after you. I thought it might just be required for dinner in bed, but I'm glad you've managed to get up to enjoy my cooking.'

I eat slowly and quietly, as Joanna sits and observes. Everything feels strange, as if the last twenty-four hours couldn't actually have happened to me. I'm in a new situation, I tell myself. It's good to be out of your comfort zone. I start to realise that

I've been so wrapped up in existing that even this situation has reminded me that I'm actually alive.

'How's your food, darling?' she asks.

I nod. 'This is good.'

'I think you're going to need more to get your strength back up. I bet you eat a lot of chicken,' she says, trying to wrap her fingers around my arm. 'For the protein, I mean.'

'I won't be going to the gym for a while.'

She suddenly stands up, taking the tray of finished food away. 'Oh, darling, whatever will happen to your gorgeous torso? I must admit I had a quick peak whilst you were asleep, purely to check it was still there.'

I rub my stomach whilst she's gone, hoping it doesn't disappear, but wondering if I would be a better person without it. Perhaps my life needs to be less about the looks – the physical representation of me and more about what else I can offer.

My mind hasn't figured out what that actually is before Joanna walks back in. 'I made you a little dessert,' she says, pushing a bowl of trifle and spoon into my hands, silently demanding that I take her creation, regardless of the lurking fat content.

'You made this? It's good.'

'It's the only dessert I ever learnt to make, somewhere in the dark depths of the eighties.' She stares at it, watching each spoonful that enters my mouth. 'Every time I make it I only remind myself of how old I am, offering up a measly throwback from two decades ago.'

'Well, I like it,' I say. I find myself leaning towards Joanna, giving her a small peck on her cheek. As I withdraw I don't regret my actions. She doesn't say anything and neither do I, as I somehow realise that the smallest of actions can mean more than words ever can.

She pats my arm. 'You know that Mitchell had a rather neat body twenty years ago?'

'Really?' I ask, refusing to believe he was ever neat.

'Oh, yes, he had more of a rugby build so he wasn't as trim as you but he was a bit of a catch back then. Of course, there seemed to be less people around back then. You knew more of the key players and the ones growing through the business ranks. Anyone with some looks and a little charm always stood out. They had to get noticed somehow and, after all, it was a time before all this mobile fucking, where the internet arranges everyone's shags.'

'Did you two, ever... you know?'

'Did we ever shag, darling?' She sweeps back her hair, this huge smile spread across her face. 'He tried to seduce me on several occasions but I wasn't interested.' Her eyes stare at the turned off television for a moment, like she's trying to see something of importance. 'I was much happier back then. For a start, I still loved my husband and I was strong and powerful, with a Detective Sergeant as my man, so anything Mitchell could offer wasn't of any concern.'

I rest the empty bowl on my lap and cover it with my hand when she tries to take it from me. 'So you don't love your husband now?'

She rubs my leg. 'Remember our pact, darling? We will never have sex again.'

I laugh and for the first time I find that rejection from a woman feels pretty good. In the future I worry that I will tell myself that this moment was down to me being incapable of sex, rather than Joanna being un-seducible. Where Mitchell failed, something in me wants to succeed. But the other part of me, the new addition, simply wants to hold her and hear the story, to know this past life that I wasn't around for.

'I want to know things,' I say. 'That's all, I promise.'

She tilts her head, the grin still there. 'Perhaps this is a whole new start for you, Ryan.'

We both nod at each other as she gets comfy beside me. 'As you grow your career you sometimes grow apart from the one you love. Perhaps we never really loved each other. Perhaps it really was just lust that formed into the practicality of marriage. You start in the same place, at the same time, but you don't always carry on the same path. It was the norm, back then.'

'He doesn't live here anymore?' I ask, already sure of that answer, having probed Joanna on how he would feel about coming home to find me in the guest bedroom.

'He got the French villa and the dogs and I got the city apartment and the Porsche, and I don't think either of us looked back. You see, money isn't the issue. When you focus on your career for twenty years it silently brings you wealth. It quietly comes in and leaves you with frequent piles of cash that you tuck away in the bank, or in property investments. Those big bonuses come around quicker than the Olympic Games and your joint income means you can always buy the best of things. The actual problem is that you don't see the years creeping by and you don't really remember the value of what you worked so hard for. In fact, you forget the value of anything. It wasn't until the turn of the millennium that I realised I had wasted the best of my youth on my career and by then it felt like it would be a waste to suddenly turn back.'

'You never wanted children?' I ask, immediately regretting it, expecting to hit a nerve.

She starts playing with my hair, organising the bed-mess. 'I can't have them and he never wanted any, so back then we seemed like a perfect match. I told myself I didn't want to adopt and he told me he wouldn't have the time to divide between his career and a family. As it turns out he never had much time for me in the last two decades, either. He's a Police Superintendent now and apparently doing his duty now takes priority over anything else.'

'Oh,' I say. 'Well I think it's his loss.'

She laughs. 'Thank you, Ryan. You know, the world really is a funny place. If our lives placed us at the same age, in the same time, I would have done anything to be with you. But fate placed us twenty-five years apart and that changes everything.'

'In what way?'

'I always wanted a son but I somehow knew it would never happen and I eventually accepted my life for what it was,' she says. She speaks with authority but her eyes deceive her, as they start to well up, her fingers trying to quickly brush the tears away, to expel the moment before history gets a chance to take note of it.

I try to move forward to hug her, but the one part of my body needed to do this is sore and tender; it feels like I'm bursting something down there, which forces me to sit back.

'It's the thought that counts, darling,' she says, as she grabs a box of tissues from the side and starts dabbing her eyes. It makes me wonder how many lonely nights she has had in this place, with only the contents of her new life for company.

'You know that there is one man alive who did offer me children?'

'Mitchell?'

She calmly nods back. 'When I told him that I didn't want any he pursued me even more, until the time came when I had to tell him I couldn't have any. I think back to that moment and realise that I was telling myself the reality that I would never have kids, as much as I was getting Mitchell off my back.'

'So, you two worked together?'

'Like I say, London seemed a lot smaller back then. He would send me flowers, visit my office and generally make a nuisance of himself. He was a lot more charming back then and significantly less sinister. But behind all of his meaningless gestures was that entirely evil man. The one you call the Quiff. As it turns out, Mitchell had just returned from an assignment in China with this man, who I later learnt was the lead scientist on some secret project. Back then your company was into a lot more biological research and not just the chemical stuff. The ability to kill as many germs as humanly possible was growing with popularity and every new year saw a new product come onto the market. It was how they made their money, but it wasn't what excited them.'

'I think one of my team knew Mitchell back then and I now think she fell for his stories.'

'Tina? Oh yes, she fell for them completely.'

'You know her?'

She gives me this knowing smile, the shades of history lined up behind it. 'There are so many intertwined memories, so many stories that overlap.'

'And I've never bothered to ask about them.'

She suddenly laughs. 'Why should you? Do you think I bothered to ask why Mitchell dropped me to start chasing this tubby Scottish girl with oversized glasses? Do you think it interested me in the slightest that she disappeared off on assignment for two years and then returned with a young child in tow.'

'Elliot?'

'Yes, darling, and believe me she wasn't the first or the last. Mitchell used what remained of his rugged looks to ship a couple of other girls out of the country, but Tina was the only one to ever return. We tried to talk to her about it but she had her dream baby boy and nothing else mattered, not even the price she paid for it.

'How do you know all this?'

She lets out a big sigh. 'I worked at G.U.E for a short while. A dear friend of mine helped me to get a job there and it was probably the worst move in my life, and when I told him I was leaving it was like a divorce. He begged me to stay, telling me he would be the next head of sales. And no matter how many times I told Jerry that he wouldn't win against Mitchell, he just refused to listen, still thinking he was the next chosen one.'

'Jerry?' I almost shout, my scattered mind putting these past lives together.

'Oh, yes, Jerry was almost a big player, but he ultimately made the wrong decisions. And as he got replaced by more senior people, his position decreased each time. These gradual demotions were like silent kicks in the teeth, until the point where he gave up and chose to wait out his pension.'

'Until I sacked him,' I say, knowing this could be a brutal end to our chat.

She just nods back. 'Yes, I heard. I'm sure Mitchell thanked you for that.'

'I didn't mean for it to happen and I wish I could change things.' I grab her hand. 'Joanna, I ruined his life just to protect my own.'

I'm thankful she grips me back, offering me that smile of wisdom and compassion in equal measure. 'Darling, Jerry made his own choices and he could have fixed his own life long ago. The thing with Jerry is that he never does anything about how he feels. He's always been one of those people who wait for fate to lend them a hand, ever hopeful and never changing. And when fate doesn't give them what they have patiently sat around for, they blame everyone else. And that's why Jerry and I drifted apart. I got fed up of sitting in all the bars scattered across Soho, waiting for him to find the courage to talk to a man.'

'So, Jerry is gay?'

Joanna laughs. 'You didn't know for sure, did you? Well there were days I'm not sure if Jerry knew. As it turns out he wasn't brave enough to do something about it, to change his life and bring some real happiness into it. First off he blamed the decades, telling me it wasn't the right time, it still wasn't accepted. Even when George Michael burst out of the closet, Jerry still refused to be himself. And then he blamed his work, saying he needed to focus on beating Mitchell to the top job. It was then, with echoes of my own husband's excuses, I chose to take myself off and build a career of my own.'

'And Jerry failed to beat Mitchell, leaving him to rot at G.U.E for a very long time.'

'Yes, he said he was staying to help Tina and that he couldn't leave this poor single mum alone. The last time we really spoke was back then, when I told him what a coward he was, and when I saw him at your sales presentation meeting I realised just how right I was. He allowed himself to become a broken man, making all the wrong decisions and never seizing the day. You must be clear that they were his choices and his alone.'

I nod, not really believing there was ever such a rich past of the people I knew. 'He said that when he retired he would go off to the Philippines.'

'That's where he will be, hiding away and still waiting for that magic opportunity to come along. People like Jerry don't really deserve the chances they are given. He still thinks he can be something special, still trying to fit himself into someone else's box. I will always remember going to his flat, just the one time. It was a small dinner party for select friends. He spent hours preparing the food, the cocktails and the music.' She suddenly grins at me, touching my knee. 'Please remember in those days preparing the music wasn't just putting a play list onto that apple thing – it actually involved some thought and patience. So, anyway, I remember looking around his place and thinking that everything was just perfect, even down to the fact he had left a couple of gay magazines scattered across the coffee table.'

'Was he trying to pick up a man?'

'Well, this is what I thought. I assumed that perhaps he had finally found a suitable companion and was bringing him into the fold that evening, or that he had invited some potential men. But the moment his eyes found what my satisfied stare pointed towards, he rushed over and bundled them away, all the time mumbling that he nearly forgot and just how tragic that would have been. The most ironic thing about it was that he hid them in his pouffe, next to the sofa. His guests happily enjoyed his hospitality, never knowing that they were sitting next to his most precious secret. There were times I wondered if he did it deliberately, as some sort of game.'

We sit in silence for a while, as I digest everything I've heard and learnt. Joanna stares calmly into space, her mind tracing back all those long lost moments.

'It turns out that there were a couple of very good looking young men at the party that night. Friends of friends, you know the sort of thing. I will swear to the moment I die that one of them fancied Jerry. He was the first to pass comment after every course, finding ways to meet Jerry's eyes. I ran to the kitchen after the main course and begged him to get the cocktails flowing quicker, that this could be his night – the moment he finally became the person he claimed he wanted to be.'

'Did he manage to pull?' I ask, not sure I want to imagine Jerry, on the cusp of discovering the nineties, trying to bed some guy.

Joanna shakes her head. 'You must be kidding. Jerry wanted to wait until he had an absolute sign. The guy was slightly younger and much better looking, which was all the excuse Jerry needed to veto any option of me setting them up. The young man tried to hang around after everyone else had left, but Jerry was having none of it, and so after a few more cosmopolitans the man left and so did I. It wasn't long after that when Tina started in the company and as time flew by she fell for the overbearing charm of Mitchell.'

I shake my head but I'm not sure what part of the tale I'm most shocked about. 'I can't even imagine Tina and Mitchell getting it on.'

'Remember that this was a long time ago, darling. Mitchell was a little slimmer and Tina a little younger. A very small part of me wondered if Mitchell was in some way genuine, but once they returned I realised whatever had happened would be damaging for decades to come. Tina had what she wanted, a dear little baby boy, but I was never sure what Mitchell got from it. He paid her no attention and only a few people ever knew what we had found out. As I left G.U.E many others did the same, so by the time a couple of winters had gone by no one really knew she had a child.'

'I didn't know,' I say. 'Not until recently. Although as her boss I should have taken more of an interest. That's one of the basic rules of management, isn't it?'

She smiles again, her experience forgiving all of my youthful decisions. 'I think it was part of the deal that she didn't really mention it. It must have brought her great sadness to have to hide away something so special.'

'It looks like everyone has been hiding something and only now I'm getting to the bottom of the puzzle. But now it's too late to fix so many things.'

She grabs my hands, taking them into hers. 'Darling, don't try to fix anything, just get out of there and do something different. You are a talented young man and I don't want to see you heading on this path of destruction. Jerry wasn't that much older than you when he started making the wrong decisions and he continued to make them for decades after that. I don't want to see you do the same. I'm on my slow path to retirement and I don't intend to spend it watching another person I care about lock horns with Mitchell.'

I smile back at Joanna as she gives me this continued frown. She's showing her age tonight, as the absence of any makeup exposes all the wrinkles and worry lines, born from those decades of deals. 'I'm not Jerry,' I say.

She drops my hands, pushing herself away. 'No, you're not, but you possess the levels of arrogance that rivalled his stupidity. The one thing you both have in common is these thoughts that you can take on Mitchell and actually win.'

'I have to,' I say, as I let out a gasp from the pain of rebalancing my body.

Joanna laughs. 'Of course, you really look in a fit state to take him on. Have you ever considered that he will be even stronger and more screwed up than he was back when I knew him. You're taking on a maniac who has a lot to lose.'

I nod back. 'And that's what I'm counting on.'

Joanna walks away, her head shaking, as I lie myself properly on the sofa. I'm desperate for some more sleep, ever hopeful that my body will find me a way out of this mess, that it will mend itself quickly. Deep down I know that it will and I know that what really worries me is that my mind needs to come up with a plan that will beat a man who has made it his mission to bully, defeat and destroy everyone who gets in his way.

I know I'm the next target, which isn't good for someone who can't be sure he's going to be able to get off this sofa any time soon.

22

After three weeks off I finally walk back into the office. Everything is different; I'm different. I feel like shit and I feel bigger, the bad kind of bigger that comes from a total lack of exercise. I've watched the skin expand around the best parts of my body, slowly encasing me in this small layer of fat. I still can't go running and the gym is out of the question for weeks.

I can return to work and so that's what I'm doing. I feel useless, my reflection on the last few weeks when I was in work reminding me that I've not been particularly successful, not unless you count my various sackings and business fuck ups as being of any worth.

I've heard nothing from Ken, with the most likely story being that he's decided to abandon me at my lowest point. Why would he want to witness my downfall when he can escape and build a new life? I thought we were best mates, together forever – until we made the end game a reality and we retired to the Bahamas – but he has turned out to be nothing more than my crooked business partner, free to move on whenever a better opportunity presented itself.

As I leave the lift onto my floor I fully expect to find out that I've been replaced. I approach my desk to see that it's no different to when I left it. I look around but there's no one about. I'm early; deliberately and uncharacteristically here as the sun is rising. I try to restart my usual routine, with a cup of coffee as the system logs me on.

It doesn't take long to tell me that I'm locked out, the first sign that things are not as they should be. I think about phoning IT support but I don't see the point. Instead, I sit at my desk and think about how many other people this happens to every single day. You don't fit in, you fail, or you're simply no longer needed – it doesn't matter the reason, but something so simple as not being able to check your emails and feel like even one of the smallest cogs in the machine is pretty shit in my book.

I head towards the lifts, the fact that my ID card still works having not escaped me. The doors open as I get there and out steps Toyah. I move back a little; genuinely surprised to see her, but she doesn't look so shocked.

I smile but she doesn't return the favour. Instead, she paces in front of me, all the time her bloodshot eyes stare into mine. As I look at her I realise that this isn't the Toyah I know; this woman has been crying and scheming, wanting to hurt me. This is the Toyah I have never seen before and she scares me.

'You played me like a fool,' she says, pointing a long, bony finger at me. Her finger nails aren't painted today and her make-up is half-arsed at best, all signs that things are not well around here.

'It was just sex, Toyah,' I say. 'It was just really good sex and I thought we both knew that. I didn't want any more, surely you knew that?'

Her face screws up as she starts her usual whining, tears already running down her face. 'I wished I did.'

I move closer, trying to hold her, feeling protective on levels I didn't know I had. She moves away quickly, her arms held up in an effort to give me nothing to hold onto.

'Toyah, we need to sort things out.'

Her head violently shakes, her long blond hair flicking around her head. In any other moment I'd find this quite attractive and it makes me think back to all the times she got into the shower with me. She'd flick her hair and then stand under the warm flowing water, slowly teasing out all those chemicals and curls until she finally looked bare, pure and innocent. I'd stand and watch, hard as a rock, as she wiped the water from her face and then slowly stepped closer to me. I can't recall the number of times I pinned her against the steamy glass and made love to her, moving our soaking wet bodies to the bedroom so that we could end in a climax of our forms entangled together, as her wet hair dripped all over my chest.

'I wish things could go back to how they were,' I blurt out.

Her head still shakes, her mind clearly made up. Her steady face shows more resolve than I have ever known. 'So that you can use and abuse me a little bit more? You sick bastard!'

I move closer, my ego no longer willing to accept any more bruises. 'We used each other, because that's what two adults do when they have consenting sex.'

She moves backwards as I advance, quickly pinning herself against the lift doors. I put an arm either side of her, my head slowly leaning towards her. 'What did you think was supposed to happen? That we would fuck a little more until eventually I gave in and we got married? Do you think on our wedding day we'd tell everyone how we met? Do you think it would be a good story to tell them how you sucked me off in the disabled toilet and that very same night I took you home and gave you a good shagging?'

She tries to push me away but I don't move. I don't want to hear her talking like some victim and I don't want to be the bad guy anymore. 'Perhaps I can do a speech to your precious mummy and daddy about the time we got a cab back to mine and you were so desperate you made me finger you all the way home. Perhaps that would be a great story, don't you think? Because those are our stories and that's what we've always been about. We've had great sex, but did you ever think I would want to go out with the girl who walks past my desk, always rubbing herself and sticking pencils into her mouth?'

She finally breaks free of me, screaming wildly as she runs down the corridor. Just before she disappears she suddenly turns back. 'I hate you so much, I will always hate you! But your time is up, Ryan. You need to go see Mitchell now. That's all I came to tell you and instead you give me more shit. You're a fucking leach and I hope he destroys you! He says this is your judgement day and I hope he's right!'

She storms off around the corner as I press the lift button. 'Judgement day is overrated,' I mutter as I patiently wait for it to arrive.

*****

I head up to the top floor, determined that if this is my end game then it will be of my choosing. I laugh at the irony that the only time I get to go up in this building is when I'm getting a bollocking or a beating. It's the lonely time, when the only company you have is the speaking lift woman. It's these moments when I realise that there has to be more to life than this; in these precious few seconds I get a rare insight into how lost

I've become. I know that I need to see Mitchell but I also know that I need to get all the bits of the puzzle out into the open, so that I can try to figure everything out.

I storm straight into the office without knocking and I find Raj already in there. I look around the room to see chaos everywhere, with Raj standing at his desk, loading the contents of his immense career into a sturdy brown box.

'Ryan, what are you doing here?'

'I need to see you.'

He shakes his head, his eyes quickly focusing back on the packing. 'Have you seen Mitchell yet? I know he's looking for you.'

I move closer to the desk. 'What's going on?'

He laughs. 'Well, as you can see I'm packing up my office.'

'They're moving you on, aren't they? You've found out too much and now they have got to you but we can stop all of this, if we just sit down and share what we know then it will all become clear. We can't let them –'

Raj slams a book on the desk, his dark eyes showing no sign of the chaos that I feel. 'What on earth are you talking about? I think your stories are somewhat wild and entirely out of context. I have been promoted to head of European Eradicatory Sales.' He picks up his favourite family photo and proudly kisses it. 'It's what we have always wanted and it's now just one step away from head of Worldwide Eradication.'

'You know nothing,' I mutter, now carefully considering my options. Either he is oblivious to what's been going on or they are rewarding his silence with a promotion. The other option and one that I don't want to even consider, is that this isn't the sinister plot I think it is and I'm acting like a fool, throwing my life away for nothing.

'Mitchell is taking up the UK position,' Raj says.

'Mitchell!' I shout back, my mind convincing me again that some foul plot must exist.

Raj walks around his desk, putting an arm on my shoulder as he takes the time to look at me properly, like he's studying me – trying to figure out just what went wrong. 'I don't think it's something that should concern you anymore, though. Look, you're a good kid but the reality is that perhaps you were slightly over-promoted. We all got a bit enthused by your passion and energy and a decent set of first year results. It was my first month here and I wanted to make some quick and bold decisions, of which some you win and some you lose.'

He starts walking, his arm gently pushing me forward. 'I think that on balance this was one of those just slightly wrong decisions.' He smiles and makes a pinching movement with his free hand. 'Just ever so slightly on the losing side but it was enough for me to think that setting you up with the flat and all the trimmings was a little too premature. Of course, that was my poor decision and not yours. I'm sure you gave it your best shot.'

'So you're just casting me to one side? That's it, just a simple good bye and fuck off.'

He releases his hold on me and opens the door. 'Look, Ryan, things are moving on quicker than you know. The UK operation is returning to the company's research roots. After all, this small island is saturated with competitor activity, but the UK does have a fantastic chemical and biological development industry. I'm sure you will agree that it isn't for the likes of you and me but for Mitchell this is where he started and I know he will bring lots of value as well as some inevitable change.'

'This is exactly what he wants, this is what he needs. There are things from his past that I don't think you know, things that are really wrong.'

Raj simply shakes his head and pushes me out the door. 'You have a lot of questions to answer, Ryan, so at this stage I suggest that the only person you worry about is yourself.'

I put my foot in the door, stopping him from shutting me out and moving on. He can't ignore me and I think now is the time for him to hear the truth, at least as well as I know it. It's a risk that he knows all of this already, but if he doesn't then I figure that his conscience and intelligence will eventually force him to do the right thing.

But Raj doesn't listen to my rumblings; instead he simply stands still, no longer fighting for control over the door. It doesn't take long to realise that someone is behind me and when I feel a tap on the shoulder I quickly turn, expecting to see Mitchell.

It turns out not to be Mitchell and instead it's two men in suits. 'Are you Ryan Castle?' one of them asks, as they both produce Police badges.

I slowly nod as I hear the door properly close behind me. 'What's this about?'

'Ryan Castle, I am arresting you in connection with the unexplained death of Jerry Cooper.'

'What?' I say, as I hear their voices in the background. They turn me around and handcuff me, but I don't really hear what they are saying. I just silently co-operate, not knowing what to think. Whatever the conspiracy theory as I knew it to be now pales into insignificance at the reality of what I've just heard.

They pull me back around and as I'm heaved away from the window the last thing I see is Raj, still packing up his boxes, as that photo of his family is carefully wrapped up and placed on top of his other things. As I'm hauled away it dawns on me that whatever Raj does or doesn't know he's already forgotten me and my wild theories.

*****

Once we're at the police station they put me in a small room. They sit at the opposite side of the table, telling me that the empty chair next to me is for my legal representation, which I should request at any point I need it. This is entirely my choice, they stress to me on several occasions, both when we first sit down and once again when they start recording.

I start to think that this is going to be quite a boring recording, should it ever get played in court, since we all sit quietly for a while. They have already given me what I assume is the standard speech, confirming who I am and explaining why I'm here, all the time setting out these subtle undertones that I'm in a lot of apparent shit. They both remain in their suit jackets, neither of them wanting to take off a layer to get comfortable, which I can't decide if this is a good or bad thing. I try my best to evaluate the situation but the only conclusion I come to is that the one on the left looks like this formal attire suits him perfectly, earning him an easy undercover position in any estate agency. It's the other one who looks completely out of place. He said his name was Luke and it's the only one I remember, mainly because it suits him far better than his shirt and tie will ever match his shaved head.

'Jerry is dead?' I say, which results in one of them leaning back and one slouching forward, both of them looking hopeful that I'm going to reveal some big plot information. 'Well I didn't kill him!' I say, putting my head in my hands, knowing that's not entirely true; my mind utterly sure that I at least killed his career.

'You didn't?' Luke asks, sounding genuinely surprised, like everyone knows it except me.

'No, of course I didn't. You have to tell me what's going on.'

'I think you need to tell us, Ryan,' the other one says, now leaning forward to join his colleague in this menacing yet intrigued pose. 'I suggest you tell us everything you know.'

'Tell you everything I know about what? I didn't know he was dead, none of us did.'

'Well, telling us where you last saw him alive would be a good place to start.'

I nod but I don't say anything. Instead I just pause and reflect, already hating myself more than I could ever imagine. 'I last saw him when I sacked him.'

'I'm sure that went down well,' Detective Luke says, with a grin almost appearing.

'No, not really, and I'm still learning what a horrible person I can really be.'

'Just how horrible? Do you want to elaborate on that?'

I sigh and curse myself, just as I realise it might be time to ask for that representation. 'I'm not horrible enough to kill him, if that's what you're thinking.'

'We're not thinking anything,' the formal one says, his eyes narrowing as he tilts his head and settles all his attention on my body, looking for any sign of me hiding something.

'Did you love him?' the other one says, his voice coming from out of nowhere.

My eyes dart between them, flicking between their evaluating stares. In this moment you could hear a pin drop in the room, with the only sound coming from the air conditioning unit as it keeps turning on and off, all the time keeping the room just above freezing. I can feel blood rushing around my body at a hundred miles an hour, all from the cold heart of a bad man. 'What kind of question is that?'

'One would think it's quite a simple question.'

'Well perhaps love isn't that easy to define,' I say, my sarcasm fuelled by a new found bravery. I'm undoubtedly still in shock and since their questions make no sense, some part of me decides that neither will my answers.

'Well let's try a different question, shall we? Did you have sexual relations with Jerry Cooper, in any location, but particularly in his apartment?'

'What?' I say and start laughing. 'This has got to be a joke. I've never even been in Jerry's apartment. I don't even know where he lives!'

'You don't know where one of your own employees lives?' Detective Luke says.

'You couldn't easily find out this information from his records?' the other one says.

'No and no,' I say. 'Trust me, I'm not a particularly good boss.'

'And you've never been to his apartment?'

I shake my head.

'For the tape please confirm what you are indicating.'

I let out a big sigh, not understanding any of this. 'I've never been to Jerry's apartment, I've never been in love with him and I've never had sex with him. I'm pretty confident that I like women and I know a few hundred or so who could provide testimonies to back that up.'

Detective Luke shakes his head and I feel like asking him if he could confirm what he just did for the tape, but I think better of it. 'We have found hair at the scene which isn't Jerry's, so we will be taking a DNA sample from you, but if you are telling the truth about having never been there then clearly it won't be yours.'

'I am telling you the truth so take the DNA sample. I've never been to his place. I've only just found out that he was gay and trust me, it wasn't from him.'

They both look at each other and then back to me. 'Well, we find that strange, since Jerry clearly had some feelings for you.'

'Any feelings Jerry had for me were probably along the lines of bitter hatred, trust me.'

Detective Luke takes out a picture from an envelope as his colleague starts to explain what I'm being given. I don't listen to what he's saying, my eager eyes only wanting to see what's now being thrown at me. Despite my innocence, my mind seems to be working overtime to try to prove that I've done nothing, like I might just be lying.

When I look at the photo I wish I'd listened to what it was, as in front of me is a photo of Jerry, but he's topless and he's definitely dead. I throw the photo across the room. 'What the hell is going on? I can't believe I'm seeing this.'

'For the record, Mr Castle is throwing the photo across the table,' one of them says.

'Why are you throwing it, Ryan?' the other one immediately asks.

I stare at the table, the past I thought I knew now making no sense. 'Why is there a photo of me on his chest?'

*****

After a few more questions and what seems like several hours in captivity, Detective Luke finally comes into my cell. 'You're free to go,' he says.

'What?' I say, not moving from my foam mattress. 'That's it? I'm not guilty?'

'It's not a crime to love someone, whatever your age or sexuality.'

'I didn't love Jerry and I'm sick of saying that I'm not gay. Not even a little bit.'

Luke walks closer to me. 'We don't really care, that's not what we're here to understand. All we want to know is if anyone was with Jerry when he died. We've already told you that it appears to have been caused by a heart attack, but the fact that he was half-naked and the door wasn't chained on the inside, all leads us to believe that someone was in there with him.'

'Well, it wasn't me.'

Luke starts to nod, but his head is tilted to one side as he continues to examine me. 'Once your DNA tests come back then I'm sure you'll be in the clear. But if not, then you need to remember what I said to you on tape, that if it proves you were at the scene and you have lied about it then the situation around his death becomes a lot more mysterious. So, in the meantime, don't try leaving the country.'

'There's only one place I'm going,' I say, getting up and leading Detective Luke to the door, knowing that I've still got a little investigating of my own to do.

23

I burst into the office, only to be met with Mitchell smiling. He knew I was coming, as his eyes had followed me from the moment he saw me walking down the long corridor.

'You bastard!' I shout, not sure what I'm actually blaming him for. My hatred for the man is clearly borne from everything Joanna has told me and everything he made me do and they now join together to convince me that he must be stopped. The events in the police station and Raj's quick exit can only ever be an icing on a very bitter cake.

He leans back in his chair, pushing out his stomach so that it touches the hard wood of his desk. 'Ryan, I'm glad you're finally here,' he says and then looks at the woman seated next to him. Her strategic placement on the corner of the desk no doubt makes her someone from Human Resources, which no doubt makes my morning even more fucked.

'So, this is a formal meeting to discuss your involvement in the tragic death of Jerry Cooper,' Mitchell says.

The HR lady quickly holds out a hand. '*Alleged* involvement.'

I sit down and offer her a smile. I know that she's not really on my side but the fact that she's not on Mitchell's, either, gives me some glimmer of hope. The mere presence of someone impartial is, in some way, a small victory in this morning's battles.

'Bollocks,' Mitchell says, turning to look her directly in the eyes. 'He's just been interviewed by the police for the death of someone he sacked, so don't give me any shit about innocent until proven otherwise. He's guilty of something.'

She doesn't move or falter as he projects a tirade of abusive words and insults, mainly about me but aimed entirely her way. I've been subjected to this so many times that it's fascinating to be an observer.

'What the fuck are you smiling at?' he says, his attention now on me. 'You're in a lot of shit and by the time I've finished with you that smile will be long gone.'

'My smile never lasts long around you,' I say. 'I'm more likely to leave your office with bruises, both mental and emotional, so I don't expect that to change today.'

He makes a grunting noise, as his eyes flick between me and the HR woman, who hasn't stopped writing things on her pad since I walked in. 'You think you're trying to be clever, do you, Ryan? Do you think that there being a witness in here will mean there's someone here to listen to your pathetic sob story?' He leans forward and grabs the pad from her lap and then throws it across the room. 'Do you really think I need to give a shit?'

The HR lady tries to speak in protest but Mitchell just smacks his hand on the desk. 'Leave the pad where it is. I'm sick of following these bullshit rules, so just sit there and make some mental fucking notes, like we did in the old days.'

The only movement she makes is to adjust her glasses and to angle her head at the floor, silently defeated far quicker than I had hoped for.

Mitchell turns back to me. 'So, Jerry is dead and about fucking time,' he says and smiles. It's the furthest I've ever seen his mouth open, his rear gold teeth glistening against the bright office lights. 'The last company employee to see him alive was you, just after you sacked that tragic excuse of a man, who was also incidentally a regular shag of yours. Now, that's an alleged web of fucked-up lies, if ever I've heard one.'

'These are your lies and you're covering things up. He knew something that you didn't want anyone else to find out and now you're desperate to bury those secrets.'

'That sad bloke didn't know what the day was half the time, so don't give me any shit about making stuff up.'

'You made me sack him,' I say, as I direct all my hope and faith to the HR lady, the only person who can change any of this.

'Oh, I made you sack him?' Mitchell says, as he starts lining up bits of paperwork across his desk. 'Did I make you fill in each of these bits of paperwork, perhaps with a gun to your head?'

I look at each sheet, all of them an individual suicide note for my career, all signed over time and all coming back to haunt me. 'You had these produced,' I say, my eyes begging the HR woman to believe me.

She simply shakes her head. 'Are these not your signatures?'

'Yes, but –'

'So why would you sign several fundamentally damaging documents if you didn't write them yourself or believe them to be accurate and fair?'

'Because he told me to,' Mitchell says in a pathetic, child-like voice.

The HR lady takes off her glasses and rubs her eyes. She looks at me and I suddenly recognise her as the person who was at my first interview for this job. And now I can only shake my head in answer to her question, as I realise that the woman who was at my arrival in this place will also be present at my demise.

She takes a deep breath, her hands rummaging through the papers. 'One of the concerns we have is that Jerry didn't sign any of these documents, which means that either he didn't know about them or didn't agree with them.'

Mitchell laughs and leans forward. 'Now can you see how "he told me to" just doesn't quite cut it? So, what's your get out plan now, Ryan?'

'You and I both know what happened. It was my mistake to ever allow you to bully me into sacking him. He knew things about the past and you used me to remove him before you try to do them all again. And now that Raj is leaving, that's exactly what you and your fucked up boss will do.'

I look at them both but neither offers me any gesture, hostile or otherwise. I can feel tears building in my eyes, tears from the knowledge that I did ruin a man's life and I most likely did play a part in his death. All of my frustrations with Jerry's inability to do his job and all of his useless comments, are now entirely overshadowed by the picture of his dead face that will haunt me forever.

Mitchell ignores my silent thoughts as he scoops up all the papers, piling them neatly on one side of his desk. 'So, you sacked your lover because he was getting in the way and then you blame me? Was it not more likely that you got fed up with him? Or was Toyah giving you grief? It really is clear that you have created a lot of shit for us to clean up.'

He sits quietly for a moment, as the HR woman sorts through her own folder of paperwork, taking out a small file of witness statements.

Mitchell grabs the folder off her, half-pulling her arm along with it. 'Oh, yes, Ryan, we knew about Toyah, too. It's one fucked up love triangle you had there.'

I can only sit and listen, wondering if anything I have ever done in this place still remains a secret. I have scattered my workplace with my personal vices and a few that seem to be made up, but entirely believable in the eyes of those who have had to work with me.

The lady nods and frowns and I think for one moment that she almost doesn't want this to be true. She, like many others, must relish the thought of the day that Mitchell isn't always right and evil isn't the overriding power around here. 'We do have statements from Toyah stating you sexually harassed her on more than one occasion, in both the disabled toilet and the stationery cupboard on the ninth floor.'

Mitchell sorts through the sheets, picking one of them up and sliding it towards me. 'This is the best one, Ryan. She talks about how you forced her to watch you strip off in said stationery cupboard, getting your kicks from your exhibitionist stunts. I mean, that is just sick, but thankfully you were disturbed by a colleague just as your filthy pants came down.'

'What did she say?' I ask, desperate to hear this above anything else. Of all the people who I've lost in the last few weeks, she is the one person I want back. Of all my hopes, her forgiveness is one of them, and now it is just possible that she had finally chosen to drop me right in my own web of shit.

'So you don't deny this happened then?' Mitchell asks. 'You really are an expert at digging your own grave.'

I smack both my hands on the desk. 'The witness to this was Sophie and I'm asking you to please tell me what she said.'

Mitchell keeps laughing as the HR lady hands me another sheet of paper. 'Sophie does agree that she found you topless and although she believes it was entirely inappropriate, she has also stated that you had an explanation that your shirt needed changing.'

'Bollocks,' Mitchell says. 'He's probably shagged her as well.'

'That's not what it says here,' my new friend from the HR department says.

Mitchell tries to grab the paper from her but she pulls it away. 'Sophie clearly states that the two of you haven't had any sexual relations and she has found you to be a professional and thoughtful line manager ever since this issue occurred.'

'Thank you,' I say and smile at her, finally able to lean back in my seat.

'Thank you?' Mitchell says, spitting all over me and then staring at her. 'I've heard enough of this crap and you sound like you're on his side now.'

'I'm here from an impartial point of view only, as you are fully aware.'

He turns directly towards her, as I prepare to see the final shot – the moment where he asserts his absolute authority. She's probably the toughest they have and he's about to clean up the HR department with one more slip of his tongue.

I decide that today isn't the day that will happen and suddenly stand up, brushing all the paper off the desk, forcing them both to look at me. 'You're about to tell her that she's trying to get into my pants, or that I'll try to shag her once we get out of here. You'll then do something big and dramatic, such as pushing the paperwork off the desk, like I just did. It's your most popular shock tactic, which means you finally get your victory before you turn all your attention to me.'

I sit back down as Mitchell turns back to face me. 'So you've finally grown some balls… well about fucking time. It's just a shame that it's a little too late.'

'Pay me off,' I say, looking solely at Mitchell. 'I'll disappear for the right figure.'

Mitchell starts laughing and looks at the HR lady. 'You want me to give you money to disappear? I tell you what I'll do, Ryan, I'll give you no money and you'll still disappear. You think you've become the big man, well you have no idea what's coming your way.'

'We're willing to make an offer,' the HR lady says, her pad back in her hand, quietly recovered from the corner of the room. She flicks through the pages as Mitchell stares in bewilderment.

'What the fuck are you talking about?'

She ignores him as she searches for a certain page and once she's found it all of her attention rests on me. 'Ryan, I think it's fair to say that there has been a fundamental breakdown in the relationship between employee and employer and it won't do either of us any good if we spend hours in investigations. It will only upset your colleagues who work for you and cause you more grief as we uncover things you might not want us to know. We're therefore willing to offer you six months' salary if you resign with immediate effect. You can blame ill health through complications from your recent operation, or simply say that you wanted a new challenge. The fact is that if you accept this offer today then we will still provide you with a positive reference.'

'Like hell we will do any of this bollocks,' Mitchell says. 'You can just stop talking now, because none of that is going to happen.'

She ignores him and continues to look at me. 'There are certain other conditions, such as the return of your company flat and car within forty-eight hours and you are also alleged to have in your possession some company stock. This will need to be left in the flat and clearly marked as G.U.E property.'

'We're taking all of that but he's not getting a fucking penny. He's a bloody murderer and we won't be paying him off.

She still ignores him, showing me the techniques I should have used and the backbone I should have found over all the months of torture from that man. 'Raj is still in charge of this building until the end of today. Therefore, Ryan, I strongly urge you to accept this offer now and allow me to process a letter to you well before this caveman takes the helm.'

'I accept,' I say, not giving any of this a second thought.

She stands up and urges me to do the same. I obey and follow her to the door, seeing that although she's shaking, it's her dignity and professionalism that will get us out of this room. Without her being here Mitchell and I would be fighting right now and I'd be losing.

'You clever little bitch,' Mitchell says. 'He might be getting away but you've just picked the wrong side in a war you have no idea how to win.'

I stop and turn, feeling somehow responsible for this woman, my guilt telling me that she has made a great sacrifice, all in the name of helping me. But I don't get a chance to say anything as she opens the door behind me and pulls me backwards.

She steps forward, returning further into the lair. 'Actually, that's where you're wrong, because once I've processed Ryan's letter and had Raj personally sign it, then I'm going to be applying for one of several positions in another division. In fact, I think you'll find that's what half of the people in this building are doing right now.'

Mitchell simply smiles. 'Well that's the best news I've heard all day. The whole lot of Human Resources can piss right off and make sure you take those chimps from marketing with you.' He stands up and thumps his chest. 'We won't need any of you in the new world I'm building, so you just spread the word that the weak should leave now, do you hear me?'

He's still shouting as she closes the door and takes a deep breath.

'Thank you, and I'm sorry, but I didn't catch your name.'

She adjusts her glasses and shakes her head. 'You know, Ryan, you paid me more attention in there than you ever did in your initial job interview. It's funny what a formal meeting can do to men like you, because in your recruitment interview the only parts of me you were interested in were my breasts and what sits below my skirt. That's why Mitchell gave you the job, because you really are a vile little pig. If you remember one thing from all of this, then remember that the only thing that separates you and that ape in there is your age.'

As she pushes me into a lift my head is shaking, my mind finding every way possible to deny her claims and prove us both wrong. 'We'll send you your things in the post.'

'But I'm moving out of my flat by tomorrow, so where will you send them?'

'I think you'll find that it was never your flat and you really should have thought of that sooner,' she says, as the doors close

'Trust me, I know that.' I push the door open button, scrambling in my suit for a pen and paper, my weary mind trying to recall my mum's address. I look up, ready to write the details down but she's already gone. I nod to myself, knowing that I've got more than I deserve from her, and so I let the doors close and the lift bring me down to reception. Security guards are waiting for me and once I'm stripped of my pass and my remaining dignity, I leave the place I called home for so many hours a week.

I stand outside and look up to the top of the building. I remember back to the first time I did that, with all my youthful energy that assured me I would climb to the top of the ladder in this company. And now, having fallen to the very bottom I can see what true failure looks like. I quietly start the engine in the car that was never mine, knowing that it won't be the failure of not making it to the top that will haunt me, but rather the failure to stand up to Mitchell and do what I knew was right so many times over.

24

As I find myself sitting on my coffee table I can't help but wonder how I will feel tomorrow, once I've handed back the keys to my car and this place. The only material thing of any value that I own in here is this table. It was the only bit of furniture I didn't have when I moved in, so I figured I might as well spend some decent money on it.

I open some of the compartments, finding even more stuff I've still got to pack. I open the smallest drawer, the one that's most hidden and find it stuffed full of condoms. I think back to just how unromantic those moments must have been, but then I never got any complaints and they all came back for more. When you're offering something so simple as a decent bit of food, from the array of posh takeaways around here, followed by some good sex, then all these minor and so obviously premeditated things are more easily tolerated. The fact that I knew Sophie would never find out that this drawer ever existed and that I would abandon it the day we ever became serious, tells me that now might be the time to grow up.

So, it's decided. I will leave the coffee table here, as a symbol of the past that I'm leaving behind. I slowly close the condom compartment, deciding they too will remain, ever hopeful that its new owners will find some laughs and enjoyment, just as I did.

I look around at all the boxes piled up and wonder how I've achieved all this on my own. In one hand I hold my phone, with the toss-up going through my head of Joanna or my mum, and in the other hand I hold the spare keys to Ken's flat. Of course I've been round there several times, but nothing has moved, offering me no hint that he has returned. The notes I've left calling him wanker and demanding he rings me have been untouched and the milk I keep replacing in the fridge remains unused, so I decide that his place is to be my new temporary home. At least in his absence it will be substantially more chilled than either of the other options and I can hopefully use it as a base to figure out where he's gone.

There's a buzz at the door but, before I can answer, Tina and Elliot storm into the flat. 'It's battle time,' Tina shouts, as she heads into the kitchen with a bag of shopping.

Elliot makes his way straight to the big television and starts making tutting noises the moment he sees the Xbox has been packed away. 'Which box is it in?' he demands, already starting a hunt of his own.

'What are you two doing here?'

'Well, we've not come to help you pack, if that's what you think!' Tina shouts from the kitchen area. 'I had to do my last move all alone and I bloody well just got on with it, so you'll get no sympathy from me.'

I go to answer, to remind her that I'm technically still wounded and that any heavy lifting could result in me tearing the muscle that desperately needs to repair itself, but I'm distracted by Elliot tapping my arm.

'Where's the Xbox, Ryan? It's like crucial I play it.'

I nod towards the right box and leave him to it. He's immediately entangled in a web of cables, blissfully ignoring his mother who's screaming that this is a temporary perk that will be removed the moment he steps out of line.

'You should cut him some slack,' I say, as I join her in the kitchen.

Tina makes no eye contact as she goes about cutting up tomatoes, preparing lunch like it's just another chore to get through. 'Don't tell me how to raise my son, okay,' she says, holding the knife towards me. She says these things in such an aggressive way, but even with a weapon in her hand I struggle to take her seriously. She's simply a woman who has been too angry for too long.

I mutter that I'm sorry and start helping with the food, somehow falling into whatever has just started happening in my flat. For a few minutes we seem to work well together, each of us taking on our individual responsibilities for the sandwiches and the drinks, finding some shared purpose in the salad bowl. 'I need to ask if you know something,' I say.

She stops her chopping and looks at me, her eyes as red as her cheeks. 'You're going to ask me if I know about Jerry, aren't you?'

I nod. 'I just can't believe it.'

'I can,' she says. 'If someone has been as unhappy and lonely for as long as he has then there comes a time when you just give up. That's what that fool did – he just stopped bothering to live for anything.'

I cringe for a moment, thinking about the other things I want to say. As I watch her work in my kitchen I realise that she knows her away around it better than I ever did. It shouldn't come as a shock but it does somehow grow my respect for her, just enough for me to consider that she might know something that can help me. 'I didn't know that he liked men and I had no idea that he liked me,' I say, ever so cautiously.

She nods, looking like she knew this day would come. 'Well it doesn't matter what he liked because he never did anything about it. Some of us never find the courage to do the things we should, and life doesn't bloody well wait, I'll tell you that much.'

'Did everyone think we loved each other?' I say, the curiosity of my reputation taking over any thoughts of the loss of a co-worker.

Tina stops her work and lets out this long sigh. 'Ryan, I'm quite sure that the whole office knew that you two weren't shagging. However, Jerry did quietly love you from the day you arrived, and it was something that was obvious to me and just about every person in London who ever saw you two share the same moment in time and space.'

'It wasn't obvious to me,' I say, as if I need to put that thought out there.

'Yes, we knew that. It was quite clear that you were too busy being Mitchell's puppet and planning your next big bonus to even think about the feelings of one little man.'

'Look where that's got me,' I say, not wanting to argue her rather sharp point.

She smiles and then nods. 'Yes, your career is down the shitter, my friend,' she says and rubs my shoulder. 'Although it couldn't have happened to a more deserving person, there is still time for you to make up for all you have done wrong.'

'You really don't like me, do you?'

Tina pauses, as if carefully considering her options of how to be as brutally honest as possible. 'You really are a shocking boss who doesn't give a toss about anyone except yourself. You fucked Toyah over, literally. You sacked Jerry just before he cost you a load of money in retirement payments and you robbed company stock to make a quick buck.'

I stand and silently take it, absorbing all the realities I know to be true.

'Did I miss anything?' she says, as she walks away with Elliot's sandwich and drink. I stand and watch from afar as she puts the food in front of him, grabbing the controller from him and taking over the game. She laughs as he shouts that she's losing him the match, to which she bundles him onto the floor, telling him he best eat quicker. They play and they forget, because that's what people who support each other do. For all the times she had a crisis in work and for all those tears in the office, I think I finally understand the reason why she did all of that during the day. I see now that when she came home, she had no choice but to be a rock of emotional stability for her young son.

It's no different to what my dad did for his family, bundling up all that resentment towards the people who never called him back and letting out all that worry about his failed deals somewhere on the North Circular. He did that just a few precious miles from home, so that when he walked in the door he was able to smile for both Mum and me. He made me feel safe, even when he was knee-deep in failure and lost in a world of frustration.

'Ken's in China,' Tina says, now back at the sink.

I suddenly focus all of my energy, concentration and jealousy on her. 'You know where he is?'

'He's gone to get proof of what Mitchell and the Quiff are up to,' she says, casually making the tea as she offers her explanation, talking as if this is normal office gossip. 'As you know, he has quite a few contacts out there, providing both of you with all that free stuff. Well, this time they need to give him some information, because Mitchell is planning something big and there are only a few of our offices in the world where he can do it.'

'Drug production?'

She smiles and nods. 'So you do actually know something.'

'Yes,' I say and stumble on my next words, wanting to get out everything that I know, despite how little time it will take. 'Joanna told me and then she told me not to mention her name to anyone. She really doesn't want to get involved.'

Tina nods. 'Yes, Joanna was there last time and back then she tried her very best not to get involved.' She starts laughing, loud enough to make Elliot turn around and shout for her to be quiet. 'You know, back in those days I actually thought that she was jealous of the attention I was getting from Mitchell. I mean, if you think I look a state now, you should have seen me back then. I had huge oversized glasses and substantially undersized cardigans.'

'I had heard,' I say. 'But you were much younger.'

'I was much more desperate, more like. I've never been the prettiest girl and when Mitchell offered me the chance to do something amazing and have a child of my own I jumped at it. I mean, come on, I was thirty and still single. It wasn't a choice at all.'

I lean towards her, my back to Elliot. 'What the hell happened?'

She drags me into the hallway and closes the door, watching for any sign that it moves, no doubt checking for any sound out of Elliot getting suspicious. As she turns back to face me her eyes are already moist, her body starting to shake as she wraps her arms around herself. 'They were dark days, Ryan. If you think I cry a lot in work now then you have no idea what I was like back then.'

'You can tell me,' I say, more determined than I have been in a long time. 'I want to help.'

She shakes her head, wiping the few tears away with her sleeve. 'You've got a bit of free time and you want revenge on Mitchell, and that's really the only reason why you're even entertaining me today. Let's be honest, if you had your job and your tongue was still stuck up his arse then we wouldn't be here right now.'

I nod, knowing this truth better than she does. 'But I've been sacked and I'm being evicted tomorrow, so I'm pretty much willing to listen right now.'

She laughs. 'At least you're being honest, for once. So let's see what you know and what I can shock you with. I'll start by asking if you knew that the gunge was never really our core business?'

'It's our main revenue stream!'

'That you know of, dear Ryan. The company started in biotechnology research and the gunge was a product that came from it. After soap and bleach it was obvious that the mass consumers would happily buy anything that promised to kill more nasties, but if you follow it through to a logical conclusion it can never be sustained.'

I silently look at her, not really understanding what she means. I always found a new product launch every six months kept my bonus payments coming in and our consumers armed with the latest germ killing device. As long as the design guys keep innovating and the marketing guys keep scaring, then I think that there will always be enough demand.

'You're not as clever as I thought but I think you get the fact that killing germs and bacteria is a need that will never go away. It's a process that's only as strong as its weakest link.'

I nod. 'You can sanitise a hospital and you can vaccinate the staff, but you'll never stop the spread of viruses from patients and visitors. That was until our patented *Building Guardians* came to save the day. You know that they guarantee to protect –'

'Stop it,' she says and then pinches my arm.

'There's another way?'

'What if you didn't have to worry about sanitising the whole planet? What if the worry of just one person slipping through the net could be avoided? If you were born immune to all major viruses and bacteria then these would never be a concern.'

My head is quickly shaking. 'That's not possible, there are too many new strains of viruses being found all the time and they adapt as quick as we fight back. And not to forget I'm pretty sure genetic modification is illegal.'

'Oh, trust me, it is! But that didn't stop Mitchell and the Quiff from trying it out.'

'On who?' I ask, already knowing the answer, already refusing to believe that it could ever have happened.

'Elliot never really gets sick, well, not from any virus or bug that was around from before he was born. Anything that's actively catalogued is of no threat to him.'

My head hasn't stopped shaking since we started talking about the impossible. It's not that I don't think it will happen, it's just my mind can't get around how Mitchell could ever be intelligent enough to think of anything like this. 'How could you do that?' I ask and start to walk away, not wanting to associate the bad things that must have happened to that young kid in my living room.

Tina follows and grabs my arm, pulling me back. 'You have no idea what happened back then. I didn't know what they were going to do, they just promised me a healthy baby and I… I was desperate.'

I push her away. 'You mean you didn't bother to ask.'

She's shaking now, tears in full flow. 'You're right, I didn't ask. I just wanted a baby and they gave it to me. I made a big mistake but don't you try to judge me. You weren't there and you have no right!'

I push her backwards and head towards my room, my cluttered mind not wanting to entertain the slightest memory of what she did back then.

She bangs the living room door, forcing me to turnaround to see what state she is in. 'He's my son and I love him! Whatever mistakes I made back then doesn't take away the fact that I brought him into this world and he is normal and healthy!'

I stand and stare at her, waiting for Elliot to burst through the door. But he doesn't come out into the hall. He doesn't come to share a thought on his mum's shady past, or to try to understand how he came to be. I assume that he knows all this; that he understands where it all started, but a part of me knows it is entirely possible that Tina has stored all of this up, just waiting for the inevitable time when she blows.

I take a deep breath, already knowing that I don't have the appetite or the right to judge her for the past. 'So why doesn't the world know about this?'

She sits herself on the floor and holds her head in her hands. 'They decided the world wasn't ready a decade ago. Look at all the shit that kicked off with sheep cloning and genetically modified tomatoes. A little blond baby immune to half the world's viruses would drive the world mad.'

'They think the planet isn't mad now? They actually think this place is ready for such a revelation now?'

She shakes her head. 'No, it isn't ready, but there are enough governments who will be willing to pay and enough competition that want to beat them to it. Why bother to tell the mass media and the general public when the people with the money and determination are the few in positions of power across the world.'

'So they want to sell Elliot and what they did to him to the scientists in major governments? And what will happen to him after that?'

She laughs and then smiles at me. 'You really do need to think bigger. They have been perfecting the drugs for the last ten years, trying to crack immunity codes for every new virus that's been catalogued. Elliot is the past and they simply want him out of the way.'

I sit alongside her. 'They can't get them all and this is still totally illegal.'

'They only need to get a few hundred more and then they will target the right governments, the ones with a little more money and a lot less principles. With the funding they could get and the other work going on around the world it won't take long before the first super baby is born, something that is immune to everything.'

We sit in silence as I contemplate if that really is a good or bad thing. As I start to run through the list of ailments that could never happen I don't see an obvious downside.

Tina is staring at me, her head shaking. 'I know what you're thinking but do you think the world is ready for this? Think about the elitist classes that would be formed, across continents and decades. Just imagine the people who are left hanging around, these people that become a burden on an unnecessary health service. Just think about when you end up in an old peoples home and the younger generations don't want to pay out precious money to keep you from catching that very inconvenient flu.'

I nod, half agreeing with her but still knowing that this will happen one day. If you follow the inevitable quest of humanity to fix everything, then the bloodthirsty path of progress will never be stalled by a few ethical concerns. I just never thought G.U.E was ever bold enough to look beyond our cocktail of fancy chemicals.

'Remember that this isn't about genetic recoding, it's about making the body immune to what can attack it from outside and cause internal illness from external factors. Even those two morons couldn't find the money to start tampering with DNA.'

'So it won't cure cancer, or maybe stop heart disease?'

She shakes her head. 'Your Dad died of a heart attack, didn't he?'

I quietly nod. 'What actually killed him was a train, but it was the stress of everything that quietly built up over time that really got him and then finally laid it all on his heavy heart.'

'I'm sorry,' she says and grabs my arm, playfully pinching it.

'And I'm sorry,' I say. 'For just about everything I've ever done to you.'

She pushes herself up and then makes an attempt to drag me up too. I struggle, still a little sore and cautious of any of my usual positions.

'You do realise that it wasn't just a case of popping some pills whilst I was pregnant, don't you?'

'I hadn't given it much thought. I assumed they did stuff whilst Elliot was, you know… in a –'

She laughs and gives me her standard frown. 'In a test tube? Well, they did some of that, but most of it happened during my pregnancy. I had to take seventeen tablets, four injections and two anal depositories a day in order to introduce his body to the different viruses. And whilst my body had to fight them off so did his, but each time it learnt ways to defend against them.'

'So are you immune, too?'

She shakes her head as she heads to the toilet. 'I bloody wish. My body was too old to adapt to so many new things, but his was young enough to learn and the drugs they gave him mean that he can retain the defensive make up to fight them off forever. Now, if you'll excuse me, another side effect of what happened to me is that I became the lucky recipient of irritable bowel syndrome, of which I am reminded of several times a day.' She grabs her stomach and smiles. 'I'm also diabetic, but I think there's a whole other reason for that.'

I leave her in peace and head into the living room. Elliot is still in his game, playing ignorant to all of this. I pick up the other controller and sit myself down with him. We select a new game and pick countries without the need for words.

Only when we're about to start does he speak, 'It's only illegal if I tell anyone.'

I nod, keeping my head fixed on the screen. 'I can't believe you picked France,' I say. 'Ken always picks France.'

*****

Just as half-time hits and well before Tina has surfaced from a lie down, there's a buzz on the intercom. I go to answer it, my mind still absorbed in all that I now know. I shout back to Elliot, telling him that I'll get some snacks and bring them over, acting as if this has been a usual weekend activity for us for quite some time.

'It's the Repo man and I've come for a clear out,' this voice comes through the intercom.

I pause, stricken with fear, already feeling trapped in a hell that's just frozen over us.

'You should be busy packing.'

'Mitchell?'

'I know they're in there so just send them down.'

'You're not coming in here.'

I hear laughter just before the clunk of the door being pulled open. 'What lovely, helpful neighbours you have here.'

'Elliot, get your stuff, now!' I shout, just as Tina appears next to me.

'What the bloody hell is going on?' she asks, with a sausage roll in her hand, her face finally looking relaxed.

'We have to leave now! Mitchell is here!'

'Oh shit!' she shouts, her face suddenly full of anger as it turns back to a patchwork of those usual worry lines. She grabs my arms, balancing herself against me. 'He'll take him. He's desperate and he'll go to jail if we can prove what he did was wrong. There are files at the office and we need them.' She suddenly starts shaking, her frantic eyes filling up. 'Oh god, Ryan, he's going to take him.'

I pull her body up straight, determined that this will not be another crisis, not now of all times. 'I know a way out but we need to leave now.'

We're soon making our way down the fire exit, hundreds of steps ahead of us. Elliot is in the lead and he keeps turning back to us to let out his frustration at my post-op and his mum's weight dragging him back.

'You have to live on the fourteenth floor!' Tina shouts.

I look out the window, to the joining block, and I immediately see the Quiff. He's about ten floors up, a mobile phone in his hand and his eyes fixed on us. 'We need to go quicker!' I shout, deciding that now is the time for my groin to experience two steps at a time. 'Elliot, you know where the car is parked? You think you can bring it to the door?'

He nods and I throw him the keys. He soon disappears into the maize of stairs; his legs carrying him double the speed I can achieve, until all I can hear are the soles of his trainers smacking against the hard floor.

'He'll get caught and how the hell are you expecting him to drive the car?'

I grab hold of Tina, using whatever energy I have left to pull her along. 'Mitchell will be trying to break into my flat right now or on his way back down in the lift, which isn't near these exits. And as for the driving… well you should just use your imagination on that.'

She uses her free hand to point at me whilst the other one takes a firm hold of the handrail. 'Don't tell me you took my son driving!'

We make it through the corridors and into the car park without seeing Mitchell. My senses feel like they're on fire as I look around the cold and dimly lit underground area, my eyes searching for any threats and my mind thinking through ways I can barricade the door and hopefully stop him.

I quickly decide to give up on the door, choosing instead to get us out of here as quickly as possible. My desperation to see my car come speeding around the corner, with a competent Elliot at the wheel, is quickly overshadowed by a deathly silence, without any sound of an engine starting.

I start to pull Tina forward, towards my parking space at the other end of the complex and as we reach the car Tina shouts for Elliot, but he's nowhere to be seen. I stare at my car, my mind momentarily removed from this crisis, as I see my beautiful BMW smashed to within an inch of its existence. The shell is all that remains and the badge is all that would make you realise what it is, as it now lies in a pool of broken glass. The leather seats are torn apart and all four tyres slashed all the way around. My eyes keep looking between Tina and back to my poor car as my mind drifts between how I will seek the ultimate revenge and how I can possibly explain this when I hand it back tomorrow.

Tina suddenly screams, pulling me back towards her. 'Elliot!' she shouts, as we both see him walking back through the door and into the car park.

228

He walks towards us as his mum continues to shout at him, but he ignores her in favour of his attempts to explain. 'I saw the broken car so I went to look for you guys but then I got lost and then –'

I see the horror in his face as he stops explaining and starts shouting. Tina is too busy yelling over his young voice to realise that someone has appeared behind us. I turn to see the Quiff running towards us, his long strides bringing him swiftly across the car park, as his hair bobs up and down.

'Run!' I shout as I push Tina towards Elliot, willing them to reunite and find a way out of here, whilst I take on the might of a guy I once saw as a distant God in my little world.

He stops nearly at my feet, his arms held out and his eyes looking at the door where we came in. I soon realise that this was probably their plan and that within a few seconds we'll find ourselves pinned between him and Mitchell. 'Why the rush?' he says.

'Tina, this way,' I shout, demanding that they come back towards me, bringing her son ever closer to the man they have tried to evade for so long. I turn to see that they're moving towards me and I also see Mitchell's face appear through the glass in the door. It's all the motivation I need to swing my arm back around, landing a fist into the Quiff's stomach. He groans and falls to the floor, allowing me to smack his face as he goes down.

I grab both Tina and Elliot and pull them towards the door to the outside. I turn back to see the Quiff still down, his shirt splattered in blood and a handkerchief over his nose. Mitchell is a few paces behind, his face entirely red as he charges towards us.

When we hit the cold evening air I look around for options, but I am met with silence and the endless tower blocks that can offer no safe haven without a code to get in or the time to explain all this over an intercom. 'Head towards the tube station!' I shout, pushing them both forward, forcing Tina into another reluctant run.

I hear the door swing open but I don't look back. I know it's Mitchell and I know how close he is. He doesn't shout as his feet smack against the pavement, bringing his fists ever closer to joining with my face. I know this will be our most real fight yet, making this a proper beating, without a mass of people or civilised work surroundings to hold him back.

A car speeds around the corner and pulls up just in front of us. I prepare myself for the fight we can't win and the unfair odds of some friend of Mitchells jumping out, but instead the window rolls down and a familiar face leans out. 'Get in!' she shouts.

'What the hell are you doing here?' I demand, as I bundle Tina into the nearest door, as Elliot and I run around to the other side.

We make it into the car but Mitchell makes a grab for the handle just as we start to accelerate. The doors automatically lock as we gain speed and the last thing I see is the welcome sight of Mitchell, his hands on his knees, his body hunched over as his desperate lungs try to take in some air.

I turn back to the driver, as she takes her eyes off the rear mirror and onto the road ahead. 'I want some answers,' I say.

She offers me a quick glance, those nearly-black eyes giving nothing away. I feel a sudden rush through my body as she also offers me a grin. 'Aren't you just pleased to see me?'

I want to say no. I want to shout out loud that I really don't trust her, but I notice that my head is already nodding. I'll always be pleased to see Sophie.

25

'I told you that I didn't want to get involved,' Joanna says, a hard finger prodding my chest. 'So please explain to me why I am now in this situation.' She looks around, taking in the array of unwelcome guests who have just piled into her life.

Tina and Elliot are on the sofa, both of them sitting on the edge and looking entirely out of place amongst the array of mismatched cushions and soft lighting from several chic lamps. She sees us looking but chooses not to speak. Instead she picks one of the plainest cushions from the scattered arrangement and places it on her lap.

I look back to Joanna who is still staring at me.

'I really need your help,' I say. 'We really need your help.'

She sighs and puffs out her chest, all the time making her disapproval clear through the shaking of her head. 'Darling, I have no interest in Tina coming back into my life. The past should stay the past, as far as I am concerned.'

'Do you think we should just allow history to repeat itself? And look at Elliot. Do you really want bad things to happen to a young kid?'

'So now you're playing the emotional guilt trip on me? That's low, even for you.'

I look down at her. 'I didn't know where else to go.'

She looks over at Elliot and soon nods, finally relenting to my needs, even if it is fuelled by the confused look of a young kid. 'I see your point. I really do. But did you have to deem it necessary for me to meet your mother?' She says, barely a whisper.

I look back over to Tina, seeing my confused mum sitting next to her. She smiles and I smile back, both of us a little clueless.

'I had no choice,' I say, as Sophie returns from the bathroom and plants herself clearly into our conversation.

Joanna looks at Sophie and then back to me. 'No choice? Everything is a choice, darling, and this was entirely the wrong one.'

'Look, she's my mum, the next of kin on my work files. Mitchell could easily have found her details and come looking for me.'

Joanna throws her arms up in the air. 'So instead of putting her into a hotel or shipping her off to a distant family member, you bring the one woman I would never want to meet around to my flat. That really helps my situation.'

I start to gently steer Joanna further away from those on the sofa and to my shock she actually obeys, as her body happily takes a step back for every one I make towards her, until we are safely in the dining area.

To my disappointment Sophie follows and grabs my arm, her gaze darting between Joanna and me, her busy mind ticking away. 'Oh, don't tell me you two have –'

Joanna laughs. 'You mean that you haven't?'

Sophie shakes her head. 'I really do think I must be the only one.'

Joanna starts grabbing at my chest, teasing a nipple. 'You really should try him out. I can promise you won't be disappointed.'

'Oh, really?' Sophie says, all the time looking at me.

'Ladies!' I shout and then look around to the small gathering of oblivious people, as I still get these uncomfortable nods back.

'So, what's your place in all of this, anyway?' Joanna asks, as she brings to bear all of her focus onto Sophie.

'Yes, that's a good question,' I say. 'You turned up just when you needed to.'

'Just good timing, I guess,' Sophie says.

'If you think we're going to accept that as an answer then you have another thing coming. Isn't that right, darling?'

Joanna slaps my arm as she realises I'm still looking at Sophie.

'Are you working with Mitchell?' I say. 'After all, he did give you the job without involving me at all.'

Her head starts shaking. 'I can promise you that my appointment had nothing to do with me secretly working for Mitchell and most likely everything to do with your inability to effectively recruit good talent into your team.'

'Oh, this one's trying to be funny,' Joanna says, edging that little bit closer to Sophie.

Sophie doesn't move, instead she just smiles. 'I assure you that I'm not on the side of the bad guys. You should consider me as one of the neutral people.'

'Are you a Police Officer?' I ask, feeling the first stirring in my trousers since they sliced me open.

Sophie starts laughing. 'You'd like to think that, wouldn't you? I bet you think that's the reason why we've never fucked.'

'Ssshhh!' I say, almost begging as I look around at my mum. She's walking about now, looking out the window as she paces around this unfamiliar world. I look at the sofa, the place where Joanna and I have made love and tested our new friendship, which has now become my mum's new sanctuary.

Joanna suddenly grabs Sophie's arm as they both start to wrestle with each other. 'Look, it's best you tell me the truth.'

Sophie pulls away but Joanna tightens her grip as this becomes some battle of youth versus wisdom. They struggle for a while, their bodies twisting and their faces scrunched up as they try to outmanoeuvre each other into some sort of obvious defeat.

'Ladies,' I say, stepping in between them as I gently prise them off each other.

'If you must know I work for the competition,' Sophie says, as she straightens up her blouse and pulls her skirt back down to what she considers an acceptable length. 'We heard rumours that G.U.E was planning something big so I got a job as close to the top as I could, so that I could figure out what is happening. It's safe to say that no one expected this.'

'You're the spy?' I say.

'The competition!' Joanna shouts. 'Oh, she's really going to be helpful.'

I nod, this time knowing that the one person I should trust is the one who allies with wisdom and the knowledge of the past. 'She's right, so why don't you just leave and go back to where you belong,' I say, as I hope that she argues with this ridiculous idea just a little, knowing that I don't ever plan on sticking with past wisdom for long.

Sophie takes a step back and looks at me, all the usual excitement drained from her face. 'I haven't told my bosses anything, you know. I want to fix this as much as you do. Whatever Mitchell is doing is dodgy as hell and we need to expose it.'

Joanna sighs at me and looks at Sophie. 'I hate to admit it but you're going to need help if you plan to take on Mitchell. He's finally lost the plot.'

I agree, all too easily accepting that Sophie should stay with me. 'It doesn't matter what our background is or what we've done, we need to stop him and we're all clear on that.'

I suddenly feel a tap on my shoulder and I turn around to see my mum looking up at me, her head shaking. 'Ryan, I'm really not clear.'

*****

I quietly close yet another drawer that has revealed nothing. 'We could be here all night,' I say, looking over at Sophie.

'Just keep looking,' she says, as she throws more piles of paper all over the floor around her. She lets out this big sigh and then pats a few beads of sweat off her forehead. She tries to brush back her hair but it's a clumsy effort with the thick black leather glove on her hand. Yet even this single act sends a shiver down my spine; the thought of her in tight underwear and just those gloves will inevitably stay with me forever.

'You're right, we could have used some more help,' she says, sitting down in Mitchell's chair as she rummages through the drawer. She throws whatever she doesn't need over the desk and floor, making no attempt to hide that someone has been in here. 'We don't have time to be covert,' she says.

'We should have brought the others,' I say, already knowing that it would never have worked. We wouldn't have got everyone into the building this late at night and I would never have explained the genuine need to break into my ex-bosses office to my mum. So it was quickly agreed that she would stay with Joanna and that they would both watch over Elliot. She didn't fully understand what was happening, nor did she ask many questions in order to find out. She seemed happy just to have a purpose, even if it was a simple fish-n-chip supper with a sulky kid who didn't want to stay at home with the oldies.

'I give up,' she says, sitting back in the chair and stretching out her arms. 'I'm not cut out for the spying game.'

I walk over to her and find myself climbing over the piles of folders and papers. 'I think you're right, this undercover stuff isn't for you,' I say, looking back over to my side of the room that looks perfectly untouched.

She slowly pulls one of the gloves off with her teeth, teasing it off with a leather finger in her mouth. She surveys the damage around her and laughs. 'After all Mitchell has done for you I bet you would love to fuck this office over.'

I walk forward, keeping my eyes on her until I'm behind her. I start massaging her back as my hands push down between her body and the chair, my fingers gently digging into her shoulder blades. I've not dared to allow myself an erection since the operation and now I'm standing behind her, rock hard and unable to control myself any longer. All my worries that I'm going to tear something down there or that my scar is going to suddenly burst open have disappeared as I forget about where we are and the danger we're in, my mind thinking only about how long I have waited for this moment of intimacy with Sophie.

'I don't fuck things over any more,' I say. 'I'm going clean and pure.'

She swings her chair around, her eyes level with the belt on my jeans. 'I'm really not sure that I believe you,' she says, as she places just one finger on the buckle. It's the hand that still has a glove on and simply the thought of what could happen makes me gasp.

I look down to see her gaze move up to my face as that one single finger works its way along the bulge that's openly fighting for escape from my jeans, until she finds its end. 'We're not going to fuck in here, Ryan,' she says, as she undoes my belt and pulls open the first of five metal buttons.

'What are you doing?' I ask, as the second button is defeated. This single act welcomes an end to the lust that has been trapped for so many months but I don't believe anything will happen and I want something far more than she can ever offer in this place. In my heart I want Sophie, but not like this, not a cheap blow job in a moment of need. I want her forever, in my arms and in my life.

I pull her hands away from my trousers but she's not looking up at me anymore, her eyes only focused on what is in front of her. 'I can't resist any longer,' she says, as she pulls at my jeans, forcing them to spring open.

I look down to see I'm still hard, my cock conspiring against me to escape that final layer; the devil's bulge begging her to continue with what my mind has forbidden.

She stands up, her eyes level with mine. I feel her heavy breathing as she moves closer in what I hope will be our first kiss, the warm leather glove pulling at the lining of my boxers. She slips it inside as I feel it working its way down.

I close my eyes as I wait for our lips to touch, and all my determination that it wouldn't happen this way disappears as I accept what I have always wanted.

But before our lips touch I wince in pain, as I feel her hand take hold of my balls and squeeze tight. My legs push upwards, instinctively trying to move my body away from the painful grasp. 'You don't change, do you?' she says, through gritted teeth.

'Aaaahhhh!' is the only sound that comes out of my mouth, as she grips tighter and slowly pulls her hand downwards. My body moves again, but this time slower, as I hold myself on the threshold of pain, my cock still rock hard as I realise I actually want more.

She suddenly lets go and pulls her hand out, her head shaking. 'Are you bloody enjoying this?'

I laugh, my manhood poking out of my boxers and my balls feeling a welcome tingle. 'Would you be annoyed if I said that I was?'

Sophie says nothing as she turns around, focusing back on the search. 'Do you know, Ryan, that you really are one giant walking penis.'

I laugh. 'Thanks for the compliment. I'm particularly happy with it.'

Sophie turns, a finger pointing at my face as her mouth opens.

'What the bloody hell is going on in here,' Tina says, her voice coming from the doorway. 'I leave you two with one job and already Ryan has got his cock out again.'

I pull myself back together, the closing up of each button reminding me of the monster that will always control me. No matter where I go or what I do I'll never stop my one track mind from bringing me to these inevitable situations.

'You should be in therapy,' Tina says, as she walks towards us.

'I couldn't agree more,' Sophie says. 'It came at me like a caged animal.'

Tina looks Sophie up and down, her head shaking. 'And I'm quite sure you did nothing to discourage it. We all know you've wanted him since the day you arrived. You're just too miserable and self-obsessed to do anything about it.'

Sophie squares up to Tina, her head towering above her. 'Oh, I'm too miserable, am I? Well what about you? Every day is another bloody crisis and it's no wonder you can't find a decent man who will ever put up with you.'

'This is becoming a habit,' I say, as I place myself in between two women for the second time this evening. The three of us wrestle for a moment before I push them apart. 'Look, we need to get out of here at some point soon, so can we just be civil until then?'

I look at both of them as they quietly nod. 'Good,' I say, looking over at Tina and the paper she is clutching in her hands. 'What is it?'

'It's everything I need. The names of all the drugs they made me take and the medical notes for every single day of my pregnancy.' She holds the papers tight as we all realise just how important they are. She looks up at me, her eyes red and her body starting to shake. 'It's a complete log of the hell I went through at the hands of those two bastards.'

Sophie takes a few strides past me and forces her arms around Tina. She refuses at first, her body pulling away, but Sophie doesn't let go as she links her hands together and keeps a tight grip. Tina soon stops moving as the crying starts, soft and muffled at first, before becoming loud and tormented, the past finally catching up with her.

As she eventually calms down, I continue searching through the papers, looking for anything that we can use against them. I think about checking Raj's office, but it's probably empty. He's on a plane right now, jetting off to his new life, leaving us behind with Mitchell as the boss and ruler of this small little division that will do things that no one else dares ask about.

'Check the bottom right drawer,' Tina says, handing me a key.

'How come you even have this?' I ask.

'I've known this day will come for a long time, so don't you think I would be just a little bit prepared? We don't all sit around sofa-masturbating all day.'

They both gather around as I play with the lock. 'I get what has happened and I get the need to uncover it, but are we really going to find anything in here? It's a bit too obvious, don't you think?'

'No, I don't think that, Ryan,' Tina says. 'Why would Mitchell hide anything when he has a willing test subject and nothing to fear?'

I open the drawer and stand back, as Tina searches through its contents. It doesn't take long before she holds up a pile of papers and hands it over to me. 'Here's your willing volunteer and it's even someone you helped to get here.'

I search through the documents, seeing plane tickets and reservations for a hotel in Beijing. I feel anger when I see Mitchell's name and my heart sinks when I see Toyah's.

'This is my entire fault and I've driven her to this,' I say, as I let Sophie and Tina flick through the papers.

Sophie looks at me, her gaze somehow giving me comfort. 'Well, we know when and where they are going, so if we can find her then we can stop this. Can't we?'

Tina doesn't nod or agree, she just laughs as she looks at one of the sheets. 'That bloody bitch. She's staying in a much nicer hotel than I ever got.'

26

'That's right, Mitchell. They are in the building now, searching through your office. I don't know what they are both doing in there but they are clearly looking for something. I could inform night security and ask them to call the police, if you like?'

Sophie nods and then shakes her head. 'Of course, I understand. No, I won't do anything until you arrive and I will keep them distracted if they try to leave. I'll see you soon.'

She hangs up and smiles. 'This is starting to become fun.'

'Do you think he bought it?' I ask, as I put all my focus onto the house over the road.

'I think he trusts me,' Sophie says.

Tina leans forward from the back seat. 'Well, let's hope he does and let's hope he is actually in this place.'

Our car falls silent as we all stare at the house, waiting and hoping for him to come storming out. It doesn't take long before lights start going on and the front door opens. Two men step out and I soon recognise the distant bulky form of Mitchell, the tall man next to him obvious as the Quiff.

As soon as they get into their car, we all duck down into our seats. My heart is pounding as the headlights shine towards us, threatening to expose the shadows of our hidden bodies. Seconds roll by slowly as they go past and for a moment I think they have stopped, as I ready myself to start the engine and speed away from yet another fight with Mitchell. But as the car disappears into the darkness I sit up, relief swelling through me as I see the brake lights in the distance.

'Are you sure she wasn't with them?' Tina asks.

'There were definitely only two of them.'

'We can't even be sure she is in there,' Sophie says.

Tina's door opens and then she leans her head through the front window. 'There's only one way to find out so get out here and stop being a pair of wimps.'

The four of us stand at the front door as I ring the bell, knowing that I am the last person she is going to want to see. 'What if someone is with her?'

'Then it's a good job you brought some muscle,' Elliot says, smiling up at me with his arms tensed, showing me where his biceps will one day form into something that could be of help in this situation.

I jab at him in the stomach, feeling somehow playful around him, despite the mess we're in. He's the younger brother I've always wanted and I find myself hoping he feels the same.

His mum quickly separates us and rings the bell again, her finger holding onto the buzzer, showing the desperation that has set in. 'I really don't think it was a good idea to bring Elliot into the hands of the enemy,' she says.

'She has to meet him and see what will happen to her.'

'Hey, giving birth to me wasn't a bad thing,' Elliot says, as he brushes his hair away from his face to get a better look at me.

I grip his shoulders. 'I'm sorry, man, I didn't mean that. I just mean that –'

Tina holds a hand over my mouth. 'Your friend Ryan here is a bit of a plonker. Now you remember what I told you about plonkers?'

Elliot laughs and nods. 'They talk shit all day long and we shouldn't listen to them.'

'Clever kid,' Sophie says, taking her turn to ring the bell. 'I don't think she's in here.'

Tina crouches down and looks through the letterbox. 'She has to be here. There is no way that Mitchell would leave her alone now that he's got her hooked.'

I step away, walking onto the lawn. I look up at all the windows and soon see a curtain twitch. I try her phone again but it's dead.

'She's in there, isn't she?' Tina says.

I nod. 'I think so.'

'Well, we're all screwed if she calls Mitchell back,' Sophie says.

'Toyah, please,' I shout, knowing that waking up the neighbours in a street like this will attract the police like flies to shit, but it's preferable to his car speeding back around the corner. 'Please, we just want to talk.'

The curtains twitch again and this time Toyah's face appears, her head already shaking as she mouths, 'Go away.'

Tina holds down the doorbell as I see Toyah's face wince at the noise.

'Please,' I say, looking up at her, our eyes locked in a silent battle that I know I have no right to win.

Her head shakes again as she walks away from the window, the curtain calmly falling back to its previous place.

'She's not going to let us in,' I say.

Tina starts to walk back to the car, dragging poor Elliot behind her. 'Let's go for Plan B then, if we can't stop her then hopefully we'll expose this before he gets her drugged to kingdom-come *and* up the duff.'

'You can't give up on her now,' I say, determined that I will not let Toyah down ever again.

'Why not,' Tina calls out without turning around. 'Mitchell will be here any minute and I am not risking him getting near Elliot. If she doesn't want to listen then that's her own choice.'

'Just like the choice you made when people tried to convince you?'

She turns around, pulling Elliot with her. As she walks back towards me she points out a finger. 'You know nothing about the choices I had to make. You will never know what I was going through.'

'But I know that people tried to help you. I know that Jerry and Joanna tried to make you see sense and that they think they failed. But wasn't it because you were just too stubborn to listen to reason?'

She pokes at my chest with the force of a decade's built-up anger. 'Don't try to bring her into this. You have no idea of the games that woman played.'

'No, I don't, but I do know that she regrets not helping you more, and if she could do it all again then she would do things differently.' I grab her hand before she pokes me again. 'Don't make the same mistakes she did.'

'What about the mistakes I made?' she says, as her arms fall by her side and the blood drains from her face. She finally looks ready to give up, defeated by those years of guilt and confusion.

I grab Elliot and rub his head. 'You didn't make any mistakes.'

She looks at me and then at Elliot, before taking him back into her arms.

'What's this? Ryan has a soft side?' Sophie says.

I smile, just as the front door opens. 'I think our luck might be changing.'

As Toyah appears in the doorway, with her arms folded, we all turn around to face her. And this small gathering of unlikely helpers wait in silence, wondering what she will say and how long we have before her new protector returns.

'Can we come in?' I ask.

To my surprise she walks away from the door, as we all walk into the house and follow her to the living room. I close the front door, looking up and down the street for any sign that Mitchell is back. The dark spaces between the street lights give little away and as I lock the door and put on the chain I realise that we have now trapped ourselves in the enemy's stronghold.

I walk into the room and see that everyone has found a seat, as they all wait in silence for something to happen. I look at Toyah, her slender frame wrapped up in an oversized jumper, her legs covered with skin tight trousers. Even though I can't properly see her body, her face alludes to the weight she has already lost – her jawline a little too pronounced and her neck a little too thin, like it might struggle to hold up even her small head.

'Are you okay?' I ask, kneeling down next to her.

'What do you care?' she says.

'We know what's going on,' I say.

'You know nothing,' she hisses and then pulls her legs up onto the chair, her body clenched into a tight ball. It's the move she always makes when she's angry, tense or upset. I always used to get around this by gently teasing my hand through any gap I could find, caressing my way up her body. I'd tickle her sides and kiss her knee, finding that she quickly unravelled for me. That won't happen now; I don't have a way in anymore. I won't get to experience the sweet taste of her breath, or kiss her olive skin anywhere I like and whenever I choose. And most of all, it's obvious that she won't ever trust me again.

'Perhaps you have something you want to tell us,' Sophie says, leaning forward and offering Toyah a smile.

'I have nothing to say to *you*,' Toyah says. 'I want you all to leave.'

'But you just let us in,' Sophie says, her body motionless as she stares back at Toyah, clearly evaluating who she believes to be a far lesser woman.

'That was my mistake.'

'I think you're about to make a big bloody mistake,' Tina says.

'Oh, and what exactly would you know? He's told me all about you! It's just embarrassing that you have stuck around for so long.'

'You little cow,' Tina says as she moves to get out of her chair, Elliot trying to hold her back. I step in her path, ready for another battle that we don't have time for.

'So, where are you going?' Sophie says, stopping everyone from moving, as we all wait to hear.

'I'm going to build a new life and achieve great things,' Toyah announces.

'Sounds great,' Sophie says. 'So first stop China and then onto the secret laboratory in the middle of nowhere. A place where the only person you know will be Mitchell. What total and utter fun that should be.'

'It has to be a secret. The world isn't ready to know what amazing things Mitchell and his team of scientists can do. But once my beautiful baby boy is born then he will become incredibly famous. He'll literally be the closest thing to superman the world has ever seen.'

Sophie laughs and shakes her head, looking only at me. 'And you found this level of intelligence to be something of an appeal?'

Toyah starts to untangle herself, finally ready for some kind of battle. But it's Tina that steps in, putting herself between the other two women.

'He's told those lies before,' she says, as she takes a firm hold of Elliot. 'He'll tell you everything will be fine and during those first few days you will believe all that he says. It's when he tells you everything will be fine after you've puked five times that day you start to wonder if he really means it. Once the egg is inside you and his gang of silent cronies have got you on the right mixture of drugs then I promise he'll lose interest.'

Toyah suddenly stands up, a shaking arm pointing at the door, her lips quivering. 'I'd like you to leave now.'

Tina walks closer to Toyah, facing directly into her past, tears streaming down her face as she tells it things she probably doesn't want to remember, but that she would have wanted to hear. 'When you can't keep the tablets down any longer, he won't be there to hold back your hair. It will be some oriental bird who doesn't speak a word of English. Someone who is only paid to keep you alive, not keep you company or comfort you, and when the time comes that they decide to move your fat and tired body permanently onto a bed, he won't even be in the same country. They'll start pumping chemicals into you like there's no tomorrow, all in the name of science and discovery. When you're dripping in sweat, your back aching as you beg them to turn you onto your side, they will simply ignore you. They won't turn off the light and they won't let you sleep, as any of that would risk you falling into a drug-fuelled coma.'

Elliot releases himself from his mother's grip, as he tries to run out of the room. Sophie manages to grab him and pulls him close to her, as I realise that Tina hasn't missed him yet.

She keeps advancing towards Toyah, taking these small and lonely steps towards what was once her younger self. 'You'll cry, desperate for them to listen to you. It's at this point that the only thing you will care about – the only thing that will keep you going – is that little thing growing inside you. But let me tell you what real fear is. Real fear is when you realise that all these people in white coats that are poking and prodding you also only care about that baby, too. At this point you become a piece of meat that is simply giving birth and once it pops out they won't even look around to see if you're still breathing!' She suddenly realises Elliot isn't in her arms, her eyes frantically searching until she finds him with Sophie. She walks over, taking hold of him. 'Oh, baby, I'm so sorry you had to hear that.'

'So what do you have to say now?' I ask, looking at Toyah.

She shakes her head. 'What a load of absolute rubbish.'

'What?' Tina says, turning back around.

'Mitchell told me you would say all of this. He told me that if you ever found me you would say crazy things and it's all because you are jealous.'

Tina storms back towards Toyah, with only the force of everyone else holding her back and stopping her from inflicting pain at the ignorance stood in front of us. 'You rotten little bitch. When they strap you to that bed and refuse to give you any painkillers I hope you remember this moment. When you scream out and they gag your mouth you just remember my face and you recall all the horrors that are yet to come!'

Toyah doesn't move, she just looks at me with this calm expression. 'I have spoken to the consultants on Skype and they are all very friendly. I have even chatted with a lovely lady who will be my fulltime midwife and carer. It's a charming little resort with a swimming pool and botanic gardens. It is actually just the relaxing break I need.'

'I can't believe this,' Tina says, as she pulls Elliot towards the door. 'She's a thousand times more gullible than I was. Back in my day it was the same promises, just with a travel brochure and a telephone chat with some old Asian bloke. She won't believe me, so fuck her. Mitchell will be back any minute so let's get the hell out of here.'

I watch Tina and Elliot leave, as she drags him along behind her. I let them go out the front door but I stay where I am, with Sophie now by my side.

'Why exactly haven't you called Mitchell?' Sophie asks.

'I don't need to,' Toyah says, sitting back down and crossing her legs. 'He said he will be home once he has dealt with something at the office.'

'That something is us but you don't have a phone, do you?' Sophie says.

'I don't need a phone!' Toyah shouts. 'Now will the both of you please leave?'

'Screw this,' I say, as I scoop Toyah up into my arms. I feel the immediate strain on my groin, as I feel my insides coming close to tearing apart. The pain forces me to drop her on the sofa, this time a lot softer than the last incident. As she struggles I gently hold her little wrists with one hand as I place the other one over her mouth.

'This looks fun,' Sophie says.

'Find some tape, quickly. And get Tina to bring the car closer.' I look back down at Toyah, as she starts kicking at me. 'I can't carry her as far as I used to.'

27

'Are you sure this is a good idea?' Sophie asks.

I ignore her at first, in favour of my continued effort of kicking at the door in front of me. I have never tried to kick a door down before and with my recent injuries I doubt this will ever be my best effort, to which I curse that Sophie is here to witness it. I still try to kick it in the right place, with all the strength my body will allow me, but nothing happens. 'We need what is in there,' I say, once I've stopped to catch my breath.

'Oh, for God's sake,' Tina says, pushing me out of the way.

Sophie laughs as I eagerly give in and move aside.

Tina looks at Elliot. 'There's one lesson you'll need to learn in life, Son, and that's if you want something doing properly then give it to a woman.' She kicks and barges at the door, her leg and shoulder each taking a turn, all the time spurred on by her desperation to change the future. She doesn't just push at the door; she attacks it, with all the years of anger and neglect coming out as pure rage against what is in her way.

'He does have neighbours,' Sophie says, her arms folded, as she stands herself a safe distance away from the battleground.

Tina stops and turns to face Sophie. 'He *did* have neighbours. We're trying to get into the apartment of a dead man, so just you pay some respect.' She doesn't wait for a response and instead wipes the sweat from the brow and takes another run up. She hits the door like a battering ram and the one solitary lock finally gives way, letting the door swing open.

We all stand there, looking into Jerry's apartment as if we expect that he's suddenly going to make an appearance, demanding to know why we're here. I had never been to Jerry's flat when he was breathing, so the thought of now entering this place feels wrong, like I'm trespassing. I always thought I'd be the last person he would ever invite here, but some of the things I've learnt in the last few days tell me I might have been wrong about that.

Tina takes hold of Elliot, carefully pulling him away from the door. 'Honey, I want you to wait outside today, okay?'

He unknowingly stamps his feet, his gaze looking over her shoulder and into the living room. 'But I've been here so many times before.'

'Today is different and I want you to remember the good times.'

He shakes his head, seemingly not taking no for an answer. 'You never think about me and you don't care that I want to pay some respect to Jerry just as much as you.'

She puts her arms around him like she's going to suck the life out of his slim body. 'We will pay our respects together, okay? We'll go to the grave and then to Ed's diner for a slap up meal, just like Jerry used to like.'

'You think she means Ed's diner in Soho?' Sophie whispers to me.

Tina suddenly turns towards Sophie. 'Yes, in Soho and is that such a big deal?' She lets go of Elliot and walks into the apartment.

Sophie reacts only by walking forward, clearly determined to be the next one in. 'Well aren't you just learning so many things you never knew,' she says and winks at me before disappearing inside.

'If Elliot is staying outside then I'd like to wait here too,' Toyah says, as she moves towards the young boy, somehow trying to tell me that she is willing to take on the role of his guardian.

He ignores her and sits himself on the floor, a pair of oversized headphones now blocking out any more adult debate.

I gently take hold of her arm and start to pull her towards the door. 'You're coming inside, because if you don't then you will run away.'

Toyah tries to resist me, her body anchoring itself in the same spot. 'This is kidnap!'

I nod, yanking her body towards me, allowing both of my hands to take hold of her waist so that I can push her into the flat. 'It's for your own good. Just think of it as a group intervention.'

Her arms suddenly extend out, her hands gripping each side of the door frame. She lets out a small whimper, her head leaning to the side. 'Please don't make me.'

I push again but she doesn't move. 'Toyah, what's your problem? You didn't even know him and I'm pretty sure the Police will have removed his body by now.'

She turns herself around, her body now a little inside the flat as her eyes well up. 'I didn't know him, but you did... and I don't want to think about that.'

I sigh and push her forward, forcing her further into Jerry's world. Once inside she looks around and starts to gasp, her knees bending and her body about to fall. I instinctively step forward, taking hold of her into my arms. To my surprise she doesn't fight back or push me away, instead she takes hold of my forearms and steadies herself. I wait until her breathing calms and then wipe away the tears on her face, as she holds her gaze into my eyes. It's these moments when I realise what I miss. The moments when we don't talk and where actions mean more than any of the shit that normally comes out of her mouth. Our time together always worked best when it was a silent movie, the moment always ruined whenever she chose to speak.

Sophie coughs in the background, forcing me to pull away from Toyah. I realise that our intimacy has never been witnessed by anyone else; our strange world has always been behind closed doors, with the only person now catching me with Toyah being the one person I don't want it to be.

'Go sit in the corner,' I say to Toyah, to which I'm thankful she obeys without question.

I turn around to look at Sophie as she stares straight at me. We don't say anything and I cannot think of the right words that can ever convey how I truly feel. She is the only woman to ever make me wish that I had never met Toyah. I look at her and I know that every other woman on the planet has only ever been practice, ahead of the day that Sophie finally arrived in my life.

'I'll start looking around,' I say, getting myself out of her empty stare as quickly as I can.

She nods but says nothing as she takes up her position at the door, her guarding eyes moving between Elliot and Toyah.

I turn my senses to the flat, realising how strong the smell is. It's like the past has been bottled up in these four walls for such a long time and now it's nothing more than a cologne of the dead. The musky smell matches the décor and the furniture; everything so old and the absence of any modern trend so noticeable. I hope that by the time I reach Jerry's age my flat will be an eclectic collection of the eras of my life;

a mix of the decades all fused together. This place looks like time stopped at some point in the seventies – the brown sofas, the mustard wallpaper and the multi-coloured rug all refusing to move out.

I go to the one place I wanted to explore – the sofas. I sit down and look around, seeing what Jerry would have seen every day, imagining that dinner party from long ago that Joanna described. I think about that day and that moment where she realised that Jerry would never face up to who he truly was. I look at the pouffe – its colour the same as the sofa – and I wonder what it hides within. It doesn't take long before I lift the fabric lid and peer inside. At first nothing looks out of the ordinary – a couple of catalogues and some bills, all ruffled from the likely police search. I shuffle things around and see that there is something hidden under that thin layer of ordinary day-to-day stuff. I soon find some gay magazines, some of them I recognise and some a little more hard-core – young guys with their cocks on show, and that's just the front cover.

I close the lid and leave the past where it should be. I feel slightly sick, but it isn't the gross man pictures, but more the proof I had been looking for that Jerry was a silent passenger in his own life. Decades rolled by where he was that sofa-masturbator, anchored to the same spot in time, refusing to see the backdrop of an ever-growing gay community around him.

'I've got it!' Tina shouts, as she runs back into the living room.

Sophie leaves her post and comes towards us, as we huddle around yet another pile of papers. Tina starts flicking through them, showing us these random pages as if we should know what they mean and how they will help us. She speaks fast and in random sentences as she tries to get out the meaning of her discovery.

I take some of the pages off her, hoping I can slowly make sense of them. 'These look like the same papers you showed us in the office.'

'Ah ha!' she shouts, grabbing them back from me. 'Except that these are the originals. I stole them from the lab soon after I gave birth to Elliot. They had so many copies that they didn't even realise one clipboard of information went missing. Once I told Jerry what had happened he agreed to keep them safe, both of us knowing that one day I could use them.'

'So these are different to the ones they kept in the office?' Sophie asks.

Tina nods and smiles at Sophie, almost as if she has forgotten their previous dramas. 'When we compare the two of them we will see that the quantities and types of drugs are different. They doctored the originals to show that it was a medical trial, but that it wasn't as extreme as it actually was. The ratios they gave me would have made a horse feel sick and now I'll be able to prove what those bastards did to me and what they plan to do to her.'

We all look around to the corner where Toyah is sitting. I almost forgot she was with us and I'm relieved to see that she hasn't ran away, but frustrated to see that the waterworks have switched back on again. Once she realises she has the full audience the tears start streaming down her face, her body rocking in the chair as she holds her legs up.

'The reality of what they were going to do to you finally sunk in, has it?' Tina asks.

Toyah continues crying, her mouth wide open, as she shakes her head.

'Well what the bloody hell is wrong with you now?' Tina says.

Toyah lets out this howl and then falls to the floor, her limp hands brushing along the carpet as she tries to mouth what is wrong.

Sophie makes a huffing sound and looks at me. 'So, how long will this latest drama take to unfold?'

I shrug my shoulders and think of my options. I can't leave Toyah sitting on the floor as she screams the place down, but I don't really want Sophie to ever see me in the same space as this girl ever again.

'I can't believe he's dead!' Toyah shouts as she pants heavily. 'His rotting body was hideous, all wrinkled and blue. I had to see it and that picture of you lying on his chest.' She starts to lift herself back up, the long whimpers still flowing out of her mouth.

'You were in here?' I ask.

She sits up and starts to claw her way towards me, her crumpled face now full of anger and smudged makeup. 'I had no choice. He told me to do it.'

'Who told you and what did you do?' I ask, as I try to put together yet more pieces of the puzzle I didn't know existed. I look to Sophie and Tina but they are still looking at Toyah.

'You never loved me and I don't know if you loved him or not. But he loved you to the point where it killed him. I'll never know what happened between you two but I'll always know how he felt. I'll know that pain until the day I die!'

I stare back at her, thinking that this is the one thing she's ever said that makes sense. 'I'm sorry,' I say, knowing that it's nowhere near enough.

'It's time for some honesty,' Tina says, prodding my arm and pushing me forward.

I look back at Sophie, knowing that I have more to say to her than I'll ever have to say to Toyah. I want to spend this energy on the future, my hopeful future with Sophie, rather than on explaining the past that no longer holds anything for me but a little lust.

Sophie looks back at me with what I think is interest. Her arms don't fold up like they normally do and she angles herself towards me, giving me every cue that I should end what never was and end it now.

I stand close to her, almost hoping no one else will hear what I have to say, despite the obvious silence that has fallen across the room. 'Toyah, look, I never loved you. It really was just sex to me. It was really good sex but nothing else would ever have happened. I never realised that you wanted more.'

She nods her head as she continues to wipe the last two years of my quiet torment away. 'Wasn't it obvious I wanted more?'

I shake my head. 'Not to me.'

'Did Mitchell use this against you?' Tina asks. 'Did he tell you that he would take care of you better than Ryan ever could?'

Toyah silently nods.

'Did he ask you to do things in exchange for him looking after you, things that would hurt Ryan?'

Her face scrunches up again, as she lets out long puffs and fans her face with her hand. When she eventually looks up at me I see that her bony face is drained of all life; the games of two sinister men have become too much for her pretty little mind. 'At first he told me that you knew about all of this and that my baby would be our baby.' She pauses, looking at me for a response, a hopeful agreement to the plan. 'Then he said you weren't the right one, on account of you preferring Jerry to me, and so he said that the baby would come in a tube and it would belong to the Quiff.'

I shake my head, not knowing what bit to think about first. 'He said that we were going to have this super baby together?'

She slowly nods. 'When he said you would be coming to China with us I got so excited, thinking about holding our baby in my arms, with your arms wrapped around me.' She starts to shake, tears in full flow – genuine tears, born out of the future she desperately wanted that's now been brutally dragged away from her. 'I just wanted us to have a baby together.'

I shake my head, not knowing whether a baby with Toyah or my apparent sexual relations with Jerry would be the biggest nightmare.

'So that's what he promised you?' Tina says.

Toyah nods, still looking at me. 'He made it sound so perfect.'

Tina sits herself next to Toyah, her bulky frame landing so close to her younger self. 'He's bloody good at that, but let me tell you he never planned for Ryan to be there. At best it would have been his sperm in a turkey baster and at worst it would have been Mitchell's drug-riddled DNA they planted inside you. Once he got you over there he would have left you, only returning a few weeks after the birth, coming into the small room they've left you in. He'll have your baby in his arms, telling you how unbelievably healthy he is. And he'll mean that literally, because you'll see all the scars and marks on his precious little arms and then you'll know the reality of what you've done. That's when Mitchell will walk back out of that room, carrying your baby with him, not giving a shit about you.'

Toyah looks at Tina and then back to me. 'So, he wouldn't have even been there with me, even if it was to be his baby?'

'Oh, kiddo, you really are as naïve as I was,' Tina says, holding out her arms and offering Toyah a hug.

Toyah ignores her, all of her energy still focused on me. I notice that her fists are clenched as she slams one foot on the floor, the soft carpet absorbing all the sound.

I think about giving her that hug myself, to hell with what Sophie thinks. I imagine us in one big group hug, making everything seem better. But before I can move I feel the jab in my face from Toyah's fist. It isn't the force that hurts, but rather the three oversized rings that bury themselves into my flesh. I step back, wiping my face, checking for blood.

'All men are fucking bastards!' Toyah shouts and then runs out of the flat.

Neither of the other two show any effort to help me, both of them looking at each other, almost smug grins on their faces.

'Mum!' Elliot shouts, as he runs back in, nearly knocking into Toyah.

'Not now, Elliot,' Tina says.

'Well on behalf of all women I think you thoroughly deserved that,' Sophie says, only offering me that dry and emotionless expression.

'But Mum!' Elliot shouts again, as he grabs onto her arm and starts pulling at her.

'What did I just say?' Tina says. 'It's victory time for women everywhere and it might just be my turn in a minute.'

'Seriously, Mum, you gotta come here.'

'What's up, Elliot,' I say, desperate for the distraction from my fellow man.

'They're here,' he says, looking more serious than a kid his age ever should.

'Who? Mitchell?'

He gives this long and enthusiastic nod. 'It's what I've been trying to tell you.'

'Oh fuck,' Sophie says.

'You didn't hear that,' Tina says, putting her hands over Elliot's ears as she pushes him outside.

'Where's Toyah gone?' I say, as we both follow them out.

'We have to find her,' Tina says. 'She's in way over her head.'

'And we're not?' I say. 'We're not going to get out of here without a fight.'

'I'll take the evidence,' Sophie says, as we all bundle into the lift.

I look at Tina, as she puts the folded papers into her pocket.

'Oh, come on,' Sophie says. 'I've already told you I'm not with Mitchell and after everything we've done so far how much more convincing do you need?'

'A lot bloody more,' Tina says, pulling Elliot closer.

Sophie looks at me, her face still void of any emotion. 'Let's think about how this will play out. Ryan, you are going to have to take on Mitchell and Tina has Elliot. So it makes sense that I take the evidence with me and that way we distribute the assets we have.'

Tina thinks for a minute, her cautious brain working all this out. She takes out the papers and looks at us both. 'Half and half.'

'See, we're all learning about compromise today,' I say, as I look into the lobby area.

I had hoped that our path out of here would be clear, that through some bit of luck we would have managed to avoid my arch rival and whatever band of thugs he has with him. But the first thing I see is Toyah in the grasp of Mitchell, as he holds her facing towards us with his hand around her neck.

I walk out of the lift, seeing no point in running back upstairs and hiding. The others follow and stay just behind me. 'I see you're using your traditional threatening pose,' I say.

Mitchell just laughs and squeezes her neck a little tighter, Toyah's hands brushing against his thick forearms, her feet on tiptoes.

'Make this quick,' the Quiff says.

'Yes, boss,' Mitchell says and then throws Toyah behind him, forcing the Quiff to awkwardly catch her, cradling her more like a lover than a hostage.

Mitchell takes a single step forward. 'You can all go if you just give me what I want. It's that simple.'

'It's never been that simple,' Tina says.

He glares back at her and it's the first time I have ever noticed them in the same space. Despite everything that happened I realise now that her torture must never have stopped, as Mitchell insisted that she stay where he can see her, or risk losing Elliot. And now all those years of built-up tension and what he did to her are focused in this one moment, but he soon turns his attention to Elliot. 'Hey, Tiger, have I got some stuff to tell you.'

I take a step forward, every part of me feeling an overwhelming need to protect him.

Mitchell pays no attention to me, the subtle move like a game of chess to him and my new position clearly poses him no threat. 'I bet you know nothing about me and it's probably time that changed,' he says, as he keeps his eyes on Elliot.

The boy stands frozen like a statue, that husky voice and big frame towering over him.

It's Tina who chooses to move first, as she runs towards Mitchell in some fit of rage, her arms outstretched as she screams wildly. For one short moment I hope Mitchell will end up on the floor, thinking that if he gets half of what the door got then we could just about win this. But before she gets close enough I hear the smack of his hand across her face. It sends her falling to the ground, as Toyah screams from behind Mitchell.

Elliot doesn't even shout his mum's name, or go towards her, instead choosing to run towards Mitchell. I grab him and pull him behind me, launching myself towards Mitchell as Elliot lands near Sophie.

I don't hear what happens next and all I can see before me is Mitchell. Our eyes lock onto each other as I get closer, like this moment has been coming for all eternity. He takes my first punch like it's a gentle slap on the face; my best not even close to his worst. Even at full health I'm not sure that I could knock him out, and with post-op pain surging through every part of my me I know that I'm fighting a losing battle.

I hit him again but he just takes it with a smile on his face, with clenched fists still hanging by his sides, waiting for the time when he lets them lose on me. 'Come on, is that all you've got?'

I make another swipe at his face, but this time he takes a step back and then pushes his right fist into my face. The force shoves me to the floor, my vision blurred as I wait for that killer kick to the stomach. When it doesn't happen I hold my hands to my nose and they come away moist, telling me that Mitchell has made his first permanent physical scar that will join the many emotional ones for years to come.

When I hear Police sirens in the distance it gives me the courage to stand up, as I think about how we can stall things long enough for them to arrive. My mind starts to play out the story we have to tell and the limited evidence we have to prove it, but as I look towards our attackers I realise all of these thoughts might be wasted.

'They'll be with us,' the Quiff says.

Mitchell laughs. 'That's means they are coming for you, Ryan. By the time they add kidnap to the rest of your charges then I imagine you'll be going away for a long time.'

I ignore him and look back to Sophie, wondering what she thinks of me as I stand here looking helpless and finally beaten. Something tells me she doesn't feel the same as she smiles back at me and then points her head towards the Quiff.

I turn back but don't see what she is thinking. All I can see is Tina getting herself back up and Mitchell towering above her, enjoying every moment of this obvious victory. He smiles and then pushes her back down, the force of his hands making her body roll along the floor. She hisses and jabs at him but he just moves away.

'You lot really are pathetic. So why don't you do us all a favour and hand over whatever documents that sad twat was hiding upstairs. And I want the boy, too.'

Tina screams, forcing herself to stand up. 'You'll never get him!'

Mitchell grabs her outstretched arm, taking her clenched fist into his thick hand. 'Relax, you bitch. You will be coming with him and you'll finally learn how to behave.'

Sophie coughs from behind me, forcing me to leave the confrontation to see what is wrong. When I look back I see her eyebrows raised and her head still pointing to the Quiff. I turn back to see that Toyah is giving me this frantic stare, her gaze darting down to the floor. My head shakes, my mind struggling to understand if they are trying to tell me something or just pointing out the distress we're already obviously in.

'Oh, for fuck's sake, Ryan,' Sophie says. 'Just be ready to punch that sad excuse for a man.'

Her words are enough to distract Mitchell from his exchange with Tina and enough to make the Quiff focus his energy onto me. I look between them, trying to figure out who will attack me first and who I'm likely to win against.

The decision is made for me as Toyah lets out a scream and then buries one of her high heels into the Quiff's foot and then bites his hand. He yells out in pain and let's go of her as I see her yank her heel out of his shoe and move away.

I take my chance, putting all my power into a swing that knocks him to the floor, blood splattering over the white wall beside him. But as the Quiff struggles, so do I as the pain throughout my body becomes too much to bear.

I turn around, ready to face Mitchell, knowing that I won't win, but hoping it will be enough of a distraction for the others to escape. As Mitchell approaches he raises a hand, readying himself for one solid blow to my temple. His arm moves but it never meets my face, as he turns to see what Sophie is doing.

I turn around to see Sophie releasing the entire contents of a fire extinguisher at him, the attack aimed solely at him, his body now covered in white foam. She's screaming as she fires everything she's got at him, her dark eyes wild in the heat of battle. It's enough to make Mitchell pull himself away from the fight as he rubs his eyes and it's enough for my lust for this woman to go up another level, totally beyond anything I knew existed in my previously small world.

'Run!' I shout, as I realise I need to focus on the moment and on our survival.

Everyone except Sophie makes their way to the exit and only when the entire contents have been released does she stop, carefully placing the extinguisher onto the floor, a satisfied grin spread across her face. 'Now, Mitchell, do you see that I'm not the quiet little princess you thought you'd hired?'

I grab her and move us both towards the door, seeing the Quiff still curled up in pain. As we make our way outside I can already hear Mitchell getting himself up, as he shouts and swears at his injured partner. I look into the distance and see a Police car racing around the corner, only a short road separating us from defeat against such overwhelming odds.

'They can't be against us,' Sophie says.

I look back to the two men inside, the seconds counting down until their recovery and then I look over to Tina, Toyah and Elliot, who have moved themselves to the other side of the road.

'We need to split up,' Tina shouts, as she pulls the other two towards an underpass. 'If these guys are on the payroll then we can't let them catch all of us.'

I suddenly feel Sophie pulling me in another direction. 'Come on, we need to run.'

'Get to Joanna's!' I shout, agreeing that we have no other choice. I turn to Sophie, allowing myself a brief second to look into her eyes, to see such determination, before we start to put some distance between us and the others.

We stagger along the road before we eventually turn a corner. I make one final look back to see the others are already in the custody of the police as Mitchell leaps out of the building and the coppers pay him no attention, telling me for certain that they're not here to help us. I feel desperation as I see the others, realising that we only had a second to make our decision and splitting up could be the only thing that saves us. The thought makes me take hold of Sophie, my only instinct now to protect her and get us to safety.

We turn the corner and start to run up a long road with flats and houses on either side of us, but there's no one around to offer any help. It's too early and we're too slow, as I beg Sophie to go faster and my own body to not let me down.

Mitchell turns that same corner and charges forward, the gap between us closing by the second. I already know that we can't outrun him and he won't give up until he has found out what we know, with the pain he knows he can cause me in the process fuelling him forward.

The thought of this and what he will do to Sophie, makes me start banging on doors. Sophie follows my lead, pressing every available buzzer. But even as I shout out I know that it's all too late. As my mind starts to accept my fate I take hold of Sophie and pull her into my body. It feels like she is where she should always have been, right beside me and always with me.

Only when Mitchell comes within striking distance do I push her away, forcing her to get behind me. She doesn't move easily, her courage refusing to leave us, as we settle for her staying by my side.

Mitchell grins and wipes away some of the foam from his suit. 'I'll get you for that, you little bitch.'

'Just you come and try it,' she says, as she throws a stone at him.

He bats it away with his forearm and then advances forward, the sheer size of him casting a dark shadow over both of us. Sophie suddenly lunges forward, her high heels as weapons, but he grabs it from her and slaps her across the face. She goes down quickly, this big grin spread across his face as he looks down at her. It offers me the only distraction I'm likely to get and so I hit him again but it's a clumsy attack that scrapes across his shoulder.

The wealth of missed signs and lost opportunities start to flash before me as Mitchell carries me into the alleyway, an Iron Gate falling open as he uses my body as a battering ram. By the time I hear the Quiff's voice I know that it's all over. I hear Sophie struggle as he likely takes hold of her. 'They'll ignore this for another few minutes, so make it quick.'

'That's all the time I'll need,' Mitchell says, before landing his fist into my head. The force of the punch sends me to the floor and as I start to fall out of consciousness I can only think about how I've let everyone down. My life went on hold for too long and now I've failed. I don't really feel the next punch as all I think about is the welcome rest as I lie my tired head down on the concrete floor.

28

'Wakey, wakey,' he says and then gives me a slap to the face. 'We really don't have long.'

I shake my head as my vision starts to come back, showing Mitchell in front of me. He stands me up, my body still limp, as I catch the foul stench of his sweat mixed with the various odours of today's fight.

It's the scent of effort and pain; a forever reminder of always being too late.

'It's such a shame it came to this, because you could have been my poodle for so much longer.' He takes a step back, allowing us to see each other properly. 'But I've got to hand it to you for making it further than most of the others ever did.'

I can only listen as I try to regain my balance, my mind running on empty and offering me no options, my spirit all but gone. He bashes our heads together and I hear Sophie's scream from somewhere nearby, followed by several graphic threats. He ignores her and takes hold of my head with both his hands, forcing me to look at him. 'You killed Jerry.'

'No,' I say, unable to shake my shattered head.

'Oh, you did. I made you, boy, so if I say you killed Jerry then that's what you did.'

'My only mistake was letting you bully me into doing the wrong thing.'

He jabs his fist at my wound and I scream in pain. I hold onto him – my tormentor bracing me, my weak body never able to get away from him. He lifts me back up to be level with his head, his eyes full of energy. 'I don't mean that you fired him, which eventually drove that sad fucker to his death. I don't even mean that your sick and twisted love triangle eventually drove him over the edge. I mean that in the light of all the overwhelming evidence against you it will be entirely obvious that you murdered Jerry.'

'No,' I say, as I force my head to shake, even with my head still clamped between his vice-like hands.

He smiles. 'But you were there when it happened and you know that the Police have taken DNA samples from you. So imagine what will happen when the test shows the hair found on his body is in fact yours.'

'No, it isn't, because the first time I've been to Jerry's place is today.'

He punches me in the stomach, forcing my abs to tense, which only serves to remind me of the deeper wound just below them. 'You'll have to trust me when I tell you that a little friend of yours dropped off some of your hairs long before his neighbours discovered his rotting corpse. The cops will pull together all the evidence and push for murder, which is just so fucking beautiful.'

'Toyah will tell them the truth,' I whisper, barely able to breath.

He shakes his head. 'Toyah will behave herself and shall I tell you why? Because she's so fucking easy to read and manipulate. If I find out she's pissed at me for what I've done, then I'll tell her to co-operate and in return I'll tell them the truth about you. But if she is pissed at you, then I'll make her see that you're about to get what's coming to you.'

'What if she's pissed at both of us?'

'What?' he asks, his head tilting as he tries to figure things out.

With his mind distracted I know that this is my only chance as I push my thumbs into his eye sockets. He cries out in pain, his hands reaching for his face as mine move to his stomach. As I fall to the floor I punch him in the balls, forcing his hands to split themselves between two injuries. I don't kneel down for long as I force myself to stand tall, pushing through this eternal barrier of our mutual hatred.

He quickly follows me back up like an angry bear, wounded but not defeated. His arms outstretch as he prepares to wrap me in another killer grip. I say no more – I will not cower or run and I will not let this man win any more battles. As his arms move in I wrap mine around his neck and as I pull his head down it meets with my raised knee. Blood pours out of his nose as his body falls limp, forcing him to sit on the ground. He stays there for a second, trying to figure things out, before he eventually falls backwards.

Pain swells out of my wound as I know something inside me has torn, but I somehow stay standing.

'Oh, for fuck's sake,' the Quiff says, as he starts to move towards me. Sophie grabs at his arm but he finally finds the strength to be half the bully Mitchell is and pushes her against the wall.

I move towards him but stumble, having no fight left to offer. I see him pick up a brick from beside me, as Sophie screams. She punches at his body but his resolve is absolute – he takes one look at Mitchell and then back to me, his raised arm about to deliver my final blow.

'Run, Sophie,' I say, but I'm not sure how loud it is. She seems to ignore me as another figure appears from the shadows. I assume it's the fake cops and I don't know if they are here to help or to cover things up, and without the energy to fight my mind resolves itself to letting the next few seconds unfold. I've done all I can, I tell myself; it's never quite been enough.

As the shadow gets closer I realise my mind is playing tricks, my blurred vision presenting me a mirage, as I think for one minute that it's Ken running towards us. And when my ears hear his voice from behind the Quiff I feel certain that I'm either unconscious or already dead.

Only when the Quiff turns, distracted by whoever has now arrived, do I start to believe that it is my closest friend, somehow here in my greatest moment of need. And when I see the Quiff's head bow down and his body fall to the side, landing next to me, do I realise that it really is Ken who has just done a few karate moves in some dodgy alleyway in the middle of London.

'I'll be right with you!' he shouts, as he kicks the Quiff again in the stomach.

Sophie starts to help me up as I watch Ken go over to Mitchell, who is starting to pick himself back up as he surveys his blood stained shirt. The hulk on the floor tries to sweep Ken's legs from under him but the fresh arrival to the fight has too much energy, as he dodges those hairy hands and lands his right foot into Mitchells groin. 'And that one's for free,' Ken says and then runs over to me.

His dark eyes and tanned face are soon all that I can see, as he offers me this smile followed by a frown. 'Shit, man, you look totally fucking awful!'

'I've been better,' I say, as they both take hold of my shoulders and pull me along until we reach the street. Ken helps me into the passenger seat of his car as I look around to see a small group of onlookers have gathered.

'Where the hell have you been?' I ask, as he leaps into the driver's seat and Sophie gets into the back. I just manage to get the seatbelt on as he starts the engine, his frantic eyes looking around at every angle.

'Don't ask,' he says as he hits the accelerator and we speed off. After turning a couple of corners he takes his eyes off the road and focuses on me, as he looks me up and down. 'Shit! Your cock's bleeding!'

I look down to see blood all over my jeans. I remember that some of it is Mitchell's but the stain around my crotch still grows by the second. My breathing starts to speed up, as I see Sophie's hands reach around the seat as she holds a tissue to where she thinks my wound is. I soon realise that it hurts like hell down there, as the lack of adrenaline from the fight makes me realise that the wound might be gushing, or at least free flowing.

'We've got to stop the bleeding,' Sophie says, as she tries to unbuckle my jeans.

I look down, unable to find the energy to help. 'Your hands are finally around my cock,' I say, my words slurred. I start to fade from consciousness again as I hear sirens and I think that it might be an ambulance, or that we're near a hospital.

'I got it, Ryan,' Ken says. 'You need to know that I got it.'

'You got what?' I ask, as I open my eyes and try to look at him, but my head won't move.

'Oh, shit!' Sophie shouts. 'That's the same car as earlier.'

Ken seems to ignore her as he holds up a memory stick. 'This is all the evidence we need of the illegal drug trials they've been covering up. When the Police see this then it won't just be Mitchell and the Quiff who are going down. This thing is fucking huge!'

I nod and try to reach out for the memory stick but my hand doesn't move that far. 'They'll take it from us,' I mutter, barely loud enough for me to hear.

'We need to get away from these guys,' Sophie says. 'We need to go now.'

'Why these guys?' Ken says, as the car accelerates.

I manage to open my eyes just as I feel a car ram into us. Sophie screams out as I sense her voice now coming from the other side of the backseat.

Ken shouts as I see him wrestling with the steering wheel, both of his hands trying to keep control. 'This cannot be happening!'

I feel the force of them ramming us again, this time bringing our car to a stop. I hear shouting between the other two; the desperate cries of the woman in the back and the angry shouting of my best friend at foes he never knew existed.

And as I hear the shattering of glass and the shouting of many men, I suddenly feel cold and my hands start to tingle. It's a strange feeling when you think the end is coming and I open my eyes for what feels like will be my last time, only to see bright lights with a smattering of blue forcing their way into my world. I close my eyes again, giving in to the welcome darkness, as I picture my dad and the bright lights of that approaching train.

As the shouting fades away I picture only my dad, his strength fading as he gives up against the overwhelming odds that hit him in his final few seconds. That one night brought an end to decades of deals and years of fighting so that he could feed his family. But that is all gone now; there will be no more queues and no more failures.

'I'm coming, Dad,' I say, as I hear the window next to me shatter. I feel glass land on my arms but it doesn't matter now. 'I failed you, Dad, and I failed Mum too. I wasn't strong enough to make a difference.'

I feel something pulling at me, someone leaning over me to get to my seatbelt. I open my eyes again to see the blinding light, my hand rising instinctively to block it out. And then I see him, I see my dad's face in front of me, that calm smile telling me that we might just make it. He takes a second to look at me, as if he is studying his lost son, acknowledging what I have become, before he gets back to work on my seatbelt. I hear the horn of the train, barely seconds away, but it doesn't scare him this time.

'I just wanted you to be proud of me. I wish I'd told you that more.'

Dad just smiles back at me as he finally releases the seatbelt, and as he takes me into his arms and pulls me from the car I know that we'll be okay. I can feel him put me on the floor, my head in his lap as I decide that it's time to finally let myself go. There will be no more queues and no more stops, but that's okay; as I drift away I know all that pointless waiting is finally over.

29

I can hear what I think is the constant beep of a machine. I lie still, calmly listening to its rhythm, freely trusting myself to the routine of that one simple sound every few seconds. It feels comforting, as if I could stay here for as long as I like, all those burdens lifted from my mind as I know exactly what comes next.

Only when I feel a hand grip mine again, as it gently squeezes me, teasing the life to come back to my body, do I decide it's time to open my eyes. I'm ready now, ready to see him. He came in my hour of need and I have so much to say – so much to thank him for. He gave me life, he taught me how to live and he came in my darkest moment.

I feel the anticipation rush through me, settling on my eyes as I try to open them. They don't do anything at first and I start to panic. I think that maybe they're taped up and perhaps I'm dead, the machine belonging to some other lucky person. I wonder if maybe I did lose the fight and that's how I saw him; the only possible answer for how I will ever see my dad again. I start to think that I'm okay with that and I try harder, willing my eyelids to move, to prove to me and whoever is on the other side that I am not in a coma or brain-dead.

I finally see the light as I blink a few times in celebration. I can see only white as I try to focus on something, to find my dad, my friends or maybe a nurse. I can hear myself shouting, moaning maybe. That familiar feeling of panic settles in as I try to figure out what is going on. Only when I see my mum looking down at me do I finally accept that I am still alive and finally safe. I curse myself for thinking about my lost Dad, well before I smile at my found Mum.

She smiles back at me, as her grip tightens. 'Joanna, look, he's finally awake.'

I hear rustling around and what sounds like something dropping on the floor, before Joanna appears before my eyes. 'Oh, darling, you're alive! We've been so worried.'

They look at each other, their satisfied smiles telling me I'm clearly not dead.

'I thought I saw Dad,' I mutter and then I try to get up. I feel pain everywhere as two pairs of hands push me back down. 'Where am I?' I ask.

Mum gives me this look and I worry that she agrees with me, that she still sees him every day in whatever her version of reality is. I start to think I'm one step closer to her twisted world, but I'm not sure it's a bad thing anymore.

'You're in hospital, of course,' she says, gripping both of my hands, resting our embrace on my chest. 'You lost a lot of blood but you're going to be okay, now that they've patched you up.'

'Oh, yes, you're nearly as good as new now, darling,' Joanna says, as they both nod at each other. She looks at my mum and I can tell that they're both satisfied I'm in working order.

I look around the white and sterile room and soon see what my eyes are hunting for – that small container fitted to the wall, with its 'Global United Eradication' logo – it tells me everything I need to know. I try to shake my mum off me, to get both of these women away so I can figure out what state I'm in. They both look like they're ready to give me a good fuss, to ask me a hundred questions. 'What about Sophie and Ken, and the others?' I ask, beating them to it.

'Everyone is fine,' Joanna says, smiling down at me as she surveys my body, surely knowing that nothing will have changed between my sleeping and waking up.

'What happened?' I ask, as I look around the room, desperate for more clues, desperate for the others to come in. I feel more frantic now, knowing he isn't here and already accepting that I'm back in my numb life. I start to move and I feel a hand on my chest, trying to calm me down, but I'm not even sure which one of them it is.

'It looks like you passed out just as things got interesting,' Joanna says.

'They rammed your car,' Mum says. 'Those bloody police were working for those bastards,' she says and then looks at Joanna, her face full of apology.

'They were bastards, darling,' Joanna says, as they smile at each other.

'Then what happened?' I ask. 'I need to know a little more than that.'

They both look at each other but don't say anything. It's like they're talking in a silent code; the unspoken language of the caring. My mum finally nods at me, seeming to know that I still want to know more. 'Well, as they attacked your car more Police showed up.'

'Jesus, how many were against us?' I ask, just as I hear a door open.

I don't get an answer as I soon see Ken looking down at me. 'Hey Bruv, you're alive!' he says and tries to grab my limp arm to give it a shake. He lets it drop back onto the bed as he frowns at my lack of energy. It forces him to look around the room as he starts muttering under his breath.

'We were just telling him what happened,' Mum says, her face full of energy with the biggest smile I have seen in a long time. I squeeze her hand and she looks down at me. All it took was for me to reach death's door and she's finally found her way back to me.

'So, where are you up to?' Ken asks.

'Windows getting smashed,' I say. 'I vaguely remember that.'

'Oh, yeah, man. Now that was completely mental!' His hands are suddenly everywhere as he tries to explain it all, my tired mind struggling to follow. 'So, anyway, as they're bashing at the windows, three more cop cars appear. By this time they've dragged me out of the car and I'm doing my best to fight them off. I'll tell you one thing for nothing – that Sophie is one tough bitch,' he says, as he looks around the room like she might be hiding somewhere. 'She took on two of them and for a second I thought she was gonna win, but that left me with the other five to deal with – '

Joanna suddenly leans in, her hand covering his mouth as she looks around at all of us in open apology for Ken's theatrics. 'I think you're somewhat exaggerating on the numbers but do continue.'

Ken shakes his head, the story clear in his mind. 'Well, anyway, I had a lot of bad guys to whoop-ass over, that's all I remember. And I had to leave you, but that was cool because we thought you were dead, anyway.'

I nod, as Ken gets disapproving stares from my two carers. 'So what happened then?'

Ken's eyes light up, as his hands move even faster. 'So, I've done some kung foo moves on a couple of the pigs, but by this point they've got their pepper spray and other shit lined up to do me some serious damage. So, anyway, I'm on like a major coke comedown, so I put my hands up whilst I wait for the right moment. There's, like, a monumental amount of shouting coming my way and I think they're all queued up to bust my ass, but then I realise that the coppers are shouting at each other.'

My mum raises her hand. 'What Ken is trying to say is that the nice police turned up.'

'Yeah, man, and the new pigs start shouting 'Special Branch' and shit like that.' He suddenly pulls Joanna closer to him. 'And that's when I see this lovely lady getting out of one of the squad cars.'

Joanna laughs. 'Well I did say that my ex-husband was a Police Officer and he owed me a favour ever since I gave him the villa *and* the dogs. It was payback time, darling.'

'So, anyway, they totally kicked ass,' Ken says, as he makes these punching motions at the nearest wall. 'We can't forget that your mum was there too.' He pulls her towards me, as if it's the first time we've met.

'You were there too?' I ask, realising that what I remember and what happened are clearly very different.

'Well we couldn't just sit around whilst you boys had all the fun,' my mum says, with a big smile. But after a few seconds she pauses, her thoughts catching up with her, as she stares into the corner of the room and tears start running down her face. 'I've not been in a Police car since –'

I lean up as far as I can and take hold of her hand, squeezing it tight. 'Say it, Mum. Please.'

She nods, like she finally knows what has to be done. 'I've not been in a Police car since your dad died,' she says and hugs me, holding me tight. These bold tears don't stop for a while as they bravely usher us into a time where she finally accepts what has happened. I will miss my dad forever but these still feel like tears of joy to me, tears that finally wash away the denial in her mind and the doubt in mine. It was the doubt of whether I could get through to her, but when my mum finally pulls away I see a new woman in front of me. Joanna rubs her shoulder and I feel that for once things might be moving in the right way.

'What happened to everyone else?' I ask.

Ken's mouth immediately opens, long before I think he's figured out what he is going to say. 'Well, Tina and Elliot are totally fine. They got held for a few days but then they got released. Elliot needs to go for some more tests but there's not gonna be any secret government plans to clone him, or any shit like that. They've even agreed to help them both to live normal lives.' He suddenly grunts. 'As normal as Tina will ever be.'

'What about Toyah?' I ask, putting everyone in order, still saving the best until last.

They all stare at each other, none of them seeming to find the right words. It's Ken who decides to speak again. 'I got this,' he says, his face nodding to the others before he looks down at me. 'Well, as you can imagine, she was pretty pissed at the whole thing. She's not having a baby, she isn't getting a free holiday to China, and she doesn't get to be with her hero. That's you, for some freaky reason that I will never understand. So she's decided to leave us and move back in with her parents, which I think is a damn shame to deprive the office of such sweet ass, to which I'm entirely blaming you.'

'She doesn't need to leave,' I say.

They all stare back at me, but after a long pause I don't think that they've heard me. I know that we will never be able to work together or be near each other, but I never intend to go back to that office or to another career. I only have to look at Joanna to know that the pursuit of that climb up the ladder demands too many sacrifices. And one glimpse at my mum leaves me sure that it's the people who matter, not your job title or bonus. Some people can be like Raj, seemingly able to keep that delicate balance between growing their family and nurturing that next promotion. But if there is one thing I've learnt is that you miss too many things; you don't see those silent opportunities when you're stuck on one path.

I look at Ken. 'If you see Toyah then tell her that she doesn't have to worry about ever seeing me at work again.'

He nods but I don't think he's planning on any noble quest to track her down just yet, not even for that ass.

I take a deep breath. 'And what about Sophie?'

'Oh, I'm still here,' she says, her voice coming from behind the small collection of people that still surround my bed.

I try to peer around them, desperate to see if what I'm hearing will hold true. They start to move, quietly clearing a path to the one thing I need more than anything. I try to lean my head up, desperate to see more than just the ceiling. I suddenly feel the bed moving, the upper-half of my body lifting up, as I see Ken's hand on the controls. The view soon gets better as I finally see her, still sitting on a chair, her legs crossed and a magazine in her hand.

'You've finally remembered me,' she says, slowing getting out of her seat and walking towards me. 'It's nice to see I made it onto the shortlist, even if I was last.'

I don't speak, not sure what to say that could ever have the impact to truly impress her, or the humility to keep her. 'Perhaps we could have a minute?' I say, looking at the others.

Ken quickly holds out his arms. 'Ladies, may I escort you to the coffee machine?'

The ladies both nod as mum taps my shoulder and kisses my forehead before grabbing Ken's arm, her face still holding that smile. 'I'm so relieved you're back.'

'It's me who's happy to have you back.'

She nods and follows Ken's lead, looking to Joanna to join them.

She doesn't move at first, holding a watchful gaze over Sophie. She walks towards her before looking back to me. 'Don't let this girl fool you. She's not as tough as she looks. Her young eyes might still respond to a little bit of makeup and that tight black suit might carry off the creases well, but believe me when I tell you that she has been a near-permanent fixture in this room.' She pulls Sophie close, the hug suddenly welcome between them both, before she stands back and looks her in the eyes. 'He's all yours, Sophie, and may you rule him well.'

Joanna doesn't wait for a response, as she takes Ken's other arm and allows herself to be escorted out of the room.

'What was that all about, Joanna?' Mum asks.

'Oh, darling, please don't worry yourself. I promise it was all just business.'

Sophie keeps herself occupied as she waits for the door to close, firstly pulling her skirt back down and then poking various parts of her face with one solitary finger. She looks at it, checking for smudging or eyelashes, or whatever women actually do.

As soon as the door closes her face is next to mine, her breathing heavy as her mouth rests near mine. I instinctively close my mouth, the fear of bed breath being yet another nail in our sinking coffin.

'Right, Mister, this Toyah thing. I want the truth and I want it now.'

I open my mouth to answer but she places a finger over it. 'I don't want any of your bullshit. You need to give me the honest yet concise version of whatever the hell you two are.' She holds the finger in place, her probing eyes still examining me. 'And if you give me any shit then I'm out of here.'

She pulls herself away and I gasp for air, filling my lungs as my head fills with the long summer months of sex with Toyah on the balcony, of the dark winters we shared in the hot bathtub and that one regrettable weekend break where she sucked me off whilst we cruised down the A13. That was three speeding points I never managed to properly explain.

The truth is that I'm lost for words and unable to put the spectrum of feelings I have towards Sophie into one small and insubstantial sentence. I don't think she sees this, favouring all those misplaced sightings of Toyah and me over the unspoken love that I felt for her from the moment I saw her. She keeps her eyes on me for another second, probably offering me that one last chance to save us, but when I don't speak she picks up her handbag and makes her way to the door. I watch as the woman I'd do anything to protect and give up every other woman on the planet for, takes one final look at me. 'Goodbye, Ryan.'

She moves quickly and I soon see her shadow on the other side of the window, the door now between us. My mind races, desperate for the one thing that will stop her leaving – those precious words that will prove to her what I truly think and feel.

'Wait!' I shout, as I struggle to get out of the bed. My body still aches, my left hand attached to a drip. I try to pull at it but the pain surges through my hand, leaving me clueless and scared. I follow the trail of the tube, desperate to figure out what they've got me hooked up to.

'Ryan,' she says, standing back in the doorway. 'Will you stop fucking about with the machinery and tell me what you are thinking.'

'You're back,' I say and smile, as I rest my head on the pillow.

She walks back towards me, the sound of those heels clicking on the floor. 'This had better be good.'

I take a deep breath and hope for the best, telling myself that it really does take a woman to know a woman. 'I promise that we'll never sleep together.'

She coughs and then laughs. 'And you really think you're capable of promising that to anything with a pulse that pays you any attention.'

I nod and keep my eyes on her. 'I promise that we will never sleep together in any way, plutonic or sexual, unless you want it to happen. What's more, I promise that I'll never sleep with another woman, dead or alive, until you tell me that it's okay.'

'Oh, really?' she says, her eyebrows rising. 'What about men?'

I laugh. 'If it helps then I promise that too, although I really don't see the need.'

She suddenly grabs my crotch, her face level with mine as she waits for any sign of movement. 'Well the jury's still out on that one.'

'I'm in a hospital bed and I'm still drugged up,' I say, holding up my left arm.

She takes a step back, reaching for something from her handbag. I watch in anticipation, knowing that I will never tire of this woman and the contents of her imagination. She pulls out her black gloves and slowly runs them down my chest before putting them on, pulling them tight with her teeth. 'You won't be able to use that excuse forever.'

I watch, my eyes mesmerised by this one simple ritual, my overworked mind desperate to keep up. But then she starts walking to the door, her handbag draped over her arms.

'Where are you going now?'

She opens the door and turns back, surveying my surroundings. 'Well if you think we're going to sleep together in some smelly hospital bed you have another thing coming. I expect to be wined, dined and suitably impressed with the lengths you'll go to prove your promise to me. And another thing, if you plan to kiss me at some point the least you could do is brush your teeth.'

She starts to close the door, as I lie in shock, wondering if I will ever be able to keep a woman like this, already knowing in my heart that I'll never give up trying.

The door re-opens, her face peering around it. 'Oh, and Ryan, I hate to bring this up but you're, well, looking a little out of shape.' She draws an imaginary line around her stomach area with her finger and then points at my body. 'I expect them to be little tight packets of muscle,' she says, scrunching her hands up. 'Gym-fit really is the minimum standard these days.'

'Anything else?' I ask.

She smiles, her face calmly nodding. 'For once and forever, just be yourself.'

'I'm going to try.'

'I have a feeling you will,' she says and then falls quiet. She watches me and I watch her, as I try to figure out what's ticking behind those eyes. She finally snaps out of it and grabs the door handle again. 'Now cover yourself up, you dirty boy. Your mother is still outside.'

She closes the door as I do what I'm told. I brush my hands through my hair and then run them down my chin, realising how much I need a shave. I start to breath into my cupped hand when I realise someone else has come into the room.

'Should I leave you two alone for a minute,' Ken says, standing by my bed.

I look at him. 'You've left me once already, don't forget.'

He starts playing an imaginary and oversized violin, as he dances around the room. 'I didn't have a choice, someone had to save the day and it sure wasn't gonna be you.'

I sit and watch him play, waiting for the imminent moment where he will tire himself out. It doesn't take long before he's standing at the foot of my bed, looking over at me. 'All right, quit it with those puppy eyes.' He runs around the bed and grabs my cheeks. 'I promise that I'll never leave you again, not even for the biggest joint in all of Southeast Asia.'

I push him away. 'Don't make promises you can't keep.'

'So all's well that ends well,' he says.

'I'm not so sure about that, Ken. Things could have gone better.'

His head's already shaking. 'No way, man. We might have lost a bit of merchandise, on account of your stupidity, but the company agreed to forget about the money we made from the rest of it because of the minor shit-storm that we've exposed. The board made a unanimous vote of no confidence in the Quiff and then proceeded to throw suitcases of cash in all directions to cover things up.'

'How the hell are they going to cover up what they did?'

He laughs and pats my head. 'You've really missed out in the last few days. Firstly, they left the Quiff and Mitchell to answer the criminal proceedings against them, absolving all corporate responsibility for anything that happened to Tina during what they are calling a phantom pregnancy.'

'She won't agree to that.'

'Well, the bag of money that landed on her doorstep seems to have turned her around to the idea. The bad guys still get into a heap of trouble but she gets a quiet life with Elliot. I think she'll buy that and besides, Jerry has left her everything in his will so I think she won't he having any more crises for a while.'

'Lucky her,' I say. 'So all we get is a pardon and the cash we already spent on the end game.'

He stays quiet for a minute and then looks at me. 'Oh, poor Ryan, he thinks he deserves more?'

'Fuck yes, I think I deserve more. Mitchell tried to frame me for the murder of Jerry, but that wasn't until he'd mentally and physically tortured me for months. He made everyone's life a living hell and then, when you think he couldn't become any more sadistic, he pursues me around London in an attempt to rip my head off.'

Ken just nods. 'You think that qualifies you for a pay out?'

I nod back, waiting for the reaction from Ken that doesn't come. I slump back in my bed, knowing that gaining Sophie was the best thing that could come from this. I start to think that a big pile of cash would make it more likely that I'll keep her, but then I remind myself that this is the old me talking.

I look back over to Ken, at least wondering if they flew him first class, but he looks ready to explode. He suddenly jumps up, as he lets out a scream. 'Let me tell you, the suitcases they deposited for me and you are so huge that you'll never have to sell another doggie fucking deodorant as long as you live!'

I laugh and try to shout back but my ribs hurt too much. Instead I just watch Ken as he dances around for both of us. And when he calms down I pull him back to the bed, needing to know one more thing. 'So what happened to the bad guys?'

Ken smiles at me. 'I've been waiting for you to ask and this might possibly be the best bit of the whole thing. So, after I'd done my moves on the Quiff and bundled you into a car, entering into a high speed pursuit with the police, it turns out that he then tried to escape. But the Police he'd bribed earlier obviously decided that their colleagues turning up, armed to the teeth and shouting loads of official shit at them, proved a bit too rich so they acted dumb and claimed they were working on a tip off.'

'And it worked?'

'Ken shrugs his shoulders. 'Details, who knows that shit. All that matters is he got caught after he went to a walk-in clinic claiming he dropped a hammer through his foot.'

'You did good, Toyah,' I say and smile.

'Anyway, man, I better go and let you get some rest,' Ken says, heading for the door.

'Wait, wait, wait… aren't you missing someone?'

He shrugs his shoulders. 'Don't think so.'

'What about Mitchell?'

'Mitchell?' he says and smiles. 'Well, that's a whole other story.'

30
ALL CHANGE PLEASE

The weirdest thing happened today. I know that's what everyone says when they want to tell you a story, but I promise that this one's for real. And I've got to say I wasn't expecting any drama, let alone this.

I was on my usual train, minding my own business. The first thing that didn't stack up was the fact that someone else got on my carriage. I've got so used to having the place to myself that when the doors opened I thought I'd fallen asleep and I was at the next station already.

We were actually still at Liverpool Street and someone else was coming into the carriage... into my little space. There are never that many people travelling towards Harlow at this time of the morning and none of them ever make it as far as the front carriage. But sure enough, this bloke got on. He didn't even bother to look around, because if he did he would have walked down to the other end that was empty, leaving me alone with my newspaper and my thoughts of the day ahead.

He just heads straight for the nearest set of four seats, the ones directly opposite mine. He's in this pin-stripe suit that I know looked good a few decades ago, but now it's all stained and shabby; it looks as worn-out as he does. It's obvious that they have both been through one awful night. He's a big bloke too, the kind that used to be muscular and now just a little too burdened.

He falls into that seat, his breathing heavy as he sets his carrier bag down on the table in front of him. He takes out this bottle of beer but he struggles to get the top off. It's a Tuesday. I feel it's important you remember that. The start of the week and he's already got himself a large Bud. He gets it open and guzzles it down, letting out this long and undisguised burp as the train pulls out of the station.

The moment he got on I decided I was going to watch him and since he was paying me no attention I figured I was safe to stare, taking him all in. That long greasy hair, gelled back as far as the eighties. It's clearly stayed with him, from a time when it was fashionable; from when he was at the height of his career, I imagine. He was probably

276

one of those promising young things, all busy climbing that ladder, chasing the old ones off the top. Even through all the added girth I can see he was probably a lot more trim back then.

Lean and mean; now angry and tired.

He stares down at his beer, obviously thinking about the battles of the day. I wonder if he has been busy fighting the young ones off that ladder that's now below him. His face scrunches up as he looks down at his battered knuckles; I think it's been a tough ride. He's been kicking the young ones away, telling them to bugger off, telling them that it's still his time. He doesn't want to give it up.

Some go quietly, like me, resolving myself to a part time job. It might be at night but it's still in the city, still not willing to let go of it all just yet. But this one – the way he gulps down his beer tells me he hasn't given up the fight against the never-ending youth that seem to line up behind us. They have these promising dreams that they think are new; they never realise that they're just recycling our ideas. They honestly doubt that it's all been done before. That other time, somewhere in the past, is simply another world to them; and they don't want to hear about it.

I feel like leaning over and telling him to stop, telling him that he's just fighting against the endless tides of progress, against the many plain suits and skinny shirts. He doesn't know when he went out of fashion – he was too busy. There's no wedding ring to be seen.

He answers his phone, talking riddles; the deal that probably went wrong. 'Those fucking bastards,' he says, finally looking over at me but not offering any sign of apology for his profanity. 'If they think I'm beaten –'

He stops to listen, his head nods then shakes. 'I don't know where he is, we got separated. I'm flying out tonight.' He holds up his hand, like he's silencing those on the other end of the line. I don't think he's used to someone else's opinions, someone else talking when it should just be him.

'Don't fucking tell me what to do and don't tell me it's over. We bury it for now and then rebuild once everything calms down.' He slams his beer bottle on the table, a stream of foul language free-flowing from his mouth. I can't hear everything but I think they're still talking whilst he's still shouting.

I lean in closer, desperate to hear the other side. But he suddenly stands up, the phone only at his mouth as he points into the air. 'You fucking bastards, you're burning me? I'm the only one with vision and the balls to carry it out and now you're running scared. Don't tell me to calm down. This really isn't a situation where you calm down.'

By the time he puts the earpiece back to where it should be I'm at the edge of my seat. It seems like I want to hear what he's missed more than he does. But there are no more words. He throws the phone across the carriage and lets out a long scream. I hear the phone shatter against the wall before it makes its final thud on the carriage floor. It seems like such a wasteful act to me, as the train continues speeding towards its destination, leaving behind whatever he did and whoever he is. The millions of footsteps, the army of cleaners and the ever-so-common rain shower will all work together to wash away every memory of whatever small and insignificant imprint we will make on that city today, or any other day.

He starts swearing again, telling this small space all of his woes, as the outside world continues to race by, putting the past forever behind us. I don't want to look anymore and so I pull myself back, never so much wanting to blend into my seat as I do now.

He eventually calms down and slumps into his own seat. I feel immediate relief but as we slow down to pull into the next station I still think about getting off. It's about time I changed my routine. He suddenly turns around, looking directly at me. 'What's your problem? You've been looking at me far too much.'

I look back at him, unable to stop that stare, now mesmerised by what I see.

'Are you fucking deaf? What's your problem?'

'I don't have a problem but I think you might,' I say, looking through the window behind him at the small army of Police Officers.

He turns around to see what I see and starts screaming as he bangs the window, freely inviting them into our little cage. The police move as the train moves, all dressed in riot gear and eager to keep up with us. As soon as the door opens he gets up to greet them, his smashed and empty bottle of beer now turned into a decent enough weapon.

He's still fighting, still rebelling against whatever has come his way. But these men want to fight back and they squeeze their way into any possible space. He slashes and bashes at them but the only thing that really stops them are the seats, as they funnel themselves into a line, like they've all joined some sort of queue so they can take it in turns to bash him back.

And when they board the train from the other end, now either side of him, he still doesn't give up. He's telling them it's not over and from somewhere deep inside him I can tell that he really believes this.

I force myself as far into my seat as I can get. 'I'm not with him!' I shout. 'I'm no one important!' We're just the somebody and the nobody who shared a carriage, that's all I think.

As they force him to the floor and bury their knees into every available part of his body, he looks up at me with these wild eyes. Wherever he's going I think it's likely to be for quite a while, but maybe that's okay. Maybe he's been fighting for long enough.

As they drag him from the train I wish him well. It seems like the right thing to do and after all the threats and swearing disappear, the last look he gives me is what I think is acceptance. I still wonder if he is only accepting the moment; if he is simply embracing the immediate future of whatever will happen to him. Or perhaps he has finally found the guts to see whatever he has done and to truly accept whoever he has become.

The train is clearly going nowhere for a while and the automated announcement competes with the scrambled messages of the driver, telling the few passengers 'All change please, all change.'

It's a lesson I think he should learn and I hope he heard it.

I hope he heard it before it really is too late.

THANKS :-)

My eternal thanks start with Rose Hicks and Laura O'Toole, for your ongoing and relentless support for my writing. It means a lot to have your faith and your keen eyes.

My most sincere thanks go to Heather Jones and Nicola Farmer, for being such great friends, constant supporters and willing readers of my work. I simply have to thank Andrew Farmer for being a fantastic friend and a pretty good photographer. New website pictures required in 2015! I'd also like to thank Harlen Holding for all his support, his humour and for reading my book in front of as many people as he can.

I owe a lot of thanks Donna Jones, for being a fellow career climber of many years. Your advice and support is always treasured and your unwavering humour has got us through a lot. And finally, I offer my endless appreciation to Ankit Goel for all his energy and passion for my work, as well as his technical skills that I simply don't have!

And thanks to every other friend, past and present, as well as a lot of colleagues, all of whom have read my work and spurred me on. I really appreciate it.

ABOUT LEE KERR

This is Lee's second book and one of ten bright ideas to be published by 2020.

He lives in London and works full time. You might spot him one day tapping away on the next big story in a coffee shop somewhere. If you see him you should say hello as he doesn't have many fans. You can see what he looks like and learn more about his work at www.leekerr.net. He's a bit of a dreamer, sometimes funny, but not when he laughs at his own jokes. He's got this crazy idea that we're all chasing something – a dream, a career, money, love, or just a better tomorrow. Do you think he's right?

If you like his second book you can…
Follow him on twitter @leekerrwrites
Like him on facebook.com/leekerr.writes
Check out www.leekerr.net for some random reading group questions.
Or simply tell a friend.

Whatever you're chasing, do it with a smile ;-)

ALSO BY LEE KERR

CHASING 30

Of all the things you could chase, what would it be?

As Josh celebrates his twenty-ninth birthday, his closest friend gives him a ring with a simple inscription: *Chasing 30*. It's supposed to be a message to tell Josh to chase something more than his talented career, to stop running from his past, and to embrace the world he has hidden on the edge of for so long. It's a plea that asks Josh to accept his sexuality and to recognise their friendship for what it could be.

But Josh refuses to admit any feelings, as he slowly pushes everyone away in favour of quietly struggling with the ideas of being a good gay, an honest son, and a real friend. He soon finds his world shattered by bizarre encounters, small adventures and interfering people, as he wakes up to see his friends have silently fought against life's complications, addictions, depression and unspoken love.

When he finally makes a stand against his grinding existence, he enters into a race against time to help his friends, and to find the courage to admit an unspoken true love for the best friend he never wanted to lose.

Printed in Great Britain
by Amazon